....

"A fascinating look at the kind of hard-core, alternative life of European street wanderers, written in a take-no-prisoners style."

— *Irish Echo*

"Hitch up and come along on Isolt's odyssey through the freaked-out diaspora of Euro-travelers. Emer Martin's debut of confident wit and casual insanity is one weird scene you're not going to regret."

— Alan Warner, author of *Morvern Callar*

"One of the finest fictional debuts of the year."

— *In Dublin*

"Emer Martin seems to write as if in a morphine vision — amid all the very real violence and pain comes a spectacular sedative of language, humor, and hope."

— Colum McCann, author of *Songdogs*

"Heaven is a rainy Sunday morning in Clontarf, a bottle of Jameson, and *Breakfast in Babylon* to read again. I loved it from start to finish."

— Niall Quinn, author of *Welcome to Gomorrah*

"This novel is gripping and unsettling but eye-opening; the mood and many of the circumstances remind me most of Louis-Ferdinand Céline's great novel of the thirties, *Journey to the End of the Night*. The pace, speed, quixotism, arbitrariness, humor, alienation . . . An auspicious, impressive debut, hot, mad, and exciting like a young writer's first work should be. She grabs you in the throat while she kicks you in the testes."

— Stephen Dixon, author of *Gould*

Breakfast in Babylon

Breakfast in Babylon

....

Emer Martin

A MARINER ORIGINAL
HOUGHTON MIFFLIN COMPANY
BOSTON · NEW YORK

For information about permission to reproduce selections from this book,
write to Permissions, Houghton Mifflin Company, 215 Park Avenue South,
New York, New York 10003.

First published in 1995 by Wolfhound Press Ltd, 68 Mountjoy Square, Dublin 1
and Wolfhound Press (UK), 18 Coleswood Road, Harpenden, Herts AL5 1EQ

Library of Congress Cataloging-in-Publication Data

Martin, Emer, date.
   Breakfast in Babylon ; a novel / Emer Martin.
      p.   cm.
   "A Mariner original."
   ISBN 0-395-87595-1
   I. Title.
PR6063.A7134B74 1997
823'.914 — dc21   97-4362 CIP

Printed in the United States of America

Book design by Robert Overholtzer

QUM 10 9 8 7 6 5 4 3 2 1

The author is grateful for permission to quote from the following:
"Search and Destroy," "Gimme Danger": Written by Iggy Pop and James
Williamson. © 1973, 1979 Bug Music, Inc./James Osterberg Music/Strait James
Music (BMI)/Administered by Bug/Mainman-Fleur Music/EMI Music Pub-
lishing Ltd./All rights for EMI Publishing Ltd. controlled and administered
by Screen Gems-EMI Music, Inc. All rights reserved. Used by permission.
"Baby It Can't Fail": Written by Iggy Pop and David Bowie. © 1986 Thousand
Mile Inc. (BMI)/Administered by Bug/Jones Music. All rights reserved. Used
by permission. "Mr. Dynamite": Written by Iggy Pop and Glen Matlock.
© 1971 James Osterberg Music (BMI)/Administered by Bug. All rights reserved.
Used by permission."Ocean": written by Lou Reed and 1973 Oakfield Avenue
Music (BMI)/EMI Music Publishing Ltd./All rights for EMI Publishing Ltd.
controlled and administered by Screen Gems-EMI Music Inc. All rights
reserved. Used by permission.

To Afshin

Contents

Part One

1

The Melon Murderer

"I AM NOT Jesus Christ. I left home younger than he, walked further and stayed out in the wilderness longer. I am a tinker. A tinker who could not stop tinking around this stretch of earth. The homecomings I have are the memories of certain events that penetrated my mind, that neither slowed nor startled me but that would not leave me. Think of the sound 'tink,' shallow and brief."

Isolt was talking to herself in the Garden of Gethsemane looking over Jerusalem. All her hard times in the city had almost turned her back into a Catholic. Standing here now she felt no Godly presence and was relieved to be spared the embarrassment of being born again. She took a last look at Jerusalem and left the garden to go home and pack.

The humidity had left the air, but she still hated Tel Aviv. She lay on the bed reading for three days. Intrusion from the outside world was neither volunteered nor sought for. The second morning she put her head in her hands and shuddered. Determined to shake her gloom, she made her way down the streets and walked along the beach feeling that something was ending in her. She bought a pack of cigarettes and sat on an iron chair on the promenade, reading and watching all the old Jewish ladies surrender their varicose veins to the evening sun.

That day she could not dissipate the thick layer of shadows that had stretched into her head, as if even her own ghosts were collapsing quietly in her soul. Stray dogs sniffed about the sand. She had a world where all the old ladies had bulging blue veins and all the dogs had cataract eyes. There were the usual conversations with the brigade of tanned, hairy perverts that maintain a diligent patrol of Tel Aviv's sea front.

"Where are you from?"

"Go away."

"English? American? Denmark?"

She settled her eyes on a battleship which was circling the horizon hypnotically. She wondered about the huge ship's motive for this rotating exercise.

"You have beautiful eyes."

"What book are you reading?"

It certainly seemed like a waste of petrol . . . Maybe the Syrians were invading.

"I think books open the mind, do you?"

"Go read one then."

"You want to come in my car for coffee in Jaffa?"

"Go away. I want to be alone."

"My friend has car, you come with us."

The ship was commencing yet another circle. She had made the mistake of acknowledging his presence.

"Please, I don't want to talk."

"You think I am a dog?"

"No, I like dogs."

"You want my friend give you books to read? My friend has books at the house."

"Fuck off!"

He jumped up in moral outrage. "You are not lady. You are stupid girl. There is not interesting talking to you and not special to look at you. You are fat and short."

She wondered if the captain of the ship had been looking overboard, dropped his contact lenses, and forced his whole crew to circle the spot in search of them. Small plastic floating through moving waves. The pervert was sulking in the distance, always alert for foreign girls who come to watch the sun go down. He was lighting a cigarette. She hoped he'd get cancer for calling her fat.

Two British lads who drank with her crowd came by. The smaller was covered in tattoos. Doomed stragglers who never got out when the summer had taken the Sunday boat from Haifa and the hostels closed and the jobs became scarce. They probably thought the same of her. She went for a beer with them but they seemed not to notice her presence so she relaxed and, savouring the one luxury of being invisible, she began to eavesdrop.

"Yeah, she's a mad cow. What age do you think she is?"

"Thirtyish, nice legs, she said she'd been to Egypt four months ago. She's been here ages."

"Probably drank the Nile dry."

"Got kids back in Leeds and everything, stupid cow. I met her on a moshav in the Golan Heights. She got fired. One morning she took the farmer's gun and went through the fields shooting all his bloody melons."

"Now the dumb bitch has invested in a metal detector and goes up and down the beach in the middle of the night looking for all the coins, watches and shit."

"Damn, if the police catch her at that . . ."

"I first met her in the Sinai. She goes to the desert a lot and smokes dope — bedouin dope — dirt cheap. Anyway I see her in the hostel and say, didn't I see you in the Sinai? She says, 'Probably, I'm always in the Sinai, I love it there, the Sinai's my garden.'"

The other shook his head, smiling. "Fucking metal detector."

"I'll drink to that," Isolt said, ordering three more beers. "But then I'll drink to anything."

At last she could leave Israel, forward into the soft rains of Europe, her body tired and her head shapeless, her thoughts less tense but without theme or direction. She spent two weeks on the Greek islands before she got to Athens. Two weeks in the company of the usual well-adjusted people one meets in budget travel. She would forget all their names soon. Their impressions would linger on, though, having found place to root throughout her brain, like unnoticed scrubweed.

In Athens she made inquiries about the infamous magic bus — a bus that for a meagre sum of gold would take her non-stop to cities in Northern Europe. Women had been known to give birth on this bus, Turkish immigrants had been stabbed and occasionally the company went bankrupt and the forever-drunken driver would bail out midway leaving everybody stranded on the wrong side of the Yugoslavian border. The man in the agency shook his head.

"They have gone bankrupt, there is a new bus under a different name."

"And what might that be?"

He shrugged glumly. "The not-so-magic bus?"

"Well, can I get it to Amsterdam?"

"Only Paris and Frankfurt."

Sitting down on the grotty travel agent's wooden bench she thought about it. She was sure some of her friends would be there hanging around. She knew the city well. She would take a train into Turkey while she was so close and afterwards go to Paris for a week, make some money begging, and head up to Holland for the winter.

She met a British guy who had Greek parents and spoke the language. They walked about the city together for a couple of days. It was in Athens when she first saw the rain and felt she was almost home. They got drunk in a fast food place. She ran back and forth to the toilet, each time looking at herself in the mirror. Each time a few minutes older. Which made her feel at least something was moving. If only the world.

The hotel room had plastic under the sheets and no locks on the door. An Irish couple cleaned the toilets in the morning. There was a freezing lobby in which she sat all day, reading a book and waiting for her train. Grey Athens outside the window, clinging to her soul. At Istanbul she stopped because of the snows. She had a note in her pocket from the Irish cleaner to give to her sister in Paris. Isolt kept that note through all the years that followed.

Nobody got stabbed, born or abandoned on the not-so-magic bus. Isolt did get sick out of the window after a Tequila race with four German backpackers. While she was deep in a coma under the seat her money and passport were stolen. She suspected the Germans but they blamed the Turkish family in the back seat. She arrived slightly dismembered in Paris, that most forgiving of cities, with no money and no identification. Locking her battered rucksack in the train station lockers with the coins one of the Germans had given her she watched them all skip off to a café to get drunk on her money; she was momentarily overcome with a sense of *déjà vu*.

How to find a friend in Paris. Does your guide book tell you this? How to search every haunt, begging spot, and familiar park bench where people once congregated. How to take your jet-lagged eyes and roll them down each street, each gutter. How to grow your stiff legs long enough to see over every house and scan four roads at once.

On the brink of despair when night had turned her search to bewildered panic, she saw Jim at the Saint-Michel fountain through a circus of beggars and their half-wild dogs. He was leaning against a car drinking a beer. His eyes opened uncharacteristically wide as he saw her limp over.

"Well, well! The dead arose and appeared to many."

"Hallo, Jim. You look awful," she said. And he did.

"Looking pretty grubby yourself, you old tart. Where have you been? London?"

"No."

"Have you anywhere to stay tonight?"

"Emm . . . Not really. You see I'm just back from Israel. I've lost some shit, well I was robbed . . . anyway I don't feel very organised."

He laughed. Thank God for Jim, she thought.

"Welcome to the Twilight Zone. You can come back to the squat I suppose."

His friend, a small Englishman in his forties, groaned. "Jesus! You Irish multiply. Let one of you in and the next thing you've got all the clan, second cousins, blood brothers, half-sisters, crowding the place out and an end to the peace."

"Yep." Jim nodded happily and nudged Isolt. "Buy us both a beer and consider the rent paid."

"Shit . . . I'm broke . . . otherwise . . ."

The Englishman rolled his eyes and gave her a bottle of beer from the pocket of his dirty overcoat. Jim put his arm around her and looked into her tired not-so-magic face.

"From the first time I saw you . . ." he sighed in his drunken stupor.

A couple of hours later they climbed through the wire and took the chain off the squat door. Isolt turned to the English guy whose name was Larry. "I suppose I'm the only female as usual?"

Jim, lighting a match and making his way up the bare stairs, laughed, "You're one of the lads at this stage. Christopher will probably have a fit. He kind of found this place and threw a tantrum when a girl moved in. He doesn't like girls, but he doesn't live here so we ignore him."

"Yeah, there's a bird from Leeds here. She's a wino but she's OK," Larry said.

Jim giggled, "Hey, dig this! The chick has a metal detector. She drags it around everywhere. It's no fucking use in Paris."

Larry and Jim glanced knowingly at each other. Larry opened a door. "She's been to Israel too."

"Good," Isolt said. "We can swap holiday snaps."

The place was candle-lit. The rooms were big but there was no water or electricity. Isolt saw her sitting there among the rubble drinking wine. The lads had described her as a wino. That was charitable of them. She was thin and long. Her nice legs were covered in sores and her slender hands had bitten nails. Her face was washed out and old-looking. All in all, in candlelight she struck Isolt as being chewed — her whole body, lovely needle-marked limbs, defeated face. Chewed. Something had swallowed her all right, devoured her, but now she had been spat out and was on the defensive for the last years of her life. Isolt knew who she was. She would have known her anywhere.

Isolt felt she was encountering a heroine in a story. A heroine on heroin — the melon murderer. And the Sinai desert was once her garden. They were introduced; her name was Becky, a Jewish English pauper from Leeds, and they would share a room. Isolt kicked about the rubbish on the floor: milk cartons, bottles of meths, discarded homemade pipes, soggy coffee filters, beer cans.

"Well, Jim. I see you brought your fungus collection with you, or do you just let the debris build up in each place of its own accord?" Her eye caught the plastic water carrier filled to the brim with cigarette butts. "Whoops! Ashtrays are full, time to move squats."

Becky looked at Isolt half-eyed. "Shit, Jim, who the hell is this? A miniature health inspector?"

Their room was the size of a grand piano. It was full of cigarette butts, wine bottles and syringes. Larry gave Isolt one of his blankets, a manky piece of cloth which smelt of hard times and no doubt previous encounters he had had under the offensive article. The nights were bitterly cold in this weary kingdom and she needed it. Two people living in the space of one piano was a bit like building a ship in a bottle. Becky's ship was sinking. Isolt had only a raft, drifting. She hated Isolt's youth, though Isolt insisted that she was on her side and growing old quickly. She accused Isolt of being a Nazi, but Isolt assured her that the room was too small to goosestep in, even for her stumpy, Catholic legs. Becky hated Catholics.

They talked into the sorry nights while methylated fires burned in the can for light and warmth. In a drunken stupor Becky spilt the meths on her hand and set it alight. The flames rolled off. She stared in surprise and tried it again, like a child.

"You read a lot of books. Who said the Irish were stupid?"

"You did."

"I did?" She was puzzled.

"You, as in you the Brits."

"Christ, don't go on with this chip on your shoulder like the bloody Scots."

"It is a well-deserved and ongoing chip on my shoulder."

"I'm not British, I'm Jewish, or at least that's what I thought before going to Israel. They didn't want me there either. It's good that you read all those books. I don't know much about anything." She kicked over an empty milk carton. "Except debris of course."

She drank some wine, sucking furiously at the mouth of the bottle, again, like a child.

"I got pregnant at seventeen back in lovely Leeds. I got married and had four kids. I kept the kitchen kosher while my husband kept his distance. Ha! Ha! Ha!" Her face looked horrible lit from beneath by the fire; she went on, "His name was Bertie, not very Jewish eh? I'm no fanatic. Becky and Bertie, cute eh?" She glared at Isolt.

Isolt nodded, waiting for more details.

"So there we were, he got drunk. I did not, then I started too. Where was I? Oh yeah, so Becky keeps the kitchen kosher, kept the kiddies and lost her looks. Man, I tell you I was beautiful once. Nothing like you. Blond, tall, the lot. So I'm boozing all the time and one day I find out he's fucking some dozy little tart who actually was my hairdresser. I wouldn't have minded so much if he had gone groping after a forty-year-old of some substance called Maude or something. No, it was a curly-haired, sixteen-year-old, disco-fluff slut called, now listen to this . . ." She put her bony finger to her lips as if to quiet the already quiet Isolt. "She called herself Tricky."

They both tried to laugh.

"That bastard used to beat me too. He used to find that I drunk all his booze and slam me against the wall. He never gave me enough for the kids or nothing. Then he stuck his little dicky in Tricky. And Becky runs off and dies in Paris."

"Do you want to die in Paris?"

"It's not top on my list of priorities right now, no."

"Oscar Wilde died here."

"Yeah, he was a faggot though."

"So?"

"His wife ran off didn't she? With the kids? Changed their names. Don't talk to me about literary figures, I saw the mini-series. I wonder what they changed their names to? I hope it didn't end in 'y.'"

"Not-so-wilde?" Isolt suggested. This appealed to Becky.

"Sure I can handle that, and they were probably drivers of your not-so-magic bus."

As they were settling to go to sleep Becky turned to Isolt. "It's Christmas Day tomorrow and you are not in Amsterdam as planned, my girl."

"You noticed?" Isolt cringed.

"Sure. You're not that fucking small."

"Well, I don't really mind. Amsterdam is just a faraway hill that's greener. Happy Christmas!" She tried to clink her bottle with Becky's, but Becky pulled hers away.

"Get lost." She looked at Isolt, the flames throwing shadows on the wall. The futility of the patterns they cast sucked at Isolt's head until she was about to scream. Becky's head drooped and she said, "Happy just another shitty day!"

"I'll drink to that." Isolt sat up and opened another bottle of wine. It was going to be a long night and they could sleep all day tomorrow.

When they were evicted the police came in with gas masks in the middle of the night and chased them all out as they slept. Jim had been cracked over the head with a baton and had to get stitches on his scalp. The doors and windows were bricked up. Anything they could not grab in the panic to get out was lost. They were all scattered on the streets for a couple of weeks hunting desperately for a new dwelling place. As they rolled their sleeping bags out under the bridge, Isolt was grateful for Larry and Jim and their constant banter.

"My friend Rory was a madman," said Jim. "He ran away from home when he was twenty-six . . ."

Larry grumbled, "Is this the guy that cooked that poor hedgehog?"

"I shared a place with him in London."

"What, with the hedgehog?"

"No, with Rory, he had a lot of stories attatched to him, a real ladies' man was Rory. We were all in London sharing a tiny room between six of us from Dublin and we all got scabies except Rory . . ."

"Oh I see," Larry said. "It was an English hedgehog and therefore an oppressor who deserved to get cooked by scabies-ridden Irishmen who came to fiddle the social security system."

Jim got serious. "No, you see Rory reckoned that eating the hedgehog stopped him getting scabies."

"Christ," said Larry. "A medical breakthrough by the Irish. That is a first. I thought you lot were still suffering from beri-beri and rickets."

An old Irishman called from the depths of the arches, "Don't you get cheeky about the Famine, young man, I was there."

Larry turned to him. "I'm not young, mate. I'm forty-five, and don't talk to me about the Irish potato famine, you may have lived through it but I read the book."

Jim peered at the old man through the darkness. "If you lived through it you must be at least one hundred and forty years old."

"I was one hundred and forty years old THEN," the old man snapped and promptly rolled over to sleep.

Nobody had seen Becky in two weeks. Somebody around the fountain said her liver had insisted on being taken to the hospital. It had occurred to Isolt last time she saw her that living did not come naturally to Becky. Her life seemed to make her awkward; she didn't know what to do with it. She was not sure if it was worth going on with all this breathing and consciousness. Then Becky never mentioned suicide, not for life's sake Isolt suspected, but perhaps because she felt that death offered nothing better. She was too tall and too blond and too worn to allow people to warm up to her. It was obvious that she had been a beauty and the way she never hid her needle-marked arms disturbed the lads. She was always bitching about men but seemed to prefer men's company to women's. She had slept with all the men in the squat at one time or another. They joked about this among themselves though they always were slightly ashamed of admitting it to each other. Everyone except Ali — no one slept with Ali — and Christopher because she hated him. Once when he was lying on the floor she took her precious metal detector and held it over his chest.

"If the bleeper goes off you have a heart."

It didn't.

"Yep. That figures," she said and strutted out of the room, Christopher staring after her slender shape with contemptuous, greedy eyes.

The only things she had taken with her from the now-demolished squat were her metal detector and her sleeping bag. She had stood on the side of the street that night when everyone was running from the police; she had not been part of the panic. Watching the action, leaning with one hand on her detector and one hand on her hip, the sleeping bag at her feet.

"The bare necessities," she told Isolt when Isolt came up to her out of the chaos. Isolt had raised her materialistic eyebrows at Becky's odd world.

Becky felt competitive with the younger girl because they were usually the only females around so many men. Isolt hated this. Becky was often rude to her, and then placated her by stealing books from Shakespeare and Co, the English bookshop. For a person who had never read a book in her life she had excellent taste.

"If the blurb on the back is depressing, complicated and obscure, I know you will read it."

Isolt inquired if Becky found her depressing, complicated and obscure.

"Oh baby! You are not complicated. I can read you like one of your damn books."

"I find the truth in the books I read, where do you find yours?"

"Listen, you are just a little kid now. I have been a woman for thirty-six years. We are the watchers and the waiters while men are busy being the doers and getters. If you get dumped on for all those years you begin to see through shit-coloured glasses, you see up the world's trouser leg, you see life as it is. Not like those damn books, what do those people know, they're all men. They're all educated people who have their acts together."

"Not all of them."

"They have their acts together enough to write and publish their shitty books."

"The watchers and the waiters, huh?"

"Yep, and the weight watchers. Ha! Ha!" She poked Isolt's beer belly.

Becky was now gone.

They found another squat just outside Paris and about twelve people moved in. This one had electricity but no water. Weeks later Becky arrived at the fountain. Isolt was at the cinema with Jim. Ali took her back and she moved straight into Isolt's room though there were plenty of others to spare. The first night she was shooting up and splattered blood on the wall. Isolt stood looking at it on her arrival.

"I took the liberty of doing some decorating while you were away, darling," she explained sluggishly.

Isolt shrugged. "Oh well, it's an improvement on the wallpaper I suppose."

"Oscar Wilde had a wallpaper problem in Paris too."

"How on earth did you know that — the mini-series?"

"You don't have a monopoly on dead faggots, you know."

Isolt did not embrace her though she was very glad to have her back and flattered that she chose her room. She sat down beside her and gave her a beer. Most of her blond hairs had turned grey in that short time. Isolt wanted to know where she had been all those weeks. She ventured to ask but Becky told her to mind her own business. Isolt wondered how she emerged from the down-hearted Parisian night with no sleeping bag, a different set of dirty clothes and the metal detector which had broken. Why carry a heavy, unfunctional machine with her when she disdained a change of clothes or a tooth-brush?

"Just keeping the wolves from the door," Becky explained, though she didn't seem to have much chance, operating as she did in a constant stupor.

When they were outside at the fountain the next evening she fell over. She stood up and fell over again. Jim picked her up and virtually cradled her.

"You've taken up break-dancing," he said.

"Break-dancing my arse," Larry frowned. "You've given yourself brain damage. That's epilepsy."

"Fuck you too, Larry," she said, all bravado. "It's this stupid country. The French refuse to obey the laws of gravity because an Englishman discovered it. They're fucking me up."

She remained at the fountain that night. Isolt ran back and forth getting bottles of wine at the Arab shop for her. She was terrified of standing up. In the end Larry and Jim carried her onto the last Metro. Isolt and Ali walked along beside them. Ali stood on the platform and shouted with his fist in the air to some curious onlookers.

"Kill the Arab."

"Shut up, Ali," Jim said. "You are an Arab."

Becky cried a little back at the squat. She snivelled and sucked on an empty wine bottle. Isolt sat on the floor and looked at her from across the room. Jim hugged her.

"It's cool to cry, Becky, we all cry sometimes."

"I don't," Larry said.

Every winter evening they would gather around Saint-Michel fountain, but in summer they would sit on the cobblestoned slope in front of the giant Pompidou Centre and watch the fire eaters, belly dancers and musicians. A huge man who was so fat his belly was rectangular would lounge about on a bed of nails, wearing a purple turban and taunting the passersby. The place was crawling with opportunistic Arabs, junkies, dealers, students, tourists and pickpockets. The Africans would congregate at the top of the slope making impassioned speeches and arguing back and forth. Usually the beggars Isolt knew would go to a self-service restaurant beside the square and have dinner. They sat at the back tables with all their bags, eating and drinking water after free water and discoursing loudly.

There were many beggars in the group. Some came and went within a week, some stayed for years, most drifted back and forth between European countries, not always in the same lifestyle. On the streets people became friends quickly and adapted just as quickly to their absences. The Europeans and Ali pooled their money together while eating in the Melodine and one of the lads went off and bought hash or acid for the evening's entertainment. The left-overs were spent on beer. Everybody was invariably broke the next morning and would go out to beg and start again. There was a party every night.

The dealer was a tiny Puerto Rican American from Detroit. He was either on a bicycle or pulling a tartan shopping cart. He came to a bench beside the Pompidou fountain every evening at eight o'clock. If there was no one there at that time he would walk right by as briskly as the White Rabbit. He would mount the escalators of the Pompidou Centre and look through the tourist telescopes. If there were more clients at the bench than he could handle he would not come down till some left. Once when he was right on the top of the fifth floor looking down, Ali the Iranian looked up and caught the telescope dead in the eye. He started hopping up and down.

"Hey man! There's our man. There's the cat man."

Christopher saw the others strain to look up. He withdrew from the telescope abruptly and fled. When he arrived at the bench he denied he had been up there looking down at them.

"Ali's crazy, man. You know that."

It was usually better not to congregate at the bench so everybody preferred to wait in the Melodine or watch the action on the slope. Jim and Larry would go alone.

"Damn, he was paranoid today, we had to go off with him to where he stashed it in a phone box. There was some fucker in there making a call and Christopher is pacing around holding his bicycle over his head in complete panic. Then he just busts into the phone box and grabs the package. The poor bugger inside was scared stiff."

The first time Isolt had met Christopher was an autumn Sunday years ago when she was sixteen years old and had just left home. She was sitting on the bench in a dismal little park in Odon. He came dragging his tartan shopping cart and wearing an out-of-date long sheepskin coat. He had a mop of curly black hair and a drooping mustache. She had been with Jim, drinking a case of beer. He stopped beside them.

"Acid?" he hissed. "Scary clowns, the cleanest."

Jim bought two hits and gave one to Isolt. It was the first time she tripped and she did not know what to expect. Christopher exchanged a few words with Jim and went on his way.

"Do you know him?" Isolt had asked.

"No, not really. I've seen him around. He's a paranoid, acid head American who lives in Versailles."

Isolt looked at the acid; it was a tiny white square of paper with a clown's face on it.

"You can get all kind of designs. Put it on your tongue and let it dissolve."

She did as she was told. "What now?"

"Welcome home, baby!" he had said, handing her another beer.

Isolt had looked at him glumly as she sipped the beer. It sounded kind of sinister to her.

The lads told her that Christopher hated women. He had a French girlfriend, though he kept her off the circuit and in the background. She was meek and thin and worshipped him. They told Isolt if she came to score to keep her mouth shut. Isolt consequently avoided Christopher as she did not relish being silenced just because she was a girl. She and Becky would give their money and let the men do the strutting about and scoring. As long as they were high every night they didn't care.

Christopher lived in a big squat in Versailles which he shared with a bunch of beggars. He rented a room in Saint-Lazare where his girlfriend lived and he rented a *chambre de bonne* in the attic of a building in the sixteenth district. He had found the squat Isolt now lived in and he called around once in a blue moon. When he did Isolt felt the situation to be different and she did not feel too inhibited to join in the conversation. He never objected, though she confessed to Becky that she never felt at ease in his presence. Becky agreed.

"He gives me the creeps. I can never hear what he's saying, he talks so low and he's always so paranoid. One acid too many if you ask me. He hates me. I can't bear to be in the same room as him. He's always telling the lads to get rid of me behind my back. That I'm trouble and a junkie. As if they can throw me out of here. He has no rank over me, I don't fall for his bullshit. This is a squat. He hasn't the guts to say it to my face. He thinks he controls that place in Versailles, not letting any women through the door. He's just like the Arabs, he'd prefer women in veils. He's afraid of women if you ask me. Just look at that droopy little girl he's got. Fucking pathetic. Stuck up, pretty French cow. She's a poor little rich kid. Hanging on to him for something, probably to piss her parents off. I know that type a mile away. The cheek of him trying to oust me. I'd like to see him try it, the spic midget. I'd punch his fucking lights out if he ever tried anything. He says I'm a junkie and will bring the law in. He can talk. I see him score smack too — that Malaysian guy says he buys some every other day."

"Christopher is a junkie?" Isolt was shocked.

"Yeah. He's pretty controlled but you see him always slugging that codeine medicine. That's to relive his monkey. He's a junkie all right and I know one when I see one. I bet all that crowd out in Versailles are junkies. He should be more sympathetic to me, he knows what it's like, the little cunt. He never complains that you're here. Maybe he likes you. Maybe Christopher is in love. Ha! Ha!"

Isolt smiled. "That's a somewhat dubious privilege."

"Stay away, girl, that's all I can say."

Isolt was flattered all the same. It was always good to hear she had one less enemy than she had previously thought.

The days went on. The grey days. They dug deep. She fell asleep. It was too heavy. More like a small death. Dreamless and dark. A long howl, being wrenched away. When she awoke she did not feel right. It was as if she had awoken somewhere different from where she first lay. The weight in her head, her shaking hands. This was Isolt's afternoon nap.

It was summer in Paris. The tourists were swarming over the monuments. A French Arab had tried to commit suicide by throwing himself off Notre Dame cathedral and he survived by landing on a Canadian tourist. It was the tourist that died.

Two Afghan guys moved into the squat. Becky slept with one of them and then went into hermitage in her room, staring at the broken metal detector.

One night Christopher the dealer brought a Vietnamese man to the squat. He was small and gentle; he wore a top hat and walked barefoot on the dirty pavements. Christopher brought them all into the sitting room and told them that this smiling little man could levitate. They sat around while the man hummed with his thin eyelids shut over his watery brown eyes. Nothing happened. Larry shook his head.

"Christ, Christopher, it's a good job he doesn't do this for a living."

Nevertheless they were all amused. Ali had a pocket piano with a four-tune instruction manual and was playing "Joy to the World." It had a puny, empty, tin sound. They were all stoned and happy. Only Becky seemed detached and irritated. The Vietnamese man opened his eyes and turned his soft face to her as if sensing her lone disenchantment.

"You are an English flower," he whispered.

"And you are a Vietnamese weed," she snapped, going back to her room. Jim stopped her.

"Come on, Becky. Lighten up, it's only a bit of a laugh."

Becky winced. "I'm thirty years old."

"Thirty-six," Isolt corrected her.

"OK, thirty-six. I'm tired of all this shit. My liver is fucked, my brain is dead, my whole body is rotting. I've nothing to look forward to but death on the streets. My husband hates me and my kids have probably forgotten me and blame me for abandoning them and all my so-called friends are freaks and misfits . . ."

"Oh well," Jim said. "At least you have heroin to fall back on."

Christopher said something snide to the Afghans that nobody could hear and they said something in Farsi to Ali. They all laughed and looked at Becky. Becky caught it and glared at them. "I hate you and your primitive culture. You too, Christopher, especially you. You should know better. I hope you die poor and alone and I hope you die soon and I hope you die screaming."

She fled from the squat. Isolt followed her down onto the street.

"Leave me alone, Irish, sit this one out. I need to be alone."

Isolt walked with her in silence. Becky turned to her. "I hate men. I hate all their big, macho world. I hate their macho Gods. All the Bible and all the rest of the stuff they say is all just macho-shit-talk. This whole world . . . Oh no! . . . Oh God! . . ."

She closed her eyes and groaned. She dug her nails into Isolt's arms and said something else. Isolt didn't know what; still she acknowledged her wisdom and began to cry.

"Don't cry, Isolt. You will be OK. You never expect anything so how can you be disappointed?"

Isolt couldn't stop crying so Becky took her to a café and bought her a beer while she snivelled into a napkin. People were staring. The waiter took his time serving them. Isolt felt that he hated them. Everybody in the café hated them. The Parisians hated them. Their own countries hated them.

"Isolt?" Becky said.

"What?" Isolt sniffed.

"I'm glad you're not a man."

Isolt squeezed her hand but Becky withdrew it. "Because you would be a right fucker if you were."

The Vietnamese guy padded quietly in holding his top hat with his two tiny hands in front of him.

Becky smiled. "Christ, look who's here. The oriental acrobat. Jesus, they're going to love us three."

The waiter exchanged glances with the patron when the little man sat softly beside them.

"Do you speak English?" Becky asked.

The gentle man smiled but said nothing. Becky threw her eyes up to heaven.

"Oh God! His conversation is about as good as his levitation stunts."

The three of them sat. Isolt ordered three more beers. Eventually Jim and Larry came down and they had a good session of it. All of them promised never to speak to Christopher again. All of them broke the promise within the week; all except Larry who never spoke to him anyway. The Vietnamese moved in on Becky's insistence.

"We can put him on the mantelpiece," she explained.

They were thrown out of the café at three o'clock in the morning and told not to come back. Isolt realised that Becky had spent thirty-six years in a world that did not want her. The strain was beginning to show.

Isolt felt she was just an eternal witness. Brought up before the great court, she would stand in the box and tell the jury of a shabby world that was hard to live in, where all the old ladies had varicose veins and all the dogs had cataract eyes. That was not the way she always saw the world. Sometimes it was the only way she could see the world.

She said to herself, "I am not the son of God. Nor would I have had it that way. The daughter of something that was there once but no longer is. All I can say is, God love you, Jesus, if your father let them do that to you. I would not have let it happen to any friend of mine. If I had had any power I would have reached out and stopped them before they wove the very first thorns in that cruel crown. I would have broken their spines."

The lies. Those sacred lies. The dreary repetition in those dark, high-ceiling classrooms. Prayers of all the wrong way of doing things. Still, for years she murmured them solemnly with all the rest of the daughters and sons, while they patiently waited for life to come trundling down the iron tracks like a noisy train. Nothing ever came.

About twenty of them were crouched in a circle on the grass around the Eiffel Tower. The drink had run out and having no miracle worker in their midst, Larry suggested that they go to an off-licence near Bastille and do a smash and grab. Jim, Becky and the infamous Rory went along — Rory who had arrived on the scene for the first time and who could not understand the undying interest Larry took in his eating habits and relationship with animals. They were back in the squat when the others came in. The smash and grab had been a success. Larry couldn't believe it.

"You really did it? I was only joking."

Everybody was laughing and slapping each other on the back. Jim and Rory were telling the story interrupting each other.

"I tell you the glass wouldn't break. Rory had to hit it about six times."

Rory shaking his head. "Ah no Jim, about ten bloody times I swear."

Isolt turned and saw Becky on the couch. She was very drunk and was sewing something with a needle and thread. Isolt looked closer over the candle-lit web of smokey air and saw what it was that she was sewing so intently. It was her leg. Jim saw Isolt's horror and hastened to explain.

"You see Rory did the smashing, Becky leapt into the window to do the grabbing and her thigh got ripped on the glass . . ."

"What did you do, Jim?" Larry eyed him suspiciously.

"I did most of the running." Jim the ever-gallant hero.

They all did the drinking. Becky was so drunk that she confessed to not feeling a thing. She finished stitching the gash in her thigh and poured some whiskey over the now-closed wound.

It was the next day that Isolt sat in the squat looking through a crack in one of the shutters. She could see Becky limping up the hill to the station with a bottle in her hand. Jim saw her sitting there.

"You're not going out?" he said gently.

"No, I think I'll leave the economy alone today."

"Still looking for that bag of money to take you to Amsterdam?"

"Still looking. This is the longest week in Paris I ever spent. Eight bloody months now."

He was walking out: "Remember, if you leave, to put the chain on the door."

Yes, she thought, the chain. The wolves are at each door. We have to chain the door. Oh silent Christ, keep the wolves away for a little while longer. I'll get to Amsterdam. Don't let the wolves come in while I am here.

Becky woke her one night to tell her that the squat was on fire. Isolt was reluctant to investigate but Becky was so insistent that she wearily got up and went to check all the rooms. Only sleeping bodies, debris and the stale smell of smoke and unwashed flesh. The Vietnamese was looking at Isolt from his corner, his emaciated legs crossed. She shuddered. He never seemed to sleep or eat. He gave her the creeps.

"Nothing, Becky, not even a lighted cigarette butt. Only an anorexic, insomniac, shell-shocked Vietnamese trying to levitate. One of these days I'll come in and find him suspended in mid-air. He's been at it long enough." Becky was not listening to her but crouched up, hugging her thin legs and chanting, "It's on fire, I swear and we don't want to see that happen . . . I've seen a Greek whose face was melted from rotting fire. I could get a bad smell from the room. Are you sick?, I asked him, is it the sweet sickliness of cancer? Go away, he said, I clean this house. I went, there is no ease to my flight. What good is good? he said, when the cheating men take everything. So I am here now but you know this is no long, yellow field, this is the burnt street. This is no overgrown ditch, those are rows of mean shops, overpriced . . . What's good is good. I remember somebody told me to come back . . . Who was it?

"Look at me for there is another fire and I am already incinerated and the lipstick won't hide it. Will I carry these burnt ashes home? Nobody believes it is human what I am. The Greek told me, this town will eat you alive, but I said, you are too late, rinse your mouth out and have them for dessert. Start again after. It won't stop through me. There is a death beat running through. Hide . . .

"My God we are all on fire . . . The hot winds prevent you from walking, just as the cold stopped you from stepping outside . . . In Israel I wanted to get back where there is rain on the windows . . . you were there too, did you? . . . Crushing insects on your legs — did you notice how some won't die? . . . Please bring me the silence, grant me some of that which you worked for. Go now hurry! Put out the fire. Find me the God of which you have spoken. He is gone from my room, leaving the smell of disappointment behind . . . Hear the flames crackling? FIRE. FIRE. FIRE. FIRE."

Isolt had not noticed that Becky's chanted whisper had become a scream. The others were standing at the door.

"She thinks the place is on fire!" Isolt gasped. "That's what she's talking about. A fire."

Larry grabbed her. "Calm down, love. She's just got the DTs or something. Maybe she took some acid earlier. Sleep in my room. Jim will stay with her."

Isolt obeyed mutely. Larry gave her a cigarette but her hands were shaking too badly to light it.

"The wolves, Larry, the wolves are at the door."

"Don't you start," he said. "One mad bird is enough around here."

He put a blanket around her. The stench brought her to her senses. He seemed to have a collection of them.

Isolt did not sleep that night. What frightened her was beyond what was happening to Becky. What frightened her was the ranting speech. It was not in Becky's words. It was not Becky's language or imagery. These were Isolt's words, Isolt's recurring fearful imagery. It was Isolt's speech that Becky screamed at her.

Could her world have slipped away? Could it have gone without her noticing it? Just like that? So that her words could be screamed at her from another body? Is that madness? Had she gone mad and not noticed it? That was possible. Does the guide book tell you how to find a world that has slipped away? Does the guide book tell you how to know when to stop sightseeing and go home? Is there an index at the back listing cheap mental health clinics for when your mind finally goes and your subconscious slips into another head and shouts back at you?

Two months later, while Jim and Isolt were at the cinema, Rory was trying to fix the metal detector and left it in the hall. Becky walked from their room all strung out on heroin. While Isolt and Jim were at the cinema and Rory was at the shop and Larry was dozing in his room, their good friend Becky tripped over her beloved metal detector, fell down the stairs and broke her neck. She died instantly, without even knowing she was dying. Rory found the body on his return. Larry said he heard her fall but there was no scream and he assumed it was only the metal detector that fell.

They left the body in its exact position. Nobody touched her. They cleared their stuff out and went, leaving her passport on her chest for identification. They rang the police from a coin box.

The police would have found a corpse of a thirty-six-year-old female with needle-marked arms outstretched on the stairs and a semi-starved Vietnamese in the living room, emaciated legs crossed, no doubt a gentle smile on his face. They would have stepped over a metal detector at the head of the stairs.

The wolves had been fed.

Isolt went with Rory to Amsterdam the next week. Jim told them that he would join them in a couple of days. He never arrived. Larry remained in Paris. Rory and Isolt spent winter in Holland working in a hostel that was on a barge and in spring they bought tickets to London. It was only here in Amsterdam, among the cobblestones, the hurtling trams and the iced-over canals, that Isolt began to realize she had lost one of the main characters of her life. It was only here she knew that eight months sharing a room and exchanging thoughts was a long time. Becky's death was the first warning, a bleak premonition. She began to love her truly in the aftermath of her life for the lesson she had been taught. She often felt compelled in that time to write down Becky's story but after much deliberation she decided against it.

Better just never to forget. She would leave writing to the writers and rely on reading and waiting and watching and tinking.

Think of the sound "tink," shallow and brief.

Isolt stood ankle deep in the smooth waters of Paris, letting the idle waves lap about her feet. Outside, the vast oceans of loneliness were pointlessly singing.

She had watched Becky stumble out to work with a bottle in her hand under the doomed sky.

"God bless your eyesight — when you saw the flames from far away, you woke us all to warn us. Though we fled for shelter in the coming years, you stood as if caught in some childhood dream, unable to move."

2

The Hoodoo Man

WHERE CHRISTOPHER was born was thousands of miles north from where Christopher was conceived. He flew in both the giant belly of a machine and the nurturing belly of his mother over the Caribbean and the Atlantic and the continent of North America, over thousands of houses and factories and schools and farms. Murders were committed and lives destroyed as he passed over; a foetus with borrowed iron wings. Helpless and naive in this double womb he was transported, without ceremony, to his future home which he liked to refer to as the Devil's Workshop; determined from a young age to be one of its evil elves.

Christopher was conceived in Puerto Rico and he arrived as a foetus in Detroit. An innocent of the womb bumping about, digesting umbilical food without awareness of greed. He turned around and sat feet first, refusing to travel upside down. His mother was lighting a cigarette and trying to feed her three other babies in her dying sister's kitchen. Christopher, with no concept of patience or guilt, stamped his feet and writhed about demonically. After only seven months and twenty days he was to be born. He had no choice; the womb began to reject him. The walls were throbbing and slippery and he was forced feet first out into the kitchen of his cancerous aunt. He ripped his mother open and was stuck to the waist half in the world and half not.

His aunts finally wrenched him out, a shiny, slimy mess gasping his first smoke-filled breaths from the burnt hamburger meat unheeded under the grill. The first sounds he experienced were the deafening, terrified screeches of his siblings. He had a layer of skin stretched over his face which his aunts removed and kept dried in an envelope. It was a sign that he would never drown at sea; sailors bought such skins as lucky charms to protect them on their treacherous voyages.

"Thank God it is a boy!" the dying aunt said.

The ambulance never came to the house. The aunts got a taxi to drive him and his mother to the hospital. His mother died on the way and was buried in a cheap coffin in a Catholic graveyard outside Detroit. The snow would pile three feet high every winter pressing heavily on the grave. She had only been in the USA two months; she had never seen a snowflake in her life. It was a miracle that Christopher survived; he was hospitalised for three months. His dying aunt thanked the lord whom she believed could witness all this and love them all. "At least he is a boy," the younger said. "He will never have to face the pain of his mother."

Christopher had been unwanted from conception. He said to many people time and time again that if his poor mother had lived in a civilized world he would have been aborted. The only fright would have been the intruding instruments of termination; he would not have felt any pain beyond the first.

The newborn was given to a Mexican woman. She lived in a house with her four daughters who were in their late teens and early twenties. He remembered a lot of make-up, hair spray and burying his head in between their breasts. He called the Mexican woman his grandmother and he loved her.

At the happy age of two he stuck a stick in the eye of the dog next door. It bit his head, huge slobbering jaws clamped his tender temple. His grandmother forced the neighbours to put the dog down, protecting him from further canine confrontation.

At the curious age of three he had his first sexual experience. He put an ant up the vagina of the five-year-old across the road. He told his grandmother and she tut-tutted and told him not to do things like that to animals or little girls till he was older. He ignored this wisdom and the next day tried to squeeze a pebble into that tiny hole.

At the avaricious age of four, though he knew better, he lay on his back at the supermarket check-out and kicked up a storm until his grandmother bought him candy. As he gulped and wiped away the tantrum tears, clutching the bag of candy, he never forgot the withering look of disgust on the cashier's face.

When he reached the bewildering age of seven his grandmother died in her sleep. His aunts screamed and wailed in mourning. He was stunned and confused; he did not know what death was.

There was a cold sky above. The morning rolled across, unfolding its light. He was led by the hand, a small child looking up, watching with dread the night's end unravel. Flushed, goose-pimpled light swam in from the far horizon. He dragged his feet on purpose, pulled along by a familiar hand in silence. He was brought to an unfamiliar house and was swallowed up by a huge green armchair with no springs. The crusts of the snow melted on his boots.

"Christopher, this is your aunt's house. Your sister and one of your brothers live here. Now you can live with them. You have to start school. You'll like it here. It'll be lots of fun."

"I want to stay with Grandma."

"Grandma is dead, Chris. She can't come back."

"I want to stay with you."

"We are all going to California, Chris. You can come and visit whenever you like. We can't take care of you there all the time. Now Grandma loved you and so do we. You be a good boy now, you hear?"

She left the house in tears.

"Waaaaaagh!" Christopher wept.

His aunt looked at him. She shook her curly head. It was a big bad world and here was another helpless child with a hungry belly. Christopher blubbered and wiped his snot on the armchair. His aunt hit him hard on the skull with the hairbrush in her hand. He felt the skull beneath the skin. He moved his skin back and forth with his tiny finger on his temple. It was the first time he thought of the skeleton inside. He stopped his weeping and snivelled. The daylight was at the window now. It brightened the room. It stood framed by the window staring with a blank, raw glare.

Christopher's aunt Carmen had been taking a beautician course when her sister came from Puerto Rico pregnant and with three young children. Carmen had dreamed of living in California, which looked the nicest of places. She wanted to do the make-up of the movie stars. Her sister arrived and two months later died in childbirth. The two aunts found someone to take the eldest boy, Fredrico. Carmen had to keep the one-year-old girl Maria and the three-year-old Henry. A Mexican woman who took pity on them offered to take the newborn son and named him Christopher. The aunt Linda had breast cancer and died five years later in the hospital. Carmen gave up her beautician course and her dreams of the sun-drenched Pacific coast. She got a job in the Ford Motor Company. She had barely time to date men and keep her curly hair straightened. The Mexican woman died and her orphaned daughters had brought Christopher back to her.

He was snivelling pitifully, sucked into the big green armchair. His boots were almost above his head and were dripping melted snow on her good carpet. He had a mop of curly hair like her own. He did not look at her. He was fingering his temple. He looked sulky. He had probably been spoiled by the old Mexican, she sighed. Her sighs hovered in the air above her. The child shuddered to witness them linger in the air as the unfamiliar room was swamped in the cruel light of day. As they dissipated, he did not pine after them, for in their flat resignation he felt no mercy.

Carmen was growing old fast. She was a factory rat. She had now three children to feed who were not the fruits of her womb. No decent man in his right mind would want to get involved in this mess. She felt if she took time to do things like straighten her hair, show affection to her wards or grieve for her dead sisters that the whole tenuous structure of her existence would fall apart.

Christopher and his siblings grew up like weeds. They were ignored by the exhausted and disappointed Carmen who took time out only to punish or admonish them. He could never stand Henry but he loved his wild sister Marie. At the age of ten he was running messages for the local motorcycle gang. Henry grew up to be a beer-guzzling factory rat who beat his girlfriends and spent his weekends watching football. Marie got pregnant at sixteen and married a Polish Vietnam Vet from the motorcycle club. The guy got a job in the car factory after the birth of a son. Christopher was having none of that.

He progressed from a paper round to minor drug dealing at the luckless age of thirteen. Carmen finally got sick of it and found his stash in a drawer in his room. She confronted him: "This yours?"

"I guess so."

"You guess so, huh? And I thought you were the most popular boy on the road with all them kids coming over every hour of the day."

Christopher grinned.

"Don't go grinning at me, young man. Either I call the police and you get a good talking to or you take your drawer and leave this house."

Christopher took his drugs and left the house. Carmen let him back in after a couple of weeks.

Christopher was fourteen when the sixties ended. He began to read the underground magazines. He took his politics from the radical left, especially the anarchists. He read an article proclaiming, "The empire is mad. And it so maddens its inhabitants that they do not comprehend its existence." This blew his mind. He read all the alternative non-fiction he could lay his grubby hands on, devouring everything from home-made bomb books to legalize hemp pamphlets. This unexpected appetite for intellectual stimulants sharpened his mind and broadened his outlook, but at the reckless age of sixteen he was addicted to heroin and had to do all he could to feed the giant monkey on his back.

Christopher stood in the snow with his friends. He was stunned.

"Your brother Fredrico, he's the dealer in that club."

Christopher had never met his brother.

"Go get some shit from him. It's your brother, man."

Christopher gasped and then collected himself.

"I never met him. He doesn't know me, man."

"Tell him you're his brother, man. He'll give you a good deal."

Christopher, trying to breathe hot air on his ungloved hands, shook his head.

"This is a fast city, man. This ain't Hollywood. Fuck it, if I tell him I'm his brother, it would throw him off. He'd think I'm trying to pull something on him."

"You don't want to see your own brother?"

Christopher sneered at his friend. He straightened his shoulders and, snatching the money out of his friend's hand, pushed the graffitied door of the club open and went inside.

It was dark as expected and some mean-looking bikers stood at the pool table. Christopher was a brave and cynical seventeen-year-old. He was on his toes but not easily intimidated. He asked the barman loudly, "Fredrico here?"

One of the guys snarled, "I'm Fredrico."

He stood close to Christopher. He was a couple of inches taller and had a beer gut. At first Christopher would not have recognised him as family. His hair was long and straight and in a ponytail.

"Give me thirty bucks' worth," he said softly, tilting his head up to look straight into those mean used-up eyes. Fredrico told him to wait. Christopher sat at the bar. The barman nodded at him. Christopher did not return the gesture. Fredrico came back. He could look a little like Carmen around the eyes but he had the wide jaw of the dead aunt whose photos were all over the house. They made the exchange and Christopher said,

"I'm your brother."

"Henry?" Fredrico looked amused.

"Christopher." He wished he had not started this.

"Christopher!" exclaimed Fredrico. "Hey!" he shouted to his friends. "This guy killed my mother." He was laughing. "You killed Mama, Christopher. In the kitchen. I can remember it."

Christopher got off the stool. He was flushed with anger; anywhere else, he would have killed Fredrico for humiliating him like this. With a dangerous black feeling in his heart and his face hardened he walked out into the snow-covered world. He could hear them all laughing at him inside and he flinched from the white daylight glare.

"Did you get the stuff?"

"Yeah, I got it. Let's get out of here and do some. I feel awful." His head was down and he felt sick to his bones.

The four friends sat in a parked van wrapped up in smelly blankets, their teeth chattering.

"These blankets stink, man."

"Yeah, let's get out of here."

They all shot up with the same needle and everybody perked up a little.

"Did you tell him you're his brother, man?"

"Yeah, I told him."

"So?"

"We're going to have Thanksgiving together. He's going to roast me a big motherfucking turkey."

"Cool." His friend nodded.

"You goofy motherfucker," Christopher snarled. "What do you think happened? No favours in this town. You don't get something for nothing."

Three of them got out and let the other doze in the blankets. They slammed the door and marched off in separate directions. The snow was frozen and uneven. It was difficult to walk on. Christopher had no gloves and felt ill-equipped to deal with this snow-covered world.

In his bedroom the curtains were closed and the day was dark and short. He lay on the bed barely breathing. He heard some winter bird call; a rough harsh sound that scraped at the chilled air. Outside the highway stretched behind his house. As long as he could remember he had heard its sounds; an inglorious procession of vehicles. When he slept they drove past always, somewhere in the back of his head, in the corner edges of his dreams. Even if he were to dream of wild prairies or peaceful mountain slopes the cars and trucks hummed through it all.

Detroit was a city for the car. Even when the cars failed the people and the industry collapsed, the cars and trucks drove on. The deadening drone that drove him towards lunacy. The apathy of awaking in the cold room, the curtains closed, the day almost gone. Christopher would not look outside, he would bury his head in his foam pillow and the black of outer space would settle so thickly behind the clouds that night would arrive with a thud.

Always on awakening he would be seized by the grip of his addiction. He would be forced to rise in the dark room, already clothed, and put on his boots. He would walk past Carmen and they would not exchange any greeting.

She was fed up with him having the audacity to waste away in her house and lead a useless life, hanging out with petty gangsters and junkies, never earning an honest dollar; his communist propaganda lying all about her. She knew that he never showered and he put his feet on the furniture. He was commonly found dozing, high as a kite, in front of the TV when she came home after a day's work at the factory. He never went to school and had a lousy attitude towards her and all authority. The things he said about the government were positively un-American. He was a pest and an ingrate. Henry was a drunk and had a foul temper but he clung to Carmen and she gave him money from time to time. Marie had settled down after her wild days of hanging out at the club and on street corners with hoodlums. Carmen enjoyed the baby, Scott. Now that Marie was a mother she could empathise and realize how hard it had been and how much had to be sacrificed. But Christopher was a junkie who talked nonsense politics all day long.

Christopher was fed up of Carmen's incessant nagging and her simple-minded view of the world. He tried to avoid her whenever possible. He had never asked her for anything since he had arrived at the bewildered age of seven. He did not feel that he owed her anything.

Christopher left the house and stuck his hands into his army jacket. He concentrated on his walk. He was aware that in a city like this a walk made a man. It was important to stick to the middle of the sidewalk, maintaining a purposeful stride. Junk affected the way you walked. Junkies had bad posture; they slunk along close to the walls, unable to bear the harsh winds that whistled through their bones. Christopher tried very hard not to fall into such habits and he used the utmost discipline to prevent himself scratching in public when high. He had observed the scratching frenzies other junkies fell into and it disgusted him. He gave up smoking tobacco cigarettes. Nicotine was an addiction that made no sense to him. There was no perceptible buzz and all the money went into the big companies that he despised. At the aloof age of seventeen, Christopher had distanced himself from the other mindless junkies and had earned himself due respect among his peers.

He sat at a topless bar for two hours a day, seven days a week between five and seven and there was nobody more punctual than those poor junkies. He gave the owner a cut and tipped amply. He sold sometimes to the dancers. He knew them all by name and would talk to them. They even liked him. Concerts were his big deal though and in the early seventies Detroit had no shortage of bands. He would tape his drugs to his stomach and smuggle them in past the guys on the door. He had an instinct for who to sell to and who to approach. He could sniff a narc a mile away. This sense never failed him. Since he was thirteen years old Christopher had gone to four or five concerts a week. He sold pot, acid, downers, uppers and smack. His curious manners and reserved nature earned him minor infamy.

He basked quietly in his legend. The bikers, who supplied him with most of his drugs and had known him since he was ten, were proud of his progress.

However, they had neglected to advise their eager prodigy of the occupational hazards. Christopher was all but deaf by the time he was seventeen. He trained himself to lip read when he was in the strip bar or whenever there was loud music in the background. He was afraid he would slip into the annoying habits of the very deaf and begin to shout during all communications; sudden death when dealing with clients. He affected a mode of speech that was almost a whisper. A drone, as subtle as the cars and trucks that rolled by perpetually on the highway outside his bedroom window.

He now had a full drooping moustache and he could sit on his hair if he bent his head back. He stopped growing early; growth abandoned him gracelessly at the embarrassing height of five foot two inches. He was imbued with such rancor because of this, it was all he could do to disguise it with his customary nonchalance, but it instilled a bitterness and mind-aching fury in him. Height mattered in this world. It gave the gangsters the edge over him that was not by rights theirs. He resented this deformity with a blind anger but there was no one on whom to target the blame. He felt picked on and singled out by nature. He hated women to tower over him but could not abide a short girl lest he be ridiculed further. Sometimes, when he was with a particular whore or dancer, he would get in a drunken rage triggered by no apparent outside force but by his sores and cankers within. He would set on her and he would slap her hard. He never had a shortage of women to come to him though. He was the dealer.

He had power over people. He sold them the drugs they wanted or needed. He had, at seventeen, all the respect of a cardinal among his shabby flock. His flock of desperate, poor, exhausted junkies or pleasure-seekers who thought they could avoid the traps of addiction. Christopher was intuitive, he could see if they were labouring with a monkey on their backs.

He could look the fiendish monkey in its demonic eye and see if it was a chimp or a baboon, if it would tug his client's hair and dig its claws into the lost soul's sunless back. Some monkeys were feeble and might be shaken off eventually after a mammoth struggle. Some monkeys were indomitable. Christopher sometimes felt that he was conversing with an array of beasts riding for free on the backs of humankind rather than with their pathetic bearers.

He could inspect the monkeys, the condition of their coats, the colour and number of teeth, the patterns of shot veins in the whites of their rabid eyes, the texture of their tongues as they drooled like inmates of an asylum, the amount of blood and dirt under their claws, the grip by which they clasped their luckless owners. He knew how near to death each of his shabby flock was. He kept his predictions to himself. He had no desire to be a prophet among those with futures that shrank into their lives; those who were shrouded in a curious doomed anti-glow, as though the light was sucked in and dismantled in the circumference of their bodies. He did not want to betray their trust as they shuffled up in as dire need as a human can be. Hollow, darting, paranoid eyes beseeched him to not rip them off, to deliver the goods without fuss. Christopher's ethics meant that he never cut his stash or sold shitty goods. He had that pristine reputation and it was deserved in the dens of iniquity that he frequented. His strict politics made him deal his drugs and exercise his power as humanely as he could. To feed the accursed monkeys without teasing or taunting their deranged souls, to show respect and mercy for even the most worthless of their bearers.

On one occasion he tried to reverse the process on himself. He stood in front of the mirror in the ladies' toilets when the club was not yet open and the girls were not around to disturb his search. He stared hard, scrutinizing the air above his shoulder. He wanted to gauge his own monkey. To identify the extent of his crisis with heroin, he probed the very atmosphere above his head with terror and trepidation. But he could not see. His own monkey would not bend to his dubious gift.

Carmen said to him many times, "You have a chip on your shoulder." He thought about this and attributed it to the fact that he was a tiny man when in his mind he believed himself to be a giant among men. The fact that his growth was stunted meant that the bikers did not automatically assume he would join their ranks. For this he was grateful as he was a loner and had no appetite for the intimidation and thuggery of a biker lifestyle.

He had run errands for them for years and had their protection if he saw fit to call on them. He had a gun but he kept it in his bedroom and rarely brought it out with him. He never would take it into the concerts. He preferred to use a simple flick knife for protection. He also carried a Swiss Army knife for emergencies which never arose but it came in handy in the meantime for peeling apples, opening beers and picking his nails. Christopher had a reputation that far exceeded his history of violence. He had been in a number of fist fights but had only once stabbed a man, when that man called him Shorty. Though he was small, people were afraid of him.

With the depths of snow in winter and the strangling humidity of summer, Christopher perceived the weather as hostile. He was always struggling against the elements in Detroit. Every season was a trial. His stamina was under constant threat of erosion from the emissions of the sky, be it the withering heat waves or vindictive snow-flakes.

The snow was a few feet high and would freeze. All its valleys and rifts would be rock hard. Detroit was a huge, industrial metropolis whose gods had abandoned it. The factories were closing down and moving to Mexico for cheap labour. The neighbourhood he lived in had most of the shops and businesses boarded up and empty. These people were blue-collar workers who did not thrive on culture. They didn't read books or listen to classical music. They watched the football and the sitcoms on TV. They watched the game shows. When the jobs were gone and they had nothing to do they got stupid. Everyone had an axe to grind. People were angry, bored out of their heads and broke. Christopher kept his mouth shut, his eyes peeled. When doing business he would slice off the tiniest sliver of an acid tab and take it to heighten his perception. It was never worth playing straight when dealing with the level of desperation and lunacy that Detroit produced.

His party days were over now. He came to look on dealing as a vocation more than a career. As a career it stank. The money was all right but he was always looking over his shoulder. Now that he was hooked he had to continue dealing to feed his insatiable monkey. The heroin made him happy, the acid heightened his perception, the uppers and downers were just for kicks, the pot he smoked so regularly that he could not imagine life without it. This was a high risk business under siege from both the law and the vicissitudes of daily existence.

"The sooner they make this stuff legal the better," he stated many times.

In the meantime he continued his good deeds: to be there every day for two hours at the club for his regulars, and to heighten people's enjoyment of music by getting them high at all the gigs.

Apart from the good deeds to be performed every day Christopher was aware of the need to wage war. The enemies were the Romans. The Romans were led by the White House. That included the CIA, the FBI and anyone in the police force or big business. They were evil and the people who served them were pawns and deserved to be wiped out for their stupidity and willingness to serve the Mad Empire. The Romans wore suits and ties. They conformed and they believed in the deity and duties that they were allotted at birth. They played the roles that were dictated to them by the government.

Romans were everywhere. They were the mainstream and Christopher was marginalised. He would not dance to their tune. He would always hate the Mad Empire. He read his anarchist books, exposés of the CIA and pamphlets on revolution. Everybody was coming back from Vietnam pissed off. He waited knowing that if he saw a chance he would grab it. Maybe he would kill a pig or a rich man before he died. He would be ready.

Between his good deeds and living in a constant state of war Christopher considered himself something of a holy man and a warrior. He was a man with a mission. He was the Hoodoo Man. Everyone looks on the Hoodoo Man with respect as he takes his rightful place at the bar to dispense alms to the needy, to kill their need, to make all their days happier and shorter. You can't hoodoo the Hoodoo Man.

It was his fate one day to come by a crate of dynamite on his rounds. He purchased it immediately and brought it to the house, perspiring with paranoia. He hauled it up the stairs panting and puffing. Carmen was alarmed; she came away from the TV and stared at him.

"What the hell kind of trouble are you bringing into this house now?"

"A case of dynamite," Christopher said, kicking open his door and putting it on the bed. He slammed the door. Carmen snorted and went back to her evening's anaesthetic of sitcoms.

Christopher plotted and plotted. Then one night with a trusted associate he drove out to a country club and using two sticks blew up the seventeenth green.. He went out a few nights later to another country club and threw a couple of sticks at random, damaging the fairway.

They shot up, dropped off the stolen car and went to a concert to mingle.

"I'm Jesus Christ!" he said to a girl and slipped her an acid.

He took her home. Carmen was asleep but as usual knew everything. In the morning she was furious.

"You want to take pussy home, get your own place, young man. It's about time you moved out. I'm a clean woman. I take a shower every day. I don't want you bringing any diseases into this house. No fleas, no crabs. You move out, you hear? Get a job."

"I have a job."

"I mean an honest job."

"I'm not dumb enough to go waste my years in the fucking factory."

"You haven't an honest bone in your body. I give you an inch and you take a mile. You don't put anything back into this house."

"I pay my fucking rent, you bitch. Now get the fuck out of my room and let me sleep."

"You're a lazy good-for-nothing. You use all those politics as an excuse not to work . . ."

"Fuck you, Carmen." Christopher got out of bed naked and shut the door on her, locking it too.

Carmen shouted through the door.

"I see you naked. You never take off your clothes. You've been up to something. I know what you have in your bedroom, Christopher. Guns and dynamite. I didn't get off the last boat you know. I'm calling the police if you don't clean it up by tonight. I don't care who you kill, God forgive me, but don't kill anyone from this house. If your poor mother could see you now. It wasn't worth her dying for you. Marie and Henry have their problems but they try to work them out. You're a bad piece of work, Christopher. God help you."

Christopher sat on his bed. The revolution was over, or at least put on hold. He hid the gun under his mattress. He called around and finally gave the dynamite to a black man who was willing to take it.

"I won't charge you. This is a point of principle. For the Cause, brother."

The man looked at him strangely and put it in his car. He was relieved to wash his hands of the whole affair. Normal duties were resumed. Christopher decided to watch some TV before going to the club.

In his dreams he took the form of a peacock. On nights of the full moon he found, if he fasted while it reigned, this transformation would occur. It was a solemn rule for him never to let a morsel pass his lips for twenty-four hours on the full moon. He was always aware of the moon. The great moon. He loved the improbability of having it in the sky hovering miraculously. Something huge beyond the banality of the city streets of Detroit. He could observe in it powers that stood away from the meddling of humans. There may have been a man on the moon but he did not stay very long and Christopher believed the moon had ignored this intrusion. He admired its splendid solitude.

He tried to curb the flow of hatred that flooded his mind and ransacked the order of thought and logic within. His life at seventeen was dislocated. He changed his diet, he looked to Eastern religions briefly, he experimented with bouts of celibacy. He could not give drugs a rest as they were his career. He might starve without them, relegated to the unhappy ranks of people relying solely on welfare, stripped of his hard-earned honour and power. There was little point in going to the school that only told him Roman facts and attempted to socialise rather than educate him. He could not leave Detroit. He knew nobody outside of the city except his aunts in California and he had lost contact with them long ago. The only jobs he could get were dumb, pointless and badly paid. He was not a worker. All he could do was continue as he was with grace and look to the moon. Maybe somewhere in the years ahead it would reveal some of its powers and make him aware of things that were now drowned in anger.

As a peacock, he strutted through Detroit. He sat in full plumage on the pool tables of the club, squawking at the bikers and shitting on the green baize. He made gifts of fallen feathers to the dancers. He stalked up and down the stage in the Grand Ballroom in front of an adulant crowd.

The snows melted in his wake. The thaw flowed in crystal clear rivers through the gutters, cleansing the city. Once he walked to his mother's grave, a place he had never been and could only imagine. He tried to sing for her but his voice was harsh. He felt upset and flew away. As he landed, crowds gasped at the splendid fan of his tail. In the distance he could hear the cars and trucks pass by in glum monotony, as reliable and as interminable as the seasons. He was a peacock standing on the steps of Carmen's house giving the official nod to passers by. He blessed them with his beauty, cursing them with his cry. He would eventually flutter up the wooden stairs to his room. The radiance of his tail would glow within the half-blocked light that filtered through the material of the curtains.

Christopher arches his back as he sleeps and clutches his genitals. In spasms he loves himself as the peacock. He perches on the windowsill and pokes his head through the curtains. He sees the moon pressing against the glass, illuminated by the mad excitement of coming to the earth it serves. Christopher breaks the glass with his beak and pecks the moon.

He comes in his sleep.

It is quiet and the ground is white and aglow. He is small among the craters and has a chalky taste in his mouth. The air is compressed into blocks of silence and the stars are twinkling. The sky is densely black. He takes off and flies and flies above the spooky lunar landscape. He cranes his long neck this way and that but he cannot see the earth. The beating of his wings is the only noise in outer space.

Candy Brown had a gap in her teeth and he had a sort of fetish for gaps. She was blond and thin and fifteen years old; her parents had been drunks along the strip. He respected her. Opening doors with her pretty smile she could score anything day or night. She was sullen and flirtatious by turns but that did not fool Christopher. He knew she was very, very tough. She took downers and this gave her an attitude which got on his nerves. She was so messed up on downers that she used to fall asleep when he was fucking her. Christopher would continue what he was doing and pull out, coming on top of her. She would get pissed off later when she discovered it. Christopher would shrug.

"I keep telling you I don't like it when you fall asleep."

"I can't help it," she would pout.

She sometimes visited him when he was on duty in the topless bar. He would straighten up when he saw her slouch in. She would kiss his cheek and he would get her a beer. It was almost like having a girlfriend. He wanted her to get a job there so he could keep an eye on her but she sneered at the idea. She made more money being an occasional whore and taking packages for the bikers.

She told him lots of stories in her sweet little voice and they made him laugh.

"One day I was hanging out at the Club, wearing a skirt that barely covered my ass. Charger asks me to change the light bulb. Silly me, I get up on the table to change the bulb, he puts his hand up my skirt and grabs my bare ass."

"Charger did that? That dirty fucker." He would shake his head, smiling.

At the unsuspecting age of eighteen, just when Christopher thought he had settled into routine for life, he was busted for cocaine possession. A poor person's life is full of surprises, he thought. They gave him the choice of a term in prison or joining the army. Christopher surprised even himself by picking the latter option. Carmen was elated.

"The US Army will make a man of you, Chris, mark my words. This is the best thing that has ever happened to you."

He was sent overseas to Germany. Sitting on the bus on the way to base in Europe the first thing he noticed was the lack of billboards. He was a bad soldier and a junkie. He was more interested in being a junkie than in anything else in the whole world and he couldn't care less about the American army. He soon found birds of a feather within the ranks to flock with. There was no shortage of heroin. He saw plenty of men puke into their trays at breakfast, put napkins over it and continue eating. The world was riddled with junkies. The army was infested with them.

Christopher did not owe any allegiance to the flag. His country was the strip of Detroit city he lived on. His country people were the bikers, whores, dancers, junkies, gangsters. He had never occupied himself outside of this. The only advantage of a war would be to have the opportunity to shoot one of his sergeants in the back during battle.

One day when Christopher was a military ambulance driver he was taking a captain to the hospital. He parked the ambulance and went into a cinema to shoot up in the toilet. High as a kite he sat down in the theatre and watched the Bugs Bunny cartoons dubbed in German before the main show. When he emerged finally the captain was dead. Christopher drove him to the hospital in a state of panic. He said he got lost. There was a full inquiry. Christopher threatened to sue the army for getting him hooked on heroin. He attained an honourable discharge. Another brilliant career down the drain. Later Christopher would tell his friends,

"I know how that bastard Nero felt when he played the violin as Rome burned. I was watching Bugs Bunny when the captain died. Me and Nero would have things to talk about."

The first night back in Detroit his brother Henry said,

"So what is it like to be in the US military?"

Christopher stuffed a giant forkful of rice into his mouth and said,

"The U-esh military ish a fucking waishte of dime."

Carmen gave him one week to find alternative accommodation.

Caught back in his old bedroom he closed the curtains. They had remained open since he had been gone. He lay down, slightly cold but too lazy to get beneath the covers. Outside the window he knew that it was snowing. Flakes that were light and soundless, but devastating none the less. He was too old to withstand the serpent tongue of a bitter woman. He was almost twenty-one. Tomorrow he would trudge through the accursed snow to the club and buy some drugs. He wouldn't go back to dealing heroin at the strip bar. He was out of sync, an outsider in a fast scene. He didn't care, it was time to move on. He was too old to take orders from those dumb bikers. As he drifted asleep he was disquieted and apprehensive. He did not know where to get his money. He was scared for the first time of the huge future that lay blankly in front of him, that started as soon as he left the room. He felt a fool in the dark. As he drowsed he heard the cars and trucks whirring by. He realised that sound had never left his head. There was a highway forged in his mind, from years and years of that sound driving on and on as he dreamed most of his life. Burrowed into the fabric of his brain, huge feats of mental engineering flung up a grey infrastructure in his head. That sound was so persistent it had been barely perceptible, forever insidious, riding the ravaged perimeters of his unconscious mind. It did not feel so good to be home.

Christopher was a year back in Detroit. He was once more established and accepted by his peers. He didn't see Candy Brown except by chance encounter. Despite the heroin use over the years she was only eighteen and her looks had not gone. They enjoyed talking together but both were involved in lives that moved too fast from day to day to get involved. Christopher decided that birds were baggage and apart from the occasional fling he did not pursue relationships. He liked to say that the exits weren't too clearly visible from the fast lane.

He was living a mile away from Carmen's house in the garage of an old couple, Riane and Alvin. Riane ruled the roost. She was a spry, little, blue-haired woman of sixty-five he had met in a Greek restaurant. He had been waiting for a contact to sell a plane ticket to in a scam of his that he conducted occasionally; they struck up a conversation and she told him that he could sleep in the garage until he found somewhere else. They were white people and the garage was full of junk. Christopher put down a mattress, placed his gun under the pillow and changed the lock so only he could enter.

She was a sharp and funny old lady. Christopher gave her a hit of acid and she loved it, she liked to see the colours and the trails of moving objects. She gave Christopher some capital and they went into business. Riane had been a criminal all her life. She could get doctors' prescription pads from the hospital and she was an expert forger. They dressed up Alvin, her seventy-eight-year-old quiet boy-friend, in a navy suit with a good leather briefcase. He would go to the pharmacy with the prescriptions and bring back the drugs. Christopher then sold them on the strip for a good price. The split went three ways and Christopher never paid rent for the garage. He was content. It paid for his habit, some gambling and he never felt obliged to rip them off. In truth Riane and he used to do acid every week and he liked her. Alvin was a doddery old soul who padded about the house clutching his pajama bottoms at the waist to keep them up. They had a big, black, beautiful Great Dane who was the pride and joy of the house and with whom Christopher made sure to cultivate a friendship for future use.

Alvin did a good job. He looked like a distinguished old millionaire in the suit. Christopher would drive him around from pharmacy to pharmacy, careful not to wear him out. At home Alvin fell asleep with his eyes half open and his mouth agape, saliva dribbling down his chin. Christopher once wanted to place a tab of LSD on his tongue to see what would happen. Riane warned him not to meddle with an old brain that was confused enough. They needed Alvin and so Christopher spared him the experiment.

Christopher was having problems with the police. There was one cop in particular who followed and threatened him. The guy was squat and red-cheeked, with yellow mustard hair under his cop hat. His eyes were small, sunken and watery-looking. Christopher thought he was the epitome of a pig. He even told the guy, "Hey, I'm not your concern. I'm committing federal crimes now. You have to change your job to get me. Go join the FBI, motherfucker."

The cop arrested him twice in one week, once for eating on the bus and once for jaywalking. He was making Christopher angry. He busted Christopher with some codeine pills and he spent twenty-one days in jail. By the time the full moon came around, Christopher shot his arm full of heroin and with an empty belly took Riane and Alvin's Great Dane out to eat the policeman.

He felt that the moon's inspiration would lead him to his victim's lair. It was a hot and humid August day and though the moon was invisible he knew it was full and he felt the pull. The neighbourhood shimmered in a mesmerising heat haze. Christopher prowled the streets clutching the dog by its neck. He was insulated by the heroin, he was the God of Revenge. He gripped the fold of hot hairy skin on the monster animal's neck. He strutted, bad medicine for bad pigs with a giant beast at his side ready to do his bidding.

The whites of his eyes were red as he trembled in anticipation of the kill.

They walked, man and beast, for two hours hunting the policeman down. Christopher groaned in exasperation.

"He'll probably pick me up for not having my dog on a leash."

He closed his thin lids over his steaming pupils. He longed for the moon to cool his war path and guide his way to the kill. His steps were sluggish and he felt a terrible thirst grip his dry throat. His spirit was waning. In utter defeat he turned back. The dog's giant tongue hung out like a desolate strip of sandpaper. Its brown eyes filmed over and rolled in its huge head. Finally a mile from home its front legs buckled and it fell, banging its chin off the burning pavement.

Christopher kicked it in the ribs in frustration, sweat waterfalling down his face and from his armpits.

"Get up, you mangy cur!" he bellowed.

He grabbed the giant head by the ears in a desperate attempt to rouse the dehydrated animal. The dog was in a seizure and Christopher took it by the hind legs and dragged it down the sidewalk. The beast was a dead weight.

"Hey! What are you doing to that poor animal?"

"None of your business, motherfucker," Christopher roared. "Now clear off or I'll shoot your fucking face off."

The car wisely sped off.

Christopher had the dying dog outside the house. Its side was bleeding and scraped. Riane was ringing the vet in despair and outrage. Alvin came out and looked glumly at the poor creature.

"I'm going to shoot it. Put it out of its misery. Riane, where's your gun?"

Riane screamed, "Gun? What? I'll put you out of your misery, you old fart."

Alvin asked again, "Riane, where's your gun?"

"Christopher took it," she gasped.

Christopher trudged inside and got Riane's gun from the garage. He came out and shot the dog in the head on the street in front of the house. Riane hammered him with her shrivelled, translucent, old lady fists. He pushed her into the wall and Alvin whimpered, "Come on, Chris, calm down. Let's bury the dog in the yard, it's got maggots on it already."

Christopher ignored him and went into the garage, locking the door. "Senile old bat," he said to Riane as she tried to pull his hair on her way in.

Christopher was listening to his beloved Iggy Pop in the garage when the nephews came.

> I'm a street walking cheetah with a head full of Napalm,
> I'm the run away son of the nuclear H-Bomb.

They came, four big men, the nephews Riane always talked about, brandishing sawn-off shot guns. When they broke the door down, Christopher leapt up sweating like a pig and roared along with the music.

> I am the world's forgotten boy,
> The one who searches and destroys.

He pulled the gun from beneath the pillow but was outnumbered. He left the house penniless and drugless with nothing but his tape recorder, his tape collection and his gun. Alvin stood at the door and said gently, "Riane is on tranquilisers to calm her down. We thought it best you should leave."

Christopher looked at him in disgust.

"She must have loved that dog more than she loved you, Alvin," he said. Alvin turned his bent, old back and went slowly into the house.

> Somebody's got to help me please,
> Somebody's got to save my soul,
> Oh baby won't you help me please.

He was back in his room at Carmen's, making occasional money doing the plane ticket scam but losing on the horses and putting it all in his left arm. He never saw Riane and Alvin again and had a bad taste in his mouth from the whole experience. He heard on the street she had passed on the prescription business to one of her nephews and they were still dragging poor old Alvin about, putting him on the front line in his pin-stripe monkey suit and empty, new briefcase.

Christopher was spending most of his time on the racetrack and apart from a few big wins was barely keeping his head above water and the wolves from the door. In truth, at twenty-four he was tired of living. He was being watched hawkishly by the police. The radical left in the country seemed lame and uninspired. The Empire was still completely and utterly mad. He was a junkie and dependent on that drug come what might. He had to put it before everything. Ronald Reagan was running for president and it looked as if the idiot might actually win. It made Christopher physically sick to even hear his voice. The Mad Emperor would destroy life for the poor people, the luckless pawns who never reaped the bounty promised to them as Americans. There were no answers and Christopher had no friends or allies. The Romans were all-powerful, the revolution was despised and written out of history. The poor had turned on themselves; witless carnivores. The rich had taken the money and run off to their exclusive townships. Christopher did not feel brave enough to fight the world with cardboard limbs.

Carmen never stopped asking him when he was going to clear off. He used to sit at his window with the gun in his hand, hypnotised by the monotony of the highway. Somehow the secret of contentment and love had eluded him. Looking at the cars and trucks speed by, he was under the impression that everyone was going somewhere and his was a cursed life of enforced stagnation. He had been relegated to the sidelines to sit without purpose, observing the movement of people driven to pursue their destinations. Like an abandoned child he sat with his sallow forehead against the rotted window frame, fingering the gun in his hand. Hands that had been broken so many times in fights or fits of anguish that the bones left unattended had reset badly. A deformed hand holding a gun limply on his lap. The other hand resting on the window pane. His twisted fingers out-stretched, his misplaced knuckles curled away from the glass. As it grew dark outside he wondered if he could work up enough spunk to shoot himself in the head.

He was busted for heroin and spent two months in prison bored and lonely; nobody came to visit. When he got out he borrowed money from the bikers. He put a small fortune on one horse and watched it lose. He dropped twelve tabs of acid and in a monster trip he had a blinding revelation and took a plane to Puerto Rico to look for his roots. Renting a house on the sea, he went alone to the Casino every day. After playing cards he would try and engage the barman in conversation just to hear his own voice.

He hated the sound of the sea. The waves breaking like gunshots on the rocky shore. Lying naked on his bed, drunk and stoned, perspiring from the heat, he would hear the waves crash relentlessly, eroding the island. The servile waves, fingers of the sea grasping at the land spastically, tearing it to bits. The tides guided by the moon in slavish homage to their own nature. There was an ugly predictability in the drag of the foam and the servant roar of the wave. Just as there were a few seconds of merciful silence, the water obediently broke on the rocks and slithered back into itself. He could find no peace beside the ocean and he could not sleep. Racked with insomnia, after two weeks he counted his money. He bought a ticket to Detroit. He walked to the Casino on his last day; on a hunch he tossed his last one hundred dollars on the roulette wheel and lost.

Christopher was stopped before he got to his house by the mustard-headed pig. They found a joint even he didn't know he had in his pocket. They beat him up in the station and let him loose. He returned to his house and found Carmen frantic. She said that there had been heavies from the club around every day to look for him. Christopher begged her for money but she had none. He went to stay in his sister Marie's house in Ann Arbor. Her husband hated him, was reluctant to even leave him alone in the same room as their son Scott. Finally he convinced an acquaintance to give him one hundred trips to sell on credit. He stole twenty-five bucks from his brother-in-law's wallet and went to the airport.

Sitting in the airport casing out the human beings on the plastic seats, he moved to an empty seat beside a white vacationer. The man was in his late thirties and divorced but flew out to Oregon every year to see his three kids. He rented a motel in Eugene every May and took them hiking. They were growing so fast and he was truly dismayed to only be able to see them annually. He was overweight and wore a baseball cap. Christopher said he was flying to Florida to see his mother. They chatted amicably for half an hour. The man was not from Detroit but from Flint. They discussed Reagan's election, the man saying he liked the refugee from Tinseltown, that he would make Americans proud of what they were again. Flint needed patriotism because it was going to the dogs with the car companies pulling out. He asked Christopher to watch his bag while he went to the bathroom. When he was gone Christopher opened the bag and found a money holder. There was six hundred dollars in one-hundred-dollar notes. Christopher quickly took four hundred and put the wallet back, zipping the bag shut. He tried to conceal his elation when the man returned. He got up and shook his hand. "Real nice talking to you, sir. I got to catch my plane. Hope it doesn't rain too much in Oregon."

The man smiled and waved. "Good luck, kid."

Christopher was off in a flash. He had got all the luck he needed from the bag.

Buying a ticket to Stuttgart in Germany, he boarded the plane and sighed with relief when it began to speed down the runway. He had one hundred dollars and one hundred trips in his breast pocket. This is the fastest I can ever go on land, he thought to himself with satisfaction. He wished it had been the night of the full moon because he would gladly have shed his dowdy skin and grown rapturous plumage as he hurtled through the treacherous night sky, safe for now in the womb of the plane, prepared for a new life in Europe.

Part Two

3

Suburbanol

TAFFY AND ISOLT sat on the train riding out of Paris towards Saint-Germain-en-Laye. The further the train rolled the bigger the houses became, the more the gardens bloomed. It was the end of summer, the second anniversary of Becky's death.

"Damn! Even the seagulls seem bigger and cleaner out here," Taffy observed.

They saw the birds perch on the fences and stone walls. Taffy looked enviously at them.

"Those are high quality seagulls."

"I thought you hated rich people, Taffy."

"I do."

They reached the last station at eleven o'clock. They were late. The Germans were the only beggars to get up early and take the best spots. Taffy was an eighteen-year-old Welsh punk with a big round baby face and light blue eyes. His hair was shaved and sculpted into a red Mohawk and his clothes were ragged and filthy. Isolt knew they wouldn't like the look of him in this town but his missing leg might win them over.

"Where do you sit?" he asked Isolt.

"Usually on the street coming away from the market beside the shoe shop. You go to the market. I just don't like all the activity. I'll meet you at that café at one o'clock."

"Two hours?"

"OK, half twelve, give it a while. I need money for tonight. I'm broke."

"OK, half twelve then. Good luck!" He hopped off.

The footpath between the shoe shop and the next establishment was narrow. Isolt sat down compactly and whisked her sign out. "*SANS RESOURCE. AIDEZ MOI, S'IL VOUS PLAIT.*" This sign worked best. When she carried the simpler sign that most others carried, "*J'AI FAIM MERCI,*" people were inclined to take it literally and give her food. Once a woman from the *boulangerie* came over to her with a cup of warm milk. Isolt had felt obliged to drink it. With her new sign she could claim to be stuck in France and need money for the ticket home. The day was very cold. She put her hands into her sleeves. The money was donated in dribs and drabs. Isolt was freezing; her face turned bright pink. Her feet went numb. She painfully moved position. Her legs and one buttock cheek were asleep. A boy passed with his friends and threw a stick of chewing gum at her.

"*Tu as faim? Tiens.*"

It ricocheted off her head and hit the ground. Isolt glowered. This was a bad day indeed. A cold useless day. She should have stayed in bed. Though that was not without its attendant miseries; to stay in the icy squat alone feeling guilty because she didn't go out to beg. A woman came up to her. "*Tu veux du travail. Viens avec moi.*"

"*Non,*" Isolt muttered looking away. The woman bristled and seemed determined.

"*Viens. J'ai du travail pour toi.*"

Isolt stiffened, this awkward scene was beginning to attract attention. The woman was a pest.

"*Je travaille maintenant,*" Isolt said, hardening her face, trying to be low key and get rid of this nasty woman. Isolt could see herself packing oranges or gutting fish for the rest of the day for a lousy meal. The work people offered beggars was to be avoided at all costs. People began to close in as the woman launched on a righteous tirade.

"*Elle ne veut pas travailler,*" she shrieked. Heavy drops of rain fell and spattered the pavement. Of course I don't want to work, Isolt thought, or else I wouldn't be sitting here. A gigantic raindrop exploding on her forehead sprang her to action. She leaped up and the woman grabbed her arm. Isolt wrenched herself free in alarm and scurried through the crowd. She stalked darkly through the heavy downpour.

*

Taffy swayed on one leg, his crutches against the wall. He had abandoned his spot early. Miserable day, he thought, no point begging in the rain, people scurry by and don't stop. Rotten grey lousy day, should have stayed in bed and experimented further with the shoebox full of drugs they had found in the squat. Heavy rain messed up his mohawk. No money for tonight. He wouldn't even bother with the fountain. Too depressing if you couldn't even get a beer for yourself. He closed his eyes and conjured up a picture of the shoebox.

Still, it wasn't so bad; he loved France. Wales had been dingy. There was never anything to do in his little town. When he left he had been roaring drunk for three days on the trot. He couldn't remember what inspired him or the haze in which he got to the coast of England, but he had taken the boat here.

He had spent his last few quid at the deserted bar on the ferry. The grey choppy sea and the white cliffs of Dover; he had felt dizzy watching them disappear. The sky had been a threatening heavy grey and the seagulls followed the boat screeching mercilessly. He had never left Wales before. I'm a mad bastard, Wild Taffy with one leg and the other one a fake. But you could never tell, I've grown so used to it I could kick you in the arse all the way to Cardiff. He chuckled, then choked back the panic that suddenly rose from the pit of his stomach. His eyes watered from all the drink and the ship rocked roughly from side to side. Alone at the bar Taffy slurped down the cider greedily. Some Americans sat on the plastic orange seats eating their own sandwiches and eyeing him curiously as he tried to engage the pimply young barman in conversation to no avail. He was finding it difficult to form sentences.

"How many times, Sir, would you tell me . . . an awful job with all this rocking, Sir . . . Whoops! Jesus! . . . back and bloody forth . . . can hardly hold on to me shagging drink . . ." The barman held on to the bar, his face green. The Americans looked on at this desolate action. There was nothing else to look at except the vicious birds circling the mast. "This boat is empty . . . it's like a frigging graveyard . . . I've known livelier boats in . . . OH GOD! . . ."

In the toilets tears streamed from his eyes as he held the iron bar and puked all over the seat and onto the floor. He straightened up and allowed himself a bit of a sob. A short yank of a sob that sounded like a sea lion barking. He had vomit on his big brown sweater. Taffy, you mad cunt, you have no other clothes. On a tear for two days and you are sailing out of the country without a bloody coat. Wait till the lads hear this one; if he could make it back to tell them, that is. He resumed his place at the bar.

"Do you ever get used to all this to-ing and fro-ing, rocking back and forth . . . Where are you from? . . . Do you live in Dover? . . . This is making me feel sick, no, I'm better now after that bit of a puke . . ." The Americans finished their sandwiches, chewing thoughtfully. The green-faced pimply young barman brooded, trapped behind the bar.

The French customs guards witnessed him flailing, wildly drunk, through the Nothing To Declare channel. He stumbled, pushing past the travel-weary straggle of tourists. They took him to a room. He gave them the temporary passport he had got in the post office. They were not pleased at the thought of letting him into the country. He had to take off his clothes.

"*Détachez votre jambe!*"

He shook his head; he could speak no French.

"*Détachez votre jambe!*" They pulled at his leg and he sobered up a little. Sitting naked on a chair while two French men pulled his leg in the dingy little office. He took his leg off and they left with it. Now he sat in the office naked, staring sleepily at his stump, and duly passed out.

Taffy was being shaken awake by a foreigner, but he was the foreigner now. He opened his eyes and the room swam. He felt awful and it was so cold. "So cold. I'm so cold. Jesus help me, it's fucking freezing," he mumbled.

He was dribbling. They had to help him dress. Pulling on his clothes roughly. He acquiesced like a sleepy child, raising his arms for them to put on his woolly sweater. Then he bolted angrily.

"Where's my fucking leg, you French bastards!"

The guards looked at each other. Taffy sat with his shrivelled-up penis and his stump turning blue from the cold. They would send him back to England and he hadn't a penny to get home. His stomach was upset and his teeth chattered.

"*Votre jambe est cassée.*"

"I don't speak fucking French. Speak English, you bastards. Give me back my leg." He wished to God he had stayed at home. A new guard walked in and handed him a plastic Monoprix bag. He felt its weight and his heart stopped as he looked inside. His leg was in pieces.

"Ahhh! . . . we were looking for ze drugs and we are sorry for your leg."

There was silence. They stared sheepishly at him. Taffy got a ringing in his ears and felt himself go deaf from shock. The men were unsure what to do. They put on his jeans and let him out into the harbour. At the train station he slept for hours on a bench, almost dead with cold, clutching the plastic bag.

"I'm Superman, Taffy the Great. The wildest one-legged man in Wales, nosing out France to my heart's content." Sober as a judge now, starved with hunger, delirious from thirst and a pain in his head like a hatchet wedged in his skull.

Taffy came to Paris on the train. This was the first charity in a new life in which he would rely on charity. The conductor never threw him off the train to hop desperately about the provinces. Instead he let him lie between the carriages. He struggled off the train in the filthy Gare du Nord to take his place in the station café with the silent Arabs and the bedraggled peasant French. He was delighted.

Taffy, the wild man, came to Paris in winter, eighteen years old, with no money, a temporary passport, a vomit-stained brown sweater, no coat, his guts in a whirl, a ringing in his ear, a hatchet in his head and his leg in a plastic bag.

Christopher was sitting in a café opposite the Gare du Nord drinking an espresso. Taffy, one leg strong as an ox, the other as extinct as the unicorn, flailed onto the street. Hop! Hop! Hop! his one arm outstretched, keeping his balance off the wall, the other clutching his leg that was clattering about in smithereens in the bag.

Christopher, leaving, saw Taffy's grand entrance to the city. With customary caution he allowed himself several minutes to observe before coming to any major decision. He could see that he was British, young, deranged but nonthreatening. Christopher didn't like attention and squirmed at the thought of all the attention this lunatic would attract. A one-legged stumbling punk in rags.

Taffy never knew how much grief he was saved when this tiny dirty American in the guise of the Good Samaritan came and took his one-legged self under that world-weary wing. A second act of charity bestowed on his red cockatooed head. Though things were by no means easy, Christopher gave him shelter in the dead of winter.

There were three large abandoned buildings surrounding a courtyard in Saint Quen. They were old and had shuttered windows. A factory nearby billowed smoke day and night; ashes fell periodically like grey snowflakes through the air they breathed. The entrance was a large green iron gate. The courtyard was full of dogs and the smell was putrid. The dog diarrhoea splashed over the cobblestones was not always avoided by the drunken inhabitants on their nightly trips back home. The first step on the stairs had dog shit caked on its rim from inebriated shoe scrapers. There was no running water. The toilet water was frozen solid and off bounds since Ali had ignored the broomstick placed by the bowl to break the ice. Viewed several hours later to the disgust of some and amusement of many a turd had frozen to the ice.

The first house on the left had its ground floor inhabited by Afghan refugees, the hardest people in Europe. In their lives they had witnessed villages destroyed and parents murdered before their eyes. They had killed their first humans before they were ten years old. They had been captured by Russians, tortured and maimed. They had fled over mountains and rivers through hostile lands. They were living in filth without papers on the ground floor. Nobody mixed with them, not even the Iranians, who shared their language. Even the most shell-shocked thug Iranian fresh from the Iran-Iraq border considered himself too good-natured and aristocratic to hang out with these brutalized, vicious, ghostlike, womanless, private men. The second floor was all German: barbaric, alcoholic and junkie Germans. They outnumbered everyone else. The Germans all had a big dog each. They were responsible for the infestation of the place with crazed, inbred, Alsatian, flea-bitten dogs. In the other two houses were old French clochards or more manic, dishevelled, huge brain-damaged Germans. The house to the left had a third floor of assorted Europeans, mainly Irish, English, Dutch and the odd demented Italian or runaway Finnish thug. The Iranians lived among these people. Christopher sometimes found his company with these beggars and deposited the baby-faced Taffy with them.

Some of these characters had girlfriends but Christopher tried to forbid girls in the place and would refuse hash and give the guy a hard time. Christopher decided women were dangerous in a male environment of an anarchist nature. Many beggars could never get a woman unless they paid for it. Jealousies festered and trouble darkened the door with females around. Nevertheless exceptions arose and a few slipped in on the lads' insistence or through their own resilience.

Christopher viewed the place as his. He had a knack of finding squats and the others knew when this one shut they would look to him to find another. He controlled the third floor and the other floors respected him as the main dealer. He frequently found people on the streets and took them home. He then felt a certain power over them, making sure they could do him no favours and even the score.

This was a multi-cultural environment of flotsam from many regions of the more ragged reaches of the globe; a herd of black sheep living precariously and resentfully on top of one another. Many lives that had gone off the rails collided here for an instant. How and ever, the prevailing factor in everyone's consciousness and memory regarding the place remained the ubiquitous dog diarrhoea. Stinking, steaming or caked dry, sometimes even frozen, it blotched the entire courtyard in random deep brown patches of about the same width and length as the spots on a big elegant giraffe.

The humans pissed into the drains and reserved their shitting for the outside world. The dogs were not so well versed in such tender etiquette. Some of the less well-brought-up humans who had been toilet trained, apparently, rather shabbily, could not restrain themselves when stoned or drunk. Woe betide them if the Afghans caught them shitting outside their windows. They would be bundled up in an Afghan rug, menaced in Farsi and stamped out like a quivering flame in the morbid, unadorned, dark rooms of the first floor.

Christopher stood, after introducing Taffy as a new member of this non-exclusive club, and looked through the shutters. His kingdom had gone astray. Wearily his eyes scanned from the factory that belched murderous black clouds into the grey sky to the mad dogs circling the courtyard.

"I should put corks in those dogs' assholes."

Ali looked up. He was one of the three Iranians who had a room on the third floor. "I hear the Afghans are eating the dogs."

Christopher, unmoved, snorted in disgust. "What the fuck kind of shit are you talking about now, Ali?"

"Seriously, man," Ali said, warming to his subject. "Begging has been really off and nobody's making money. The French don't like the look of the Afghans. Killers, man! They can see it in their eyes. The old ladies don't give them money. All the Afghans are hungry, man! I think they sneak out and quietly cut their throats. Then bring them in and skin and cook them downstairs. Dogs are disappearing, man! This is true."

Christopher surveyed the outside world and said in a low pained voice, "Ali, how can they cook the dogs? They've no shit to cook them with. Where would all the smoke from the fire go, huh?"

Ali, unperturbed, his eyes closing, leaning back on some cushions, said, "Wow, man! you're right. They must eat those dogs raw. Those guys are tough I'm telling you."

Taffy sat quietly in the corner in shock. He had never even met foreigners before and now he was here. Taffy hoped those men they talked of would eventually eat all the dogs. Negotiating around the dog diarrhoea on one leg was too difficult.

A third act of charity that cemented Taffy to Paris for a long time happened within a week of his arriving in the city. An old lady took him to her room. She saw him sitting and begging and invited him to hop up six flights of narrow stairs. Her lame husband had died years ago and the wooden crutches were unused and gathering dust. They were a little short for him and he feared he looked like a hunchback when he used them, but as vain as he was three legs were better than one. If he had to be a hunchback, Christopher remarked, this was certainly the city to do it in.

Taffy and Isolt did not go into the café. The day had not been lucrative enough for indulgence and they were too vulnerable to suburban town stares. They chose instead to sit on the wall of the moat of the huge château at the park, rolling cigarettes.

"The suburbs may be good for others but I hate working here."

Taffy agreed, "Miserable."

"I'm never leaving Paris again."

"Me neither."

"There's too many wicked people living in the suburbs."

"Wouldn't it be grand to own a castle like that," Taffy said, happy with the thought.

"You see, Parisians are city people and mind their own business, minimal interference," Isolt said. "Here and in the rest of the markets people always stop and bother you. It's all right for the Germans or the real filthy, hopeless-looking beggars but for me, I'm a girl and relatively normal-looking, that's a guarantee that they will stop and try to salvage me. I have to stick to the big city, people pester me less. Especially if I sit in a busy Metro station tunnel at rush hour. People give the money but don't have time to stop."

"But if you're in those tunnels and the police come by there's no escape."

"The police don't do much with me. They usually just move me on."

"If I had lots of money, I'd buy a castle like that."

Isolt looked at the château. "God, imagine living there."

"We could put all our friends in it."

"Yeah, and hold big banquets where everyone drank wine from goblets and ate with their fingers."

"Just sit there all day with all our friends getting smashed."

"That's what we do anyway."

"We wouldn't have to beg."

"There would be big roaring fires in the fireplace and we would just eat and have bands come in to entertain us."

"A big video screen with lots of films to choose from. Everyone would have their own room too."

"We would have to have servants to clean up periodically."

"Yeah, we'd make these snotty French people be our servants and we'd fill the huge hall with sheep and goats and dogs."

"Maybe not dogs."

"Yeah, we'd have a room full of drugs and a doctor on hand with a neverending supply of clean needles and prescriptions."

"There we would be in the castle eating and drinking and doing drugs with all the people we like."

"What if we all got enormously fat?"

"We would have a rule that we had to all tie our legs together and jump everywhere to keep fit."

"I could just throw away me crutches, it would be the same thing."

The rain began to fall again and reluctantly they left their castle unclaimed and went down to the RER station. Isolt slid under the barrier and held his crutches as Taffy jumped. The train station workers watched but as usual did nothing.

"I hate rich people," Taffy declared, mesmerized by the flow of mansions fleeting past the rain-streaked windows. Isolt put her legs on the seat and tried to find a sleeping position.

"Taffy, you hate car owners and up."

Isolt dozed uncomfortably. Taffy stared mournfully out the window till he was no longer looking at the landscape but mesmerized by the individual drops making their jerky, haphazard paths across the window — some blown by the wind joining with others to streak rapidly to the end, others caught wobbling in one spot. He wondered if his friends were sitting now in a warm pub in the tiny town in Wales. If they still wondered what had happened to him on that three-day tear. He wondered if his family cared.

This rain was falling too in Paris when they got off the train. They stole a can of tuna and bought a baguette for dinner. The rain had diluted the dog diarrhoea in the courtyard. They turned on the heaters in the room and ate ravenously. Warm and full they found a miniscule piece of hash on the floor and rolled a tiny joint.

"Let's try more of that shoebox," Taffy said.

There was a box of drugs stashed beneath the couch. A welcome find for those interested in home entertainment. It belonged to no one in particular but was guarded and monitored by all. Its contents were drugs and tablets of all shapes and sizes. Loose pills, pills in foil packets, plastic containers of pills. Most had no recognisable names. The box had been sitting waiting in the corner when they first found the squat. In the beginning it was viewed with suspicion. Gradually curiosity propelled them to throw caution to the wind and explore the potential of this cardboard receptacle of possible unearthly highs.

"Have you tried these reds?" Taffy asked, the box on his lap.

"Yes, nothing perceptible. Freddie thinks they're just an antihistamine."

"Whatever that is."

"I just don't want to fuck with antibiotics," Isolt said, kneeling at his feet rooting through the selection.

"I just don't want to grow breasts," Taffy said.

Isolt nodded vigorously. "I'd thought of that. What if they were hormones and we all started changing sex."

Taffy was bug-eyed and incredulous. "Oh Jesus! Now that would be a right mess."

"Wouldn't it just. Have you tried these flat white ones in the silver packet?"

"No, let's go for it." Taffy extracted the packages. "There's a few packets of these. You take six to start with and I'll take six."

"Right!"

They tore open the packets and popped the pills into their hands, washing them down with Evian.

"Don't grow a beard," Taffy said.

Isolt stroked her chin. "Well, I hope they do something. Has anybody got a high off anything in this wretched box?"

"Nope, and if they do they are so drunk and stoned they don't know the difference."

"We're both clean. That microscopic joint couldn't amount to much."

They sat back and looked at each other.

"What now?" Isolt said.

"I'm bored," said Taffy.

"I wish we had some decent drugs."

"Or a TV."

"I'd take drugs over TV any day."

"The government should give them out free. If I was president I'd give them out free."

"It would certainly reduce the health risk of unwarranted experimentation of this kind."

"If I was president everything would be free."

"That's some campaign slogan, Taffy." Isolt got up and began searching the room for undrunk alcohol.

She got down on all fours scrutinizing the carpet for hash pieces.

She had her eye close to the floor and began putting possibles on the arm of the chair for later inspection.

"Make yourself useful and see which of those are hash and which dog shit or mud." She handed him a lighter. Taffy set to work and lit a brown piece, leaning over to smell the smoke.

"Dog shit."

"Here, I think I got something. We can light it up and wait for the others to come home."

She put the minuscule fragments in with some tobacco and rolled. Placing it to her lips Taffy lit the end and she inhaled. A strong smell of burning rubber filled the air.

"I think you're smoking a bit of Ali's boot."

Isolt made a face.

"Ali's sole is falling apart."

"How very sad."

"No, I meant his boot. Sole of his boot. We did that two days ago. It looks exactly like hash. We've all been smoking Ali's boot."

"This definitely wouldn't happen if you were president, would it Taffy?"

"No way!"

"Nobody would ever smoke Ali's boot again." Isolt sighed. "If only we could get into Christopher's room."

"He's never there."

"I know. But he uses it to cut his hash. There are always splinters that fly when he chops those big bricks."

"God, I'd kill for a beer now," Taffy moaned.

"Maybe the others will bring some. They should be home soon. Unless they made loads of money and went to a film."

"Do you know what I want to come back as?"

"No."

"In my next life."

"What?"

"Do you know what would be great?"

"A very rich man."

"No, even better."

"President."

"No, less hassle than that."

"For Christ's sake, what?"

"A dealer's carpet," he said triumphantly, closing his eyes, his baby face radiant with this latest fantasy. "A dealer's carpet. All you'd have to do is lie there and get beer spilt on you and hash dropped on you all day. And dealers listen to music all the time."

"How extraordinarily beautiful," Isolt said.

They took six more pills and waited. After a while Taffy asked Isolt how she felt.

"Hmmm . . . kind of ordinary."

"Yes, I feel ordinary too."

They sat and thought about how they felt.

"Maybe we should call them Suburbanol."

Taffy laughed. "Yeah, Suburbanol."

Isolt closed her eyes and said, "Suburbanol. For that ordinary feeling."

Hours passed and Payman was the first to come home. A solitary human, drenched in a deep sorrow, quiet as a mouse. He always wore a heavy green parka coat and a woolly hat. He had a long black beard. Christopher had brought him home and at first everyone objected. The squat was full and Payman was hardly an asset, hardly the life and soul of the party. Hardly anything at all except a bulk of living tissue whose aura of tragedy and sad manner made them all feel a little guilty.

Payman usually talked only to himself. This could start in the middle of the night. He would suddenly uncurl from his green parka and sit up, his huge Persian eyes open without blinking, and begin to talk in Farsi. When the others asked Ali what he was saying Ali would just say "Spooky, man! Spooky! Payman's spooky," and launch into a monologue about himself which no one could bear to listen to. Ali and Payman had deserted the fighting at the Iran-Iraq border and both had ended up on the third floor with the Europeans. Ali was impossible to get rid of. The lads tolerated him because they knew he would always be there. He was so infuriating that he was a character and they accepted him as such.

Payman was not like Ali. Payman was a gloomy soul padding about the world in the throes of a living hell. Christopher would not let anyone touch Payman. He would invite him to his rented room in Saint-Lazare and they would get high on Christopher's heroin. Christopher interpreted Payman's sorrowful silence as a mark of dignity. Payman had seen the troubles of life and was suitably respectful. Payman was in mourning. Christopher understood that. He felt that being in Payman's presence alone in the tiny attic room, high on his beloved opiates, was something akin to being in a church. They would sit scratching and drowsing. Sometimes Christopher broke the silence and whispered a story or observation. Payman, hunched up against the wall, would stare dolefully ahead and offer no recognition of the disturbance. Observing this Christopher would feel slightly embarrassed. He believed Payman to be constantly meditating on his rotten life. Christopher would follow suit and retreat into silence to contemplate his own misery. At midnight there was non-stop porn on the black and white portable TV. They would sit together watching, scratching and drowsing, every now and then breaking the monotony to get higher.

Isolt handed a packet of the white pills to Payman.

"*Essayez.*"

"*Ça va?*" he asked.

"*Oui, ça va,*" she said.

"I wonder if he will feel ordinary on them," Taffy pondered as Payman munched down all the pills, grunting.

Jim and Larry came in soaked to the skin.

"I'm sick of all this weather," Jim said. "That dog shite is running all over the gaff. Maybe I'll head down south."

Christopher and Ali came in. Jim turned and grinned. "What a lovely couple. When's the wedding?"

Christopher growled. He wore a black raincoat down to his feet. The hood was pulled up and his face framed by the elasticated rim of the hood which had puffed up into a triangular peak. He looked like an evil goblin. Everybody smiled at him. He stood in a puddle that was forming around his feet. They all sat, taking off their dripping coats. Christopher sat in the furthest corner and blew his nose in his shirt sleeve.

"Jesus! If you want a tissue I'll find you one," Isolt said.

"I stole this shirt four months ago. It's Pierre Cardin. Nice shirt. Nice blue stripes. I've never taken it off." He held up his shredded sleeve. "All the buttons have gone except one. No one's ever worn one of Pierre's shirts as much as I have. Pierre Cardin would be pissed off to see his shitty shirt now." He smiled gleefully. "Yes, Pierre Cardin would be one sorry motherfucker if he saw what I've done to his shirt." He shook his head and rolled a joint.

"Want to come down south?" Jim asked.

"No, I don't."

"Why not?"

"Too many fuckheads."

"I agree," Larry said, taking a can of beer from his pocket.

"Those Arabs run all the shit down there," Christopher said. "Dodgy motherfuckers. Not to be trusted. I've had my trouble with the Arabs. They had to learn the hard way. One was fucking with me every day. I'd go to the fountain to sell my acid. He'd take one and never pay. Hanging around all evening out of his head. I got mighty sick of him I can tell you. So I get nine hits and with a minute drop of glue stuck them together. I never thought it would work, but he snatched it out of my hand and stuck it on his fat wet tongue. I could almost see it all come apart in his mouth. Man, I can tell you he didn't hang around long that night."

"Nine hits!" Jim thought out loud with wonder.

Christopher handed a piece of hash to Larry. "Roll one for the group. I'll smoke this one myself."

Isolt frisbeed white pills to Jim and Larry.

"These are OK."

"Yeah? How do you feel?"

"Ordinary."

Taffy laughed. "We're calling them Suburbanol."

"For that ordinary feeling," Isolt said.

The others ate them. Ali looked hurt.

"Where's mine, man?"

"None left," Isolt said. "Here's the shoebox, do something useful in the interests of science."

Ali pouted.

"Ordinary feelings are wasted on you, Ali," Isolt told him.

Jim gave Ali one from his packet. "Larry, give him one from yours."

"No, I won't," Larry said.

Ali ate one. "This is not going to do much, man," he grumbled.

Christopher inhaled the joint with satisfaction. "Once an Arab and his friends that used to sell some bogus shit around the fountain to the tourists started encroaching on my territory. Bothering my clients. I was plotting against them when one night they followed me into a dark street and stuck a knife to my eye and took my stash and my cash. I followed them and when one broke off from the crowd I followed him. The only weapon I had was a can of shaving cream. Man, I pummelled that poor fucker so much his cheek was torn and hanging off. I only stopped when I saw blood come from his eyes and got scared. I took what money he had on him. I took his watch and ripped a gold chain off his neck. He wasn't saying anything this fucker, just bubbling blood. Frothing at the mouth. I saw his friends at the fountain next night. I had my knife in my sleeve. They never came near me. Scared shitless. I only saw the guy once again, in a café a year later. A huge scar on his face. I lost my money and drugs and my Swiss Army knife that night and I think of that sometimes and it makes me mad but that fucker has to look in the mirror every morning to shave. He has to think of me every day of his shitty life. Until death, no less."

"Another of Christopher's delightful little bedtime stories," Isolt said. "Thank you for sharing that with us."

"I'm just illustrating a point, my dear, before you go running off on your stumpy little legs down south. They fuck with birds more."

"I can deal with them. Unlike everyone else I don't hate Arabs. It's not logical to hate an entire race."

"Yeah, man! Arabs are bad news. A nuisance," Ali nodded.

"You are an Arab, Ali," Jim said.

"I'm not. I'm Persian. We have to fight the Arabs." He puffed out his chest and roared, "Kill the Arab!"

"Shut up, Ali! You are an Arab."

"Man, that's like me saying you are British. You don't like that."

"I am British, Ali," Jim said.

"No way, man, you're Irish," Ali protested, frustrated.

"As Irish as you're Arab, Ali."

"No, man. I'm not Arab. Persians don't even speak Arabic, man!"

"It doesn't matter, Ali. Persians and Arabs, as far as I'm concerned, it's all the same culture. You look like them and you act like them."

Ali was upset.

"That's right!" Christopher said, "you could barely put a cigarette paper between them."

"No, man! Persians are Persians. Arabs are dogs, man. No Arabs come into the squat but Persians live here with you guys."

"No French Arab in his right mind would want to live here, that's why. They have their own scene. They're more attached to this country than we are," Isolt argued.

"I wish the Afghans would stop playing all that shitty Arab music all day," Larry said.

Ali screamed: "Afghans are not Arabs either."

Everyone laughed.

The door opened and Rory came in. He was a good-looking Irishman with shoulder-length black hair and blue eyes — the same Rory who had fled to Amsterdam with Isolt the winter after Becky died. They had squatted together for a year in London after that. Isolt had returned to Paris the following spring. Now here was Rory, slightly drunk and dripping wet. He shook himself like a dog and everyone complained. Rory hated to beg. He never stayed long in Paris. He always met a woman and eventually disappeared with her to her country. He would promise life-long love, move in with her parents, get bored after a couple of months and leave. He wore cowboy boots and now and then left to work as a motorcycle courier in London. He once drove his bike all the way to Greece. There he was arrested for busking. The police cut his hair and he got thin and pale during two weeks in prison. Rory couldn't play the guitar too well and he never practiced. He played it only to attract women. It worked. All the hippy girls at the fountain and around the Pompidou centre came to him. Rory kept swearing that he would be rich one day. And every time he left Paris he swore that he would never return. He galloped off regularly into the sunset with a new wide-eyed young adoring girl. But Rory could never stay away from Paris too long and he would slither back at sunrise without the girl.

He took out three plastic containers of methylated spirits.

"Three bottles of meths. I got them at the Arab shop. Fucking expensive."

"Yeah, well you don't buy them too fucking often." Christopher hated Rory.

Rory ignored him. "I'm going to make coffee and warm up. It's filthy weather outside, it is."

He rummaged in the debris and extracted some coffee filters and a box of coffee. He went to the chair with no seat that operated as a cooker. Instead of a seat there was an iron mesh and another beneath it. He poured the methylated spirits into the sawn-off pipe with tinfoil at the bottom and dropped a lit match in. As it burned he poured Evian into the teapot and placed it on the iron mesh seat. Then he put the burning spirits beneath it and sat back to wait for it to boil. He warmed his hands over the flames.

"Man, we could live here after the collapse of civilisation and survive," he said with satisfaction.

"Evian might be difficult to come by," Isolt said. "And the Arab shops might not have such accommodating hours."

"They work like the Pakis in London," Rory said.

"The Koreans in America," Christopher said.

"Well, they deserve it. France, England and the U.S. have all gone running around other people's countries behaving much worse than staying open till midnight."

"The Koreans stay open all night long where I come from, sweet thing. Get down off the soap box," Christopher said. "Rory, got any drugs?"

"No."

"Well how can I stay in business with everyone smoking my hash?" Rory was silent.

"Got any money, Rory?" Christopher stared at him.

"I just spent it all on meths and coffee."

"Fucking liar."

"I'll give you fifty francs — that's all I have left."

Christopher sighed and took a piece of hash from the cuff of his sweater. "Here, this is seventy francs' worth. So everyone's smoking yours tonight. I'll make my own joints as usual."

Rory gave him the money. He handed Jim the hash. "Roll one up. I'll make coffee. Got any beer?"

Jim looked at Larry. Larry rolled his eyes and dug in his giant overcoat. "This is my last one."

Christopher looked at him while burning the hash for his private joint: "You're all fucking liars."

Rory dunked a mound of coffee in the filter. He placed it on the coffee pot and poured. Taffy was staring at Larry.

"No, Taffy," Larry said as he took a beer from his pocket. "This is definitely my last one."

"Just smoke the joint, Taffy," Isolt said.

Taffy nodded at her. "OK."

Hunched in the corner, Christopher took a bottle of Dinacode cough medicine from his bag and drank, wincing horribly. He quickly took a slug of Perrier to rinse it off his guts. The substance was sticky. Rory talked of a girl he had met.

"She says she is seventeen. I think she has run away. I was playing her some songs. She reminds me of that German girl I lived with."

"Don't bring her here. You and your birds are trouble," Christopher told him.

Rory sipped his coffee, looking at Jim, who shrugged noncommittally. Christopher shifted uncomfortably and winced. He hiccupped loudly, his whole body jerking.

"Yeah, Rory. I don't like those floozies you fuck. They're trouble, underage and they call the cops when you start beating them."

Rory snapped, "I never hit a woman in my life."

"Fucking liar."

Jim broke in. "Hey, ease up, lads, don't ruin a good joint. Pour us some coffee, Rory, don't hog it all to yourself."

Ali said, "Man, I had a girlfriend once. I had two. They were twins, really tall and blond. I got them both with babies at the same time. They were Swedish birds. Flashy. They begged me to go back with them and be father to their children. I went for a while. They both had twins. Four babies, man! I thought I was tripping. Lots of Persians go to Sweden, man! I have relatives there. Very rich people, they own half the forests in Sweden. They gave me a forest and I put the two girls and four babies there. All blond, man! I swear! I couldn't handle it, the babies grew so fast I was tripping over them all the time. Man, I said to them as they got older, "Cut my veins. Drink my blood. You will trip forever.'"

"When was this, Ali, pray tell?" Jim asked.

"Last year, man!"

"You were in jail for four months last year, Ali."

"I had no papers. They stopped me begging and threw me in jail." Ali nodded enthusiastically.

"What was that like?" Isolt asked.

"Nice place. Clean. Good food."

"So when did you have time last year in those six months you were a free man to disappear unbeknownst to us, get two tall blond Swedish babes up the spout and raise a family in a Scandinavian forest, Ali?" Jim asked.

"There are twelve months in a year, Jim," Isolt said.

"What?"

"Not ten months."

"Huh?"

"Nothing. Never mind."

"Twelve months in a year, Jim." Christopher imitated her in a high falsetto voice.

Ali sighed, "Yeah, those kids sure did grow up fast."

Rory said, rolling another joint, "When was your last girlfriend, Larry?"

"None of your beeswax, mate," Larry replied.

Ali sat up. "What beeswax? I kept these bees once. I went to a bee-keeping conference in Belgium, man . . ."

"No, Ali. You are not telling this one," Larry said.

"I haven't heard this one," Taffy said.

"You don't want to, mate." Larry was stern.

Taffy said, "I never had a girlfriend. Unless you count a couple of blow jobs behind the disco wall and a bag of chips on the way home afterwards."

"I haven't had a bird in ages. I might have to buy one soon," Jim laughed.

"Birds are baggage," Christopher said.

"Yeah. First they would do anything for you, then you stay with them and all they do is whine," Rory said.

"OK! OK! let's not launch into a diatribe against women," Isolt said.

"Poor Isolt," Jim laughed.

Christopher turned to Payman who was sitting as still as a bony winter tree on a windless day: "Payman, you ever had a girlfriend?"

Payman lifted his head up a little and said quietly, "Yes."

Everybody was taken aback. Payman rarely joined in group conversations. All eyes fixed upon him with interest.

"What happened, Payman? Where is she now?" Christopher probed cautiously, but there was no answer: "*Où est votre petite amie maintenant, Payman?*"

Payman lowered his head slightly and seemed to think of this. Thirty seconds passed before he answered. He spoke just as softly in the same reverent tone as before.

"She die."

They all looked stupefied. Then everyone at the same time burst out laughing. Christopher hunched over rocking back and forth, slapping his thigh. Larry wiping the tears from his eyes. Jim shaking his head.

"Oh Jesus!" Rory laughed, moving to make more coffee. "That's gas, that is. That takes the biscuit. The Iranians are a fierce shower. What were youse lot shouting about when I came in? I could hear yiz all the way up the stairs."

"We were complaining about the horrible kebab music the Afghans play day and night," Isolt told him.

"Maybe we can fix that," Rory grinned.

"Please do," Jim said.

Rory took a Perrier bottle and rooted through the debris until he found a long plastic pink ribbon. "This is from flowers I gave a bird ages ago." He tied it to the top of the bottle.

"That won't work," Jim told him.

"I know exactly what I'm doing," he said.

"What the fuck are you doing?" Christopher said. "If the Afghans come up here I'm not being a hero. You get thrown to the lions, motherfucker."

"Trust me," Rory assured them, walking to the windows and opening the shutters onto the torrential rain. Christopher snorted. Rory threw the bottle out and jerked his wrist. Glass smashed on the first floor. He quickly reeled it in and slammed the shutters closed.

The music stopped abruptly. Everybody sneaked up to the windows and tried to peep outside. Even Payman stared as two Afghans ran about in the pelting tumultuous rain, furious, murder in their hearts, pulling open the iron gate, staring down the road, visibility nil. Another, with his bare hands hungering for the guilty neck ran in and out of the three houses. The dogs raced in circles, frenzied, barking out of their minds. The black polluted rain fell in thick drops, hitting the cobblestones and bouncing back up into the night. Christopher noted the full moon. The Afghans slithered about in the diarrhoea kicking the lousy dogs.

"Man!" whispered Ali. "Tonight the doors were open on the first floor. I look in and see bones everywhere. About the size of dog bones. The Afghans, man, are eating the dogs. They eat them raw. Dogs are disappearing, man, I swear on this!"

Isolt crouched beside him and whispered, "Ali, do you feel the tablet Jim gave you?"

"No, man!"

"Do you feel ordinary?"

"No, man!"

"I didn't think so."

They watched the rain fall and fall, pounding the earth, soaking the Afghans' heads and running down inside their coats. The dogs trying to run for shelter inside. Some huddled against the wall cowering. The Afghans running inside pushing the lunatic dogs out. The gutters gurgling and creaking, bloated with thunderous torrents. The moon held in the sky by invisible forces.

Payman, the mad grieving Persian, was ranting into Jim's ear in a strange ancient tongue while Jim decided to himself to head south.

The Afghans brooded in the dark small rooms of the first floor, trying to block the window with wood and plastic that kept falling down. Rain fell incessantly. Dogs whined and scraped outside until the Germans came drunkenly home. The dogs shook themselves and slept on the second floor whimpering with trembling limbs and hairy dog eyelids jittering in their sleep. The Afghans did not turn the music back on but sat entombed in silence or talking in low voices before trying to get some sleep thousands of miles away from their war-torn home.

4

The South

PARIS WAS not a city to leave lightly. Especially if you have a roof overhead. A roof overhead and a double layer of barbarian Germans and Afghan refugees underfoot. A roof overhead, barbarians and refugees underfoot and a herd of mad dogs at the door. But something could snatch you away. Things happen in the undertow of the world that you can never anticipate. You could be walking directly towards the city and find yourself side-stepping into the unknown and staying there.

There had been several attempts to get down south. Always something would come up at the last minute and they would decide to postpone it for a day. The obstacles ranged from hangovers to acute lethargy, with little scope in between. Isolt approached the train station casually with the lads. With some surprise she found herself on a TGV express train in the first class carriage as it pulled out of the station flanked by huge grim walls, slicing through the city. The trains moved so fast that they only stopped once, in Lyon, before arriving in Marseilles. They were thrown off at Lyon and reboarded a few carriages down. They were discovered before the train took off and once more had to walk the plank. They waited for the next train in a grey foggy Lyon and took window seats in first class.

Jim had taken a puppy with him from the raggedy wild pack of Alsatians in the courtyard. The conductor was not happy but it was hard for them to be intimidated by a French ticket inspector. He fumed and they looked at him with a modicum of detached curiosity.

The dog urinated on the floor, spreading out its small wobbly legs, its eyes pitifully fixed on Jim. Jim did not admonish the creature.

"Tourists," Jim said. "Sorry we don't speak French. Do you speak English?"

They begged their way along the coast, sleeping on the beaches from Marseilles to Nice: Jim, Rory, Isolt and a Finnish guy called John. John had deserted the Foreign Legion. If you remain in the Legion for the five-year term you can receive a new identity, papers to stay in France and a pension. If you desert they hunt you down and the French government punishes you severely. John left two months before his five years were up. Jim was fascinated by this logic.

"You spend four years and eight months in the army and desert with only two months to go. Now you are a marked man for life. Why?"

"I was fed up. Could not take one more day" was all he was prepared to say.

"That's crazy!" Jim said.

"So?" John shrugged.

"Jim thinks there are only ten months in a year," Isolt observed.

Rory laughed. "Yeah! Jim doesn't like to be confined to the Roman calendar. Jim's no Roman."

"Jim can't count," Isolt said.

On Nice beach one evening the lads sold Isolt to a Tunisian for a lump of hash. The Tunisian took her by the arm.

"*Viens! Viens!*"

Isolt looked at Rory and Jim imploringly.

"Don't worry! Just stay put," Jim advised her soothingly. Then loudly, to the impatient Tunisian, "She will come after she has a smoke." Then turning to Isolt, "How do you say that in French?"

Isolt bristled. "Ha! Ha!"

Rory and John burst out laughing. Jim rolled a joint, grinning, saying to the man in his heavy Dublin accent,

"*Bientôt, mon ami, bientôt.*"

"*Bientôt* up your arse, Jim, you fucker," Isolt raged. She got up with the Tunisian still holding her arm. "*Enculé!*" she rasped, wrenching her kidnapped limb free. "*Va t'en!*" She wedged herself between John and Rory. He came behind her and grabbed her shoulders. He was getting frantic.

"*Viens! Viens!*"

The beach was deserted and the dark blue dusk was rapidly blackening. The Tunisian took from his purple slacks his shrivelled cock.

"*Alors, une pipe,*" he was saying, trying to push it in her face, clamping his legs around her head. Isolt wriggled away and threw a rock at him. He ducked, still holding his cock, shrieking.

"*Pipe! Pipe!*"

The next rock hit his shoulder, another his leg. He scurried away in front of some tourists who were walking along the shore. The lads rolled around laughing. Isolt sat back down on the rocky beach.

"He's going to be a pest for the rest of my stay here."

"Free hash, baby!" Jim handed her the joint.

"Poor bastard," Rory said.

"What is a 'peep' anyway?" asked John.

"Something none of you have had in a long time," Isolt snapped, smoking furiously, the night completely blackening around her.

They gained an addition to their group a few days later. A bonfire had been built on the beach and they sat around it drinking. It was hard to get the fire going. They scavenged the area for dry wood. As Isolt kicked about the stones she noticed a fat girl with three sticks in her arms. The girl was shivering. Isolt eyed the sticks covetously.

"Come sit at the fire," Isolt said across the tiny patch of darkness that separated them.

The girl waddled towards the fire and said to the others in a London accent, "She said I could sit by your fire."

"It's not really a fire. It's more of a smoke," Rory said.

The fat girl threw the sticks on the smoldering pile and remained standing.

"Sit down. Have a beer," said Jim, staring at her huge goose-pimpled calves. As she sat Rory looked at Jim and made a face.

John asked, "Got any drugs?"

She shook her big head. The sticks began to catch alight.

One night as they slept in their bags by the dying fire Isolt began to dream — an ugly, middle-aged, pot-bellied son greets his short, fat, worn, old mother in his one-roomed bed-sit. Outside the window the street is run down and there are prostitutes and drug dealers at the corners. The mother is horrified and her big-eared, crooked-nosed, hairy son is clutching a large Humpty Dumpty doll.

"Meet Humpty Dumpty, Mother, remember him? Imagine, he's been with me all these years."

The mother recoils as her chubby son holds out the stuffed toy.

"I still remember the day you gave him to me. He has always been my only real friend." He withdraws the doll and kisses it on the purple dome of its bald head.

"This is an awful room, son," she sobs. "How could it all have ended up like this?"

In a tiny bed beside the window he places the toy beneath the sheets and tucks it in. Bending down, he nuzzles its pink felt nose gently.

"There you go, Humpty, poor thing, off to sleep now and no bad dreams."

He kisses the yellow two fingered cloth hand.

The mother stares at the scene through tears and with terrible grief takes the door handle to leave. The dirty, ragged son rushes over and taking her gently by the shoulders he guides her to the bed. They both kneel on the bed looking out of the window at the neighbourhood with boarded-up shop windows and sick-looking whores, stamping the ground occasionally for warmth like cart-horses. The dealers swarm around each other and disperse. They hiss their goods to passers-by who quicken their pace and narrow their eyes. The street lights for the evening come on.

"At last!" the son says. "At last we are alone, Mother, what we always wanted. Without that bastard to kick us to a pulp. You and I can enjoy this peaceful winter evening alone, as we always dreamed."

All the dead squirrels darted about gathering nuts and all the dead flowers bloomed. On my felt, purple, dome, egg-head I have no ears to hear the dead birds that must be singing merrily in the proud fallen trees. My foam insides churn to think I have no muscle and bones to let me run without a care through the grass that is shrinking back into the earth under the black sun. If I had a voice box I could curse this stuck-on felt mouth that leads nowhere. No tongue to taste the bitter berries of the charred bush. I am an egg with stuffed limbs. I have no breasts, no womb. I have nowhere that goes in and nowhere that goes out. I have no eyelids to close over my big arched eyes. I have to watch everything. I can never rest again. How can I go home?

Isolt awoke and fretted awhile in the cold night. She had dreamed Humpty's dream. Wires had got crossed and Humpty's unconscious had swum into hers. The fire was dead. She listened to the new girl Melonie's resounding snore and was reluctant to submit herself once more to sleep and the taunts of wandering unconscious minds that used her as host for their pitiful lost dreams.

Jim stood the next day on the ashes of the fire and announced, "We need a new drug!"

He stomped off, taking his bag with him, and his little dog trotted in his wake. Rory came back after his icy morning swim. "Where's Jim?" he asked.

Isolt said, "He's gone to look for a new drug."

"I know a strange way to get high but it can be scary," Melonie said.

They bought asthmatic cigarettes and made tea. They drank the liquid.

"This is really foul stuff," John said.

"Wait," said Melonie.

Isolt walked through the chilly afternoon streets. She sat down at her spot in front of the supermarket. She hesitated before she sat. She wondered if it was the moment she sat and took out her sign that she became a beggar, or did she walk like a beggar and look upon others as a beggar would? Once a beggar always a beggar, she thought, not without a hint of pride.

Christopher walked towards her and threw her a coin.

"What are you doing down south?" she asked, squinting up at his silhouette outlined by the harsh sunlight.

"You look flustered, Isolt."

"Not flustered, Christopher, rather I'm perplexed."

"Go on."

"When you are no longer engaged in the actual act of begging are you still a beggar?"

"Well, you certainly aren't a chartered accountant."

"Do you define yourself by the means by which you accumulate money? Is a doctor still a doctor when she is not performing her doctorly duties?"

"Begging is not a privilege, it is a right. When the Spanish Inquisition tried to punish beggars the Catholic hierarchy objected. Ask and you shall receive. You are always permitted to ask, people are not forced to give. That is entirely their choice according to their conscience. It is the thief who forces the giver. Beggars let the choosers decide. If everyone who passed you gave one franc you would only have to sit for ten minutes and it would not hurt anyone. Then everyone who was short of money or in a fix could just sit down for a while and have enough for a meal. There should be a law, it wouldn't damage a soul."

Jim walked by and Isolt waved to him happily. He looked a little strangely at her and gave a small wave, jerking his hand in her direction.

"I wonder why he didn't come and say hello when he saw you were here."

"He looked a bit panicky all right."

"And he's without the dog. We all drank some strange concoction earlier — maybe it worked on him. I don't feel anything at all." She looked at her hands, holding them in front of the sun. "I feel a little sweatier. I feel fatter too. My arms look thicker."

"You've put on weight since the first time I met you."

Isolt was crestfallen. "This is true. My lifestyle. All I do is drink beer and wine and smoke dope and then get the munchies and eat and eat. All I eat is baguettes and cheese. It's so cheap and good but I have bloated."

She put her head back and felt a roll of flesh in her neck. She could feel all her flab. Her bulging stomach and sagging thighs. Her thick, blubbery arms. She felt nauseated.

"In Paris I walked a lot. Here I just go from the beach to this begging spot."

"You are a short girl, you should watch your weight more."

Isolt looked down at her body in dismay. She fantasized about having a huge knife and chopping all the excess skin off.

"This is terrible. I can't sit here any more."

She got up and walked off, forgetting her bag.

When she got to the beach she stood on the promenade. The grey sea met the grey stones.

"Christopher, this is not a nice beach. There is no sand. Even if you swim, which I don't. It's too frigging cold. I don't know what we're all doing at this resort in the dead of winter."

She walked down onto the beach, scurrying across the rocks, stumbling occasionally. As she moved she felt her thighs wobble and the cheeks of her arse vibrate and flap. She felt her belly bounce up and down and her stretchy breasts flap against each another. All her flesh jiggled. She wanted to take a marker and trace where her figure should be and cut off the excess. She arched her back and felt a fold of flesh just above her hips.

"Even if you want to swim there are rocks all the way under the sea. I don't know why Nice is so popular."

Isolt pulled at all the flesh under her chin that she didn't want. She wanted the real her to rise like a skinny phoenix out of this fatty mound that she had become.

"I have to become thin. I must not eat for three days. Just fruit for a month and I must have as much exercise as I can get."

She took out a pen from her jacket pocket and wrote on her arm as a reminder. AS MUCH EXERCISE AS YOU CAN GET and underneath it she scrawled EAT ONLY FRUIT. DRINK ONLY WATER. She rolled down her sleeve.

She then threw herself onto the rocks and tried to do press-ups. Rolling over she did some sit-ups. The rocks were hurting her back; some were pointy and sharp. She knelt and swung her hips this way and that, panting and puffing, her face red and contorted, grabbing her stomach and kneading it like putty. She was horror-stricken by her own obesity. She took off her boots and socks to look at her feet. They were not fat, she remarked with relief, but she was aghast suddenly at the tufts of black hair on each big toe. She rolled up her jeans as much as she could to reveal plump, hairy calves. She pulled up her sweater; there was a black line of pubic hair snaking from her belly button down over the blue-white, bulbous bubble of her belly.

"Aaaaaaggggggh!!!!!!!!" she roared, racing fully clothed into the grey embrace of the sea.

*

Jim was sniffing. Why was he sniffing so much, when there really was no need? A bird on the beach looked at him, cocking its head on its side. A great big dirty seagull.

"JIM," it squawked.

He leaped up in fright and pounded up the steps of the promenade. He walked purposefully through the streets, a sweat breaking out on his forehead, his heart pounding. He realised he had left his bag and his dog on the beach. But the thought of the bird made him whimper in terror and he kept walking. When he became part of the crowd on the pavement he concentrated on keeping pace. Now and then he believed people were saying his name when they talked. His head swung from side to side to see who kept calling him. He walked by Isolt who was sitting in her usual spot in front of the supermarket. He saw to his surprise that she was sitting talking to herself, gesticulating and wrapped up in a heated discussion. She waved. He waved back warily and went on.

All afternoon he paced the city centre in circles. Every group he saw seemed to be talking about him. This made him furious. What discussions were they having? What conclusions were they coming to behind his back?

An elderly woman in a fur coat was coming towards him glaring hatefully. The poodle in her arms yapped suddenly, "JIM! JIM!"

He took flight and ran as fast as he could. He swung around the corner and saw an alley that led directly onto the beach. He went to dash down it and ran straight into a brick wall, knocking himself out.

At the same time an American tourist family were leaving McDonald's with their food. The father took his Big Mac out of the bag. He opened the box and opened his mouth wide to take a bite. Rory came from nowhere, dishevelled and wild-eyed, pounced and snatched the burger from his very hands, then grabbing a milk-shake from the astonished child marched off, eating savagely.

Melonie found Isolt on the beach. "What are you doing?"

Isolt glanced up at her. "I'm breaking the stones open so I can eat the chocolate out of the middle."

"You're soaking wet."

"I was in the sea."

"I thought you boycotted the sea."

Isolt pushed some stones into her mouth. "Mmmmm!"

She held a large rock and was using it to hammer the smaller ones.

"Where's your bag?" Melonie asked.

"I left it somewhere."

"How are you going to sleep without your sleeping bag?"

"I don't know."

"Have you seen the others?"

"No. Jim walked by me ages ago. He looked panicky."

"Help me build a fire before it gets dark."

"I'm too hot." She put more stones into her mouth.

"You'll need one later."

"Leave me alone."

"This is a strange drug, isn't it?"

Isolt stopped what she was doing. "Very." She suddenly gave a short shriek of a laugh. Then she covered her mouth quickly, feeling guilty. She stared at the stones.

"We have to make a fire. I have some hash as well. It will calm you down. I should have warned you not to do the drugs without hash."

Isolt put out her hand and Melonie pulled her up.

"How do you feel?" Isolt asked.

"I don't feel any different. Then I will see a house and I walk up to it. Then it will disappear. That's been happening all day. I've been smoking hash so it's kept me mellower than ever before. I have conversations with my mother and some friends have talked to me who are dead. I can understand that you think there is chocolate in the stones. I bet you can even taste it. I saw people staring from the promenade at you. You were sucking and licking the rocks and trying to break them open. I had to laugh. I knew it would be an hallucination."

Isolt was unsettled. "When the waves slam the stones I keep thinking the sea is calling my name." She frowned and followed as Melonie picked sticks for a fire. Black shapes darted by the corner of her eye. It was dark when they were finished building the fire.

Melonie pointed. "Look over there. It's Jim's dog."

Isolt saw a pathetic shape in the darkness. She whistled. The dog started to run, then it hesitated. It looked back into the blackness and back towards them. It began to bark. Then after a while it came, fumbling, trying to drag Jim's bag. Melonie went over and carried the bag back. The dog wagged its tail and leapt around her in excitement.

"This dog is starving and we have no food."

"Jim's a shit." Isolt petted the mangy shivering creature.

Isolt twitched her head. Shadows that moved agile as spiders whisked by the edge of her vision. "Melonie, what would you think if I told you that there were mind parasites that eat your dreams?"

Melonie lit the fire. "I'll roll a joint. Hang in there."

Isolt closed her eyes and felt her head cave in.

"Oooooh!"

Melonie put a joint into her hand. "Have a smoke. Relax!"

Isolt smoked. Christopher came to the fire.

"Girls, girls. Has it come to this?"

"What do you mean?" Isolt asked.

"Wot?" Melonie said.

"Where are the men? Have they gone to war? You have been abandoned. Easy prey here for the Arab."

Isolt handed the joint to Melonie. "Pass it on." She nodded at Christopher. Melonie looked around and then back to Isolt. "Who do you see?"

"Christopher is here."

"Is he a dead guy?"

"Of course not! He's here. Don't tell me you can't see him. Are you blind with that drug?"

"Why should I see him? I'm not inside your brain. Only the dead come to see me."

"You said your mother talks to you. Is she dead?"

"That's right, I did say that. No, she's very much alive unfortunately. She just comes to ruin my good high as usual. Ha! Ha! She was always very good at that." She stood up. "I'll leave you to it. I have to find more wood. Scream if you are attacked. Christopher here won't be much good to you."

Christopher leered at her across the fire.

"You're scared now to be alone. What's so good about being a girl? I've kind of done a survey on that. I've asked loads of birds. What's so good about being a girl?"

"I don't know what good it is."

"Some girls say that if you're pretty you can get things for free. That doesn't apply to you of course."

Becky spoke from behind. "I'll tell you what's so good about being a girl. You aren't a man."

Christopher snapped, "Stay out of this, Becky. You sure made a mess of things. You lost that perfectly good squat for one. I was going to move in. It could have kept us all over winter."

Isolt froze. She did not have the courage to turn around and see her dead friend.

"Becky!" she choked.

Christopher was stern. "She's gone and good riddance. Now answer me, what's so good about being a girl?"

"God, I don't know. She was right though. I wouldn't want to be a man. But it's hard, people are so dismissive, even other women."

"You are a girl, not a woman."

"Surely that's for me to decide."

"No. You are a walking recipe of vulnerability and failure. You are a poor, plain, fat, young, short girl with no man to protect you."

Isolt crawled closer to him. "And once you see it. Once your eyes are opened you can never retreat again. It's like going mad. Everything you read, everything you see on TV, all the films, all the conversations you take part in. You want to talk about it all the time and it starts to get on people's nerves. You hate the culture that spawned you and there is no escape to any other system that will improve your status. If I was black I might go to Africa, somewhere where I would never see a white person again. As women we have to live in such close proximity to those who hate us and keep us down. To finally realise the enormity of the whole rotten deal is like going mad."

"Hey woman! Take control. What are you sitting there rambling for? Save the fire."

It was Rory; he took her shoulders and leaned down and kissed her on the ear with a squeaking sound.

"What's so good about being a girl, Rory?"

"People like me can sweep you off your feet."

Melonie came back laden with wood. Rory was elated; he kissed her big cheek.

"Melonie, your drug was marvellous. I had such a day."

"Melonie, what's so good about being a girl?" Isolt asked.

Melonie thought about it, then shrugged. "Fucking nothing."

Rory laughed. "Oh, I wouldn't say that. I'd like to have tits, then I could feel them all day long."

Isolt pointed a finger in the air. "The time has come the walrus said to talk of many things, of shoes and ships and sealing wax and cabbages and kings, and why our vision floundered in the light of all these things."

Rory extracted four bottles of red wine from his bag. "Look what I snatched today." Isolt took one as he opened it and drank.

Suddenly Jim's dog dashed off in a frenzy to greet Jim who was walking towards them, grinning sheepishly. His face was swollen and he had several scabs, and a stitched-up gash from his forehead to his chin. The others stared and winced when he sat down. Rory handed him a bottle.

"Jesus!"

"Oh Jim!"

"What the hell?"

Jim shrugged; the dog was trying to lick the scabs, but he pushed it away. "So I won't make the front page of *Vogue,* what's new?"

"Jesus, that's a right mess."

"I ran into a wall at about fifty miles an hour. I was running from a horrible old bag and her poodle who knew my name. I turned the corner and I swear I saw an alley with dustbins and back doors and everything, it led onto the sea which I could see clearly too. I ran straight into a wall. Jesus, next thing I know I'm in a fucking ambulance with the siren going and everything. They stitched me up at the hospital. I didn't know what the fuck was going on. Imagine trying to tell the doctor, 'You see sir, a poodle called my name and I was freaked out so I ran into my own personal solid brick mirage.' And in fucking French too. I was going to tell them that I was jumped by the Arabs, but the doctor and some of the nurses were Arab and they were all so nice to me I said it was some Frenchies who beat me up and took all my money and shit. I just got back from the police station now. God, everyone was so fucking nice and sympathetic. I told them I was a student who was touring France and they were all so sorry this happened to me and ashamed. I was glad to get out of there, I can tell you."

Isolt laughed. "I saw you earlier. You did look in a bit of a state."

"I saw you just sitting down at your spot ranting and raving to yourself, your arms flying about."

"I know. I hallucinated that Christopher was there and I was talking to him. I must have looked a right nut. No wonder I didn't get a fucking centime the whole time I was there."

"I found her on the beach later attracting a crowd, she was breaking the stones open so she could eat the chocolate out of them," Melonie said and they all laughed.

They drank the wine and smoked the hash.

"What about these Buddhists and Eastern religions — they seem OK. Do you believe in reincarnation?" Rory asked. Isolt shook her head.

"I spent ten years fighting to keep the Catholics from the door and I felt so drained from the struggle that I tend to recoil in horror from any set system of belief. Perhaps the only moral stance in view of the evidence is to maintain that my life is on no greater scale than that of a tomato. At death I shall be flung into the ground to rot like one and the afterlife will be identical to the one I had before I was born. Nothing."

"It's a bit much to believe that not one of our greatest minds or inventors had anything more promising than a tomato afterlife," Rory protested.

"Why? Next time you look and feel superior to a tomato think of this: it was our species that killed all life. We weren't worth it to the earth. We were nature's suicide impulse. We found in its belly enough chemicals to destroy everything."

"So you don't believe in any religion?" Jim asked.

"Religion is the incinerator of the soul."

Jim laughed. "Every time I talk to you, you fall asleep and I am left sitting there thinking it's a shitty world."

"It is a shitty world," stated Melonie.

"But it's good to know this," Isolt continued. "Armageddon is human nature. Beginning before the industrial revolution, before the Greeks and Romans, before the wheel; they were only instruments of it. Most humans have been dumb animals who obeyed the process without realising that even their own hearts and the clock ticking in the room were a death beat."

"But where do you find your hope? What prevents you from going mad? What gets you up in the morning to start another day?" Rory asked.

"I have no hope. I can only live on the streets. I might really go mad if I was forced to rejoin the ranks of society."

"I love this lifestyle," Jim said. "I've never had a job. I've been living like this for almost seven years now."

"I hate it," said Rory. "Well, it's a bit of crack. I consider myself a recreational beggar. I'm only doing this scene for a while. I don't want to end up like those old blokes. Zipped up in a plastic bag one winter when I'm forty."

"It's a shitty world," Melonie sighed, feeling she had to contribute something too.

"A horrible place to be killing time," Rory assured her.

"And we can't even conduct that murder with grace," Isolt laughed.

"I don't know. I've had my moments." Jim touched her arm.

They drank some wine and thought of all this a while.

"Oh no, Isolt, you grim little girl, you've depressed us all."

"I don't think so, Jim. You don't strike me as one of the dumb animals content to rot in whatever machine your culture affords you."

"You sound like a religious nut ranting on and on about Armageddon being just around the corner," Rory taunted.

"Not around the corner but here and now. We are Armageddon, that's the delusion. We try to avoid it and it's impossible because we are the death machine. Since the first person was conceived, our killing hands, our crushing feet, our greedy stomachs, our loud mouths, our lazy brains. We are the grimy night, our own brilliant ideas brought it down around us. How can we avert the end or even delay it for very long when we are the catastrophe that's happening? How can we tackle the problems without confronting ourselves antagonistically at every step? Simple! The human species is Armageddon and the individual is a cog in the destruction machine. We hate each other. We live in fear of being denied material goods, of different races, of different philosophies, of death. We seem to be more death than life."

"How do you think we could stop it?" Rory asked a little nervously.

"If I had one shred of faith in a possibility of avoidance, believe me, I would go out and try to prevent it. But I am a facet of the apocalypse. I consume, I use energy, I pollute, I may even breed. I've never sown a seed in my life. Even those that do won't counteract the multitude who can't. From the wheel to the multinationalist corporation. Kodak, Coca-Cola, Christianity, all unadulterated highly structured cannibalism. This gives me a terrible feeling about being alive. You want to save the planet, salvage the environment? The only way possible now would be to wipe out the entire human race. Otherwise it's useless. Just lie back and watch the show."

"So you think we should never protest or try to change?" Rory asked.

"No," Isolt assured him emphatically.

"Well, what's the point then?" he pleaded.

"I don't know if there is a point. Just that it's better to be a spanner in the works than a cog in the machine."

"A spanner in the works?" Jim said incredulously.

"What about music?" Rory gestured to his guitar.

"You only use music to get laid," Jim laughed.

"Well, she reads books. What about Art?"

"I never thought I'd ever hear a beggar say, 'What about Art?'" Melonie snorted.

"I don't see myself as a beggar." Rory was hurt.

"Yeah! He's a fucking astronaut. Ha! Ha! A real spacer all right," Jim hooted.

Isolt could foresee an argument and was on a roll. She interjected quickly, "Art is tolerable. We have to express ourselves. It doesn't slow the process down but it makes the knowledge bearable. Now take tourists . . ."

"Yeah!" Rory nodded. "Tourists are everywhere."

"Exactly, Rory. Tourists destroy what they set out to see. They are peasants forced by big industry to travel great distances when otherwise they would have been content to remain at home. Poured out of their coach buses, disorientated and upsetting the rhythm of the communities they blunder into. We all resent them but we are convinced that we can't do without them. Tourists want no surprises.

They need to go six thousand miles and still eat the same hamburger, sleep in the same hotel."

"Oh God!" exclaimed Rory. "I just remembered something about hamburgers."

"What?" said Isolt sharply, not cherishing the interruption.

"Nothing, nothing. I'll tell you later."

"Bought leisure. Money leisure. Exhausting leisure. Tourism at the turn of the century will be the world's biggest industry. To push people onto one another en masse, to places that they have no affinity with. To destroy local communities with huge outside bulks of brain-washed consumers who need T-shirts and souvenirs to remind them where they've been. Multi-national hotels reap the rewards that the locals are conned into thinking are theirs. They mock each culture by taking the crudest and most diluted parts and reproducing them for sale without any encouragement of understanding. Plastic Eiffel Towers made not by French people but with cheap labour in the Third World. Tourists are being forced out of their homes during their only time to relax and cajoled into a foreign holiday. They return after being insulted, sneered at and ripped off by the natives convinced that they have seen another place but it has been sterilized for their arrival. They will claim some knowledge which is false of those cultures. How many times do people come back from Paris and all they can say is that the natives were rude and the prices expensive?"

"The French are rude," Jim said.

"OK! OK!" Isolt sighed, "we live for the most part off the charity of the French which is forthcoming. There are more people visiting more places now than in the whole history of the world. The more popular the destiny the more cleaned up and generic it will become. No surprises, no discomfort. Bewildered sheep destroying the world."

"Who is behind it? Who's pulling the strings?" Rory asked.

"A body of multi-nationals supported by you and me every time we buy anything from any supermarket shelf. No one in particular. Most involved are blissfully unaware of the magnitude of the outcome, from the corporate boss on the golf course to the office cleaning lady making it all shine with toxic chemicals in her window spray."

"So why don't you just go and kill yourself?" Jim asked.

"I do despair. I just try to avoid doing damage myself and I try not to buy anything unnecessary."

"Can that save the world?" Melonie asked.

"No. I told you, you want to save the world? the whale? the dolphin? the frog? the rain forest? Then kill all humans. Let the other species thrive until the sun dies naturally."

"But we can't kill all humans," Jim said.

"No. Not a feasible solution," Isolt said.

"Well, I have to crash. I'm exhausted. Give us a kiss good night," Rory said. Jim leaned towards him and kissed him on the cheek. Rory shrugged.

"No more volunteers?" he inquired.

"I have no bag to sleep in." Isolt despondently stretched herself across the stones.

"Have mine," Jim offered.

"I can't do that."

"Share it," Melonie said.

They lay in the bag and Melonie zipped them up. Jim turned on his side with his back to her. Isolt put her arm around him, aroused by the situation. She lightly stroked his belly through his shirt. He turned and kissed her mouth. She almost touched her fingers to his wound. He flinched and her fingertips hovered in the night an inch from his battered face. They groped silently, eyes closed in the darkness. Neither undid any clothes. She felt his erection through his jeans and pushed her tongue into his mouth. Her tongue touched and tangled around his own sour-tasting tongue. There was a bitter taste to his saliva. His swollen lip quivered with pain.

Morning was glaring and Rory was hovering over them.

"Well, well! Young love."

Jim sat up blinking and in agony. His face was monstrously swollen and had bled overnight. Isolt reluctantly slithered out of the bag and onto the cold jagged rocks.

"It's too cold for this lark. I'm going to Paris," she moaned.

"John never returned," Rory said.

"After that experience he probably begged the Foreign Legion to take him back," Jim said.

"So when are you two getting married?" Rory asked.

"Shut up, Rory," Jim snarled.

"Was she a virgin, Jim?"

"Shut up, Rory," Isolt said. She felt too embarrassed to look at Jim. "That was the strangest drug."

"Let's do it again," Rory said.

"Are you serious?" Isolt said.

"I'm on for it," enthused Melonie.

"Jim?" Rory looked at him, clapping his hands together.

Jim groaned. "Shit. Why not?"

Isolt stamped her feet for warmth. "I've lost all my stuff. I'm going to bunk a train back to Paris."

Rory said, "Back to Christopher. Hey, do you know that's who she kept on seeing last night when she was ranting and raving?"

Jim grinned. "You do look a bit different, Isolt. Are you in love?" But he could not look at her straight. Isolt ignored him.

"Let's go for breakfast and then I'll get the train."

None of them had any money so Isolt left them at the station. She planned to jump trains all the way to Paris.

Before she left she went to the toilets and looked in the mirror for the first time in weeks. Almost normal weight. Yesterday she had been obese. She washed her hands of Jim's blood. There was a scab in her fingernail. She feared she had clawed at his wound as they slept. Her face; it was growing old. There were tiny cracks in the skin beneath the eyes.

Do I belong to it? It is growing old. And I am receding.

On the train she was overcome with anguish. Her mother's silver ring. She had never once taken it off but this time she had put it on the sink's rim to wash the blood from her hands and had forgotten it. Believing herself to be hollow, craving obliteration, she tried to find company in the rushes of stark trees and houses that danced briefly in front of the grimy windows. The conductor mistook her grief for sorrow at the loss of her ticket and let her stay on till Paris. Why had she taken the ring off? She never took it off. Never. She had left her guardian angel on the sink. Her finger bore the ring's whitish indentation — the last trace of her Irish past.

I loved you. I loved you more than the world you gave me to.

Things were not all right. She was dazed. Touched by the loss of her mother's ring. By the agony of every step she took through the carriage. By the tiny sound of her soul rattling about in her hollow body as she desended the steps of the train.

People greeted their loved ones. The station was crowded, decorated for Christmas already. She had nowhere to sleep. The squat was most likely dead and she did not want to be cast adrift in that area after the last Metro. She was too late for the fountain. She saw signs for Frankfurt, Amsterdam, Milan. They seemed to be big friendless cities like Paris. She walked outside, leaving the station. There was a street with men and women prostitutes lined up against the walls. Half of them Asian. They have come so far, Isolt thought. She felt as she walked that she had not left the station, rather that that giant building — with its hubbub of people, Christmas decorations, warmth of reunions, people coming home or returning to their own cities, those innocents excited at the promise of foreign soil, station workers on shifts all knowing what to do and where to go when it was finished — had somehow abandoned her.

Isolt walked for a few more hours that night until, exhausted, she squeezed in through the gate of a park beside Notre Dame and slept fitfully in the cold on a bench beneath a tree, beset with visions and dreams.

There you came. Who were you? Rising all those evenings from the moth-swollen air. Their fur wings nauseating your lips. Trembling against your neck. Your skin soft yellow. Looking at me from the top window, as the shadows invaded your room and the street took the night. Standing with your one broken hand on the window pane where the two darknesses met. Inside darkness, outside darkness, both as unforgiving. Watching me mount the steps into the hall to my big room, which made me feel as if I was shrinking every time I stepped inside. I who had nothing ever to fill it. No pictures for the wall. In full view of January's torment. You who did not seem to mind the dark.

And when I tried to wave, you turned to stone.

5

Breakfast in Babylon

ISOLT SLEPT on the bench that morning dreaming of her home which she had left and never revisited. The dream is a view from a Dublin corner — a man in gray cord trousers carries leaves on branches across the road to be burned. In the distance cars with bruised side panels drive off the pier into the roaring gray water; goodbye to the white sky, farewell to a moment of seagull cry. The drabness that is in everything circles the planet outside. The man stands close to the burning heap, blinded by the smoke; he does not budge. There are other men, sawing down trees.

Straight ahead the forest falls away as the city opens its arms and an ice-cream van melody limps through the sullen world. The shrill cries of the Legion of Mary gossiping about the end of the world. Men drill through their female souls to where the glistening sewage flows.

The trees gather rank and with the help of the wind they bend and sway, moan and chant in a cold and desolate sing-song. And the Reverend Father Blank of the Imperial Church of the Holy Nothingness gathers his shabby flock and half-heartedly, out of time, they march towards the emptiness that was always present in the good times of their lives.

There is a damp little bar where everyone comes and sits, to while away the centuries over a pint glass of erosion and a beer-stained drink mat. If all ceases for a second they can feel their hearts beating and their deaths singing in the trees. If it all ceases for a minute they can feel their deaths breathing and their hearts trembling in the trees —

She was being shaken awake by the park caretaker. His face was reddened by outrage and the cold November chill. She thought of the story of Lazarus. On being brought back to life he wept. Imagine the pain of undoing death. Her back aching, she sat up stiffly, still struggling from the hard bench, still struggling to emerge from the dream, the cutting down of the trees, humans flapping about in their idiotic preoccupations, helpless. She began rubbing her numb body back to circulation, glancing up at the park attendant in disbelief as he told her of the fine for sleeping on a bench. She told him if she could afford the fine she wouldn't be sleeping there in the first place.

This is France, he was shouting, insulted immediately by her accented command of his language.

Thanking him curtly for his orientation tip she proceeded to limp on bloodless legs towards the gate. His face softened; the excitement of waking a young girl on the bench had promised him a diversion in his duties. Now she was depriving him of his reason to be angry and thus leaving the monotony of his day exactly where it had stood before. Go to your consulate, he was shouting at her, hurt by her apparent indifference to his sudden chivalry. Finally as she looked back he waved his hand.

"*Paff!*" he said. He shrugged at a jogger warming up nearby, looking for an alley. "*Ce pays est pourri par les étrangers.*"

The jogger did not react to this sentiment and started out on his run, his long hairy arms swinging idiotically at his sides.

Isolt witnessed all this as she hobbled out of the park. Paff indeed! she thought. She was being followed. This was not paranoia. Turning around she caught her hunter in the eye. A small Arab, about thirty-ish, was beside her smiling. She sagged with gloom. It was too early to have to deal with this intrusion so soon after the last.

"Where are you from?"

She walked on.

"You speak English? You should not sleep in park. It is very dangerous."

He kept beside her.

"This town is full of bad men."

"And you've come along to save me from them all. Right?"

"I will buy you coffee."

"No thanks. I'd never get rid of you then."

"Come. You are a nice girl. Very beautiful. Do you want a croissant?" He put his hand on her arm.

"Don't touch me. You have no right to. You keep your women under lock and key, then you think you can treat western women like whores."

"Are you racist?"

"No. Now leave me alone."

"Is it my frizzy hair you don't like?"

Isolt laughed at this. "Get the fuck away from me."

He kept following her, this time brushing his hand on her arse. Isolt swung around.

"Fuck off!"

"I like a strong woman."

"Listen to me. I don't want a fucking croissant or coffee and I don't want to sleep with you."

"Friend. I want you for friend. Just friend."

"No."

"You are racist?"

"I'm going to get the police if you don't leave me alone."

The thought of this dampened his ardour. She marched off in fury towards the Metro at Saint-Michel.

"*Salope!*" he shouted after her, "*Putain!*"

Isolt ducked under the barricade and went down the steps. Warming up, she let the first few trains pass by. She had cramps. On the train the motion made her more tense. The pain swelled into a dull ache in her womb. An iron claw dragging down on her insides. She had no money for painkillers or tampons. To soothe the pain she jiggled her legs. Breathing deeply, sucking in the foul air of the crowded rush hour carriage, she pinched her thigh hard to distract herself from the pain in her womb. Letting her breath go, she reflected that yesterday's depression and extreme reaction to the loss of her mother's ring, even the unsettling dreams, were more understandable considering the arrival of her period today. This provided her with a modicum of solace. Through the gasps of pain, the repetitive gnawing of unseen teeth, the iron claw pulling and pushing deep in her belly, she organised herself. Find a toilet and go beg. Noble objectives to dispel the current crises.

Isolt emerged from the labyrinthine metro system at Sèvres-Babylone. She walked into the Bon Marché department store and went into the Ladies. There was only a small spot of blood. Rolling up a giant wad of toilet paper she wrapped it around the crotch of her knickers. She washed her hands, looking at herself in the mirror. Then she went through the shop stealing a pen and three small plastic alarm clocks. Occupied as she was by her stealth, the pain still nagged and every now and then would become an intrusive stabbing.

She wandered outside and scanned the ground for some cardboard to make a begging sign. There was a box in the alley beside the department store and she tore the lid off. She crouched down wincing with the pain. *SANS RESOURCE AIDEZ MOI.* When she had filled in the letters enough to render them adequately visible she went in front of the store and sat between the fish stand and the fruit stall.

A child came up, sent by her mother, and gave her a punnet of strawberries. She ate a couple ravenously until some smart alec walked by and commented.

"Sans resource et vous mangez des fraises!"

She put them behind her back and squinted into the clamour of the day. Her pain distanced her from the sights and sounds of the sales-people and the shoppers. She was wholly absorbed by her bleeding womb, watching the throng of feet stamp by. Her forehead was set in a deep frown trying to pace the violent cramps and ease them into a steady throb of dull agony. She took the money given and nodded her thanks, barely glancing up. She shoved the change into her pocket, biting her lip, every now and then groping for a strawberry, not wanting to move till she had enough.

Time was the only cure. Tomorrow she would not feel this bad. Six hours from now and this would be manageable. The present agony would soon be a vague memory. Pain stretched the span into a life time, agony an evil spell that conjured an eternity out of a space in time. The acute discomfort felt every month, however, was not profound. Once it was over she dispelled the fears and wavering emotions and did not reflect on them. They could not torture her forever.

She took one of her alarm clocks out but there was no battery in any of them. She asked the next person who gave her money for the time. The woman looked surprised and told her.

A giant approached. She knew him to see but had rarely spoken to him. His head was completely bald. He was seven foot two inches.

"Hey, woman! Get up, the blues are coming."

She stood up looking around.

"Hey, Freddie."

He seemed embarrassed. Her head barely reached his chest.

"Down this street?" she asked, trying to avert the pathos of the situation.

"Yeah!" he nodded, getting businesslike. "They almost got me but I ran. They followed in the van. We better get out of here."

The blues were a group of men whose lousy job was to cruise the streets in a long gray van picking up destitutes. They wore navy blue overalls, hence the nickname. God forbid if they caught them in the morning. The beggars would sit in a cage in the van and waste the day driving around as they filled the dreaded vehicle with beggars and winos. At about eight o'clock this mundane mystery tour would wind up in the suburbs as they herded everyone into a building. They stripped and hosed everyone down, boiling the clothes in disinfectant and feeding them all watery soup with chunks of rotting horse meat and a mug of cheap wine that tasted like nail varnish remover to stop the alcoholics from losing the soggy remnants of their minds. Then came bedtime in the dormitories. Coughing, scratching, weeping, spitting, the stench of diarrhoea and incontinence from the plastic mattresses, the fear of a fist in the face or a phlegmy word of madness in the ear. Men and women with discoloured veiny skin hanging sloppily from their bones, holes hollowed in their legs, ancient and deep. The very skin of their yellow eyeballs baggy and wrinkled, the pupils burst, the lackluster irises stained. The random loose groans tracing the horror of each day and weaving the fabric of each ugly night.

God forbid, if lying on her back on the mattress in her hot wet urine, a terrible woman shrills out a garbled sound forking into the huge grub-infested air that pins them all down to their own immovable plastic rafts drifting away and away in bad company over the edges of the earth.

Morning. The clothes returned stinking of chemicals, and out into the bright light of the dreadful suburbs far away from the city, shuffling in shock in the direction of the RER station.

Freddie and Isolt sat upstairs in the Bon Marché restaurant over a nice pot of tea. Isolt squirmed self-consciously on the seat, hoping she wasn't leaking.

"You know what they say about the blues," Freddie said quietly and seriously. "Go in with one flea, come out with ten."

Isolt laughed and poured the tea. It spilt over the lid.

"Shit! A man on the moon and they can't even invent a cafeteria tea-pot that doesn't spill."

"You have to hold the lid up while you pour."

Isolt took his advice and it worked. She looked up at him and he flinched in embarrassment. Nervously he ducked his bald head and slurped some tea noisily. She noticed cuts and stubble behind his ear.

"Why do you shave your head?"

"I kept getting lice." And as if this was not sufficient justification he added, "It was going bald anyway."

Isolt shifted in her seat and gasped, "I got pains."

He reached into his pockets and surreptitiously extracted a plastic container, twisting the lid open. Isolt watched this closely. He had hands like shovels. He quickly pushed four pills over to her.

"DF118s," he said. "They'll kill your pain."

Isolt snatched them up. She knew Freddie vaguely. He hung close to Christopher. He was famous for washing his teeth in the fountains. Isolt was sure the French hated to see that. A filthy, bald, English giant scrubbing away at his crooked molars, foaming at the mouth, lobbing a white ball of spit into their precious fountains and bending down graciously to rinse his toothbrush in the spray.

She swallowed the pills. "Thanks."

He looked around. "The others should be here shortly."

"What others?"

"Oh, I dunno — we kind of get together here every morning now. A lot of the lads beg around Sèvres-Babylone. They take a break around now for breakfast."

"Who?"

"I don't know if you know any of them."

Isolt excused herself, "I got to go take a piss," and briskly made her way to the toilets. It was a mess. All soaked through the paper and onto her jeans.

"Fuck!" She leaned against the partition wall. She cleaned up as best she could. At least her jacket covered her jeans. She ran out and bought a box of tampons and stole a pair of plastic sunglasses with fake gold frames while she was waiting in the queue. Racing back to the department store she rushed into the toilets. When she returned to the restaurant Freddie was gone. She slumped disconsolately in the chair and sipped the cold tea.

Isolt drowsed happily in her chair. She wished Freddie hadn't gone. Those tablets had worked and given her a buzz too. She would like more. Larry tapped her on the shoulder. "Woman! What are you doing here? You're meant to be down south."

"Yeah? Well I came up yesterday."

"How come?"

"To have breakfast in Babylon."

He smiled. "Hold on while I get a cup of tea. Though there is no such thing as a cup of tea. Which will I have? A nice cup of tea or a lovely cup of tea?"

Isolt grunted. "Well, here in Babylon our expectations are considerably lower."

When he came back he was with two others.

"This is Fred and this is Jack."

Isolt nodded. Larry continued. "This is Isolt."

They all shook hands formally when they put down their trays. Both had British accents. One was black and had a beard. They paid scant attention to her. She was used to this. Most men on the begging circuit did not know how to talk to women or else they discounted them entirely. A girl had to fight to establish herself. Larry knew her too well to behave in this manner. He leaned over to her and said,

"Tell the Irish contingent to come back north, all is forgiven."

"I thought you'd be pleased to be surrounded by your countrymen."

"What we have here is two pathetic specimens. An epileptic and a black man. Neither will admit to the offence."

"I'm not epileptic," Fred sighed. "Look, I know what happened last night. I took too much acid, that's all."

"Nearly ruined the trip," Jack said. "Jittering about like a fucking fish out of water."

Fred glowered into his already lukewarm milky tea. He was of slight build and had mousy thin hair. He wore a white overcoat with black threads, an orange V-neck sweater with an orange T-shirt underneath. He had a silver identity necklace with "Fred" scratched poetically on the disc. Jack wore a tight brown knitted jumper with a navy stripe ringing the middle and dark blue denim trousers. His face was brown and even managed some freckles. He had a flat upturned nose and an oval head.

Larry sighed and continued, "And Jack here is not black of course."

Jack's eyes glinted with fury.

"Aren't you?" Isolt asked.

"No."

"Yes you are," Fred said.

"No I'm not."

"Why deny it?" Isolt asked.

"Because I'm not."

"Your skin is black," Larry said leaning over and pointing to his fingers holding the tea cup.

"Well, it's brown anyway," Isolt said, trying to be helpful.

"It's fucking not," Jack bristled.

"What's so good about being white?"

"I don't know."

"Then why try?" Fred said, exasperated.

"I'm not trying."

"But you say you're not black," Larry told him.

"I'm not."

"You should be proud of it," Isolt said, wondering if this was a joke on her behalf.

"I'm British and proud of it," Jack stated emphatically.

"Well maybe, but your ancestors came from Africa."

"No. I'm British through and through."

"Jesus," Fred said. "Your sister is a whore. You are a beggar. You don't even live there any more. What did Britain do for you?"

"It's the best fucking country on earth, that's what," he exclaimed passionately.

"Not if it produced you," Isolt retorted.

The two others snorted with laughter.

"Look," said Jack. "I know what I am. British. Made in England. I never even knew any black people."

"What about your family?" Isolt asked.

"They're not black either."

"Kind of hard to believe, Jack," Larry sighed, pouring himself more tea.

Fred perked up. "Maybe you're from Afghanistan, you could kind of pass for one of them with the beard and all."

"Where are you from?" Isolt asked Fred.

"Scunthorpe," Fred said.

"Who took the cunt out of Scunthorpe?" Larry said, more of a statement than a question. Fred threw his eyes up to heaven smiling slightly. Isolt decided not to think about it. Jack, who was still wrestling with racial inner demons, burst out, thumping his fist on the table, causing other diners to glance around.

"I'm fucking British and proud of it. I love my Queen and I would fight to protect the Union Jack."

"But you wouldn't live there, eh?" Larry said.

"I don't have to, it's a free country."

"What do the other blacks think of this?" Fred asked. "Do they pity you?"

"I don't associate with black people."

"I shouldn't wonder," Isolt said.

A tall long-haired guy approached the table with a tray and sat down. Larry did the introductions.

"This is Cloggie from Holland, she's a Paddy from Ireland and Jack here is from somewhere in the Congo."

"Jesus, Larry!" Isolt said. "It's a good job you don't work for the United Nations."

"So what's your gimmick, Cloggie?" Isolt asked.

"Cloggie used to work for the space shuttle," Larry told her.

"So how long will it take to put a beggar on the moon?" Isolt said.

Cloggie smiled. "No, no. This is not true. He is joking. I was an economist."

"Oh, it's all the same thing," Larry said.

"So after studying economics you decided to become a beggar? I gather you weren't an A student."

"Christ, this one's a sarky cow," Jack said.

"Everybody has a story to tell." Cloggie winked at her.

Isolt wondered why he winked.

"Where did you stay last night?" Larry asked her.

"In the park beside Notre Dame."

"Beside it?"

"Well, it's just across the river."

"Any trouble?"

"Park attendant tried to fine me for sleeping on a bench."

They all laughed. Isolt smiled. She had resented that wink and had taken a dislike to Cloggie for the moment.

"I met Freddie the Giant. He warned me about the blues. He was in here a while ago. I don't know where he went."

"He's a strange one," Cloggie nodded.

"He's another one of Christopher's bleeding prodigies," Jack said.

"Christopher put him in the squat with us. He's dead quiet but he goes berserk when he drinks and he drinks every fucking chance he gets," Larry said. "I'm surprised he warned you. He hates birds."

"Tweet-tweet!" Isolt said.

"It's embarrassing," Fred said. "He starts shouting at them on the street and remember when American Michele came around?"

They all reminisced smiling.

"My God, that sure was something," Cloggie said. "He called her an ugly cunt."

"He said he'd never seen cunt so ugly," Larry said.

"He told her he could smell her period a mile off," Jack said.

Isolt reacted inwardly to this with terror.

"Well," Jack confessed. "She did have a really smelly period."

"Is the squat still open?" Isolt asked to change the subject.

"Yeah, but all of us are in hotels now," Larry told her. "It was getting out of hand. Christopher kept lording over it and dumping more and more really bad alcoholics and sick old men on the third floor. The dogs kept multiplying and they ate up a big supply of hash that one of the Germans had smuggled down from Holland and they started acting weird. Freddie the Giant feuded with the Afghans one night when he was pissed and they nailed a rat to our door. I just couldn't take it. Might as well be nabbed by the blues, it was like being in a doss house. The place was infested by winos, weird dogs and Afghans practising Voodoo."

"Yes," Cloggie said. "And one girl gets raped."

"That's right," Larry said. "This German has a bird with him and he's always slapping her about. She was black and blue, poor cow, but she's a bad junkie and she stays put. Anyway he buggers off one night and doesn't come back. She wanders about crying and wailing for the bastard."

"Those birds are begging for it," Jack said. "They don't have to stay. Fuck all the hype about battered wives. They love it, they keep coming back for more."

"So," Larry said. "One night all the Krauts, you know how they are, want to shut her up so they gang rape her and cut her up badly."

"Gunther told me they cut off one of her nipples as a souvenir. He said Omi has it. He says it looks like a raisin or a prune or something," Jack said.

"Ouch!" Isolt said.

"Funny," leered Jack. "That's what she said when they scraped her off the ceiling."

The men laughed.

"Fuck," Isolt said.

"Yeah, fuck is right," Larry continued. "So she stumbled off the next morning half dead. We never heard of her since but the four of us and Taffy decided to split in case the police would bust in."

"Did you know when it was happening?" Isolt asked.

"Shit, Isolt," Larry said. "You know how the Germans are. It always sounds like Dante's fucking Inferno down there. What could we have done? The shortest of those cunts is six foot four."

"She should have gone when her old man buggered off. She shouldn't have stayed without his protection," Jack stated.

"Well, from the sound of it he didn't do much of a job protecting her," Isolt said.

"Sweetheart," Jack sneered. "He kept the others off her and her nipples on her."

Cloggie winked at her. Isolt stood up, glancing down at the chair in case she had leaked. She was paranoid today; it was so heavy she could feel the blood ooze out. "I don't know about you people but I got begging to do. This is getting too fucking depressing anyway."

"OK love!" Larry said. "See you at Saint-Michel."

"That reminds me," Isolt said. "I got three alarm clocks here. Anyone want to buy one?"

"What do we want with alarm clocks?" Jack asked.

"To get your lazy arses up in the mornings and beat the German beggars to the best spots."

"If we have to set a fucking alarm clock every night," Larry said, "we might as well get a job."

Isolt took them out and showed them.

"They're small. You can carry them around in your pocket so you always know what time it is."

"How much do you sell it for?" Cloggie asked.

"Twenty francs. They cost one hundred and thirty and I'm not bargaining. Take it or leave it."

"OK! I buy one." Cloggie took out a giant handful of change and started counting.

"I'll give you fifteen," Jack said, reaching for one.

"Fuck off Jack," Isolt said, snatching it away. "I've just given it to Cloggie for twenty. That's a decent price."

Jack counted out twenty francs in one franc pieces or smaller. Isolt stood checking Cloggie's amount in equally small change.

"God, you lousy beggars. Doesn't anyone ever give you a ten franc piece?" she moaned.

Fred was glumly counting his money. "I've only got twelve francs."

Isolt decided that he had offended her the least out of the three newcomers.

"Done," she said, handing one to him. He dumped the change into her hand. It wasn't even eight francs but she didn't say anything.

"Hey!" Cloggie was outraged. "That's not fair. I want some money back. We gave twenty and he only gave twelve. I want my eight francs."

"You are not an economist now, Cloggie, you are a beggar," Isolt replied sternly.

"Yeah," said Larry. "And beggars can't be choosers."

She turned affectionately to Larry.

"What about you, Larry? I could go get one for you as a present. Don't you want to beat those industrious German beggars to their spots?"

"The early bird catches the worm," Jack said.

"Thank you, Jack," Isolt said. "We should go into sales together."

"Who wants a worm anyhow. Really?" Cloggie laughed alone at his own joke.

"No love," Larry said. "Not even for free. I'm forty-eight years old and that's the only way I measure time. Never hour by hour."

"Well, you wouldn't want to," Jack said. "Forty-eight years is a lot of fucking hours to keep track of, mate."

"I hope the blues are far away," Isolt said.

"Yeah," Jack said. "I expect they've picked up all the old geezers by now and they're all comparing what colleges they went to. Oxford or Cambridge, old chap?"

"Yes indeed," said Cloggie. "Some of those crazy old men are philosophers and have degrees."

"A lot more in their noodles than the blues anyway," Larry grunted.

"Are you going back out to throw yourself to the lions?" Isolt asked them.

"I am," Larry said. "I didn't make fucking nothing. Just enough for me bleeding tea."

"I just got ripped off on a frigging alarm clock," Jack said.

"How much do you have?" Cloggie asked her.

"What you just gave me and whatever I begged. I didn't count it."

"Don't you count as you go along?" Fred asked.

Isolt was aghast. "No. Do you?"

"Sure," Fred said. "Every time someone gives I look at the coins and I add it up in my head and say thanks out loud." He acted it out, his head bent and his hand out. Glancing at his empty hand, he muttered softly, "Ten *francs. Merci.* Twelve *francs. Merci.* Thirteen *francs. Merci.* Eighteen *francs. Merci.*"

"Jesus," Larry shook his head. "You cold bastard."

"I don't count centimes," Fred continued. "So I always have more than I think. It's like a surprise for myself. When I get to one hundred and fifty francs I quit. Enough for a few smokes, some hash, a meal and a few beers."

"Who would you say gives the most?" Isolt asked.

"Old ladies," Jack said promptly.

The others nodded their heads in affirmation.

"Old ladies, God bless them, they're the best," Larry said. "They're givers, they're all alone, nobody talks to them or pays them any mind, old man died years ago, kids never visit. They know what life's about or what it's not about at any rate. They think when they see you sitting there down and out that you could be their kids or grand-kids. Well acquainted with life's twists and turns they are. It makes their day to go to the market and give the leftovers to the beggars. It's the highlight of their crappy lives. They hardly leave the house after the shopping's done. They want that, the 'merci' and the smile I give them. They're so fucking lonely. They need the contact. And for my regulars, a special nod of recognition and a *comment ça va?* How's your father and the rest of it. Ha! Ha! They love it, it makes them feel included. That's how bad their lives have got after all those years servicing the husband and the kids and the home. My heart breaks to see them come up day after day and give me their change. Sometimes if I'm away from a certain spot for a couple of weeks they come up all smiles and say, 'Where were you? I thought something had happened.' They know what money's worth at this stage, they know how good it is to give. Breaks my heart."

"Same with me," Isolt said. "Little old ladies giving me my drug money."

Everyone smiled. They all lit up more cigarettes. Isolt had none but it was no shame to scab some for the moment.

"One time this woman passes by and shakes her umbrella at me," Fred said. "She shouts *'C'est pour l'alcool?' 'Non,'* I say, *'C'est pour les drogues.'* You should have copped her face."

They laughed.

"Never businessmen," Larry said. "Men hardly ever give money and never pretty, young girls. They think they have it all. When those pretty girls get old and shrivelled and bent over they will start to give. Those businessmen will never be givers."

"Most of my big money, when it comes, comes from men," Isolt said.

"Every now and then, they will give me a hundred-franc note."

"They're just thinking of fucking you when they lay it on like that," Jack said to Isolt.

"They can think away," Isolt said. "Suits me fine for a note."

"Whore," Jack said.

"I'm going for one more tea before I go," Cloggie said. "Who wants one?"

They all agreed except Isolt. When Cloggie got up to get the tea Larry turned to Isolt, who was still standing up.

"What's your hurry?"

"I lost all my shit down south. I need to get a sleeping bag, some clothes and try to get a hotel room. Which one are you in?"

"George V. Over beside Polly Magoo's."

"All right. I'll see if I can rent that out. How much?"

"Well, find someone to share with. Stay with us tonight. Me and Jack unfortunately have to share a room. Cloggie and Fred share another. It's one hundred and twenty for a double."

"Where's Taffy?"

"Fuck knows. Haven't seen him for days. When's Jim and Rory coming up? You never told us how the south was."

"Shite!" Isolt said. "I don't know when that lot will come here. There was a girl with us. A fat girl. She was all right. And you know John?"

"Finnish John the Foreign Legion refugee?"

"Finnish John the Foreign Legion refugee," Jack repeated, throwing his eyes up to heaven. "Now I've heard everything."

"Well, he disappeared during a trip two nights ago. I wonder has he showed up yet."

"You know what," said Fred to Jack. "Your lot don't give money either."

"My lot?" Jack said.

"Yeah. You know, the blacks. They don't ever give me any money."

"Blacks aren't my lot, mate. I don't have nothing to do with no blacks," Jack said. "I'm as British as you are. Born and bred in that great land."

"Maybe," said Larry, "they don't feel sorry enough for us whiteys begging 'cos they have it worse. Do they give to you, Jack?"

"Not if they don't give to you, mate." Jack's tone was strained.

"They just give me little cards with the names of churches on them. Never any dosh. Do you go to those churches? Gospel are they?"

"The blacks here are mostly first and second generation Africans," Isolt said.

"Well, I'm Church of England," Jack protested.

"What?" said Fred, "They let you in?"

"I'm fucking English, aren't I?"

Isolt could feel it starting all over again.

"Hey, I'm off. Thanks for the cigarettes. We've come a full circle. He's not black and Fred's not epileptic."

"I'm not epileptic," said Fred. "For fuck's sake."

"He's as much epileptic as you're black, right Jack?" Larry said.

"He is epileptic. I fucking saw him in spasms last night. Had to turn him on his side so he wouldn't swallow his tongue," Jack said.

"Look here, Florence fucking Nightingale," Fred said, "we were tripping, that's all."

"Better epileptic than black," Jack said.

"That's a sad statement of our times," Larry said sombrely. He turned to Isolt.

"Hey, woman, always in a rush. We'll catch you later. Are you going to get a clock for yourself?"

"No." Isolt shook her head. "I'm like you, no patience for time."

"No time for time." Jack lit another cigarette.

"Why kill time when you can kill yourself," Fred stated.

She could see Cloggie coming with more pots of tea. She left before he came to the table, marvelling that she had just sold alarm clocks to beggars. Isolt resumed her position between the fish stand and the fruit stall. Her strawberries were still there. There were three left and she ate them. She stared into the garbled symphony of people selling and buying, eyeing each other, shouting their prices into the startling frost of noon, converting every word uttered into steam. The hundreds of jelly blind fish eyes gazing, bereft of any final visions; the over-ripe and under-ripe fruit slipped quickly and surreptitiously into the brown bags of consumers; chemicals, poisons — all toxic for efficiency — electronic goods made off the broken backs of the Third World, built-in obsolescence keeping the product rolling; the soaps and sprays and powders preying on vanities, over-packaged, sucking the earth dry of resources, all the perfumes watered down.

Purses open, spewing forth currency, pockets dug into, coins clattering about. We believe lies, we buy things we don't use, we throb with twentieth-century gloom. Clothes in the window, stick-thin, impossibly tall dummies spreading guilt among the roly-poly, lustful gazers. Hands that reach out have money in them, wanting a product in return. Cars speed by, belching pollution, offending the world with horns and engines, so we can go faster, speed things up. Things, things, money, money. This is Babylon. We are all in exile from our very souls here in the chaos. So it doesn't hurt to take shelter in the belly of the beast and have breakfast.

To have breakfast. To while away the centuries over a nice cup of lukewarm erosion. If it all ceases for a second you can feel your heart trembling and your death bleating in the trees. If it all ceases for a minute you can feel your death enclosing and your heart crying for mercy in the trees.

The sales coup of the century. Alarm clocks to beggars.

Roll up, roll up, it's a competitive business, only the disheveled need apply. Start every morning under the bridge with an electronic beeping noise. Freedom from the rat race is but an illusion. Weep, weep! Though we cry we have known it all along.

Here over a lovely cup of tea we can partake of breakfast in Babylon, resting a while where time is not of the essence, where the only opportunity is in eternity.

Prepare yourselves, for the beggars have just bought alarm clocks.

And every now and then through the banal panic, a tiny old lady bursts towards her, knowing that what really matters is giving for nothing. A stark life form side-stepping out of Babylon in the wink of an eye, dragging only sustenance in a tartan shopping cart, bending down wrinkled and wrapped up for winter, all beads, bald patches and solitude these old women, dropping what's left after all the morning's frantic exchanges into her grateful hand.

6

....

Where Picasso Ends
and Christopher Begins

ISOLT HAD never begged so hard. Five hours sitting in four different locations — the last in a Metro tunnel during rush hour. She bought a pair of black leggings, a three-pack of knickers, a towel, shampoo and conditioner and some make up in the Tati at Montparnasse. To-night could be her big date. She felt good sitting with her plastic bags full of unopened and unworn items on the Metro, like a normal commuter. Soon she wouldn't look or smell so much like a beggar.

From the bridge she could see the Eiffel Tower. She was attracted to Christopher. She was attracted to the idea of being very, very old. At this very moment on the bridge she felt compelled to dive into the Seine. To throw life off course. Walk down one street or walk down another.

Isolt felt herself being drawn towards Christopher just as she had been been drawn to the gash in Jim's face; she had carried his scabs in her fingernails unawares. Her friend Becky had hated Christopher because he was cruel. She had sensed Isolt's initial infatuation to-wards him and didn't like it. Becky had heard the death beat running through their lives. Her death had been a warning to Isolt to go look for shelter but she was not sure how.

She left the tower and hurried on to the American church on the quays.

*

The American church had a small college attached to it. Isolt walked down the steps, through the hall and ducked into the showers without catching anyone's eye. As she shampooed her hair she wished she had remembered to buy a razor for she felt monstrously hairy compared to all these young American girls. They were rich and she was poor. All those hairless First-Worlders laughing and talking shit. They came across as naive, patronizing and phoney.

Christopher had none of these traits; he was the only poor American she had ever met. She rinsed the conditioner from her hair and stood for a blissful moment under the thumping hot water. She had not had a shower in two months.

Stepping out naked, she caught an unwanted glimpse of her lumpy body in the full-length mirror; red patches from the scalding water splotched all over her fish-white flesh. She shut this out of her mind and vigorously dried herself with the towel. These Americans were so super-confident; the world was their oyster and their parents' credit cards were their pearls. They had huge brightly-coloured soft towels and a million and one products in their designer make-up bags, they knew each other and chatted merrily like birds. Isolt was jealous of their camaraderie and their ease with the world. She put on her new knickers and leggings, all the time holding in her stomach. She sniffed her bra; it smelt of smoke, but she had to put it on anyway as she had no other. She wished she had a new jumper that didn't smell of sweat; she almost cried putting on her filthy black jacket, she felt so alone. The girls were looking at her discreetly. She had meant to ask them for a lend of a hairbrush but now that they had spotted her sniffing her bra she was ashamed to ask.

She combed her shoulder-length hair roughly with her fingers. The confidence she had obtained earlier from her rampant consuming was ebbing away. Covering her face in foundation she immediately perked up; it was an improvement. Her red nose and the tiny broken veins on her cheeks were smoothed over. There had always been something about her face that had stubbornly defied prettiness. Her gray eyes were slanty and her cheeks were too big; vast expanses of cheek on either side of the nose, they were great plains, herds of wildebeest could graze on her cheeks. If she had a child with cheeks like that she would mercifully drown it.

There was nothing seriously physically wrong with her — too

chubby perhaps but not fat like poor Melonie — yet she still felt deformed, handicapped, especially when she saw the beautiful women in the advertisements everywhere. Isolt was plain though the make-up was making her look pretty. She put eyeliner on the pink little rim of her socket, blinking a little as her eye watered; she put some brown eye-shadow over the whole eyelid, putting an extra shimmer green stripe in the middle. Then with the satisfaction of opening a virginal mascara she brushed her eyelashes until they were thick and black, sticking the brush back into the tube, imagining the hymen breaking, screwed the lid on. She coated her lips in slut-red lipstick, pouting involuntarily in the mirror.

Presentable and blemish-free, she avoided the full-length mirror on her way out. An American girl was using a giant can of hairspray. Sealing in your rotten thoughts with poison, Isolt thought unfairly as she stomped out, not quite a new woman but a refurbished specimen for the time being.

The pavements were wet with drizzle, their colour a damp, dark brown under the yellow street lights. Cars and trucks passed on towards oblivion. She felt oppressed by the traffic and the city at night. The sight of the Eiffel Tower failed to elate her wizened spirit. Europe was going home for the night desensitized by the day's labours. Everyone was scurrying for shelter huddled under ominous black umbrellas.

November was a month of anticipation and a surrendering towards the long winter. The coming of winter had always struck a dead note in everyone at the fountain. It wasn't so bad in December when it was icily bitter and taken for granted. Soon it would seem as if there were no other seasons, no other city but a gray, cold one. A dread nestled sourly in their stomachs as they saw the last curled and burnt autumn leaves cling to the great trees. There was a rush indoors to squats and cheap hotels which seemed harder to find every year. The younger people could still stamp their feet, getting drunk and stoned at the fountain, laughing furtively, cherishing the glow of inebriation. The older ones were pensive, subdued with a terror that dried out their insides. The pressure was on for the lads to beg an extra one hundred francs rent a day and that was by no means an easy thing to do.

This night Isolt approached the fountain from the Metro exit by the oil-black River Seine, wading head down through the drizzle. She saw Ali talking to Taffy and walked into their midst. Ali stared into her eyes.

"Woman. Where have you been? Have you got a cigarette? I dreamt of you last night. It is so good to break bread together again."

Isolt nodded. "Yes, yes, Ali. Half a brain." She gave him her tobacco pouch.

"Woman. My beard has grown shorter and your hair has grown longer. What could that possibly mean?"

"It means we have nothing in common, Ali, now settle down."

She kissed Taffy on the cheek. He had a black rat sitting on his shoulder.

"It's my girlfriend's," he explained. "I got this French girl now. I was kipping on the street and I woke up and this punk chick was trying to undo my pants. I let her suck my willie in a fucking doorway. You wouldn't believe it, would you?"

"Well, it wouldn't happen in Wales," Isolt conceded.

"Fuck no. So me and her share a room in a squat with all the French punks."

"I thought you hated the French punks."

"Yeah. Well, they are fucking pussies compared to the Brits. All their shaved heads and buying their clothes with the zips and rips and pins already in them. Fuck 'em, eh? And then they all kiss each other on the cheek whenever they meet. Have you seen them fight? It's just push, push. They never hit each other. One picked a fight with me 'cos I stole this bird I have now from him. I threw down me crutches and hopped up and head-butted the cunt good and proper."

He took the rat off his shoulder and fed it some beer from a straw.

"Does your girlfriend speak English?" Isolt asked.

"Naw. And I don't speak French neither. She just gives me blow jobs and I take care of her rats. She's got three now."

Isolt laughed. "What's that one called?"

Taffy nodded to Ali. "I was going to call it Ali but Ali said to call it Yahweh."

"Yahweh? He must be talking to the born-agains. Hey Ali, you can't be a Christian with a name like Ali."

"*Allah akbar*," Ali roared, his hands in the air. "Kill the Arab."

"Isn't he an Arab?" Taffy asked.

"Persian," Isolt said. "Has Christopher been here yet?"

"Aggggggggh!" Ali howled. "From the great warriors of Persia I am descended."

"There must have been too much in-breeding," Isolt said, as they watched Ali jump around them sword-fighting an invisible adversary.

"Swish! Swish!" he panted.

"I never met a normal Iranian," Taffy said as the rat crawled into the neck of his jacket. "Him and Payman — they're both crazy."

"Well," Isolt said, "you don't really meet a normal anything around here."

"Hey Yahweh, you're tickling." He squirmed. "You know, I'm saving up to buy a parrot. I'm going to let it sit on me shoulder when I beg."

"That should work. You should teach it some French. That would kill them. The French would love that. A one-legged punk with a French-speaking parrot."

"That's brilliant," Taffy said. " 'Cept I don't know any French."

"Just teach it to say *'Parlez-vous français.'* Honestly, you'd make a fortune."

"*Parlez-vous français?* Yeah, I could do that, excellent."

Someone had thrown something into the fountain. It was brimming over with red soapsuds. People were having sud fights. Ali climbed halfway up the winged statue of Saint Michel. He sat on the saint's back and roared at the onlookers.

"*Allah akbar,* you idiots!"

He was covered in red suds. Taffy threw down his crutches and scrambled up the side of the monument. His stump was no handicap, he was able to put his full weight on it; he pulled himself past Ali and onto the extended arm of Saint Michel. Ali was still sword-fighting, clinging to the wings. Taffy took something out of his pocket and put it on the finger of the stone saint. It was a condom. So, Isolt thought, it's not just all blow jobs for Taffy. The crowd cheered and Taffy threw both of his arms triumphantly in the air.

"*Allah akbar,* you idiots."

The crowd was delighted. Ali, who had not seen Taffy's ascent, believed the hour of glory was his, his face was touchingly resplendent with pride. Isolt watched as the rat fell out from under Taffy's jacket and plunged unceremoniously into the red frothy mess. Isolt peered into the fountain and down the bubbly tunnel the rat had made in the suds. She had no intention of leaping in after it on this, the night of her big date. The police came along and Taffy and Ali climbed down. Isolt handed Taffy his crutches and patted Ali on the back.

"Well done, both of you."

"Hey!" Ali bowed. "Any time. No problem. Just say the word."

"Taffy, Yahweh fell into the fountain."

"Jesus. Where?"

"There." Isolt pointed to the edge.

Taffy bent down and stuck his arms in the sodden froth. "Can rats swim?" he called back frantically.

"No, man," Ali said. "That's how the Pied Piper killed them." He turned to Isolt. "Hey, woman, remember the Pied Piper man? He killed the rats. He brought them to the edge of the sea and they all jumped in. It was a crazy scene, man. All those rats jumping and jumping. I have never seen anything like it in all my life . . ."

"You weren't there, Ali. It's a story," Isolt said, and Taffy whooped with delight as he pulled Yahweh out by the tail.

"I've got him. I've got him." He sat on the side of the wet fountain. "Actually it's a her but in rats it makes no difference."

"It looks dead." Isolt inspected it but not too close for fear it would resurrect and claw out her eye.

"Shit," Taffy said and threw it over his shoulder back into the fountain. "She's going to kill me. I'll have to say it ran out under a car or something."

"No blow job tonight," Isolt commiserated.

"Hey, man," Ali mused, "didn't that weird guy take the children too? I seem to remember something more than rats."

"Who?" Taffy asked.

"The Pied Piper man. Remember him? Don't you read the papers? He was crazy. I hope they got him in the end. I remember he got the children too."

"It's not just the blow jobs. She's always thumping and punching me." Taffy was inconsolable.

"Why don't you head-butt her?" Isolt advised.

Taffy considered it but shook his head.

"If I whacked her she wouldn't touch my willie any more."

"I admit it's a dilemma," Isolt nodded.

Taffy and Ali were wet and shivering. Christopher came up behind Isolt. He kissed her on the cheek and turned to the other two.

"You both look like drowned rats," he said.

They all looked startled at this. Ali's eyes opened wide.

"Hey man, you are the Pied Piper."

Christopher grew annoyed. "Ali, where's Payman? Payman? I want to speak to Payman."

"Payman's dead. Dead. He fell from the wings of an angel and drowned. You the Pied Piper. State your price."

Christopher threw his eyes up to heaven and adressed Isolt. "What stone did you crawl out from under?"

Before Isolt could think of an appropriate answer Payman shuffled up in his perennial green parka. Christopher took this other pitiful Iranian to the side and they began to converse. Isolt watched. She felt tense and didn't know how to act.

"Are you on the streets this weather?" she asked Ali.

"Sometimes yes," he said. "But I met these Christian ladies and they let me sleep on the Jesus bus."

Isolt laughed. He meant the born-again Christian ladies who mingled on the square with the junkies and beggars, trying to convert them. They had an orange double-decker bus covered in Jesus slogans which they drove around and gave out food and pamphlets. They were part of the scene here. Human flotsam floating among the various groups, fellow losers.

Christopher was over to the side doing deals with various punters. Isolt did not dare to go over. Payman approached and Ali began to rant in Farsi. Payman spat on the ground in disgust.

Taffy spoke to her. "I have to go home. I can't wait for the van. I'm freezing me tits off."

"OK, good luck," Isolt said as he made his way, soggy and ratless, past the Germans and their dogs. Isolt hoped she could talk to Christopher and establish something before Larry and his friends arrived to witness it, though with Ali here there was not much privacy, he always told everyone everything. Ali begged just enough each day for one tab of acid and a litre of beer, he bummed cigarettes and kept them in a variety packet that he never shared. He survived on nothing but the food from the Red Cross van that came every night in winter at eight o'clock.

Christopher did not come to her in a dream. The first time she laid eyes on him he was not instantly recognisable. As once she was sucked from the darkness of all history and slipped squalling and unnoticed into a living shape, he too battled from the infinite range of strangers into the circle of her acquaintances. Not destined but coincidental. Only after a few years of seeing him around the city did she pay attention to stories involving him. She began to long for their lives to cross significantly and cling in the cramped part of eternity they inhabited; cling, and then she was sure she would have to let go against her will, his lifeline breaking from hers. As if strapped to the elastic of fate, he would eventually spring back towards the void of his grisly future and his death, out of earshot of her narrow world. Isolt was looking for adventure.

She loved his voice, it was a melodious whisper. She imagined him inside her when he began to talk, breathing through her. She loved his gnarled monkey hands. She imagined, as she watched him deal, a dirty fingernail grazing her nipple. To touch his sallow skin and feel his muddy glazed eyes on her body. He was dying, she guessed. She wanted to love him as he choked.

She might suffer the consequences of her deed but life demanded recklessness to jolt her out of this present rut. When Becky died it had excited her to have been so close to a death. As the years went on it had hurt her to have lost a friend. Eight months of friendship day in and day out on the streets was a long time. She had not made many others. She missed her. It was time to move back towards some sort of intensity. She was fed up watching others fumble and lose their footing, of always being poor and of only having poor people to talk to. Christopher was different.

It began to rain once more. She followed the general procession of the beggars across the road. They stood huddled beneath the arches. Ali came with her; he had the dead rat in his hand and was completely wet.

"I saved it, man. I rescued the rat. Have you got a cigarette I could borrow?"

Payman walked away; he still braved the old Saint-Quen squat. He moved in the eye of the hurricane aided by his only solace, the heroin he had just bought from Christopher.

"Put that away," Christopher snarled at Ali.

Ali looked frightened and quickly shoved the dead rat into his pocket.

Isolt stood rooted to the spot. "Are you going to wait for the van?" she asked lamely.

"I don't eat that shit," Christopher said. "Are you hungry?"

"No, not really," Isolt lied.

"Well, you look as if you have quite an appetite for such a short girl."

Isolt wondered if he was insinuating that she was overweight. She howled inwardly with humiliation.

"Jesus. You're in a great mood," she said.

"Yeah. Well . . ." He frowned. "Listen, come with me. You can do me a favour. You want to do me a favour?"

"Sure." She rejoiced.

As they walked off cutting separate paths in the infuriating drizzle Ali came up beside her and throwing the rat in her path hissed with all the menacing lunacy his soul could muster.

"Man. Don't follow the Pied Piper."

As Isolt brushed off this cheap trick she wondered what she was, a rat or a child?

Christopher sent Isolt into a pharmacy to buy two bottles of codeine cough medicine. He was too scruffy to go in himself. He drank half of one down in the Metro and gave her the other half. His mood improved considerably. They took the Metro to Saint-Lazare and had a coffee in one of the cafés opposite the station. Isolt no longer felt hungry.

"I have something to show you," he said. "Proof of my identity as a force in this city. My credentials. It's a public street — you have nothing to fear. Come on."

Isolt paid the bill and Christopher exited with her close behind. He looked around furtively when he stepped outside and then practically threw himself in one direction and stopped beside a phone box.

"What are you going to do now?" Isolt had her hands in her pockets and was cold. "Ring into headquarters?"

"No, no. Just wait. Look at this." He crouched down, pressing his finger to the ground, lighting his lighter beside his finger. Isolt could see a scab in his mop of curly hair.

"Don't tell me. A secret passage."

"Cut the attitude, sweet thing, and look."

Isolt sighed and crouched with him. Under his dirty fingernail was a large C carved in the cement.

"I did this when it was wet four years ago."

Isolt stared at it in silence.

"It's my initial." He pleaded for a glimmer of understanding.

Isolt looked up, their faces about two inches apart; he had wide pores on his nose.

He stood up abruptly: "I'm a fossil in this city." He seemed sincere, genuinely eager for her to understand. Isolt was dumbfounded.

"Well," she said. "I can see you're not a tourist anyway."

"C is for Christopher. I'm thirty-three years old. The age of Christ."

"Watch out for the guys in the skirts and the funny helmets."

"Believe me, they are around every corner."

They walked towards the station. Christopher lit a joint and they stood and smoked it.

"You're burning my head up with crazy ideas. You're making me hungry," he said to her as they stood in the wet dark air by the seedy Metro stairs.

They had to climb six flights of back stairs to his *chambre de bonne*. These rooms were the old servant rooms before the building was split up into apartments. There was one Turkish toilet at the end of the hall for general use. The walls in the halls and on the way up the stairs were light green — kind of nightmarish, mental hospital green.

These were rooms for a poor student, a struggling poet, an unmarried mother, a chronic alcoholic. These rooms were one step away from the street. These were living quarters for refugees, immigrants, exiles.

Christopher entered his room and left Isolt waiting in the green corridor. He rummaged about inside, came back panting and led her inside the narrow space. There was a sink to the left as she entered. A large part of the enamel was shattered. There was an orange plastic bucket beneath it to catch the water. The bucket was full to the rim with an opaque black fluid. Clay was caked all over the floor and cardboard boxes of clay were stacked up to the side. The room was about a metre and a half in width and four metres in length. The debris on the floor was a nebulous concoction of newspapers, fruit peels, scraps of clothes, tools, empty whiskey cartons and other indiscernible items. The last lodger had dragged planks of wood up the six flights of stairs and built a bed wall-to-wall near the roof, like a second floor with a wooden ladder as access. You could not sit up on this second floor, it was too close to the roof. Christopher used it to store more debris. It was packed with stolen boxes of blenders and juicers. The window was a tiny square high up on the wall. One of its panes was broken. The view was of other rooftops and dismal little attic rooms.

"Eiffel Tower view," Christopher stated proudly.

Isolt hung off the ladder straining to look out: "I can't see it."

"You see the aerial with all the little red lights on it in the distance?"

"Yes."

"That's the aerial of the Eiffel Tower."

"It must be a great comfort to you."

The previous owner had been a Venezuelan homosexual and he had pasted magazine pages of male ballet dancers on the roof wall-to-wall, and behind the sink. Everytime you looked up you were bombarded with black and white images of leaping men clad in tights, with giant bulging penises. There was one chair facing a tiny black and white portable TV, which sat on a crate with an old towel draped over it. There was a blue camping gas canister and a saucepan lying beside a sack of muddy potatoes. A potato which had been left in the sink for several months was in an unrecognisable state of decomposition. The walls were covered in peeling brown wallpaper and painted over in a random spattering of DayGlo orange, pink and green stripes, blotches, stars, suns, moons and splashes. A huge map of Paris on one wall had red thumbtacks stuck in strategic positions. On the other wall there was a large Pablo Picasso print taped over the lunatic's paint job. Uncleaned paintbrushes stuck to the carpet and small overturned paint cans were set in petrified DayGlo puddles. Christopher had painted over parts of the Picasso print and drawn a large green stripe that emanated from the figure's shoulder over the poster's border and extended up the wall.

"See," he said, tracing the line with his finger, his eyes gleaming. "I wanted to blend the painting into the wall. Can you spot the point where Picasso ends and Christopher begins?" He stood back in admiration: "Clever, eh? And I added bits where Picasso kind of got his colours wrong."

"Picasso got his colours wrong," Isolt repeated.

Christopher pointed to the floor. "Take your rightful place."

Isolt plonked herself down in front of the tool box and a bicycle wheel. Christopher sat on the one chair in the room. He rolled a joint. They drank the other medicine bottle. Isolt winced. It was sickeningly sticky and foul-tasting. She almost retched.

Christopher nodded: "Yes, it's horrible stuff but it keeps the monkeys from the door."

He sealed the joint with a lick of his tongue. He rolled the tiniest joints using only one paper. He had never bothered learning all the fancy joint rolling for communal purposes.

"Do you do dope?" He turned on the TV, twisted through the stations, settled on one and turned the volume down.

"What kind?" Isolt asked.

"The big H."

"Heroin?"

"Heroin?" He imitated her. "Horse. Mary Jane. Smack. Dope. What the fuck do you want me to call it?"

"Do you do it?"

He shrugged. "Not every day." Then he looked at her: "Do you have any?"

"No," she said.

"I sold my last bag to Payman. I need money for a trip to Amsterdam to get some more supplies. Christmas is a busy time in my business. All the lads crawling out of the woodwork for the peak begging season. The woodwork squeaks and out come the freaks, isn't that right? Well, we'll just have to do with the codeine buzz to get us through the night. Don't smoke so much tobacco. The smoke clogs up the room. Inhibits my breathing. And I need to breathe." He inhaled deeply and spoke in a constricted dope voice: "Here, kill it. I'll start another."

They smoked and talked till three in the morning. Isolt lay down on the ground with her jacket and boots still on. She attempted to curl into a foetal position. He turned off the TV and the light, which was a bulb hanging from a thick black flex and draped over a wooden support beam for the bed at the roof. He threw a light blue stinking sleeping bag over her and flung himself on top of her.

"Oh, Isolt. I was bummed out when you went down South. Freddie said you'd be fucking some filthy Arab there. Man, I was bummed out."

Isolt lay face down on the dirty carpet, an orange peel sticking into her eye, feeling him as a dead weight — crushing her. She turned over and looked at his frantic face framed by the prancing ballerinas with huge bulging genitals. He got under the cover and squashed his lips against hers, groping for her tits. She told him that she had her period. He took his dick out of his trousers, took her head by the hair and pushed it down. She felt his flaccid penis by her cheek and turned and sucked it. He kept pushing her head down roughly. She felt it get hard and gagged. As he held her tightly by the hair she felt decapitated. She could see the executioner by the guillotine take her severed head out of the basket by the hair and display it dripping, eyes rolled back and tongue hanging out, to the rapturous mob. She saw the old woman sitting knitting by the basket, one plain, one purl. Her gums ached, he came without warning in her mouth. She swallowed, trying not to taste the gooey sperm in case she threw up.

"Thanks. It's been so long," he muttered, embarrassed, and letting go her hair turned his back on her. She slithered back up banging her head off the steel tool box.

"Ouch!" she cried.

"Careful," he mumbled.

"Oh fuck off."

They both sniggered.

Isolt took a swig of Perrier to rinse her mouth. She made sure it was a fresh bottle. The whole place was lined with Perrier bottles. He couldn't be bothered to go to the end of the hall to piss and so he used the empties and sealed them. Since he drank at least three litres a day and relieved himself constantly they built up at an alarming rate.

Once he had bothered to cart a whole load down the six flights and abandon them in the outside world. He wondered if anyone had opened the tops and got the stench in the face of stale year-old piss. There were, he knew, people desperate enough to empty them out and take them back for a refund. Especially a lucrative load like that.

The map of Paris with all the red thumbtacks strategically placed, he explained, was a system of transport he had developed. He had ten bicycles chained at different points about the city, so wherever he was, he always had access to a set of wheels. When he removed one and took it to another part of town, he came back and changed the thumbtack. Sometimes he forgot and lost track of the ever-shifting patterns. On one occasion he lost a key to his cryptonite lock and had to abandon the bike, taking only the wheels and the handlebars. He returned months later to see the frame still chained to the wrought iron fence, except they had painted the fence and unable to move the frame, they had painted it green also.

In the morning Christopher left at eight o'clock to steal some whiskey at the local supermarket. Isolt felt he gave her a look of disgust when he came back. He sat down on the chair and turned on the TV, keeping the volume down. She lay on the floor.

"You don't look so great without all that paint on your face."

"How come you're stealing whiskey? I thought you didn't drink."

"I don't. I'm out of money to buy drugs so I have to sell the whiskey. I usually go up to Holland every month to buy. Since Marie-Claire and I are on the rocks I've been blowing all my cash on heroin. That's bad news, man. I've been down, Isolt, I've been down."

"Why did she leave you?"

"Well, truth is she was doing all these pills and getting an attitude. You know the way pills give you an attitude. She was a thief. All that shit up there," he pointed to the bed on the roof, "is hers. You know those downers put you in a kind of fog. She started getting uppity. Talking back. Whining. Too big for her boots. Damn, when I met her she was just a frightened little mouse. I taught her everything. She even learnt fucking English from me. I liked her 'cos she was tall, you know. I like tall birds. It flatters me to be with one. I stuck with her out of pity. Her father was a big shot architect and her mother a publisher. They were rich. I never had me a bird of that calibre before. When I was fucking her I used to think of her father and all the fucking houses he dreamt up. Thinking of the inheritance, my dick was a skyscraper." He laughed. "She was kind of precious. They treated her like a kid all the time. They were split up too. A broken family. It was pity. That's the God's truth. I stayed because I was the only goddamn thing she had in the world that she liked.

"She used to come up to me and buy an acid tab every week. Fifty francs. That's what I thought of her. Every time I saw her. Here comes fifty francs. Fifty of the easiest goddamn francs I ever made in my life and that's no joke.

"Like I said, she was tall, so I started to talk to her. She was real shy. Kind of pathetic. She used to have one of those bags, you know those bags the French birds wear, a little panda bear shoulder bag. It looked so goddamn childish. She was always eating bags of crisps and shitty fast food. I taught her the importance of diet. I turned her into a vegetarian. I had her living on nuts and berries. Actually she became anorexic I think. We got bicycles. She stole about ten of them. She was a good thief. She had been a thief long before she met me too. You know how these rich girls are when Daddy won't pay them heed. Tall, elegant French girl. It was a cinch for her to rip places off. We used to go to Amsterdam together. She was brave. She used to carry all the stuff for me. You know she looked the part. She was pretty, stick thin, man. I like them thin. Like little girls. No titties. Vulnerable. I could reach out and snap her in two.

"Well, she got a little too brave for her own good. I was getting sick of her. It was the pills. I gave them to her to sell to her school friends, then she goes and gets hooked. Stupid bitch. She gets busted trying to cash a cheque with stolen cards and cheque books. Four months in jail. She wrote to me every day. Man, she must have been bored. Every shitty little detail of her life. Told me she had the girls in her cell eating garlic for their health. Can you imagine? Shit, that was my preaching, man. Garlic was my gospel. She said everything had been her fault and when she would be released she would make it all up to me. That's a fucking lie. She got out and I guess I stood her up a few times. I was getting high you know, with Payman or Freddie or someone. I forget who. She wouldn't give up the pills either. I hate those things and she hated me doing heroin. Better heroin any day than those pills, man. She still had that shitty attitude. I never hit the bitch though, in spite of herself, I might add.

"She never moved about during sex. That was one thing that struck me. She would just lie there and not move and when I was finished she would pull on her pants and it was business as usual. Sometimes I used to test her. I would watch her wipe off methodically with tissues and get dressed again and put on her coat and then I would tell her I wanted to fuck her again, that my dick was getting hard. It got my dick hard just knowing what I was doing. She would just strip and lie down without a word. That was lovely. I liked that in her, no fuss. She was good to me. We had some laughs. I kept her laughing, man. That's the truth.

"Well, this room is in her name. So were all the others. I've lost all of them. I haven't paid rent here in months, they want me out. I suppose I'm squatting here. The squat in Versailles is gone too. The health inspectors closed it down. Now that is a shame. They were the happiest days of my life. We had a good crowd out there. Freddie the Giant's just about the most generous man I ever met. Maggot from England, he was a kind of sleazy character, I liked him mind you, long leather coat, sort of a fascist. His father was Irish. He told me that when his father used to go every year on holiday to Ireland he used to refuse to take Maggot along after the age of ten. He told him he was too English. That killed me. His own father. Then there was Dutch Mark, Tony, Fats and Stripe, they were all from Holland, except Fats who was German. They were the core. There were others who drifted in and out but they were my men. The apostles. I wanted Payman to come in on it but he was happy enough in Saint Quen with all your rabble. The fucking Irish and Germans and Afghans. I have a soft spot for ol' Payman as you know. He's seen some things, man, that you can tell. Witnessed some atrocities. I feel I can communicate with him. You're too young to understand that, sweet thing. Anyway women don't respect each other in the same way."

"OK! OK! What happened to the squat?"

"Yeah, I was happy. Me and Marie-Claire were getting on fine. She was the only bird allowed in and I didn't like to bring her too often. I was doing so many drugs I wasn't all that interested in pussy to tell the truth. Freddie used to call her Miss Lovely. But he couldn't be around her because he'd insult her. You know how he is with birds. She was dead scared of him. He made her cry once with his name-calling. He felt awful about that because he just can't help himself. It's how he reacts to women. So he used to nick her presents and say to me, 'This is for Miss Lovely,' earrings and watches and candy and shit. She used to wrap up pieces of hash in coloured paper and little parcels of downers for him with a bow on it, girlie stuff you know, and give it to me for him. I liked that. That way there was peace 'cos Freddie don't like women. We spent many a night in that squat with all the lads bad-mouthing the fairer sex. The lads called me a turncoat for associating so closely with one but I'm not prejudiced and Marie-Claire was good to me many a time. Though I've had enough now. As I said I'm tired of being responsible for someone else's welfare. I've got to look out for yours truly. This is a crucial point in my life . . ."

"What about the squat?" Isolt guessed that he had done some dope in the toilet down the hall before coming in to the room after his whiskey heist. He looked stoned and he was so chatty. She was kind of pissed off he didn't share but then he was in need.

"Yeah. Well. That's a sad story. They were the best days. The stars were aligned in my favor for the first time in my life since I was seven years old. My dealing was on top form. Marie-Claire and I were going on excursions, cycling our bikes and she was co-operating fully. Good and obedient. I was surrounded by a good bunch of lads. My apostles, I used to call them. They laughed at that. They liked it. I could tell. I was the guru, so to speak. I gave the orders, decided who moved in and who could stay. A strict rule — NO BIRDS. Except for me and I tried not to abuse my privilege. They used to joke, 'We've been Christopherized,' they used to say. That was good, eh? CHRISTO-PHERIZED.

"I had some cats and a dog. The squat was in a regular neighbour-hood and Versailles is a rich town. The neighbours hated us. The lads got careless and lazy. I tried to prevent it but I knew they were doing it behind my back. Even though that was one of the main rules. They were begging in their own neighbourhood. That's like shitting on your own doorstep. It doesn't exactly make those people feel up-wardly mobile to be shopping and see their neighbour slouched outside the market with a sign saying he's no resources, know what I mean? Ha! Ha! And there was no fucking toilet so everyone shit in the garden. The neighbours started to complain about the smell in the summer. It did get bad, I admit that.

"The garden was overgrown. Grass and weeds ass deep. My dog had problems getting through the fucking jungle it had become. So to build up some muscle on the animal I tied an iron trash-can lid to its back so that it would have to drag that around and get stronger to cope with the fucking weeds. The next-door neighbour snatched my dog. Said it was cruelty to animals. She said she would report me to the fucking authorities. I can't afford that. Minimum contact, that's what it's about, baby. I'm illegal here. No papers. I let her have it without a fight. Truth is I was getting sick of the mutt anyway. I could never train it properly and the lads embarrassed me by laughing at its efforts to make it through the shitty garden."

"What was its name?"

"Shit, I didn't even know its sex for that matter and I forget its name. I don't think it had one to tell you the truth. I'm a cat person. Dogs, man, they're not so bright."

"Then what?"

"Too many British blokes, friends of Maggot, moved in. The Brits have no respect, man. I lost control. I was hanging out too much with Miss Lovely. They would just stick their asses out of the fucking second floor windows and take a dump right there and then. I reckon that must have been the last straw for the neighbours. The health inspectors closed it down. It was the end of an era. My luck has been downhill ever since. Yeah, well, that's the lesson for the day. Every good thing comes to an end. I've lived my life by clichés. Man, I miss that place. Haven't been so content since I was seven years old and living with Grandma.

"Versailles is gone. I almost feel sick with grief to look at it on the map. A poor man's life is full of surprises. The squat in Saint Quen is a zoo. I got Freddie in there despite protests from the other residents. Poor Freddie, I couldn't have him in here, he's too big. Marie-Claire and I are fighting now. I forget why. I'm getting ready to dump her. I need to get out of dealing. It's doing things to my personality. I'm paranoid. You know I've been doing it almost twenty years. It's all I know. I can't afford to get busted and get deported. I can't go back to the States. Europe is civilized. This is child's play for me here. I need to move to a new phase in my life. I don't want a bitch dragging me down. Birds are baggage, man. Even you, babe, you don't say a word but I can feel when I'm hurting you. I don't need that. Don't fall in love with me. I get sick of all that. I've my own cross to bear. I'm thirty-three, I've got to watch out. This is the year they could really crucify me."

He paused, collecting himself. Gaunt and weary.

"I need a break, Isolt. I have a proposal to make to you. You see I'm burnt out. I'm getting old. Thirty-three ain't no joke. Freddie and I talk about it all the time. He's around my age and a future on the streets is not on. Payman too. Payman's kind of crazy though. His chances are dim. Freddie is sick, his liver is troubling him. I need to get legal. I've got some schemes up my sleeve that I think could work. Freddie could help me, he thinks they are good ideas, but first I want papers. I can't do nothing without them. That's where you come into the Grand Scheme."

Isolt rolled a cigarette from her tobacco pouch.

"What can I do?"

"Marry me."

"Go and shite!"

"I'm serious."

"What's in it for me?"

"The good old US of A. The Devil's Workshop. The you-knighted, be-knighted un-tied states. You could be a member of Uncle Sam's little club."

"I don't want to go there."

"You're a well-travelled lady now. I thought you might add it to your repertoire, so to speak."

"What about money?"

"Money?"

"Give me money instead."

"I don't have any fucking money. What do you think I've just been trying to explain to you? Don't turn this into something it's not. I haven't just been blabbering on for my own amusement. I've been honest with you. You're just too young and simple-minded to deal with. Money! Shit! I can see you will fit right in in America."

"I'll think about it," Isolt said, pleased with this new turn of events. It would give her badly needed leverage.

"Well hurry up, because I don't need so much of your company, it's getting on my nerves."

Christopher said that birds were baggage. Isolt ruffled her feathers and tagged along.

If anything of real significance happened in the weeks that followed it was contained in their conversations. Christopher talking and Isolt content to listen. They formed a routine very quickly. Christopher relied on routines and took great pleasure in seeing every small detail through. They got up and both went on errands to steal whiskey. They went begging. They scoured the city for chemists who would sell them codeine cough syrup. They had coffee somewhere and drank the medicine. Washing the mess down as it clung to their throats like glue. Isolt would change her clothes, wash up and put on make-up in the Air France terminal near Invalides where they had big toilets and wash basins. Sometimes she took a shower in the American church and he sold whiskey to the Spanish caretaker who tried to buy Isolt from him too. Christopher laughed at this pathos. "He asked me how much you were but I said I didn't have the change." Jim and Rory were not back from the South yet. She wondered where her allegiance would lie then. Now and then she would meet the lads for breakfast in Babylon. Christopher never came, he would stay out begging. She made much more money than he did. He tried to punish her but she was always happy and proud to make money and didn't care. Most nights they ate indoors on the little one-ring camping stove. They shopped in the big late night supermarket by the Pompidou Centre, stealing some things and buying others. Potatoes, peanuts in their shells, broccoli, carrots, tomatoes, cucumbers, avocadoes, onions, garlic, apples, oranges, bananas, honey, and six litres of Perrier a day. Christopher made her drink water to clear up her skin. She was always back and forth to the Turkish toilet at the end of the nightmarish green hall. The wooden floor was so creaky. She stumbled against the mental-hospital coloured walls, stoned and paranoid every night.

Once when they were sitting in the attic room with the TV on there was a pounding at the door.

"*Christopher, c'est Marie-Claire.*"

Christopher froze.

"Christopher, I know zat you are in zere. I hear ze TV. Christopher."

He looked panic-stricken and trapped.

"Christopher. I just want to talk. Please. You must let me talk to you. Please Christopher."

Christopher put his head in his hands.

"Christopher, I cannot talk in ze corridor. I cannot say it here. Please, Christopher, you must let me come into your room. I came all ze way to here for you."

Finally she kicked the door and shouted.

"Goodbye Christopher! Have a nice trip."

She stamped heavily down the wooden corridor. They listened to her footsteps pound the flights of stairs till they faded.

"Sorry," Isolt said.

"Man, what did she mean, Have a nice trip? Shit! Maybe I should go after her. Have a nice trip? That crazy bitch. Hey, did you hear the way she kicked the door? Feisty, huh? She wouldn't have done that when I met her. I made her what she is. I taught her to have guts. Though from that pounding down the hall she must be wearing those cowboy boots again. She bought those boots and I wouldn't let her wear them. They make too much noise. I'll fucking nice trip her. Shit, if you weren't here sitting on your fat ass looking at me with your big, round, stupid face I could have let her in and sorted her out. Shit. Fuck you, Isolt."

"I could have crawled up onto the bed."

"Yeah. I suppose. Damn, if she saw you she would go crazy. Crayzee."

Isolt was sick of him talking about this little rich kid all the time. She was jealous and truth be told she admired the girl, her drug smuggling and massive stealing heists. Marie-Claire, a tall, beautiful, thin Parisian wild child. It was like something out of a bad French film. They loved those naughty schoolgirls. The younger and naughtier the better. The French were paedophiles, Isolt thought angrily. The incident depressed them both.

Christopher took his blow job with a vengeance that night; it made

Isolt cry but she did not let on. Crying while sucking dick. Isolt wished she was dead.

He would not screw her. He only did it once. He told her he didn't really like pussies. The way they got wet and slimy repulsed him. Women were smelly down there. He said sex detracted from his personality. That all the great men abstained for a reason. Women spelt woe-men, woe to men. You wouldn't see the Pope or the Dalai Lama having a female confidante. Women weren't very bright and they were insecure. They belonged only in the background. It was a man's world. They had nothing to say to interest him as they had no lives beyond their men. When he came it zapped his strength. It killed him a little every time. He felt so awful after coming. It drained his brains. It made him wise when he wanted to stay young and foolish. He was a loner. The Hoodoo Man. And you can't hoodoo the Hoodoo Man. He wanted to be disciplined to live a clean life. He had given up tobacco and alcohol and he wanted to be strong enough to give up sex. Still he liked the nightly blowjob routine. Rounded off the evening nicely. Couldn't resist really. He hated himself afterwards. Back to square one. He hated to even look at Isolt afterwards. She was the shame. Lying there begging to be fucked with her sad, little eyes. A darling little lamb to be slaughtered, lying on his floor. Making a face when she swallowed his come just to get at him. He chose not to fuck her. Might as well be fucking a shoe full of liver. He preferred it in the mouth. Made her look so helpless. Sometimes he would come on her face. He usually apologized afterwards. Sorry to subject you to my own perversions. She never complained. It was more detached somehow in the mouth. Less of the woman involved. More like a glorious blowing machine. Give shape to those big fat cheeks. She should thank him really. He almost burst out laughing every time he saw her choke.

He had wanted to run after Marie-Claire. He loved her. He was ashamed to be seen with Isolt. She was a short girl and she was shabby. Her clothes were raggedy and out of place in the fashion-conscious French society, her hair was neither long nor short, her skin was unclear from alcohol, tobacco and bad diet. She did not hold herself very well, she slouched and he had to shout at her to pick up her feet a couple of times every evening. The French girls put her to shame. Marie-Claire had been a classic beauty. It was a shame things had fallen apart. He had gone to so much trouble to mould her in his image. Diet, manners, language. But he didn't want to marry her for papers. There were several reasons he needed Isolt for that. It would be complicated to marry a girlfriend for papers. Sex was too big an issue. Isolt was perfect for the job but she had to be educated if he was to spend time with her. He spent hours lecturing her.

"I've been on top of more women with a soft dick than with a hard one. I'm not ashamed of this because I'm an addict. I consider myself a closet anarchist. I have been a guru to many men. I'm a figure of importance, a respected entity. I have moved in many circles. I hold court. I give people the official nod. I'm a small-time loser, a two-time user. I was born under a bad star.

> Look out honey 'cos I'm using technology,
> Aint got time to make no apologies.

"That's Iggy. My favourite. You wouldn't know nothing about that baby. Detroit sounds. You know I see myself very close to Jesus Christ. Jesus forgot to instruct people about diet. I have come to take up where he got stopped. He was killed by the Romans. The Romans are my enemy too. The suits and ties out there. Slaves to all that paperwork and bureaucracy. The keepers of the Mad Empire. The bringers of famine. Capitalism. Babylon. False gods. Worship of money and material possessions. I have all the local monsters eating out of my hand. I keep myself clean of sex, alcohol, material goods, tobacco, meat, dairy, so my karma is ripe for big events. I am a master of deception. I have a past. I have killed a man. I am the Midnight Rambler, sweet thing. I have stuck my knife down the throat of many a punter who tried to take control. I decide who speaks and when. I am a king demon. A crazy man. I am a king man with rings on my fingers and nails through my toes. I remain aloof from the affairs of commuters and consumers.

> I am the world's forgotten boy,
> The one who searches and destroys.

"I am the dealer. People wait for me. They woo me. I'm always fair with my drugs. I am the only punctual dealer in the world. (Mind you, I have no drugs at the moment which is no great advertisement.)

I come, do my business and leave. No stories, no jokes, no fooling, no flirting, business only. Sometimes I crack a smile but only a select few get the benefit of the doubt.

"I was conceived on a Third World Caribbean island and carved in the Devil's Workshop, moulded out of hard times in the meanest city in the USA. The fifth largest city of the Mad Empire. Detroit was Rock 'n' Roll. Iggy and the Stooges. MC5. I saw them all. Got them all high when I was only a kid. Europe is civilized and I have proof, after all I'm still alive after ten years here on the streets.

> I'm a street walking cheetah with a heat full of napalm,
> I'm the runaway son of the nuclear H-bomb.

"I steal everything. I steal anything I can. That is fundamental to my politics. What I do not steal I borrow and break. What I cannot borrow I will keep anyway and never give back. What I cannot steal or borrow I destroy. Anything that does not fit into these categories is beneath my contempt.

"I hate this world but I believe firmly that my legend is alive in it. Maybe you are too young to understand. Too simple-minded. Too green. Green as the hills, that's you, sweet thing. Just off the last boat.

"I don't love anybody. I like to have power. I get respect. I take all the risks so that people may be injected with short term bliss. I elevate the quality of many bedraggled lives, alleviating some of the drudgery of the streets. And if you criticize it as a short term relief, well, it's more than God and all the heavens above have ever done for those poor cunts. I am the angel of mercy. A prophet in the great traditions of prophets. I have a mission, Isolt, so don't try to deflect me. Be good. Co-operate. I have a mission to bring down every government and undermine the present global economic system. I want to change life on earth as we know it."

His halo was bent and singed. His mop of wild, blue-black hair had not one single gray strand. He had scabs on his scalp and dirty fingernails. Even the beggars said he was a filthy bastard. His stinking, baggy, black trousers always hung half way down his arse. His shirt sleeves were shredded and his collar so heavily caked with dirt that his neck was permanently ringed. He shaved once a week but never washed. His mustache glistened with snot and his huge wings were clogged with oil.

He constantly sang his own praises and expected a chorus. The mottled bunch who would provide him with this service were always the weakest of the crew. They were his prey and they looked up to him. The stronger humoured him and sneered behind his back but he did not tolerate woman or man to block his way or put him down. The intelligent kept their distance. The initiated always came to bad ends under his dysfunctional umbrella.

Christopher was wrong, Isolt knew some of those songs as well as he did. She knew the one he liked the best. She could sing it to herself out of his earshot.

> Somebody's got to help me please,
> Somebody's got to save my soul,
> Oh baby won't you help me please.

"I have been a dealer for a long time in this city, always on the same turf. Six years, that's a long time to survive. There's a photo of me in every police station in Paris. I have spent many a night inside the jails here. I have even been up in court for stealing whiskey. All this with no papers or visa."

He looked at Isolt sitting among his own refuse, hanging on to every word, always in a stupor, entranced by his sunken past. Sunk like a huge galleon in murky waters. Far beneath the surface it rotted and he could only swim down and salvage bits, bringing them to the surface as memories. He was afraid he would drift and lose the point where it all lay. Indescribable what he saw toppled over on the shifting sea bed, when he could swim unnoticed among time's sharks and view the very rooms of all that had been before, the broken skeletons of drowned associates trapped beneath the wood. What could he tell this feeble little girl of all these horrors?

He instructed her as to the moon's importance but never told her of his secret transmogrification. He would never trust any soul with that knowledge. He was the peacock. He had angel's feathers, a devil's voice and he walked like a thief. It was late into the night again. He spent so much time lecturing her.

Trying to get her to understand, he was asking her a question. A question that he himself was not sure how it should be answered. In this room where Picasso had ended and Christopher had begun, the transition to him was barely decipherable. She was being Christopherized and loving it. She was sucking his dick like mother's milk. He leaned over looking into her wide, green face; he had forgotten his question. He felt blank and confused. Where was he? She reminded him. Jail, visas, papers, he had never been badly burnt in this city. Yes, yes that was it, so the question was — Was he too slippery a snake for the simple-minded Parisian police or too small a fish in a nasty big pool?

7

Winter Fairground

THEY SOLD the expensive whiskey to the whores. Isolt walked down Rue Saint-Denis with her black bag clinking. Approaching a bored cluster of prostitutes in the door way she said the magic word, "Whiskey?" She waited in the doorway ignored by the other whores while one went up and got money. There she stood with a bag full of stolen whiskey in the company of these scornful creatures, feeling dodgy, an impostor in the underworld. When she told Christopher of these fears he laughed.

"Shit, girl! You are a beggar in the overworld and an impostor in the underworld. There is no hope for a poor girl like you."

They sold the regular whiskey to the beggars at the fountain for a low price. Christopher did all the selling to that market maintaining that he needed to retain some visibility as a dealer. The beggars would come the next night with cut faces and black eyes complaining that they drank the poison and got into fights or fell down steps. "We preferred the other stuff you sold," they said and Christopher smiled and told them that as soon as they bought enough whiskey he could go get the goodies in Holland.

Finally, Isolt and Christopher accumulated enough money to send Christopher to Amsterdam to buy his drugs. He was elated at the prospect of putting his career back on track. Jim, Rory and Melonie came back to Paris for the peak begging season. Isolt stayed at one of the cheap hotels with them and shared a room with Melonie.

Christopher stayed longer than she expected. At one point she considered the possibility that he had flown the coop or maybe been busted and was in jail. She did not miss him at all and began to dread the day he would return. Nevertheless she felt compelled to stay with him and finish what she had started. She could not confide in anyone. Melonie was nice but they never managed to get that close. She feared most of all the return to the attic room stacked with his refuse. It was akin to walking into his mind. She was trapped in there, in the horrible little hole with a phoney view. In there he had full control since it was she who was in his mind. Her mind became a minuscule part of his, another piece of the debris; she had nothing of her own. She submitted to his sordid appetites without a whimper.

There were days — when Melonie was out of the room — that she gazed at herself in the mirror. After a while her personality disappeared. It dropped off right before her eyes, her face a mushy heap. Beyond this point something so hideous would manifest itself in her features that she would jolt away from the glass and lie on the lumpy bed mute with apprehension. The hotel had a tiny lobby with a sour-faced woman behind the desk. It was a narrow six-floor building with just space for two rooms on every floor. The double rooms had two single beds with a table in between and a wardrobe with a mirrored door. There were no chairs and there was no carpet. No lampshade to shelter the eye from the naked bulb that hung from the centre of the ceiling like a light in a torture chamber. The place was infested with mice. There were bugs in the mattresses that sucked her blood as she slept. There were mind parasites that ate her dreams. The mirrors failed to reflect her good points. Bad neighbours paced the roof above, arguing among themselves, causing the dangling bulb to sway back and forth slightly, or on closer inspection to trace dim little circles full of sorrow in the moth-infested air. Many a time there were sounds of uncontrollable weeping behind the walls. Mean-spirited ghosts of former residents took possession of her as she slept and led her dreams into uncharted territory, off the path and into the depths of the forest where they abandoned her without pity. She did not have the map home. The unknown was crouching in the next room.

In the days before they had a hotel they had no choice but to stay out drinking. Jim, Melonie, Isolt, Rory and his new American girlfriend,

Kim, were on the streets together for a while. Kim was tall, handsome and drank like a fish. Eventually they would head down to Les Halles. There was one Metro entrance that stayed open in winter. Not wanting to be bothered all night by lunatic clochards, they would walk on the tracks through the long twisting tunnels to other stations. There were big rats that crossed their path. Jim's dog, now almost fully grown, had to be carried through, afraid of this dark journey. Sometimes a cleaning car would come down the tracks and they would stand in the gaps at the side, backs against the soot-black walls.

Other nights as they walked to the open station they would test all the car doors and, if one was open, two of them would sleep there. One night when Melonie wasn't around, Rory and Kim found a car and Jim and Isolt were determined to do so too. They were lucky. Isolt clambered into the back and Jim stretched out across the two front seats, his dog cowering on the floor. They smoked a joint and Jim stuck it out in the ashtray.

"This will give him a fright when he finds it."

"How do you know it is a he?" Isolt asked.

"Big car."

"Big car, little dick."

"So that's how it goes. My dick must be a monster."

"No car, no pussy."

"Shit, don't I know that. No girl wants to be with a beggar. That's why beggars have dogs. Dogs are girlfriend substitutes, some warm body to snuggle up to at night. Christ, how does Rory do it? This one may be American but she has legs right up to her neck."

"Yeah. She's kind of tight though. She has all those travellers' cheques she doesn't want to break out. She won't beg so she says she needs them. Pretty pathetic if you ask me."

Jim laughed: "Rory will get her to beg in no time. She'll break down when she sees how much we can make coming up to Christmas."

"She'll have to if she wants to drink all the time at that pace," Isolt said.

"Yeah. And she never chips in for hash, I notice. Yet she's started smoking it the last few nights. Ah sure, God love her, ending up with us lot on her European trip."

They lay in silence. Jim shifted about in the front.

"Isolt. I don't suppose I can sleep back there with you? The gear stick keeps sticking up my arse."

Isolt hesitated. "All right, but there's not much room for two."

Jim scrambled in and they lay squashed, Isolt with her head to the seat. The dog peered between the two seats wagging its bushy tail. Jim kissed her neck and she shivered.

"Turn around and let me see you," he said.

She did not budge. She lay very still. He put his arm around her and she cringed. He felt this.

"You're not into it, huh?"

She was silent.

"I thought maybe after that night down south, you know, maybe you and me could like, you know . . ."

"Please Jim! No," Isolt muttered to the seat.

"Sure." He was embarrassed.

He climbed back into the front and they did not speak again that night.

In the morning Jim got out of the car early with his dog to take a piss. He came back and the car was gone. He knew immediately what had happened. His heart sank and then he laughed at the thought.

Isolt woke up as the car's owner was putting the key in the ignition. She was summoning up the nerve to jump out of the car when he pulled into traffic. She lay very still hoping he would not look behind and find a girl sprawled out on his back seat. She guessed that he was going to work and would drive for half an hour and then stop. She needed to piss. The traffic was jammed and she tried to breathe quietly in the back. Her bladder was bursting. As the car began to speed up, she realized that they were on a freeway. Oh my God! Isolt thought, with my luck the guy is driving to fucking Spain to see his dying mother. Maybe he would stop for petrol. The pain in her kidneys had reached such a point that she grabbed her crotch and pressed it hard. After an eternity he pulled off the freeway and seemed to be stopping at traffic lights. She could wait no longer. She leapt up and reached for the lock. The man swung around and exclaimed in fright, "*Putain!*"

He tried to grab her shoulder but she wriggled out onto the street and ran. As she glanced behind, she saw him standing by his car staring after her as the other cars honked their horns.

She jumped into somebody's garden and pulled down her jeans. She pissed as two young children put their toys to rest to watch. Isolt saw a plump woman come running out with a broom. She could have somehow controlled the thunderous flow but then she would only have had to find another garden. She continued urinating as the woman brought the broom down full force on her back, shouting for the police. Isolt turned and stood up, giving the woman a view of her front. She zipped up her jeans and brazenly walked out the little gate. The woman stood rooted to the spot with her hand over her mouth. Isolt left her petrified with the idiot broom clutched and poised in the air and her hand at her face.

She walked down the street realising that she had left her bag in the car. It had the few things she had accumulated since she had lost her other one a month ago. After escaping without a scuffle from the car and with her bladder now deliciously empty she could not care less.

She approached a woman who looked as if she was out shopping.

"*Excusez moi, quel est le nom de cette ville?*"

The woman looked sharply at this scruffy young girl.

"Versailles," she replied haughtily.

"*Ah bon? Merci beaucoup, et où est la gare?*"

The woman pointed her towards the station and Isolt thanked her again, sauntering off in the early morning that glistened of winter suburbia.

She ducked under the turnstile. Surprisingly, she had the carriage to herself. It must be Saturday or Sunday, she thought. As the train rattled on towards Paris she sat with her feet on the opposite seat, her legs spread apart. Her cheeks vibrated on the seat with the train's motion. Thinking of the woman staring in shock at her bushy triangle, she became aroused. Maybe she had a vocation as a flasher. She put her hands in her jeans and began to masturbate with the rhythm of the train; bringing herself off in a frenzy of ecstasy with the sun shining in the windows, halfway to Paris.

Isolt did not leave the hotel till late in the afternoon. Somebody was in her begging spot and she found a place beside the opera house instead. It was seldom that she made absolutely nothing. Today was such an occasion. After half an hour she got up and moved into the Metro tunnels. The police moved her on. She returned to the hotel and knocked on Jim, Rory and Kim's door. Jim and Rory were still in bed, hungover and coming down off acid.

"How do you feel?" Isolt asked.

"I feel peeled," Rory said. "Nervous and delicate. Not my usual robust self at all, at all. I can't handle the outside world today."

"Where's Kim?"

"Off on her usual marathon begging session. She was so surprised at how much she made the first time that I can't stop her. She's become superbeggar. At it about four or five hours a day. I think she thinks it's a job."

"Jesus!" said Isolt, who usually started to get fidgety after forty minutes unless she had some dope.

"You've got to hand it to the Yanks. Entrepreneurs every one of them. She's bringing home the money big time. She tells me she wants us to go to Greece. So she's saving."

"Are you going to go?" Isolt asked.

"I swear it's getting to be too much like work. I'm starting to dread going out to beg."

"You had trouble in Greece before," Isolt said. "They cut your hair."

"And locked me up for two months, just for busking."

"You were only there two months," Jim reminded him.

"Well, a month at least," Rory said.

"Last time it was two weeks."

"Well, it felt like fucking two years, OK?"

"I'm hungry," Isolt said. "But I made nothing. I can't wait till eight o'clock for the stupid van. It's only five now."

"Me too," said Jim. "I have pains in my stomach but I just couldn't get up. I haven't eaten since breakfast in Babylon yesterday morning."

"Have you any money?" Isolt asked. "I'll go out and get a baguette and a can of beans or something and bring them back. I'll get some chips too. I'll pay you back tomorrow."

"I'm broke." Rory shrugged.

"Me too," Jim added.

Isolt sighed and stretched across the end of Jim's bed stroking his dog, which trembled under her hand.

"We could eat this sorry dog. How long have you had her? Three months, isn't it? Have you decided what to call her?"

"Sheba!"

"Sheba?" Isolt feigned astonishment.

"Sheba!" Jim said emphatically, and to prove it he called "Sheba! Here, Sheba!"

The dog wiggled up the bed and nuzzled Jim. It put its head between its two front paws and fell on its side. Jim rubbed its stomach and it lay with its legs pointing upwards. Isolt could swear the creature was actually grinning.

"Jesus Christ!" She shook her head.

"I feel weak with hunger," Rory moaned, getting up and searching the room for money. He was wearing his jeans and sweater in bed. The room was cold.

"Once I was so hungry I ate an entire tube of toothpaste and threw up," Jim told them proudly, getting out of bed himself.

Isolt laughed. "Does Kim have her loot stashed here? We could take some and give it back later."

Rory's face changed. "No way. She keeps it locked in a little wooden box in the drawer."

"Doesn't trust you, eh?"

"You're a shit-stirrer," Jim smiled.

"Why does she put up with Jim and his mutt in the room? Surely she needs to bonk in peace."

Rory was strained: "It's cheaper this way. And anyway I don't care who listens to me bonk. They might learn something. You two did it in a sleeping bag on a beach in the south. Don't think I didn't hear that."

Isolt was flustered. "Well, you couldn't have heard much."

"Hey now, boys and girls," Jim said. "We're all hungry and cranky. We'll feel better after we eat."

They were all standing up and Jim and Rory put on their jackets. Sheba danced around, leaping up on Jim with excitement. He tied a piece of rope to its collar.

"Why don't you just buy a fucking lead, Jim?" Isolt suggested. "They're not that expensive."

"Looks harder this way," Jim said. "What's the plan? Go to the fountain and put the nip on someone?"

"We could give blood," Isolt said. "Afterwards they give you food and a beer."

"Now why didn't I think of that?" Rory put his arm around her as they walked.

"Have you done it before?" Jim asked her.

"I tried but I was underweight. That was two years ago. I'm not any more, that's for sure."

"You used to be too skinny. You're just right now."

"Ah, would you listen to him!" Rory grinned. "Why don't you two hook up?"

Isolt got a sudden vision of Jim and herself suspended on meat hooks.

"She won't have me," Jim responded cordially.

"Christopher's fucking evil," Rory said to her.

Isolt didn't answer.

The blood van was on the square beside the fountain. They were starving and when they saw it their mouths watered and their pace quickened. A nurse stopped them at the door. She consulted a doctor who came out and looked them up and down.

"*Non, merci.*" He shook his head.

"*Pourquoi, Monsieur?*" Jim asked.

"You are too dirty," the young doctor replied in English.

"But blood is in the inside," Jim protested.

"Ask him for the meal anyway," Rory prompted.

"Hey, Mister!" Jim called after the doctor who was retreating back into the van to attend to his duties.

"Doctor," he sternly corrected Jim.

"*Nous avons faim.* We wanted to eat. *Manger,* you know, eat. *S'il vous-plâit, Doctor.*"

"I am a doctor not a priest," the young doctor said.

"You're a miserable old fucker, that's what you are," Rory said.

The doctor didn't need the antagonism and disappeared. The three stood there in defeat.

"I think I'm going to faint," Isolt said. "I have to pay the rent tonight too and I don't have a bean."

"Just avoid the cow at the reception," Jim advised her. "They won't throw you out just for being one day late."

"Let's go back to the hotel and eat all Kim's toiletries," Isolt said.

"Maybe she'll be back and we can ask her for some of her millions," Jim said.

"That skinflint?"

"What's wrong with you?" Rory eyed Isolt. "You don't like Americans or something?"

"I'm with Christopher. He's American."

"He's from another planet," Jim said.

Rory walked along: "I hate the Greeks. Ali hates the Arabs. Taffy hates the English. Isolt hates the Americans. Larry hates the Germans. Christopher hates the Brits. The Brits hate the Irish. The French hate the Italians. The Americans hate the Japanese. Payman hates himself. Jim hates everybody and everybody hates the French. Jack is black and he says he's not. This is the world we live in."

"Black Jack," Jim conceded. "Now there's a puzzle."

"There are two hundred and sixty-five million Americans. I've only talked to about ten. I don't have anything against them," Isolt protested. "I laugh at them. That's all. I take the piss. They're so out of place here, you know . . . I might go to the States. I'd like to go. It would be my next move."

"Well," Rory said, "talking of being out of place, I think the Frenchies would shoot an Irish beggar before they'd shoot an American tourist any day."

"I wouldn't bet on it," Isolt said.

They reached the hotel. Isolt walked briskly by the reception avoiding eye contact with the woman behind the desk.

"I take people as they come," Isolt continued on the way up the stairs. "Sometimes I say things I don't mean. I sober up and regret it all. All the hatred I have is towards myself."

"Hence filthy Christopher the self-elected prophet and piss-artist," Jim scowled. "He hates birds. You're as bad as Black Jack. You are a bird hopping along beside a bird hater."

"He is a cat lover you know," Rory said. "Cats prowl after little birds and tear their heads off."

"You two are getting very good with your metaphors lately. What, do you practice at it or something? Life's not that simple. Don't judge me."

"We're warning you, that's all," Jim said, as they arrived at the door. "Christopher's crazy. You're in over your head."

Isolt drowning, sinking into the wreckage of Christopher's past.

Kim was reading French *Vogue* on the bed. She brightened up when Rory came in. He kissed her on the lips and they embraced on the bed. Isolt and Jim sat down on the single bed opposite. Isolt picked up the magazine and flicked through it backwards.

"I'm trying to improve my French," Kim said sheepishly. "Books are too hard to read."

Isolt noticed Jim looking over her shoulder. "Pretty girls, eh?" she said to him.

"Naw. Too scrawny. If you got up on one of them they'd break."

"Liar," Isolt said.

She flicked through to the beginning and handed it back to Kim. "Babylon. All those women's magazines make you more stupid and fatuous than you start out, and Lord knows none of us can afford that."

"Watch out," Jim warned. "She's on her soap box again."

"She's probably right," agreed Rory, looking at one of the models inside. "Still, wouldn't mind having me a piece of that."

"You'd risk Babylon for her?" Kim asked him mockingly.

"Yep! I'd like to have breakfast in Babylon with her every morning."

"And lunch and dinner and tea and supper," Jim agreed.

"Speaking of breakfast and lunch and dinner and tea and supper . . ." Isolt hinted.

"Oh yeah," Rory said. "Maybe Kim, you could lend us some dough. We're fucking starving and none of us had any luck today."

"We tampered with the economy to no avail," Isolt said.

"The general public were not interested in filling our empty stomachs," Jim added.

"Nor did they want our blood in their veins," Isolt continued.

"We went to the blood donor van and they knocked us back," Rory told her as he stroked her hair fondly.

"Thank God," Kim said. "You still had acid in your system. I wouldn't like to get your blood."

Rory massaged her back. Jim and Isolt looked at her from the bed. Kim pursed her lips. She always felt this Eurotrash crowd were trying to con her. Stab her in the back.

"You didn't even go out today, I bet," she pouted.

"We did. Just a bad day. I swear. I was moved on by cops. I didn't have a chance," Rory told her. "We don't even have cigarettes."

Kim looked at him in disgust. "Don't lie to me, Rory."

"Look! Just a bleeding sandwich for Christ's sake." Rory raised his voice.

Kim's eyes filled with tears. "Don't shout at me," she pleaded.

"Well, you go off and buy your fucking *Vogue*. Which if you ask me is a misappropriation of begging funds. What did you write on your sign? PLEASE HELP ME. I'M OUT OF MONEY TO BUY THIS MONTH'S ISSUE OF *VOGUE*."

"You spend all yours on booze and drugs," she retorted.

Jim and Isolt sat on the bed marveling at Rory's aptitude for fucking up the situation.

"You haven't begged in three days, Rory," Kim said, getting off the bed. "I've bought you dinner every night. You wouldn't support me so why should I support you and your goddamned friends?"

"I taught you how to beg, you bitch," Rory snarled.

"Well, thanks for passing on the secrets of such a highly skilled profession."

"Just a fucking baguette," Rory glowered.

"And some beans perhaps," Isolt interjected.

"No." Kim was close to tears. "It's a point of principle now. You can't just use me like this."

Rory's face darkened. "You are refusing three friends, who are your only friends in this city, a fucking loaf of bread."

She put on her coat and took her *Vogue*. She threw a packet of cigarettes on Jim's bed.

"Don't be so dramatic. It's seven-thirty. The van will be at the fountain in half an hour. You can eat then. There's some cigarettes."

She left the room. "Bye," she said to them. No one answered.

They sat in silence for a while smoking cigarettes.

"Let's go and wait for the van," Isolt volunteered.

"Fuck that fucking van," Rory fumed.

"You sure smooth-talked her," Jim mocked. "Losing your touch with the ladies."

Rory got up and ripped open the drawer on the bedside table. He took out a small decorated wooden box and clutched it in his lap.

"That's the safe?" Isolt asked.

"She's no fool. She always takes the key," Jim said.

Rory took a hair clip from the table and stuck it in the lock. He fiddled for a while.

"Shit, this always works in the movies."

"Give it to me," Jim said. He tried and then he pulled the lid hard. There was a loud cracking noise.

Rory panicked: "You've broken it, you fucker."

Jim pulled the broken lid off and they looked inside. There were at least four thousand francs and five hundred dollars in travellers' cheques. Jim gave out a low whistle.

"Jesus fuck me blind." He shook his head.

"I can see this is the end of another beautiful relationship," Isolt said to Rory.

"Not necessarily. Why don't we split the money and Jim and you go off to Hamburg to Gunther's squat up there. He's always telling us to come. I'll tell her you both nicked it. I was out of the room or something."

"I want to stay in Paris for the moment."

Jim lay on the bed and closed his eyes. "Oh no! It's fucking tempting but . . . Oh shit! . . . It's not even Christmas yet . . ."

"So?" Rory said. "Begging'll be good up there as well. You kept saying you were sick of France and the scene here."

"What if you marry the bird and I can't be best man at your wedding? Don't you care about that, man?"

"Look! Seriously. You've broken the stupid box. She'll go crazy even if we don't take the money. She wants to go to Greece in January? Well let her go. We'll leave her the travellers' cheques, they're no use to us. She has to go back to college in the States anyway at Easter, I think. So you can come back whenever."

Isolt was counting the money. "She could come back any minute. Make up your minds."

Jim looked at Isolt: "Well, I've nothing here, have I?"

Isolt said: "There's four thousand five hundred francs here in cash. Divide it by three or we should take a thousand each and give Jim the rest since he has to take the blame and get a train to Hamburg."

"Done," Jim said, clapping his hands and starting to run around the room throwing his stuff into his bag, Sheba yapping at his heels.

Their hunger all but forgotten, they helped him pack and when he was done they all left the room and went to the train station. Jim bought a ticket for Hamburg and they sat in a café beside the station drinking beers and eating sandwiches.

"I'll buy for you, Jim," Isolt said.

"Gunther won't believe it when he sees you at his door." Rory munched away whole-heartedly without a trace of guilt. You cold bastard, Isolt thought, you will probably fuck her tonight as well, after she stops crying. The more thrilling for your deceit.

"I hope there's room for me and Sheba in the squat." Jim drank his beer and looked around nervously. "What if he's moved and I'm stuck in Hamburg? I hope this is the right address I've got here. I can't read his fucking writing."

"Just take a taxi from the station. You can afford it," Isolt said. "It'll be all right."

"I hope it's cool." Jim shook his head. "What if she reports me to the police?"

"I won't let her, don't worry. I have her wrapped around my little finger."

Rory held up his little finger.

Isolt looked at it doubtfully. She couldn't imagine big, handsome Kim twined snake-like on that grubby appendage.

"Yeah, you displayed that power over her tonight," Jim said sarcastically.

Rory shrugged. "Look, she's lying on the bed reading fucking *Cosmopolitan* or *Vogue* or whatever shit, like the Queen of Sheba, no offence to your dog, and she has all that fucking money and she won't buy her old man a lousy sandwich to share with his friends. She can go back to college at Easter and say what a bohemian little chick she was in Europe. She'll be telling these stories for years. How she lived with a gorgeous Irishman in the fucking Latin quarter in Paris and hung out with all the street characters and did drugs. This will be just another story to impress her friends. How she was robbed by the gorgeous Irishman's shifty friend who lived in the room with them with his pathetic, flea-bag mongrel.

"She's only using me too, man. She'll end up with some college kid who can take her out to eat and bring her to the cinema without dodging in the back door and drive her around in a nice car. Us lot, we're stuck in this game. We don't have anywhere to go. We'll never get decent jobs or nothing. We've been on the streets too long. We all got bad habits, you know. She'll be all right, she can't see beyond my dick at the moment. She shouldn't have refused food to the hungry man who shares her bed, to her drinking companions and temporary confidantes. It wouldn't have taken much. The bitch deserves it and I intend to fuck her brains out too while I can, 'cos in a few years' time I won't get no more twenty-year-old college kids with bright futures. She'll be gone soon and Jim, you can come back. I'll write and tell you, OK? She's just passing pussy but we've been friends since national school and our oul' fellahs drink in the same bar back in Dublin. Take the money and run, boy. Don't worry. Have a good time with it."

Jim sat there unimpressed: "What do you mean shifty friend and flea-bag mongrel?"

Isolt and Rory took care of the bill. It was a cold and windy night. Jim came up from the toilets and shuddered as he looked outside. He seemed reluctant to move.

"Don't you have a jumper?" Isolt asked.

"No," he said quietly. His eyes pleaded with her.

Rory took off his and gave it to him. "Here, man."

Jim took it grudgingly. It was a sign that his fate was decided and he would have to go. He put it on over his shirt, then he put on his filthy, denim jacket with all the heavy metal sewn-on patches. His back was a grave stone for Bon Scott, some singer who had choked in his own vomit. The birth date, a dash and then the death date, an embroidered face and an unlikely assertion that he lives on coupled with a conflicting request beneath that he may rest in peace. The three walked through the howling wind to the station. Sheba was almost blown into the traffic. She was reluctant to keep walking. Jim dragged her along with the rope. Isolt ran into a pharmacy and bought some codeine for herself and toothpaste. She handed him the toothpaste.

"Something to eat on the train."

As they stood at the bottom of the platform, Jim said, "You know it'll be weird to be meeting real Germans. Not like our mad, junkie Germans here. Law-abiding Germans. That will be strange." He paused: "Isolt, come with me, come on, for the laugh."

Isolt was surprised. "No, Jim, I can't."

They stood and watched as he walked up the platform beside the train. The entire sum of his worldly possessions was over his shoulder in a green bag, his lousy dog at his heels. Twenty-four years old, slightly drunk, thin mousy hair hanging limply to his shoulders, Jim was going to Germany for the first time in his life. A new country, an unknown language, a dubious address, with a borrowed sweater to keep him from winter's ruthless ravages and his sewn-on cloth patches to connect him to the world. Scooping the squirming Sheba up under one arm, he turned as he was about to board the train and gave them a thumbs-up sign and a weak attempt at a smile. They waved from way down the platform. He hesitated and then pulled himself on. Isolt watched as his denim tombstone back disappeared into the train, two brown, frail, little dog legs sticking out under his arm, pedaling the air needlessly.

"I hope he'll be all right. He seemed so frightened all of a sudden."

"Shit, what about me?" Rory said. "I should be on that train if I had any sense."

They watched as the train rattled out of the huge station with all the birds perched on the roof taking flight and flapping about in the roar. It entered the night sharp as a needle and was lost to their sight, its puny lights trailing into the abyss.

Omi belonged to the wild tribe of mad, junkie Germans at the fountain. Abandoned in a roadside café when he was two years old, he was placed in different foster families. When he was fourteen he killed his foster parents with a shotgun on a farm outside Cologne. They had been making him work too hard. At eighteen he was released and he raped a forty-six-year-old woman that very night. He wouldn't pay money for a prostitute. He was too prudish. He was shooting heroin every four hours and supporting his habit by breaking and entering with an acquaintance from his prison days. When he contracted HIV in the mid-eighties he used it to his advantage, even tattooing the three letters on his neck. Nobody would fight him. He carried a needle and threatened people with it; he wore heavy bicycle chains around his neck and his arms. Five foot, eleven inches, stocky with cropped blond hair, tiny blue, piggy eyes set close together, an upturned nose and a mouth as small as an asshole; he had a toothbrush mustache like Hitler's. He was covered in scars and self-made ink tattoos. To show off, he liked to inject opiates into a vein on his forehead. He had pronounced muscles and his strength was legendary.

He broke a bottle into a Japanese tourist's face. The police at the fountain descended on him within seconds. He had broken the rules by attacking a tourist. It took eight young policemen to put him into a van. They stuck guns to his head and he just pushed them away. They sprayed CS gas into his face and he did not flinch but kept on kicking. They sat on him and cuffed his legs and arms and beat him with their batons. Omi was back the next day, his face swollen with blows and his arm in a makeshift sling.

He drank whiskey, shot heroin and sucked down a medicine called Elixir for diarrhoea. It came in small, green bottles and gave a good four hour buzz but you had to drink the whole bottle and risk constipation for days. Omi was so hooked, his insides so destroyed, that he had to drink a bottle just to have a bowel movement and this was a medicine to cure diarrhoea. Omi didn't care, in fact he didn't possess many faculties of emotion.

He had raped a woman again in Germany when he was twenty-two. She was alone in the house with her two toddlers when he had broken in. He was on the run for that crime.

Omi hung out with the roughest of the Germans at the fountain. He was the worst of them. They barely tolerated him but they had no choice as he always stuck around drinking a bottle of whiskey every night, roaring at everybody in pathological spurts of rage. He caused them trouble by association but they were afraid to kill him. Omi was invincible.

The first time he laid eyes on Melonie he was transfixed. She was young, fat and sloppy and had thick, black, greasy hair with pretty brown eyes and clear skin. Melonie took a good bit of abuse from the lads because of her weight. She did a lot of speed, which she got from a wiry, jittery little French punk called Speedy. Rory told her she was the only fat speed freak in history. The speed made her smell bad. She whined too much and got paranoid when she was coming down. When the lads spoke among themselves she would pester them, afraid they were laughing at her.

Wot? Wot? Wot? She was always saying "What?" in her London accent and they imitated her, which infuriated her further. They nicknamed her Melanoma. When she got too upset at all this jibing she would sulk and go stay with Taffy and the French punks. The French punks liked her. They deferred to her and she got them speed. They respected her as a crazy, big, foreign girl.

For days Omi stared at Melonie when she came to the fountain. He began to attach himself to her group which consisted mainly of Rory, Larry, Taffy, Payman, Ali, Isolt, Kim, Black Jack, Fred and Cloggie. They were amused to have him around the first night. He kept Ali subdued which was a blessing in itself. The next night they were alarmed. They decided to lose him by going to drink beer on the steps of Trocadéro. He followed and sat with them, glugging down his little green bottle of diarrhoea tonic and staring at Melonie. Melonie said she had to go ring her mother. She got up and Omi asked Cloggie, who spoke German, where she was going. Cloggie, amused, called after Melonie. She came back.

"Wot?"

"This gentleman has pointed out that it is not good for you to go to the phone by yourself. It is too dangerous."

Melonie stared at Omi in astonishment.

"Wot?"

Omi stood up and grinned somewhat toothlessly at her.

He escorted Melonie to the nearest public phone. Omi was protecting her because he said it was a bad neighbourhood. The only reason the neighbourhood was considered bad was because his type and her type gathered there to drink nightly at its fountains, take in the majestic view of the Eiffel Tower and listen to the Africans drumming. As she talked nervously to her mother on the phone, getting into arguments and long distance tears, he paced up and down outside, his chains rattling, literally growling at passers-by. All this to protect her, yet he was the most dangerous person on the street. Conversation was limited. He spoke no English and she no German. She spoke a few words of French, he didn't. She was terrified.

"Omi has fallen in love with you," Isolt said.

"Wot?"

"You heard me."

"What the fuck can I do about it?"

He followed her home to the hotel every night. He began to resent Isolt always being there while he attempted to administer the good night kiss. Melonie insisted she could not be alone with him. He would rape her. He had the reputation and he was HIV positive. Cloggie told Isolt one night at the fountain that Omi had told him to tell her he would stab her with an infected needle if she continued in her already reluctant role as bodyguard.

"This can't go on. He'll rape and infect her," Isolt protested.

."It's not your lookout. You could get killed too," Cloggie said.

"Melonie, you'll have to leave town," Isolt advised.

"Wot?"

"Go back to Spain or the South or Italy or back to your mother in England."

"I'm better off with him than I am with me bloody Mum."

"Go join Jim in the Hamburg squat," Rory said.

"Can I beg up there?"

"Sure," Rory said. "Jim wrote and said he's grand and he's even getting social security and the government is sending him to German classes."

"Fucking paradise." Fred nodded admiringly.

"You've no choice girl," Larry told her.

"It's stay here and get AIDS or go there and attend German classes," Isolt said.

"Go on, Melanoma. It's time your fat ass was surgically removed from the streets of Paris." Black Jack smirked.

Speedy was upset to hear of her departure. He came to the station with Kim and Isolt to see her off.

"Love has driven you away," Kim teased.

"Jesus, that cunt Omi! He falls in love with someone and they have to leave the country," Melonie pouted.

"Tell Jim he's a fuckhead thief," Kim said. "And if he comes back I'll call the police."

"Wot?"

Speedy gave her a little something for the journey and the train took off.

Omi found out. Someone in the group had told a member of the German contingent and they had told Omi. Everybody knew where Gunther's squat was. Then they were warned that Omi had stolen a car and was driving up to Germany to kill them all.

Jim went down the narrow wallpapered stairs to the front door. He saw a shape through the frosted glass and opened the door rubbing his eyes. To his surprise he was handed a telegram:

Omi stolen car Stop coming to Germany Stop to kill you Stop

He slammed the door shut with his foot and went running up the stairs shouting to the others, waving the piece of paper. They shambled out of the house, pulling on their jackets and calling the dogs. There were five of them and they went to the pub down the road to assess the danger. Melonie sat in shock and all she could say was the proverbial "Wot?"

Gunther had a cunning plan. "Ve vill just sit here, man, and send lookouts in shifts to keep an eye on the gaff. Then ven he arrives ve call the police from the bar. He is vanted for rape of a voman. Ya?"

Jim marvelled at German efficiency. They ordered beers all around. However, no one would volunteer to be a lookout and so they abandoned the ingenious master plan and got drunk.

At seven o'clock that evening Omi walked into the pub. Melonie began to cry.

"Quit blubbering or I vill kill you too," Gunther hissed.

"Wot?" she continued snivelling.

"Vot? Vot? Vot?" Gunther howled at her in exasperation.

Omi sat down at the table.

"Trinke?" Jim's voice was trembling but obviously his German classes were not a complete waste of time.

People in the bar were staring at this unlikely apparition. He was wearing no shirt despite it being December and had chains draped over his scarred torso. Jim cursed Customs for letting him through. One of the Germans told Omi that people were sniggering at him. Omi looked around. They all are, Omi. All of these people are mocking you. Omi began to get angry. They think you look ridiculous, Omi. They are all having a good laugh at your expense. Let's get them, Omi. We can show them. Teach them not to fuck with Omi the invincible. We're on your side, Omi. The others caught on to his ploy. Gunther whispered to Jim.

"Ve have to fight everybody in the bar."

"Wha?" exclaimed Jim.

"Wot?" said Melonie.

Omi got up and punched an innocent bystander. The others followed suit and a massive brawl ensued. The police came and arrested them. They spent the night in jail but it was worth it. They were all in the same cell except Melonie who was back in the squat with the dogs.

Omi was embracing them and slapping them on the back. He was close to tears. They were his brothers in arms.

Omi the invincible proved to be quite vincible in the end. He was sentenced to life for the rape and for stabbing a guard with a dirty needle. They later heard that his Elixir habit continued while in prison until he grew so sick his circulation was cut off. He developed gangrene and had both of his legs amputated from the hips down. The thought of Omi lying on a thin mattress, dying of AIDS in his cell with no legs, was proof to Melonie that sometimes there was justice in the world.

Later on, the others would laugh when they contemplated the scene. Isolt, Larry and Black Jack shuffling into the Post Office, imbued with an air of self-importance for the task that had to be undertaken. They did not smile as the poor Post Office clerk took down the cryptic message of these bedraggled specimens, an old grey tramp, a short shabby girl, a black man in rags.

Omi stolen car Stop coming to Germany Stop to kill you Stop

When Isolt heard that Christopher was back she avoided the fountain. He came to her hotel one morning.

"Do we have a deal or not, greenhorn?"

Isolt sat on her bed biting the skin beside her nails.

"Deal?" she frowned.

"I need papers." He stood with the door closed behind him. She looked at the grey sky behind the curtainless window. It had not changed for days but he had dragged more darkness into the room when he entered.

"You've missed some small dramas here."

"Jim took off with some bimbo's money."

"He did indeed."

They fell into a lethargic quietness.

"You missed Omi and Melonie's great romance."

"She was a fat girl."

Isolt sighed and placed both hands flat over her belly.

"You fucked Jim down South, Rory told me."

"We didn't take our clothes off. We just kissed."

"Do you feel attracted to him sexually?"

"No. Not at all."

"Well, you can fuck anyone you want. I just want to marry you for papers. But I swear, Isolt, I will treat you different if you do marry me. I will always have a place for you to stay. If I have another girlfriend I will tell her you are my wife and she must make room for you. Even if that means making her get out of our bed for you. If you marry me I will consider you above all the other females in this world." He lit a joint and they snorted some heroin together. Instantly he became a lighter presence in the room.

"I know it's hard for you. You're just a wee girl and you might feel I don't treat you right but I am honest with you. You have to pay your dues. How old are you?"

"Twenty."

"Twenty! Shit," he laughed, shaking his head. "Yeah, you got a lot of due paying to do, girl. You've already paid some by not being so pretty but you got a long way to go before the final pay-off. I'll tell you something, I know I'm not easy, a man with a mission who can't be deflected and all that good shit . . . The Hoodoo Man . . ."

"And you can't hoodoo the Hoodoo Man."

"Yeah. See? You're learning. Now you can pay some of your dues by marrying me."

"The morning after Jim and I kissed, I left for Paris. I was washing my hands in the train station and I took off my mother's ring. I never did that before. It was silver so I didn't have to. I left it there. I forgot it. I only remembered when the train started moving and it was too late. I've worn it for four years, since I left home. I feel empty without it."

Christopher stood to go.

"You're just a wee girl. You don't know nothing. You've never even known real friendship the way a man does. You whine about losing a piece of silver, you don't know nothing. I killed my mother. It was not worth it for her, my life has been a waste. You're so simple-minded. You read all those books, well that's a bad thing, having your nose stuck in fiction at your age. Will you marry me?"

"Yes. But I'll have to move back in with you."

"All right. I can live with that if you follow my rules and don't become a hindrance."

He walked out. Before he closed the door behind him, he said, "Books aren't good for an ignorant girl."

They had set up a winter fairground in Paris. Isolt and Christopher would walk through, their breath visible on the icy air. Ancient skies, old stone statues, candyfloss stands. He kept watch through the window of the English bookshop for her, as she stole the day's newspaper for him. Each evening she would change her clothes in the Air France terminal, and they would walk all the way to the fountain. The asylum of dogs and people, crushing up to the Red Cross van that gave them soup and a food bag. On Christmas Day they put an extra orange in. If it was raining they huddled under the arches, hassled by the police. On the way home he read the newspaper and she sat staring out of the windows, watching the black tunnels. Sometimes she could see through gaps in the huge walls, other trains. They seemed to have come from another world.

She could feel content and empty, looking out of windows.

Walking in silence across the Seine, far away she could see the lights of the fairground wheel.

In the night the TV was on and he changed the channels incessantly. He dreamed up new insults as she rolled herself more cigarettes. Now and then she would borrow his newspaper and turn to the obituaries. She enjoyed in them the feeling of completion. Relatives issuing strange pleas, "Rose says — No flowers please."

Ali said he had been sitting talking to Payman on the fifth floor of an abandoned building near the Saint Quen squat. Ali and Payman had been in the same war but not together. Payman had driven a tank. Sometimes when Ali talked his hands shook and he made machine gun sounds through his teeth in mid-sentence. He was not aware that he did this. Payman carried a copy of the Tehran telephone directory which he read at intervals. Ali was talking to Payman and was making the machine gun noise, his arms outstretched and vibrating. They were sitting on the floor in a big empty room. Payman got up off the freezing floor and, leaving his directory, walked out of the room. Ali thought he was taking a leak.

Ali waited twenty minutes for him to come back. He had been in the middle of a story when Payman had exited without a word. Ali heard sirens and went to the window to see what the commotion was. Five floors below Payman was crumpled up on the cement. He was folded over like an old rag. Ali took the book and ran. Maybe the police would think he had murdered Payman, thrown him five flights to his grave. When the ambulance men prised open his hand they found the remnants of a human nipple clasped inside. He had picked it off the floor in the squat. He had kept it pressed between the pages of the telephone directory.

Ali was wild that night at the fountain. Nobody believed him. He was hyper and weeping intermittently. Christopher sent Fred and Larry to verify the story with the police. The police told them about the nipple and wanted information. They were questioned but said only that they were friends of the deceased, he was Iranian and that they had heard a rumor of his suicide at the fountain. They did not know his second name. They never asked how he would be buried.

Isolt was sitting with Ali at the fountain the next evening. His story was verified and he was basking in minor celebrity status. Everyone wanted to hear it from his lips.

"Man, mid-sentence, I swear he left mid-sentence and I thought he needed to piss and I wait and the next thing man I hear sirens. Sirens, man! He's lying in the alley like a rotten apple core. I ran. Me and Payman are old war buddies, man. The second biggest war since World War II. We fought side by side and after escaped into Afghanistan. We fought for the mujahideen, fought the Russians, man. Lived in the cold mountains. Slept on the bare snow. They paid us one gram of heroin and a virgin a day, man. Hey, have you got a cigarette I could borrow? Me and Payman go back a long way."

When Freddie the Giant was told of the news he said, "I'm not surprised. Ali makes me feel like committing suicide too."

Christopher was shaken. Payman had been his hero. He had taken Payman under his oily wing and had often included him in his evening schedules with Isolt and Freddie.

"The monkey on his back wouldn't let him die," he said. "In the end heroin was all that kept that man alive. He would have been gone years ago without it."

The three mulled regularly about the dilemma of Payman's life and death. Had all of life been unknown to him? No place ever became familiar, no face ever recognisable in any sort of comforting way. No peace sought, no turmoil of interest. Every movement projected a reluctance to be performed. Was he a ghost numbed by a machine-built world? Was it the war? Or before the war? Did the trauma trigger the terrible melancholy or had it always clung to him, a shadow in the skies of every living moment? Had all those living moments been repugnant to his soul? Had Payman ever laughed or smiled or had he been an uncomfortable child dislocated from joy?

His gesture had deemed life not worth living. He had not wanted life, but what had caused him to want something else so much? What hidden reservoirs were tapped to release the immense energy needed to die? So suddenly, so silently, so finally. A breathless leap from an open window. From the tired-out unknown of life to the final unknown death. A transition that rendered his action heroic. Payman the explorer.

If anyone should rest in peace, it was he. If anyone should truly cease to exist, it was he. Organic life repudiated him, machines bewildered him, night and day disturbed him, rest eluded him, nothing was of interest to him, no influence could save him. Was his soul missing from the plan? Was it invisible to God? Was it not located on the map of all souls? Was there an empty space inside him with an absent soul?

He had no place, no sense of connection. No sewn-on patches on his jacket to align him to any tribe. Alienated and isolated, severely suffocated by depression, he had managed to catch his hideous monkey off guard for a split second and snatch the opportunity to die.

8

The Cottage
Behind the Big House

IN THE WAKE of his grief for Payman, Christopher had landlord trouble. He had not paid the rent in months, and recently any
attempt to pay had been rebuffed. The landlord came knocking one
night and shouted through the door that he would come with the
police tomorrow. Christopher packed a few bags and he and Isolt
took them to a hotel. They had to make quite a few trips with the
tartan shopping carts taking heaters, TV, the white chair, all of Marie-
Claire's stolen stuff, records, etc. The landlord came alone and was
satisfied to see them struggle out with a couple of blenders, the tool
box and a lamp shade still in its wrapping. However on entering
the room, the boxes of clay, Perrier bottles, decomposed potato in
the broken sink, orange plastic bucket of black slime beneath, and
assortment of debris were too much for him. He warned them
that they would have to clear it all out. Christopher snorted deri-
sively.

"He's throwing me and my old lady out on the streets and now he
thinks I should perform free cleaning services too. Shit, this guy has
balls."

The landlord looked up and saw the roof plastered with prancing
male ballerinas.

Within days of his eviction the squat in Saint Quen was raided by
police. Freddie the Giant was out on the streets and his health was

growing worse. His skin had turned yellow and he suffered from temporary memory loss. Christopher scoured every day for a new squat.

"I have to get the Giant off the streets. He's in bad shape."

He found a squat in the suburb of Meudon, a mile and a half from the RER station. It was a tiny cottage attached to the back of a large old house. There was running water but no electricity, there was one bedroom without any windows, a living room, a tiny kitchen and a bathroom, a blocked-up fireplace and no furniture. The place smelt musty and neglected. Freddie could have cried with gratitude. Christopher frowned and organised trips back and forth with all his stuff.

"For such a self-proclaimed monk, you sure have a lot of material shit," Isolt complained.

Christopher and Isolt took the bedroom; Freddie took the living room. Christopher sold his drugs and Isolt and Freddie begged. Isolt still stole whiskey for old times' sake. Occasionally when she walked down Rue Saint Denis, the women approached and asked her if they could get a bottle. She began to feel obliged to have some on her, as if it was a service she had to perform.

One night Freddie came home in the rain without shoes. His thick, ingrown, brown toenails curled into burning red toes. He said he had seen a man without shoes and seeing as it was such an awful wet night, he had given him his own. Then he himself had become a man without shoes, walking home in the winter weather. He now tied plastic bags over his feet.

Christopher was a creature of habit and had been swept around in fate's erratic tides of late. He was unstable and spending more money on heroin than was wise in his position. He didn't seem to be saving anything for his next trip to Amsterdam. Isolt sat reading in the evenings by the gas light. Christopher dozed off in his white chair in the corner. Every time Freddie moved, the plastic bags on his feet rustled. Rain hit the window and the glass shook from the wind's blind pummelling. Isolt had a feeling that this tiny ship of fools was bound to spring a leak very soon.

Freddie the Giant sighed from his jaundiced corner. He glowed yellow. It broke Christopher's heart to see the curious doomed anti-glow of the dying, the light sucked in and dismantled in the circumference of Freddie's body. He had taken off his shirt and there was discolouring where his liver was. His bald head trembled as he drank a beer. In the gas light he had a grotesque, freakish quality.

"Why are you sighing?" Christopher asked kindly.

"I'm pissed off," the Giant answered.

"With what?" Christopher would have done anything in his means to help him.

"With life in general and Paris in particular."

"Quote of the week," Christopher said.

"And it's only Monday," Isolt added.

The two men sighed in unison. Isolt bent her head down over her book and tried to concentrate on the story. The bedroom had a corrugated iron roof and the noise of the rain was tremendous, but easily distanced. Christopher was sitting staring at Freddie the Giant's bloated, crinkly, plastic shoes. Freddie the Giant lay on his back looking at the damp patches on the ceiling. There was a patch shaped like a sperm and one shaped like Australia. A sea-horse balancing on a goose directly above his head. Two women wrestling, one with a third breast in the right corner. There was a Saint Patrick with his bishop's hat strangling a snake.

If Isolt needed to be rescued, there was nobody coming. If she needed to be discovered, there was nobody looking. If she needed help, she was in the wrong place.

The three lived calmly for the first week in the dilapidated little cottage. Then they had a visitor. A rich, young Frenchman who owned the house and the cottage attached to it. His hair was parted in the middle and down to his shoulders. He wore loose, designer suits and walked with a slouching, casual gait. He always kept his hands in his pockets and only took them out to sweep back the hair from his face which he did with monotonous regularity. It was his twitch. He was twenty-six and gave the impression of being the lay-about son of rich, conservative parents. Christopher told him that he spoke no French.

"May I come in?" he asked.

Christopher let him in and closed the door. He directed him into the living room with the gas lamp on the floor. Every movement caused huge shadows to glide across the wall. He sat on Christopher's white office chair, the only chair in the room. He peered at Isolt, who said hello. He stared at Freddie the Giant stretched across the floor in a stupor, seven foot two inches from his bald, yellow head to the crinkly plastic shopping bags tied to his feet.

"My name is Didier," he said nicely.

"My name is Isolt, this here is Freddie . . ."

"Hush, woman!" Christopher glared at her.

Didier looked at him puzzled.

"What can we do for you?" Christopher stood at the door; he had a chair leg in his hands. Didier looked at Isolt again and then tried to see into the bedroom.

"There are only three of us here," Christopher said. "We're squatting."

"*Ah bon?* Squatting? Well, yes, you see zis is my house," he said nervously.

"Nobody had used the house in a long time. It's falling apart," Christopher said slowly.

"Ah, yes, zis is true. You see, we kill ze house soon, you know, how you say, knock it over?"

"When?" Christopher demanded to know.

"When?" Didier was unsteady.

"When will you demolish the house?"

"Ah, dee-mol-eesh, yes zat is it. Ah yes, well maybe ze summer, *bientôt.*"

"We'll stay till then. We won't give you no trouble when it's time to leave. It's February, man, and it's fucking cold outside. We are all beggars, we *faire la manche*. This man here is very sick. He needs food and shelter."

Didier looked at Freddie the Giant and nodded.

"Ah yes, I see."

Christopher had sized him up and came over to him. Didier looked up in alarm but was relieved to see Christopher no longer had the piece of wood in his hand.

"Am I in your chair?" Didier inquired.

"Yes. That's OK. I can stand."

Didier took out a little tin box and showed its contents to Christopher.

"Do you smoke zis?"

Christopher nodded. Didier gave him the box and Christopher opened it and rolled a joint. Didier sat on the floor, making sure to sit on one of the many plastic bags in case he soiled his cream-coloured suit. "I do ze coke. You know cocaine? Come to ze house sometime and I will give you a snort, as you English say."

He put his finger to his nose and sniffed. The French were very expressive, Isolt noted. They had rubber faces, controlling their wrinkles and contorting their eyebrows to express a point. Christopher grinned from his throne.

"Cool. I appreciate that offer."

Freddie groaned.

"He should to go to ze hospital. Has he ze hepatitis? He is a bad colour."

"Maybe, maybe." Christopher smoked the joint.

"He hasn't left the house in two days," Isolt said. "I gave him a cigarette and he forgot about it, he just kept it in his hand twirling it about without lighting it. He asked me for another one two minutes later. Christopher and I can't carry him. He's too big. Do you have a car? We could take him."

Didier took the joint. "A car, yes. My license is not so good. You know I was drinking alcohol and ze flics zey find me." He giggled. "But my friend has car. We will come tomorrow at about nine in ze night."

"No," Christopher said darkly. "We can take care of it ourselves. I've known Freddie for years. He has bouts of this. Like malaria."

"I do not want him to die in my house." Didier was quite relaxed, shrugging his shoulders and flicking his hand through his hair. "My parents zey pay me to take care of zer places."

He stood up, brushing himself off. He handed Isolt the joint.

"You are welcome to stay for ze winter. I will come tomorrow for your friend."

Christopher saw him off.

They heard the door slam and Christopher waited in the hallway. Freddie looked at Isolt with pity. "He's going to kill you."

Christopher came back in, his face contorted with hate.

"You fucking cunt." He grabbed her by her shoulders and hauled her up. His monstrous face pressed right up to hers as he slammed her against the wall. "You fucking, fat, stupid, little cunt. I'm going to hurt you. You have to be punished for this."

Isolt stuttered in shock; she tried to wriggle away but he held her tightly. "Wha . . . ?"

"Don't play with me. I said HUSH when he came in and you start prattling again. You talked out of place. When anyone comes in I am the fucking boss here. I am the only one who communicates with him. Freddie knew that, he doesn't have to be told. You blather off all our names to him, you little whore. He could have been a fucking cop for all you know. I am going to hurt you now. I can make your life hell. You've no fucking discipline. *I'm Isolt and this is Freddie. Christopher and I can't carry him. He's sick.* Now he's back tomorrow with his fucking friends. How can I hurt you? Huh? Are you even worth a fucking beating? I'm going to fucking knock some fucking sense into you, whore."

Isolt whimpered, "I . . . I . . . I'll leave you if you touch me, Christopher. Go marry Freddie. You love him more than you've ever loved a woman."

"Cry. Cry. That's all birds are good for."

"I'm not crying." Isolt fought back tears.

"All bravado and street smarts and thinking they're tough. One good smack and they're putty in your hands. Snivelling and whinging. Of course I love Freddie more than you, you silly bitch. I loved two birds in my life. Candy Brown, a whore who would squash you and your tears like an ant. She never cried, I'll guarantee that. All her tears had been fucked and slapped and doped out of her by the time she was fourteen. And Miss Lovely, an angel who would put you to shame with her poise. You have about as much poise and sex appeal as a duck. I won't beat you up because we are to be married. We are going to check at the city hall tomorrow and see what it entails. The sooner I get rid of you the better. I can't stand to even look at you. You disgust me. I don't want you to undress any more in front of me, the sight of your body makes me sick every time. You have no discipline and it shows all over you. Look at the lines on your face, the bags under your eyes. Jesus, I don't want to see what you will be at twenty-five, a fucking mess. Only your youth is holding up your face and body and you're no spring chicken, soon it will all be mush and you will be an ugly lady. Hear that, Isolt? An ugly lady with a banged-out pussy that no one wants to finish off. What do they tell you in those books you read? What lies for simple bitches such as you? What fairy tales do you stuff your ignorant little bird brain with? 'Cos you ain't no intellectual. Poor Freddie here doesn't even like to be around cunts and you burden us with your presence. That's what's making him sick all this time. You're killing him with your bad pussy odour. You're turning him yellow with your cunty little stories and comments. We don't need you here. Freddie and me don't need you. You are a burden to us both. Now go to the room. Go to the room and leave us alone for pity's sake. I'm sleeping here tonight to take care of Freddie in case he needs anything. You will kill him with all this trauma. Tomorrow, Freddie, you will get up and we will walk to the hospital, OK?"

"OK!' Freddie nodded.

"Go now. Get out of here," he shouted at Isolt.

Isolt ran into the bedroom. She fell on the floor and grabbed her belly in both hands. She squeezed and squeezed the fat, sobbing and rolling around. She bit at her nails, tearing them off till her hands bled. She smeared her face in blood, snot and tears. Her teeth chattered, she had the hiccups.

Lost in some haze of self-pity, she lay exhausted on the musty floor. There were lice in the carpet and they crawled into her eye. She sat up and swept them off. There were no lice in the carpet. They had inspected it closely before.

Isolt saw the gas light in the other room extinguished. She listened numbly as she heard them settle to sleep, talking in low voices. The rain grew heavier. It pelted the corrugated roof of the room, making a terrible din.

"Mother," she said to the darkness.

She wanted to forgive herself and to have compassion. She wondered why she didn't just leave. To walk out and wash her smeared face in the rain. To abandon all her possessions yet again. To be free of Christopher. She should go up to Hamburg like everyone else seemed to be doing and avail of Gunther's hospitality and free government German lessons.

What was she doing here? Trying to hoodoo the Hoodoo Man?

Trying to find the meaning of life with a man who saw a poor man with no shoes in the awful, wet weather and then became him? They were both so far gone that she found their company dreary. She was used to shutting off when Christopher ranted on in his barely discernible low voice. The nightly scene all took on a bland nightmarish quality, him whispering away either boastfully or hatefully and Freddie staring at the ceiling pointing out his visions in the damp patches, while the rain pounded deafeningly on the iron roof. She would watch Christopher's red chapped lips move in the monstrous cacophony. The visitor had been a welcome respite.

From where she sat she saw two darknesses. The immediate darkness in the other room, a built-up darkness, stacked on itself in particles. She could discern shapes within the darkness and different shades of its make-up. Then there was the other darkness: the dense, impenetrable black yawn of sorrow that lay like a heavy, sunless cloak over the entire earth. She craved it. She would have found it sooner or later. It was in her nature to seek it, like a mad bee after the blackest honey.

Freddie the Giant was too sick to stand up the next morning. At ten o'clock at night Didier, true to his word, arrived with two friends. The three young Frenchmen were getting a kick out of their descent into the underworld. They watched Christopher fuss about with his baggy, black pants hanging halfway down his arse and his big mop of curly hair. Isolt sat silently in the corner, a watcher and a waiter. They carried the bald, yellow giant to the car. Christopher stood and watched it pull off with its precious cargo.

"I hope they bring him to a hospital and not just dump him in a ditch. All they want is him off their property. Fucking capitalists."

Isolt sat quietly, knowing they were ordinary men and not gangsters. Christopher snorted some heroin. He did not offer Isolt a line. She knew she was not to speak. She read her book and went to bed. He slept in the living room. Her hands were throbbing still where she had torn off the skin around her nails.

She had a dream that she squeezed off all excess flesh from her head downwards. She squeezed it until it hung in great fleshy dugs from the soles of her feet. She then dug a hole in the back garden of her family's house in Ireland. She buried the excess flesh and covered up the hole with fresh clay. A flock of geese approached her, hissing. She could not run because she was physically attached to the horror she had just buried. She saw a Madonna and Child sit on the stone bench playing with a snake. Saint Patrick ran up screeching fanatically, snatched the snake from their loving hands and strangled it. The Madonna and Child became an ugly, dilapidated man holding a small, obese, homey-looking woman in his hairy arms. Isolt clawed the earth beneath her feet to free herself and escape the flock of geese. Instead of finding her own flesh she found a small wooden coffin containing a Humpty Dumpty rag doll. It was lying amid a multitude of tiny seahorse skeletons. She cradled the doll as the geese surrounded her, pecking and tearing her flesh. The grass was shrinking back into the earth and there were men sawing down the trees of her childhood garden. She tried to prize her eyes open and finally succeeded — blinking in the darkness, trying to make sure she would not succumb to sleep again. She crept into the living room. It was a night of the full moon. Christopher did not stir. He lay curled as a foetus but with his fists clenched and his eyelids twitching like a dog's. She put her throbbing hand on the windowpane, where the two darknesses met. Inside darkness, outside darkness, both equally unforgiving.

Christopher and Isolt did not associate together the week Freddie the Giant was in the hospital. She would leave the house, beg and then hang out with Rory, Larry and the others. She saw Christopher at the fountain selling his drugs but they barely exchanged glances. When she returned home every night he would be reading the newspaper or trying to fix the electricity so he could watch TV, his tools out all over the floor. She bought a torch and read in her windowless room.

Freddie came back after a week. He was still yellow but much improved. Neither Isolt nor Christopher had got around to visiting him. They began talking together again, albeit somewhat warily, the night he came back. Freddie had many containers of pills to take. Christopher read over each label with the scrutiny of a passionate amateur.

"I always wanted to be a pharmacist. Have my own place. That was one of my dreams. I have great faith in drugs."

One night not long after Freddie's homecoming, when Christopher was at the fountain, one of his old Versailles comrades, Dutch Mark, approached and said he wanted to talk business. Christopher jumped at the chance to talk to someone who shared his glory days. He brought him to the cottage, telling Isolt to give him some time before she came back. Dutch Mark told Christopher that he had a parcel of heroin to sell and a parcel of coke. He said he was going straight in Holland and wanted to open a restaurant. This would be the money he needed to start it. Christopher listened carefully to this beggar turned restaurateur. Dutch Mark had never dealt drugs and had no connections. He had bought this bulk off some men in Amsterdam and wanted Christopher to sell it. They would split the profits. Christopher could barely contain his enthusiasm for the arrangement. He had spent all his money and was almost out of hash and acid to sell. This was a juicy apple falling right into his lap. Dutch Mark told him that he would give him the stuff tomorrow and come back down every week to take his share of the money. They agreed on the selling price and how much each would get. Freddie, who lay on the floor for most of the transactions, got up and made them tea. He said he would give Christopher a hand in getting the stuff off the ground. Dutch Mark left and Isolt passed him by as she was walking to the cottage from the RER.

She came in the door to find the other two elated.

"We'll make a fortune on this and we didn't even have to smuggle it down," Christopher grinned at her.

"Where are you going to sell it?"

"On my usual stomping ground, the fountain I guess."

"Your man next door does coke. Sell that to him. It's not a beggar's drug. They want sedation, they don't want to be alerted to their immediate surroundings."

"Good idea. I'll go suggest it to him. He's lots of dough."

"You'll be rich. We can go to the Bahamas for our honeymoon."

"Ha! Ha! You wish. Actually Freddie and I can put our schemes to work."

"What schemes? Don't tell me you're going to put Freddie and yourself through college to study pharmacy."

"Don't breathe a word of this to anyone. When I was in the US

Army at Stuttgart you could order things cheap from the US, like Harley-Davidsons. Now whenever I see one parked here in Paris there's always a little crowd gathered to admire it. They cream when they see a Harley. To them it's the America they love, James Dean, Marilyn Monroe, Brando. I don't think you can get them in France. I would go to some American on the base in Germany and give him the money to order one from the States and a little extra for himself of course. Maybe get two guys and two bikes. Freddie and I would drive them back to France and put an ad in the newspaper, selling for triple the price we bought. You know, maybe even eventually run a little legal bicycle shop on Avenue de la Grande Armée with all the other bike shops. That's a dream of mine, to own a bicycle shop. I have to get legit though. We must find out about the marriage business. You go tomorrow to the Hotel de Ville and ask there. If I'm going to cross borders all the time I need papers."

"OK," Isolt nodded. "Though it all sounds like junkie dreams to me. A step up from the usual 'go to Colombia and bring back a kilo' fantasy."

Freddie handed her a beer which she accepted gratefully. Christopher looked agitated. "I don't like to see either of you drink so much beer all the time. It keeps her fat and it will kill you, Freddie. It's healthier to smoke a joint to get a buzz."

"We do that too," Isolt said.

Christopher told Isolt to put on her good clothes. Isolt was amused.

"I've no more good clothes than you do."

Christopher said he had been out this morning and had stolen a shirt and a tie.

"What? Did you steal me an evening gown too?"

She put on a yellow sweater.

"Quit blabbering, woman. Don't you have a skirt?"

"No. I haven't worn a skirt since school. I thought you didn't approve of skirts anyway. It didn't suit your Islamic-like ideals of how women should be presented."

"It serves a purpose," Christopher said. "Damn, if I was a girl I'd be a fucking millionaire. Females are just too dumb to see it. I'd use my pussy to my advantage. Birds don't realize what a gold mine they have between their legs."

"Well, that just demonstrates that you haven't a clue what it feels like to have one."

"Well, to tell you the truth, Isolt, I can't take seriously any individual who doesn't have a member between his legs. It's dicks that make a human great. But if you don't have one, there is a minor consolation, you have a piece of equipment that can satisfy one and you should use it to your advantage."

"It's precisely those sentiments that have caused all the trouble in this world, Christopher. Worship of the phallus. Every city has to have its penis. Paris, the Eiffel Tower. London, Nelson's Column. Washington has the Monument. To show the mortals that it is the penis that rules, with no room for deviations. When the nuclear holocaust comes it won't be a forty-foot clitoris you'll see flying through the air."

She found a pair of black ski pants, sniffed them and dusted them off. "You'll have to look the other way. I know how my body offends you."

"That was a cruel thing I said, Isolt." Christopher lowered his head.

"It was, but you meant it and you can't apologise for it. Why don't you just go fuck Freddie if you love men so much? Why don't you leave women alone?"

"I liked Marie-Claire. I liked the way she looked."

"Vulnerable."

"I guess I'd a bad start with the weaker sex. Killing my mother got me off on the wrong footing. Something I have to pay for with women the rest of my life. That's why I put up with girlfriends I suppose. Guilt. Otherwise I would be a monk. I thought you were a thug. That's why I picked you. I thought you were tough. Seeing as you hung out with all the lads and took care of your own corner, so to speak. You stood your ground. I liked that. I liked your wit. I thought you'd have more stories of going to men's houses and then stealing their wallets when they had their pants off. That sort of thing. I was disappointed. That's what I was looking for, a kind of con-artist chick. Instead I find out you are an angel. That's why I didn't want to marry

Marie Claire, 'cos she was an angel. I always thought women were either angels or whores. Now I find out they're all angels."

Christopher put on his shirt and Isolt did his tie. She knew how to do one better than he as she had worn one every day as part of her school uniform.

"Look at this noose that the Romans wear every day to remind them of their servitude to Babylon and capitalism." He tugged at his tie. After shaving and splashing water on his face, he trimmed his hair and mustache over the kitchen sink with a scissors.

"Those hairs will be there till we leave," Freddie complained. He was the tidiest of the three. He made a pot of tea on the camping stove. They drank a cup and smoked a joint before they left.

"Now don't go out while we're gone," Christopher told Freddie on the way out the door. "I'll bring you back food and tobacco. You have to keep warm until you're better."

They went to the city hall but found a giant barbed-wire fence of bureaucracy denying them access to the garden of marital delights. Neither had residency in France nor papers of domicile or employment. They didn't understand half of what was needed. Deflated and with a myriad of forms they left the windowless corridors of power and smoked a joint at the station.

"OK. We've one more thing to do and then you can run off on your stumpy little Catholic legs and beg."

"Don't take it out on me."

"You know the problem with you, Isolt? You're so fucking middle-class." He was cracking peanuts out of their shells. He stood about four feet away from her. He ate the nuts and threw the shells at her. This made him laugh. Isolt did not react. She did not see how she could. He sneered at her and threw the shells, aiming for her face. There were a few people on either side of the platform.

"People are beginning to stare, Christopher."

"You're so fucking middle-class. And what have I told you about saying my name in public?"

She sat on the bench staring away from him, avoiding the eyes of anybody else, as the shells struck her. A middle-aged woman came up to Christopher and scolded him for making a mess.

"*Ramassez tout ça,*" she said. The train came and saved him.

"You're so fucking middle-class. That's your problem." Christopher took out some of the forms and began to try and decipher them. He handed some to Isolt. After about three minutes she handed them back.

"You need a hieroglyphics expert to figure all that shit out," she said and turned to look out of the window at the black tunnels.

Isolt arrived at the little cottage behind the big house. Didier was in the living room with two friends. Christopher was sitting on his throne holding court. There were lines of cocaine cut up on a mirror with a razor. One of Didier's friends was female. Isolt had thought for an instant it was Marie-Claire. She was thin and pretty with a sensitive face and a high forehead, she wore no make-up and had long brown hair. Christopher waved Isolt in.

"Come in. Come in. This is the girl who refuses to believe Eve was taken from Adam's rib. She thinks Eve got a bum deal. We call her El Ribbo for short. El Ribbo, sit down and do a line."

Isolt took a rolled-up note and snorted a line.

She went to the kitchen and ran the tap, putting her finger under it and water up her nose. She sniffed hard. Freddie was stooped over pouring hot water from the saucepan into a teapot.

"You're not his butler, Freddie. I can take you food as well, for as long as you have to rest. Why should you make the tea every time he snaps his fingers?"

Freddie, alarmed at this mutiny, said, "Christopher is a good man, Isolt."

"You're right," Isolt said. "Oh look! The hairs are still in the sink where he cut them."

"Dutch Mark came by earlier."

"I can see that. In fact I can feel it. It feels good," she sniffed.

"Yes, it does," Freddie snickered.

"Is Didier paying for it?"

"Christopher's trying to get him to take all the coke in bulk. This is just a sampler."

"Five of us snorting for free. That's generous of him."

"Christopher's a kind man."

"He must be."

"He likes you more than he lets on."

"How touching."

Freddie walked into the living room, the machine-gun rattle of the mugs on the tin tray announcing his arrival. Isolt followed him. She wondered if she would be allowed to speak. Christopher was in fine fettle. Didier and his friends were snorting up a storm. Didier was listening to Christopher's stories intently, pushing his hand through his hair, laughing feverishly. Isolt took the mirror when it was handed to her and did another line. She decided that it was safest to communicate with Freddie the Giant, though she would like to talk to the woman. She was starved for female company since Melonie and Kim left. She wished sometimes she could talk to the prostitutes she sold whiskey to but they seemed out of her league. Perhaps if Becky had not tripped over her metal detector and died they would still be friends. It was impossible to imagine Becky alive at this point. The grieving was over. She could think of her without longing; though it was tempting to think of her as still alive.

At about three in the morning everybody was out of their respective trees. Freddie the Giant leaned over to the French girl and told her she was ugly. The girl stared in shock as he proceeded to tell her that she had a face made of play-dough and though she had big tits she was still an ugly cunt. Christopher scolded him and advised the others that it was a bad habit Freddie had, to insult all females regardless of face or tit size.

"As you see, the girl's tits are small, not big. He doesn't know what he's saying. He is a sick Giant and should be treated with pity not scorn."

The mood was broken and half an hour later the little group left, grinding their teeth, Didier twitching madly.

Christopher, Isolt and Freddie were too wired to sleep, so they stayed up talking. At six a.m. the wretched birds were awake and twittering. Freddie was snoring and Christopher put a sleeping bag over him. It was freezing cold. Isolt went to the bedroom and slithered into her sleeping bag shivering, her teeth chattering. Christopher came in and coaxed her into giving him a blow job. He had the courtesy to remain in the sleeping bag with her afterwards. Isolt was grateful for that; she knew it was a cold, cold morning with no promise in either the grey air outside or the imbecile birds chirping fruitlessly in the trees.

Didier gave him money for the parcel of coke and Christopher had a rapturous vision of himself cruising down the Autobahn on a Harley Davidson, the wind blowing the scabs out of his curly hair, the Giant on a bike behind him, no longer yellow but rosy-cheeked, his bald head shining, forever a grateful apostle. They celebrated by doing a half-dozen lines or so of the brown powder heroin.

Dutch Mark sat on the floor. He was a tall, good-looking man with long, blond hair tied in a ponytail. Christopher gave him his half of the money for the coke. They all did a line of smack. Dutch Mark and Christopher talked about the good old days in the Versailles squat. They laughed and slapped their thighs. Freddie made tea. Isolt watched and waited. Dutch Mark left satisfied.

Christopher said: "We've got to sell that shit. I don't want to stand at the fountain with it on me. That Malaysian dealer was busted last month. He used to keep it in the shoulder pads of his baseball jacket. They found it. The police had been after him for ages. They would arrest him but never find it. He told me when they found it he felt like a celebrity, everybody in the station came to have a look at him, slapping him on the back and smiling, they were so fucking happy."

"I could go tell everyone you got smack and to come to the house to get it. That way you don't have to go out," Isolt suggested.

"Well, then we'd have every junkie howling at the door long after it had gone. Word gets around. We'd be busted for hash or anything we have here."

Isolt nodded. "I know, but with all this on our hands surely we have to keep the wolves from the door, not the junkies."

Christopher snorted. "They're one and the same, sweet thing. They're one and the same."

For two weeks they had a ball. They stayed high, only venturing into the squinting daylight for the supermarket. They were hibernating. Covering themselves in euphoric leaves and drifting away on treacherous waves. The three in the little cottage, building a ship in a bottle. A Puerto Rican captain, a gentle giant, a stowaway girl; blinkered horses tied to the rotting deck.

Dutch Mark was at the door.

He was not amused. "I came all the way here from Holland for nothing? I do not think so, my friends."

Christopher sat on the chair smoking a joint, his head down.

"Well, man. The shit's hard to get rid of. Especially in this climate. Seriously, Mark, police presence is heavy at the fountain these days. They're looking for me. Come back in two weeks and you'll have your money."

"Give me my stuff back. I will find someone else. We will call it quits."

"Well, I gave it to someone else."

"You can't be serious?"

"Sure. That's what I did with the coke. He came through. He'll come through in this too. I guarantee it. I appreciate your concern. A lot is at stake here but these things take time, man. That you have to understand."

"Who is this guy?"

"Mark! Mark! I won't tell you that. Look, come back in two weeks and I guarantee you you'll have your bread. Settle down. This is smack you're talking about here. It's mucho complicated. Trust me."

"I understand there are difficulties but we made a deal. I said I needed it in three weeks and you said you could do it."

"Well, I didn't foresee these minor technical details. You have no choice in this matter. Be cool, Mark."

"I have to have the fucking money. I have other people waiting for it in Holland. There will be big trouble. They will break my legs."

Christopher looked at him closely. "I thought you said you had paid for it and were just waiting on profits."

"I never said that. No, I still have some people to pay off."

"Look, give us a week, OK? I can't do anything before then. Wait in Paris so they can't get you."

"I have obligations in Holland. But OK, one week. I will be back. I gave this deal to you because I always admired your honesty. I thought you would be straight with me."

"Yeah, well, sure. You'll get your dough. Trust me."

"I will give them your name, Christopher, if you fuck it up. I will not let them torture me."

He got up and left.

Christopher came clattering back into the room after closing the door; he was sweating and wide-eyed.

"Did he say torture?"

Isolt and Freddie nodded. Christopher paced up and down the room.

"I thought it was just that fucking yuppie, Mr. Restaurant, I was dealing with. I thought, fuck him, he can't touch me. Now there's more involved. Heavies. Damn. I've been double-crossed."

"Give him your half of the money from the coke," Isolt suggested.

"What do you think we've been spending?"

"Jesus, Christopher, we only buy potatoes and carrots and apples."

"They add up, God damn it."

"Not to five thousand francs, they don't," Isolt said.

"Not to mention your beer every day," Christopher added.

"Christ, Christopher, just give him the fucking money," Isolt said.

"It's mine. I made the deal. It was a cinch. Shit, I've been double-crossed. Now I got a monkey on my back big time. I can't kick while trying to get the rest of it. That's impossible."

"How much do we owe?"

Christopher was grateful for that "we." "Ten thousand francs."

"We snorted twenty thousand between the three of us in two weeks?" Isolt was shocked.

"If I give him the three thousand eight hundred I have left then I still owe six thousand. Where am I going to get that with a monkey on my back?"

"Won't codeine work this time?"

"Shit, woman, you don't realise we've been loading our systems morning, noon and night. Codeine is not going to have any effect after that."

"I wonder if I have a monkey? I've never done it steadily for so long. Just bits here and there. It did occur to me when we were doing it but I didn't want to break the magic."

"Shit, I wish you could magic up ten thousand francs," Christopher snapped. Then he perked up. "Sell your ass, Isolt. I swear just for a week. Me and Freddie would look out for you. You could bring them here. We'd be in the bedroom. You could fuck them in this room. Wear a condom. Nothing would happen. You'd make the money in a week, a young chick like you. No problem. I'd do it and so would Freddie but no one would buy our sorry asses. You'd save our lives. I'm serious, it's the only way out of this mess. I'd forever be in your debt. I'd never be mean to you again. It would be a really brave thing to do, Isolt. Courage like that is hard to come by."

Isolt looked at him incredulously and saw he was quite serious.

"I'd rather you get tortured personally."

Isolt went clean. She did not experience much except her joints aching, a runny nose and a cold. She was a little irritable but that could be put down to the fear of impending doom.

She begged for hours and she and Christopher got back to stealing six bottles of whiskey a day between them. Freddie dragged himself out to sit at the local market. Christopher tried to beg but he never incited much pity and made barely enough to buy apples and Perrier every day. He and Freddie had to keep buying heroin in small doses and make it last. They were drinking the foul codeine once more. Freddie the Giant was sinking into chronic depression, so much so that Christopher fed him with the whiskey money and let him spend his own begging money on porno movies. The drugs were taking their toll. They could not seem to accumulate without it being whittled away again on hash or codeine or a bag of smack.

"We're digging holes by the seashore," Christopher fretted.

He went next door to borrow the money from Didier, but Didier said he was going on a holiday to Thailand for a month with his friend and couldn't afford to extend the loan. Christopher pleaded with him, saying it was for Freddie the Giant's liver transplant, but Didier had been around and knew a junkie when he saw one.

They lived with a sickening countdown to the moment Dutch Mark would come knocking at the door.

There was a knock on the door. The unmistakable rat-tat-tat of Dutch Mark looking for his pound of junkie flesh. Christopher let him in and he walked straight into the living room and sat on the one chair in the room, the white chair. Isolt was shocked to see Christopher sit on the floor by the wall. They sat at Mark's feet like children waiting for Grandma's bed-time story to begin.

"My money?"

"I can give you three thousand francs," Christopher said.

"The rest?"

"We shot it all up, Mark. We never sold it."

"I trusted you. I believed you had the integrity for the job."

"Never trust a junkie, Mark."

"Give me the three thousand."

Christopher pulled the notes from his pocket and handed them to Freddie who handed them to Mark.

"You owe seven thousand, my friend."

"Fuck it, Mark. We can't do it. We'll kill ourselves. We're beggars for Chrissake. You know how it is, you've been there. Freddie the Giant's sick as a dog. I have to nurse him. You know seven thousand begging is impossible."

"You were a dealer not a beggar, I thought."

"Well, I've fallen on hard times. I have a monkey on my back. I fucked it all up. My girlfriend left me and I went to pieces. Remember Miss Lovely? Have some compassion. All this stress is killing Freddie. We walk around waiting for the sky to fall on our heads."

"Perhaps you should have thought of that when you did all my drugs by yourselves. When you hoovered all my lovely fucking drugs up your noses."

"Mark, man, you have a chance. This restaurant business. You've cleaned up your act, you look straight. You can find the money somewhere to appease those heavies. We can't. We have no chance. Once a beggar always a beggar. Except in your case of course. We'll probably die on the streets. All of us. Look, take my girlfriend and fuck her and we'll call it quits."

"I don't want the girl. I want my money, my friend."

"You're no friend of ours. I'm going to have to ask you to leave my house," Christopher sighed heavily.

Dutch Mark stood up. "You will not get away with ripping me off. There will be hell to pay. I will give them your name and description. They will come and deal with you. I wash my hands of the matter. Don't try to run. They will find you. Have the seven thousand ready for them or else."

"Get out of here," Christopher snarled.

Dutch Mark left, closing the door quietly. Christopher found it ominous that he did not slam it.

"Do you mind not using me as bartering merchandise?"

Christopher was distracted, he didn't even look at Isolt. "Settle down, El Ribbo, don't get flustered, it was just a gesture."

"Times are hard. I'll have to sell the museum," Christopher said to the Giant and the little girl. He opened a little English/French dictionary and flicked through the pages.

"Here is my collection of acid tabs. The museum."

Isolt crawled over to have a look as he showed it to Freddie.

"There's a Batman, a Garfield, a ying-yang, a Superman, a butterfly, a snake, a scary clown, a poppy, a cannabis sign, a Pink Panther and many, many more. Oh, here's my favourite, look, a Bugs Bunny. My mentor. Where's my Statue of Liberty? I've even got a Nancy Reagan head: that proved to be unpopular though. It freaked people out to ingest her." He flicked back through the pages. They were little squares of paper with tiny designs. "Ah, here it is, Liberty." He showed it to Isolt and she smiled at it. "Times are hard when you have to sell the museum. I count fifteen in all. I'll sell them tonight though I hate to do this. It took me years to collect. Nice, huh?"

Christopher stood at the fountain and a young American passed by.

"Acid?" Christopher hissed.

The American stopped and said that he wanted to have a party and did Christopher know where he could get all different types of acid as a novelty. He was thinking of going to Amsterdam. Christopher couldn't believe his ears. He laughed in astonishment.

"I got fifteen different rare types on me now, man."

The American was incredulous.

"No shit?"

"Eight hundred francs for the lot. This is your lucky day, man. Don't fuck it up."

They went to a café and had a coffee. The guy studied photography in San Francisco. They talked about the US. Christopher said he sometimes missed it and would like to visit but he would never live there again.

"San Francisco is not Detroit," the guy said.

"I am Detroit," Christopher said. "You can't get more Detroit than me."

The guy laughed. "I come from Basking Ridge, New Jersey, man. I'd never go back there. They say New Jersey is the armpit of the USA."

"Then Detroit is the balls," Christopher smiled.

They made the deal. The guy even paid for the coffee.

None of them slept well at night. They were afraid of being murdered in their sleeping bags. Christopher sat on vigil with a broken chair-leg by Freddie.

"Sleep, man. I'll protect you. You need to sleep."

"I can't," the Giant groaned.

Christopher understood. "I've had thirty-three years of shit. The thought of another thirty-three is too much. I've had it. I might kill myself."

Freddie sighed deeply: "How can I owe seven thousand francs? It's daft. I have never in my life had that amount in my possession, either in cash or material goods."

"Dutch Mark is inviting bad karma onto himself. To hassle down-and-outs like us for money. To threaten a sick man. That's not cool to pressure beggars. Something bad will come to him, mark my words. I hope it's soon. I hope he doesn't wait years and years and then not understand why this bad thing happened. If he can link it to us he will learn a lesson. That's why you must live a clean life, so if you do a bad thing you will feel the consequences immediately and can deal with it and learn from it. This delayed reaction is dangerous. I do a bad thing and I get it in the face right away. Like this drug business. I hope Mark is living clean for his own sake."

"I don't want to die on the streets, Christopher. I'm terrified. Don't let that happen. Keep a roof over my head. I'm so sick I can't control any of what's happening. I'm tired of living too. I'm the same age as you, thirty-three. I've had enough, there is no future. I'm ready."

"Don't talk like that. Maybe you should go back to the hospital. You seemed better after that. A little yellow around the edges but that's to be expected."

"I think it was the walking home in the rain barefoot that finally did me in."

"Freddie, you are a saint. I believe that. You are the most generous man I ever met."

"No, Christopher. I feel awful about bawling out every bird I meet. God forgive me, I've hurt a lot of women in the past few years. I've made them cry for no reason."

"Don't worry about birds, Giant. They're bloodsuckers with hearts of stone. Why don't you ever pick on Isolt? I would have liked to see you do it."

"Isolt's all right. She's not like the others."

"Anything with a snatch is one and the same to me."

"I haven't had a woman in a year. I just watch porno movies and jerk off. I haven't had a woman I didn't have to pay for in ten years."

"Can't live with them, can't live without them, huh? Women are liars at heart. Barefoot and pregnant is what they should be at all times. Chained to the kitchen stove.

"When I left Detroit and arrived in Stuttgart I went on to the army base and sold my acid. I still had contacts there, you dig? I knew my way around. I was in this bar and I saw a middle-aged woman drinking, a right old whore she was. She had a fourteen-year-old girl with her drinking a 7-Up. This was back in my drinking days you understand. I don't drink no more. I went up to the mother and I said in English, 'Can I fuck your daughter?'

"They took me home and I had a fucking threesome with mother and daughter. I shit you not. Hell, I moved in. I guess I kind of overstayed my welcome 'cos after a month or so of this set-up some biker guys came up to me in the factory and said that her ol' man was getting out of prison and would not be pleased to find me poking his old lady, not to mention his little girl.

"I was in a bar that night getting wasted. This other bird picked me up. I was so drunk I couldn't get my dick hard. She was pissed off. Next night I was drinking JD and she comes in with another guy. She says to me real coldly, 'You still here?' I say to her, 'Bitch, I live here.' Ha! Ha!

"She walked into the bedroom with her man and told me to get the fuck out of there. I smashed her glass table with the bottle and started smashing up the whole apartment. All the little perfume bottles on the dressing table. Everything. She calls the police and they drag me out. I tell them that it's my old lady and she came home with another man. She was screaming at them, 'He's not my old man. I've never seen him before. Lock him up, he smashed up my house.' I could understand that much in German anyway. The police took me and let me sleep it off in the cells.

"I came the next morning to France. Man, I was bummed out. It was Christmas Eve and I was in Paris starving and sleeping rough. I stole food and slept anywhere I could, covering myself with newspapers. I used to get cardboard boxes and sleep in them. Then after two months I met Maggot, an English bloke, and he turned me on to begging. I was drinking wine and still sleeping in boxes. But I had ambition. I went clean. I gave up alcohol. I saved my begging money and went to Amsterdam. I went into a biker club and they liked me. They gave me an acid contact. There was hardly any acid in Paris and everyone wanted to try it. I saw a gap in the market and it was easy to smuggle. I think I became a minor cult figure in the Parisian underground. Then came Miss Lovely. I had a big squat in Versailles. All the local monsters were eating out of my hand. I was a respected entity. That was the high point of my career. Maybe of my life. Damn.

"Where did it all go, huh? Can you tell me that? Everything I worked for slipped out from between my fingers. For six years just running around trying to keep from getting busted and to keep the wolves from the door. I lost it all. My career, my houses, my squats, my attic rooms, Miss Lovely.

"I've lived a hard life, Freddie, and I'm tired. I can't see how I can gather momentum again. I'm getting old. Maybe if El Ribbo will marry me and I get papers. I'm weary though and that's the God's truth. Life just drags on and on. I can't see another thirty-three years of all that shit. I lived fast. The pressure of trying to accumulate all that money and the huge monkey on my back has broken me. All those years wheeling and dealing. If it wasn't for you, Freddie, I would call it a day and commit suicide. It would be a relief. I never enjoyed my life and I wasted it. Who would miss me? Not a soul. My family in Detroit probably think I'm dead long ago. I've never contacted them since Germany. Miss Lovely might, huh? Well she's young and she has her own life to live now. I just put her on the right track. Hopefully she'll stay out of prison.

"Freddie, what can I do? This winter has lasted forever. I've had it. I can't take no more, I swear. I wish I was dead. May God have mercy on me. Have mercy on the poor Hoodoo Man."

Freddie was crying.

"Don't cry, Freddie, I'll take care of you. You'll always have a roof over your head. Don't you worry."

"I'm crying for you, Christopher."

9

The Lesson
of the Blind Midget

ISOLT MET Christopher on Rue Saint Denis outside the Chinese take-away. Her black bag was light and empty as she had just sold her last whiskey to a gummy old hooker in a doorway. They were pestering her for more. There never was enough to go around.

"Let's order and split. I don't want to be around this area," Isolt told him.

"Chill, baby, chill. Don't get flustered. We're going to buy rice here and go to a Vietnamese cafeteria for the meal. The rice is much cheaper here."

They put a carton of rice in Isolt's bag and walked to the cafeteria. As they were sitting at the table Christopher glanced around surreptitiously and dove into the bag; he snatched the carton, tearing the lid off, and dumped the contents onto the plate. It landed in a perfect rectangular mould. He quickly mashed it up and put the carton back into the bag.

"If you don't do this quickly they'll suss it's not their rice. I've been caught before."

"And what do they do?" Isolt asked. "Call the police?"

"You're taking the piss now, Isolt. No need for that. It's twice as cheap and light and fluffy. I'm no fool."

They ate in silence for a while.

"You have a big appetite," Christopher said. "That's a bad sign in a girl."

"Why? Are you afraid I'll gobble you up?"

"No. It just seems a mite unseemly. Shows no self-control and you need to shed those pounds big time. Women shouldn't take up too much space. Now don't get on your high horse. Even women know this. It's funny, their place is already so tiny in the world and they instinctively diet to make themselves smaller. They all want to be so thin and not eat. I think women want to disappear."

"The givers of life don't want to live," Isolt said sarcastically.

"They are the bearers of life. The giving is in men's balls."

"There is an egg too. Do you know how small the sperm is compared to the egg?"

"What egg?"

"You know nothing of biology, do you? You haven't the faintest idea about the inside of a female body."

"I know all I want to know about that mess. I only need occupy myself with the outside of that particular machine."

"You said to me yesterday that I needed to change a tampon every time I pissed. Why?"

"Jesus, girl. How could the piss come out if you're all plugged up?"

"How many holes does a woman have?"

Christopher was blushing and turning around.

"Hush, people are listening. Down there? Two of course."

"Three!" Isolt said triumphantly. "The one that leads to the womb is different from the urinary tract."

"This is making me sick. I'm trying to eat. I never found another one. Two is all I've counted. I'll believe it when I see it. And I'm not going rooting in yours so don't be getting your hopes up. Now talk about something else, please. We rarely go out to eat. This should be my treat but it's self-service and you paid for your own before I could intervene, so eager were you to stuff your fat face."

"What's the occasion?"

His face darkened. "Some Dutch thugs were asking for me at the fountain. They were told I'd gone home. They set off on the C train in our direction."

"Freddie's there."

"I know, I know. He's sick again. I told him not to answer the door. They can't do anything to him, he's too ill. We'll go later and see if they're waiting for me or what."

"We were all so frightened and now we leave the poor Giant alone."

"They won't torture him, Isolt; he's dying anyway."

"We have to go back, call the police, do something."

"Jesus. I shouldn't have told you. You're too young to understand the more subtle things in life."

Isolt sat staring at him in bewilderment. Christopher shifted uncomfortably under her gaze.

"You've stopped shovelling your food into your mouth all of a sudden," he said resentfully.

"You're meant to be his friend."

"I am. Just the other day I gave him money to get laid."

Christopher lowered his voice. "Freddie had a hard time finding a prostitute that would do it. He was in bad shape. In the end he got one with no teeth. She didn't even make him wear a rubber. He said as he was doing it her wig came off. She had short grey hair. He said she had a big operation scar over her stomach. She probably had no womb. There was a gerbil cage behind him and when he started nailing her the gerbil jumped onto the wheel and started running on the spot, no less."

Isolt smiled: "Jesus, that must have been a sight to behold."

"I love Freddie more than anyone else in the world. More than my dead mother. He's more than a friend. I've been looking out for him for years. I've always given him money and fed him and given him places to stay. I love him like a son."

"Then let's go protect him."

"No."

"I'm going."

Christopher took his knife up from his plate. "I'll kill you if you do. They won't harm him. I need you for papers. I've put up with you so far. You can do as you please soon. First we must marry, then you're free. Now pack up your leftovers in the carton and we'll take them home to Freddie. We're going to a movie first, you can choose which one, we needn't sneak in the back door to a random picture. Happy?"

"If I leave now and go home, what will you do?"

"I'll beat the shit out of you."

Isolt was sickened by her own absence of power.

*

The cottage was dark. They hid behind some dustbins and studied that darkness. The living room window was black and heavily curtained. The frosted bathroom window was also black and similarly curtained by a towel nailed to the wall inside. There was no sign of light.

"They might be waiting for us inside," Christopher whispered.

It had been raining and Isolt's socks were wet inside her shoes. She hunkered down, her thighs aching; she had three pronged fingers touching the grainy wet cement for support.

"Let's call an ambulance. That way if they're there we'll see them and if they're not, Freddie needs to be taken to the hospital anyway. We should have done it days ago."

"The ambulance won't enter without police and I have all my affairs in there, including my passport. That's not an option, we have to wait and stake them out." They remained hunkered down — two shadowy, hunch-backed dwarfs behind the rubbish bins. After ten minutes Isolt sat on the wet ground.

"Why not wake Didier up and send him in?"

"That's not a bad idea. Let them kill him."

They crept around to the front door of the big house.

"They could be watching us now," Isolt said.

They rang the bell, cringing at its confident chimes that seemed to go on forever.

"Faggot," Christopher sneered.

There was no answer.

"He must still be in Thailand, the asshole."

"Let's go back behind the bins." Isolt looked around nervously.

"You're just full of good ideas tonight."

Isolt felt the pain of the night's every moment. The tedium and terror made her nauseated. She burped burps that tasted of sulphur. The wet soaked through her clothes, through her skin and seeped into her bones. Christopher remained crouched and murderously attentive. At long last, when they heard the first bird's call in the dark morning, he stood and crossed over to the cottage door. He listened for a second, then came back.

"Isolt. You knock. They won't touch a girl. They're waiting for me."

Isolt hauled herself up with much miserable effort and stumbled over on dead legs to pound on the door. Christopher remained behind the bins. Isolt finally took out her key and stuck it into the lock. She didn't care what was inside. She needed to take off her wet jeans and sleep in some warmth.

"Freddie?" she shouted. "Freddie."

The silence was ominous. Christopher was behind her. He grabbed the chair leg that was always behind the door and leapt into the pitch-black living room. He ran to the bedroom. Isolt fumbled for matches and lit the gas lamp. Christopher dashed into the kitchen and bathroom wielding his primitive weapon. He returned panting. They looked at Freddie stretched out peacefully and obliviously. Isolt walked over to where he lay, his shoulders propped up against the wall and his head dangling to the side. She held the lamp up over him. He was dead.

Christopher took the white chair outside and sat down. Isolt took the carton of leftovers out of her black bag and placed it beside the corpse. She packed her stuff and went outside to Christopher. Light was creeping in under the edges of the sky, like a golden hand lifting the lid of darkness up off the world. The birds were jubilant.

"What are you doing, Christopher?" she asked.

"Oh! . . . eh . . ." He jumped off the chair and plunged back inside the cottage. Isolt took the chair in one arm and closed the front door, putting the chain on.

"Get your stuff. We'll pay our last respects and leave," she said.

Christopher opened the carton of Vietnamese food and shovelled a handful into his mouth. He did not close his mouth or chew and when he leaned over it fell out again. He emptied the rest of the contents over the Giant's lifeless chest.

"What are you doing, Christopher?"

"He was a son to me, like I was the father I never had."

"It's not the first time in history a father allowed his son to be killed."

Christopher was weeping. Isolt did not reach out to him for she knew he was not there. He was far away, faltering through some dark orbit, his giant wings in tatters, fleeing in terror a damaged moon.

Freddie's corpse was still stiff. He had bruises over his long naked chest and face, blood dried around his nose, and his teeth had been knocked out. They must have beaten him up not realising he was so ill and fled when he died. They could be still out there. Freddie's lip was curled up over his broken teeth; it made his face look monstrous. Isolt thought of the gerbil running on the wheel. She felt pity for the toothless, wombless woman having this doomed monstrosity fire his last load into her.

Christopher ran about the house in a frenzy, trying to stuff all he could into his numerous shopping carts.

"Leave it, Christopher. We can't take it all. We have to clear out before the corpse rots or the Dutch return."

"My toolbox! My TV!"

"All right, Mr. Monk, take those. Let's go."

They packed four shopping-carts and put them in the hall. To try to tidy and sort out the debris was impossible. They wrapped some used syringes in tissue and put them in a plastic bag along with the contents of the ashtrays. At last they stood over the fallen Giant.

"Should we say a prayer?" Christopher asked sheepishly.

"What about checking his pockets?" Isolt said.

Christopher stuck his hands in the filthy denim pockets of the corpse.

"Look! A piece of hash."

They sat and rolled a joint. Isolt glanced at the ceiling which still harboured the frozen visions the giant interpreted each night. Christopher made a clumsy attempt at the sign of the cross and blew the smoke into the corpse's cavernous mouth. The smoke swam inside the mouth and left it, billowing into the air. Isolt watched.

"I hate to ruin the moment but don't waste it all on the poor dead bastard."

Christopher handed it to her. They sat on the floor with the corpse between them.

Christopher repeated, "I feel we should say a prayer."

"OK, make one up."

He was uncomfortable. "You're the book reader. The Irish Catholic. You must know something."

"I do, but none worth repeating."

"I remember something. I went to a Polish Catholic school as a kid. The Hail Holy Queen."

"Say it then."

Christopher stood up and clasped his hands. Isolt stood too.
"Ahem," he coughed.

"Hail Holy Queen, mother of mercy,
Hail our life, our sweetness and our hope,
To thee we cry, poor banished children of Eve,
To thee we send up our mournings and sufferings,
In this Valley of tears . . .

"Then it got kind of obscure, I could never remember the rest.

"Goodbye Giant,
I'll never forget you cried for me,
I loved you like a son,
I swear you were a saint,
I did my best to shelter you,
I couldn't cure your liver,
I could have protected you from your murderers,
I don't know why I didn't,
I feel I killed you or let you be killed,
Though it was in my power to save you.
I don't know, Freddie,
You wouldn't have lasted long anyway.
You should have had a little more discipline in your life,
I think,
I lectured you many a time,
All those porno flicks you jacked off to,
That's bad news man,
But you were a saint anyway,
Despite hurting all those birds,
You were better than any of those bitches,
Of that I am sure.
So goodbye, Freddie. You were the gentle Giant.
You were the one junkie I could trust.
Blessed Virgin, pray for us now and at the hour of our death,
And now is the hour of Freddie's death, or thereabouts.
In the name of the Father and of the Son . . .

"And the other one, who was that? The Virgin Mother?"

"No," Isolt said. "The Holy Trinity's an all-male club excluding
mothers, even if they are virgins."

"Who was it then?"

"The Holy Ghost."

"Where did he come in? I don't remember him."

"He was the dove that came down to Mary's window and got her pregnant."

"A bird got her pregnant?"

"It's just a story. Let's get out of here before we're up there in the clouds with Freddie."

"Let me finish."

"Fine." Isolt sighed as Christopher began.

> "Goodbye, I'll miss you, Freddie.
> Maybe the Dutch will be satisfied,
> And not come after us,
> You died so that we may live,
> If it works out that way,
> You were dying anyway,
> This way you died for a reason.
> Amen!"

Isolt turned to him. "Is that why you wouldn't come to his rescue? You thought he was the sacrificial lamb for those pricks?"

"Shit, Isolt, let's get out of here. Don't judge me. I don't know."

"Let's put his passport on his chest and call the police from a phone box. That's what we did when Becky died."

"I guess you loved her like I loved him."

"She was my best friend once. I never felt like a guardian. Still I would have saved her at any cost."

They left the cottage each dragging two shopping carts and Isolt had a bag of her own. They rang the police and then the British Embassy to tell them one of their subjects was dead at that address. As they sat in the RER station with all their stuff, Isolt turned to Christopher.

"I feel terrible. First time I met him he preserved my freedom, then he stopped my pain. I didn't rescue him. This is not the first time a father has allowed his son to be killed. We have a mother-hating, son-killing civilization. God the father not having been spawned by a woman demonstrated the refusal to deify the female. Adam gave birth to Eve. The Greeks had Zeus giving birth through his head. The snake was a symbol of the Goddess. In Ireland Saint Patrick rid the country of snakes. There were no snakes. He was driving femininity from the Godhead. That interfering Welshman polluting us with the Roman religion.

"Abraham would kill his son for God the Father. Where was that boy's mother? The sons were all sent to war throughout recorded history to be butchered. Woman were beaten and denied freedom. Even the new twentieth-century religions of Freud and his apostles believe their sons want to kill them and sleep with their wives. Men charge sons with such treachery, see the mother-child relationship in such a twisted way they hate the mother and would kill their sons. How could there be so much war if men weren't willing to sacrifice their sons?"

Christopher did not reply at first. As far as he was concerned the wolves had been fed and the full moon was not for two weeks.

"He liked you, Isolt. So hush with your ravings. We have to be silent now and grieve for him. You were the one female he did not insult. He said you were all right, that you were different from the rest."

"Well, I'm not."

"Yeah, I know. That's what I think too. You know one time when I was begging and you were down south, I was bummed out. I thought you were never coming back. A mother walked by with her little girl. And she gave the girl money to give to me. I swear the kid looked like a four-year-old version of you. I said out loud, 'Isolt!' as she gave me the money. That's exactly how you must have looked as a kid."

They looked down the tracks for the train but the tracks were empty.

Christopher sat back down. "This winter has gone on forever. And I don't know if spring will come now."

They booked into one of the cheap hotels, sleeping in separate beds. Christopher warned Isolt not to tell a soul about Freddie dying. He didn't want the attention. Christopher could not sleep. He sketched pictures of Freddie's face with the lip curled up and kept a collection of them in his bedside drawer. He was still scared of the Dutch exacting revenge so he let her sell the whiskey at the fountain.

She scored the hash and met him in a café and gave it to him. Every evening he remained back at the hotel drinking cough medicine.

There were two new dealers at the fountain; they were young Scottish boys. One was eighteen years old and one was twenty. They were tough and feared and worked together. George, the elder, had a fine Alsatian dog. Even the rowdy Germans were impressed. Christopher was upset that he had been replaced so completely. Six years he had stuck it out as dealer on the same turf and now nobody even asked for him. Everything had gone after Marie-Claire left him. Too much heroin. He hadn't saved his money to keep himself regularly supplied with merchandise. While he floundered about for a couple of months with no sure supply of hash there were young cats out there sharpening their claws. Things were bad indeed for the Hoodoo Man. He still had Isolt to train in. She did not have the class of Marie-Claire but she was truly easy-going and never moody. For a bird, that was a breath of fresh air.

Isolt hated her afternoon naps but she could not resist the impulse to escape. She would lie on the thin mattress of her hotel bed and get lost in a dark, oppressive sleep — straining against the tugging of the waking world.

Christopher was fretting in the corner of the room watching her come to her senses. She slept all the time, maybe as much as fifteen hours a day. When she was awake she had her nose stuck in novels or else she plodded about seeking out her friends, drinking and chattering. She was not a healthy influence for him as he reached this crossroads in his life. His time was running out at thirty-three years of age. Her inanity enraged him. This was the Hoodoo Man's cross, this half-wit slob of a beggar girl. One day he would rise above it all.

"What?" Isolt mumbled, stirring from the sticky web of sleep.

"I didn't say nothing," Christopher growled.

Isolt slid off the bed fully dressed. "Jesus! It's dark already."

Christopher took a breath, paused, then winced: "Isolt. I'm going to tell you something."

"What?"

"I went back to the cottage behind the big house in Meudon —

just to check on things. I opened the door and the smell hit me. Ugly, man, an ugly, godawful smell. I went to the living room and there was the fallen Giant exactly where he had been slain. I walked over to it, this dreadful shell as if a whole symphony was exploding in my head. The moment was magnified. I felt I was being observed. I knelt down and brushed my fingertips off his bare, purple hand. That touch. God help me. Nothing survives the death of the body. Nothing could escape from the weight of that terrible thing. I felt it. The Giant's all gone. Nothing except memories. Ach! I can't bear it. Alleluia! I thought I could hear a chorus singing, A-Lay-fucking-Loo-yaa. I backed off and stood up. I was being watched, I heard a rustling under some newspapers. RATS. They were staring at me. Two rats. I ran and left the door open.

"I rang the fire engine. Wandered about for hours. Went back. The door was closed. I went in. The smell was there but the Giant was gone. The Giant'd been there two weeks. I think his eyes were gone. I don't want to think about it. Remember the lip was curled. Well, there were no lips at all. Just a gap. Shit. I spent yesterday in a trance. Something snapped in me. I thought I was having a nervous break-down. I can't even tell you where I slept last night. I just lay down somewhere on the street and dozed. I walked miles and miles through the city. I couldn't look anyone in the eye. Today on the Metro I was sitting in front of this fifteen-year-old girl. She had a nice, slim body and expensive clothes. So I look at her face to see if that's pretty too. She was looking right at me. I must have looked crazed. How could she know I had just witnessed my best and last friend, lipless, eyeless, toothless, peeling and rotten. Some simple-minded, well-dressed, pretty girl. How could she know? The ugliness. All our lives on the street. I wish I had never been born. If I had been aborted like I should have been, my mother would have lived and taken care of my family. I broke my own family by my birth. Love has been nothing but confusion. I am living in wartime."

Isolt was lying on her bed with her eyes shut. She was silent for some time and then she said, "We should go to London, get married, and I'll get a job and go to the States."

Christopher whispered: "Leave Paris?"

"Look, we can't figure out the marriage bureaucracy here. We can do it in London. Then you can come back. There were some weirdo bikers at the fountain looking for you. Jim said they might have been Dutch. Nobody knows the story yet, but you need to leave the city for a bit. Didier was at the fountain later that night. He said the police found Freddie murdered in his house. He told them about us living there. Didier was freaking out. The police probably want us for the murder or something. We have to leave the city."

"Dig a tunnel under the sink and escape this town."

"Precisely." Isolt was brushing her hair and now she tied it back. "Look, I can make a ponytail now."

Christopher did not look.

Isolt left him fretting in his corner over the image of the neglected corpse of the dead Giant. She was not a nurturer. She did not take Christopher on hand so that she might reform or help him. Isolt was not an earth mother. If she thought of motherhood at all it was as if her womb was a raindrop, falling through time itself, ready to hit a surface and explode forming other smaller raindrops which would fall in turn and on and on . . . The huge falling ocean dissipating into a tiny, evaporating moist particle.

She turned a corner into a tabac to buy tobacco and papers. Looking at all the men in the cafés she wondered what all the women were doing at home. God has had a hysterectomy. We are all homeless until the stolen womb is reinstated.

Christopher had followed her. He was frantic.

"I've no drugs at all. How much money did you make today?"

"One hundred and thirty, but I have two whiskeys I'm off to sell now."

"I need some heroin."

"Look, I'll buy you a bottle of codeine. I'll even go into the chemist and get it for you. I haven't eaten yet. Let's go sell the bottles and eat in the Chinese on Rue Saint Denis."

"I'd really like some heroin. I feel suicidal. I want something to knock me out."

"Have a bottle of whiskey."

"You know I don't drink no more. You don't want to see me drunk, El Ribbo, I'll beat the shit out of you. Now give me the money. I'm sick of you sucking my brain dry for chit-chat and stories. You owe me. I'm giving you that green card, the key to the US. What do I get in return?"

"Europe. Just like you wanted. It was all your idea. If you want something to knock you out and you can't drink, why don't I hit you over the head with the bottle? I want something to eat, that's thirty francs, then some hash, that's one hundred francs, a few beers with the lads, that's fifty francs at least. So I need two hundred francs including this tobacco. I can give you maybe fifty francs."

"Fifty francs!!!"

"Look, if you come with me you can eat. I'll give you fifty francs for your codeine. I'll score the hash, meet you and give you half. Jesus, Christopher, that's reasonable. You're not my pimp."

"OK, done." He walked beside her, keeping a tight grip on her elbow.

Later that evening, after Isolt had scored hash from the Scottish dealers, she met Christopher hiding out in the café. He looked terrible. He stood reading *The Telegraph*, his tiny coffee cup empty on the counter. He kept his little finger entwined in the white delft handle in case the waiter took it away and he would lose his right to stand there.

"I need a little company. I think I'm cracking up." He choked back a sob.

Isolt said, "All right, let's go smoke a joint."

They took the Saint-Michel Metro one stop to Musée d'Orsay and sat at the end of that platform, smoking in relative silence. Isolt was in the mood for a few beers and some joking around. Christopher was a burden. They stepped up onto the next train. When the doors opened in Saint-Michel there was a blind dwarf with heavy glasses and a white stick; his clothes were soiled and crumpled and he clutched a plastic shopping bag. Isolt stepped off beside him and observed his hobbled step onto the train. She said to Christopher, "At least we are not as badly off as that."

Christopher snorted. "Girl. There are three hundred people on the platform who all look as if they're doing all right. This is a lesson. Why do you have to compare yourself to the most miserable motherfucker in the entire place to feel good about yourself?"

Isolt laughed. "OK. I'll see you later."

"We're going home now, Isolt."

"I need some beers and light company."

"Where is your heart? Your loyalty? I have just seen and smelt my best friend's two-week-old rat-eaten corpse. Any time now I need to grieve for Freddie by thinking about him, I have to overcome that stinking spectacle. He cried for my troubles and all I can associate him with is a carcass. Something I don't want to think about. I don't even want to catch anybody's eyes in case I see their corpse. I can't be alone. I'm scared of what I might do. No lips, no eyes. That touch of death. My fingers are still cold with it. I knew automatically that this was my next real step. My own death. Maybe your death too. Christ, I hope I don't kill anyone. Just to wake me up from this frame of mind . . ."

"You're going to be a barrel of laughs tonight. OK, I'll come back to the hotel on one condition, that I can drink my beer without a lecture on the evils of alcohol."

"Thank you, Isolt. You will not go unrewarded for this. I love you."

"No, you don't."

"No, I don't."

In the Arab shop as Isolt stocked up on bottles of beer, Christopher hovered around her. "If you drink all that beer you'll be getting up and down all night having to piss. That would drive me crazy if I was you."

When they got back to the hotel Isolt drank her beers, went up and down the stairs to the toilet and listened to Christopher rant and rave. They smoked the hash and finally lay down on their respective beds. To Isolt's surprise Christopher came to her and instead of a blow job he wanted to have sex.

"I'll plug you good like an old pork pig, you frog leg, puff-ball girl." He laughed recklessly as he climbed on top.

As Isolt turned the corner she saw Taffy begging in the street. He sat grinning with his stump on display, his crutches leaning against the wall, his red and green mohawk haircut, a nose ring and now a beautiful red, blue and yellow parrot on his shoulder.

"Fokdewueeen! Fokdewueeen!"

Isolt stalled, puzzled. "What is your bird saying?"

Taffy was proud as punch. "I trained her. I trained her meself."

"Fokdewueeen! Fokdewueeen!"

"Is that French?" Isolt asked, straining her ears.

"French? No." Taffy looked a little sheepish. "I know you told me to teach it French but . . . what the fuck, I didn't."

"Well what language is it?"

"Listen," Taffy instructed patiently.

"Fokdewueeen! Fokdewueeen!"

"Fokeweeen?" Isolt said.

"Fuck the queen."

"Fokdewueeen! Fokdewueeen!"

Isolt laughed. "Oh! Fuck the queen!"

"Fokdewueeen! Fokdewueeen!"

"Does it have to keep doing that? It's getting on my nerves."

"No — not all the time. My girlfriend hates it. It ate one of her rats. Still it's a good begging prop. Are you going to the fountain?"

"No, to the Cluny. Why don't you come? I'm sure they'll allow the bird in. I'll buy you a beer."

"All right." He stood up. The bird spread its wings and Taffy ducked. "Ahh! don't do that. I keep thinking it's going to shit on me."

Isolt and Taffy walked together to the Cluny café, the one place that didn't seem to mind their presence on a regular basis. Paranoia was a symptom of the beggar lifestyle. Everywhere she went she felt like a beggar, even if she was paying money for goods and services. The Cluny staff knew they were beggars but they always sat in the corner away from the bar and drank their weight in beer. Jack, the robust owner, would give a free beer to any of the girls that would kiss him. Isolt obliged every time even if he was a bit slobbery and old. The waiters came and talked, occasionally slipping out to the street for a joint with them. One time one of them gave all the centime tips in the plate to Fred on the way out. There was nowhere else like that in Paris, and sometimes they even ran out on the bill, or angered Jack by snorting coke and smack from off the table tops, bringing in their dogs in heat to drag their periods across the café floor. They would lie low for a while and then come back in ones or twos on their best behaviour until forgiven.

Melonie had taken a break from Gunther's squat and the humbling kindness of the German government. She had brought hash down and wanted to sell it. It was her eighteenth birthday.

"It smells funny," Fred said.

"Don't like to think where she put it," Cloggie intoned.

"Where's Ali?" Melonie asked.

"He ran off with the Christian Ladies on the Born Again bus," Rory said.

"Yeah! Ali used to be all messed up on drugs. Now he's all messed up on Jesus," Larry said.

"It's no improvement," sighed Fred, who was standing up behind them. "Last time I met him he was trying to tell me about the fall of paradise and he was getting the story all fucked up. Something about a geezer called Saddam in a park with his bird, Eve."

"Fuck paradise!" Melonie said. "If I was Eve I'd eat the apple all over again. Paradise is a sell-out."

"A fucking holiday brochure," agreed Rory.

"Fokdewueeen!"

"Wot?" Melonie said in shock.

"Jesus, that bird of yours gets on my tits," Fred grumbled to a grinning proud Taffy.

"Sit down mate, you're making me nervous," Larry said to Fred.

Fred stared at him.

"Why don't you sit down, man?" Cloggie begged.

"I forgot," Fred said.

"Ali is going to marry one of the hags on the bus. Ali, of all people, a convert. Settling down," Isolt told Melonie.

"He was saying he had a pain in his stomach," Rory said. "And one of the ladies just put her hand on it and it was healed."

"I wonder what would happen if he had a pain in his dick." Isolt raised her eyebrows.

"Do you know who I was thinking about the other day, Isolt?" Melonie smiled. "That Finnish bloke who vanished without trace the night we did the weird drugs down south."

"Oh yeah! Did anyone ever hear tell of him again?" Isolt asked.

Rory shrugged. "Finnish John, the Foreign Legion refugee? God knows where that poor bastard went. Probably freaked out really badly and lost it. Maybe he's dead. I wonder why he never showed up again? I forgot all about him."

"Scary how you can disappear without a trace," Melonie said. "And where is that awful cunt, Black Jack?" she inquired as she tipped her litre beer towards her and glugged at its surface.

"Black Jack. Jesus. What a disaster! He's sulking, I guess," Larry said. "He must be the most annoying wanker I have ever had the displeasure to room with. Filthy little bollix. He and Ali were fighting and he gave Ali a knife and said, "Go ahead and stab me." So Ali stuck it in his arm and when he tried to make a big thing out of it, we told him he was an idiot. Then last night we were all sitting around watching this fire-eater on a unicycle and Black Jack was sitting in a lotus position in front of him and kind of out from the crowd. Suddenly in all the swirling of the flames his hair caught alight. He didn't notice at first why we were all pissing ourselves laughing. Then you should have seen his face. He leapt up and started slapping his head and squealing like a pig. He ran and leapt into the fountain at Place des Innocents."

"Why are you all so mean to him?" Isolt said.

"Mean to who?" Black Jack was behind her.

Rory laughed and winked at Isolt. "Isolt, have you heard Black Jack's new name? It's Jack Thing."

"Don't you start, mate," Black Jack glowered.

Rory took up his guitar and started strumming to the tune of "Wild Thing,"

> Jack Thing,
> You are disgusting,
> You are so boring,
> And your feet stink,
> I think I hate you,
> But I wanna know for sure.

Amid the laughter Black Jack stomped off to the bar to get a beer. He and Melonie were always the butt of everyone's jokes. They were the easiest ones in the crowd to be cruel to. Isolt couldn't figure out why, just a certain vulnerability and their irritating personalities and they kept coming back for more.

"Hey, Melanoma. You're back. I thought I smelt something fishy," Black Jack said.

"Wot?"

"Leave off her, Jack, she's got some goodies," Rory said.

"It smells funny." Fred sniffed the air.

"Don't think about it. It does the job," Larry said.

"Why don't you sit down?" Jack asked Fred.

"Couldn't be bothered," Fred shrugged.

"He forgot," Rory sneered. "His epileptic brain is a bit soggy."

"I'm not epileptic," Fred said.

"Fokdewueeen!" the bird screeched and fluttered its wings.

"Rory told me Freddie's dead," Melonie said.

"Yeah," Isolt nodded. "Didier told us he was found in the house. He OD'd I guess."

"How come you didn't find him?" Larry asked. "I mean you and Christopher and Freddie were thick as thieves in that house."

"We moved out ages before. Christopher wanted to live back in Paris. I think they had a falling out over drugs or money."

"I heard he was murdered," Fred said.

"Christopher killed him." Rory winked at Isolt.

"Payman and Freddie are both dead since I left, and Omi, thank God, is dying," Melonie said.

"Christopher's apostles are dropping like flies," Isolt sighed.

"I'm sorry about Freddie," Taffy said to Isolt.

Rory was dismissive: "I never liked the guy, he was an embarrassment. You could never bring birds around him."

"Can't say I liked him much either," Melonie admitted.

"There's room in hell for all of us," Larry said wisely.

Poubelle Pete came in and sat down with them.

"Any good pickings?" Isolt asked him. She turned to Melonie: "He picks through the bins all day."

"I hope you wash your hands, mate," Larry said.

They all looked at his hands; they were grey with dirt and his long fingernails were blackened. His hair was matted together and torn apart to make dread locks. His face was smeared with dirt and his wool sweater was long and ripped at the sleeves. His denim jeans were so encased with filth they looked like leather. He was only about twenty-five years old and too proud to beg. The son of two teachers in Wolverhampton, England, he had dropped acid in polytechnic and never looked back. He followed the itinerant, New-Age convoy around Britain but fell out with them for mysterious reasons, went to India and Nepal for a year and had arrived recently in France.

"I'll buy you a beer, Pete." Isolt dug in her pockets.

Jack the Patron threw his eyes up to heaven when he saw the new addition. He asked Isolt if her friend ever took a shower. Isolt told him she doubted if he did. Jack wanted a kiss to let him stay. Isolt obliged, leaning forward to kiss his flabby cheek; he turned his head and caught her lips. Isolt made a face and carried the beer back to the table.

"So!" Poubelle Pete said, taking his beer and slurping it noisily. "I hear you might be splitting to London."

"Yeah." Isolt nodded. "I'm all Parised out, I think."

"I hate the English," Taffy stated.

"You can't beg in England," Black Jack said.

"I can get the dole."

"I'll tell you how." Black Jack puffed up his chest.

"No," Larry insisted, "don't start him off on that subject. He's king of the Department of Health and Social Security. He goes on for hours and hours, he knows every loophole on every form."

"Where are you going to stay?" Melonie asked.

"With Jim Glass. You lot remember him, he was here for ages."

"Jim's cool." Rory nodded. "Is he still with that ugly Belgian chick?"

"Yep! Then I'll find a squat. Rory and I went through it all before, remember, Rory? Just after Becky died and we left Amsterdam."

"That's right. Christ, that was about two and a half years ago. It doesn't seem that long at all. Maybe I'll go over too and do a bit of motorcycle courier shit. Though I have to get a new bike. I'll have to save up. How much money will you be taking over?"

"Too much," Isolt said.

"Is head-the-ball going too?" Rory asked.

"Christopher? Yes, he is."

They all groaned.

"Christopher is OK, we have a good laugh together," Isolt defended him.

"You're both as crazy as each other anyway," Larry conceded.

"I'm tired of begging. I want to go off on a trip somewhere."

"Where?" Taffy asked, feeding beer to the bird from the end of a straw.

"Maybe America," Isolt said.

"Americans are dumb," Fred stated.

"I hate Americans," Taffy agreed.

"They're not playing with a full deck," Larry said.

"Not the full shilling," Rory nodded.

"Three sandwiches short of a picnic," Black Jack added.

"Well, I don't see any of yous lot up for a Nobel Prize lately," Isolt snorted.

"Look at Ronald Reagan, and he's their President. He's a laughing-stock," Black Jack said.

"You lot have Thatcher," Isolt said.

"That's why I'm in France," Fred said.

"Look at you. You're voluntarily moving to Thatcher's Britain to make some dough to go to Reagan's America," Black Jack said.

"Reagan went out last year," Isolt said.

"I'm boycotting Britain until Thatcher falls from power," Black Jack said.

"I'm sure she misses you," Larry said. "A black beggar on the dole."

"I'm not black," Black Jack hissed.

"Oh, God, he's still at this nonsense." Melonie sighed and signaled for a waiter.

A waiter came over and they ordered another round of litre beers.

"Will you miss me?" Isolt asked.

"I'm used to missing people," Larry said.

"Go to Hamburg to Jim," Rory said. "England is a dump."

"At least it's not fucking Ireland," Fred said.

"I want to make money and I know I won't in Hamburg," Isolt told him. "Maybe learn to type. Get my act together. Take a word processing course. I don't want to beg again."

"Me neither," Rory said. "I should buy a bike and get back to the real world. I hate begging. It's becoming boring having to go out every day. It almost feels like a job."

"Yeah," Black Jack nodded. "I might go down and do some grape-picking this year."

"I guess I could go back to Scunthorpe and do a government training thing in carpentry or something," Fred said.

"When you learn German they place you in jobs sometimes.

Jim does this janitor's job part time. I might make money cleaning houses. Either that or dealing," Melonie said.

"Does Jim still have that pathetic mutt?" Isolt asked.

Melonie nodded. "It's grown up now. The thing is scared of its own shadow."

"I have to get my act together," Poubelle Pete nodded solemnly. "I might save up for a horse and cart."

They all laughed. Poubelle Pete looked puzzled.

"A horse and cart!" Rory shook his head.

"That just shows how far you've gone, mate," Larry said. "That's going further down the scale."

Poubelle Pete smiled. "But I've dreamt about it these past years. Whenever I think I've gone daft in the head. A horse and cart. That's my only realisable dream."

Isolt raised her heavy glass with both hands: "I propose a toast. To a realisable dream, a horse and cart for every woman, child and man in the land."

They raised their glasses, clinking them, and drank greedily.

Hung over, Isolt walked the next morning to the Pompidou Centre. She felt weak and her stomach was upset. A cigarette tasted chalky and only made her feel worse. She entered the big modern building from the side, glided down the escalator and went to the record listening room on the ground floor. The drinking had gone on last night till the bar closed at three A.M. and then she had dragged them all for another beer at a twenty-four-hour café. They had all begged off at four A.M. and she had been left with a near-catatonic Poubelle Pete for company and a last beer.

She had stood at sunrise watching Poubelle Pete vomit into a bin beside the Seine and she had taken a marker and drawn an X on it so that he would know not to root in it the next day on his rounds. He said it was amazing the things people threw away. Engagement rings and a goldfish skeleton in a margarine tub. Then he collapsed under a bridge and she had tried to sleep there with him but had risen after a few hours, freezing cold.

They came to the Pompidou a couple of times a week. The record listening place was free and warm and the only chance they got to listen to music of their choice. Isolt chose a Velvet Underground album and sat down. She put her earphones on and closed her eyes.

> I am a lazy son,
> I never get things done,
> But here comes the ocean,
> Here comes the sea.

She sat with her eyes closed, concentrating until the music was over. The Pompidou Centre was a beggar's home away from home. She drank some water at the fountain and descended to the basement toilet. When she washed her hands, she noticed that her face was blotchy and puffy and she turned away in disgust.

Walking through the streets back to the hotel she thought of Christopher's trancelike walk after he had touched Freddie's corpse. Christopher said he had felt shrunken in the streets, that the buildings rose like cliffs on either side and though he was invisible to the crowds as he meandered through them, he had felt a presence watching his progress from miles above. Perhaps a giant rat as tall as a skyscraper eyeing him hungrily, perhaps Freddie's ghost or perhaps even a God. Isolt felt tiny among the buildings, as if she was moving through a remote canyon, but she did not feel she was being observed. In fact the only things now that made her feel she even existed were her upset stomach and flushed cheeks. She went into the hotel room. Christopher was sleeping on his bed so without a word she flopped down on her own and slept till it was dark.

Christopher took all his belongings to the American church. He set them up. Blenders, juicers, black and white portable TV, lampshade, bicycle wheel and his white chair, among other things, were stacked in the downstairs lobby. He sold two bottles of whiskey to the janitor for the price he normally sold one, just for the privilege of having a sale.

The blenders and juicers were bought immediately by the American students. A young man named Chip came and offered him one hundred francs for the TV. They agreed to one hundred and fifty. Chip had nothing on him but a five-hundred-franc note. Christopher called George the janitor over but he had no change.

"Hold on. You watch my stuff and I'll get change from upstairs."

Christopher mounted the wide staircase and when he got to the top he went out the front door and did not stop running till he reached the market crowds.

"Five hundred francs for a TV, a chair, a lampshade and a bicycle wheel. The guy can't complain."

He hadn't felt so pleased with himself in a long time.

Isolt found a note in the lining of her jacket. She recognised it at once. It was the note given to her in the autumn she was in Athens three and a half years ago by an Irish couple who cleaned the toilets of the hotel. She was meant to give it to the girl's sister in Paris. She thought she had lost it and had always felt guilty that she had not delivered it. She could lose her mother's silver ring yet in spite of herself keep a random note. A go-between for strangers between Athens and Paris. The girl was supposed to work in the furniture section of the Samaritaine department store. The manager said she had left to work in an English book shop beside Concorde. On her way out she spotted Ali in his shiny black top hat and Mexican poncho.

"Ali, what are you doing here?"

"Isolt, man, good to see you."

They kissed twice on the cheeks.

"So Ali, news is you've given up drugs and are going straight."

"Straight as an arrow, man."

"What, pray, are you doing in the furniture section of Samaritaine? Shopping for your bridal suite?"

"Sort of, man. I'm marrying this old lady soon. I'll have papers in France."

"Do you have sex with her and everything?" Isolt asked.

"I have sex with Jesus Christ, man," Ali enthused. "Drrrrrrrrrr!"

He made machine gun sounds. He was holding a roll of wallpaper; he opened it a little and showed Isolt the pattern.

"I'm buying wall-paper for the double-decker bus. Do you like it? Trippy, huh?"

Isolt inspected it. "Very trippy indeed, Ali." She showed him the note. "I've just found this important message I have to deliver to someone's sister at Place de la Concorde. I'm on a mission — do you want to escort me?"

Ali snatched the note from her hand and stuffed it in his mouth and ate it.

"Mmmmm, thanks Isolt. Must protect all secrets."

Isolt stared at him for a while and then turned to leave.

"Good luck with the redecoration of Christianity, Ali."

"Yeah, man. Jesus loves you. Break a leg." He waved after her.

The hotel room was smothered in Christopher's newspapers.

Isolt bristled to see them. "You think you're a radical and you read all that shit."

"I don't know of any decent radical papers. I still would overthrow the government despite what I read."

"Not to ameliorate the situation. You just want a bigger piece of the pie. You're a fake."

"I keep telling you, I'm a closet anarchist."

They sat in most nights, scoring points, getting stoned. It was time to leave. They procrastinated. They tried to save more money. They were saving nothing. Christopher was waiting to leave on a full moon.

Finally Isolt bought a rucksack and packed. Christopher stuffed his paperwork into the rucksack along with his rags, then he strapped his tool-kit to his bicycle frame. They went to Saint-Lazare. At the entrance of the train station there was a wild man blackened by dirt lying on the steps. His teeth were broken and rotten and his face twisted. His matted hair was crawling with creatures; he had a dirty, long brown beard; his nose was broken. Though it was winter he wore no shirt and his exposed torso was covered in scars and fresh cuts. He writhed on the ground calling out to passersby for money. People were too afraid to approach.

Christopher was excited by this spectacle.

"Look. That man is Barabbas."

"Do you know him?"

"No. But he is the living embodiment of Barabbas. He's the modern, mortal Barabbas."

Christopher took a ten-franc coin from Isolt and went up to him. Barabbas twisted and turned in the dirt; he roared at Christopher as he approached and Christopher leaned over and offered the coin. Barabbas snatched it out of his hand and spat on the ground. As

Christopher walked back to Isolt, the man flung the coin at the wall and it ricocheted off the brick and down onto the street. Christopher was thrilled: "Barabbas," he said, "Fucking Barabbas."

Isolt shook her head. "I thought we were a mess."

Christopher admonished her: "Girl, remember the lesson of the blind midget."

They had no tickets for the train and were made to stand in the carriage intersection. Isolt looked out of the window while he read a newspaper. The countryside rolled by. She was thinking of Christopher and she did not know what she was doing. *It's no use, my arms are too weak. I can't catch and I can't throw.* She remained looking out of the window for the entire duration of the journey. Always amazed that there was any countryside left at all.

They stood on the boat deck and saw France disappear before their very eyes. Christopher shuddered.

"The end of an era." He sighed.

Isolt thought of Taffy and how he had left the English coast with two legs and arrived in France with one. She associated this awful car ferry with him and his story. Riding away on Taffy's waves towards a dingy land even he had wanted to hobble away from. She felt it already, seeing the crew and the tourist families and the faded promotional posters on the ship's walls; the English boredom. The seagulls whirled chaotically about the mast. They glided loosely on wind currents and dove squawking onto the deck. The boat left a silver slug-trail in the metallic green sea. It was getting dark. Night formed around them like a fragile shell.

"The French were kind to me," Christopher said. "Once when I was really down and out and just arrived in Paris, I was sleeping on a bench in the Metro. A woman came up to me, a respectable woman, nicely dressed, middle-aged and she put a fifty-franc note into the top pocket of my jacket. That was a brave thing to do. I saw her out of the corner of my eye as she left like a thief in the night. Imagine a woman like that touching a man like me, down in the Metro. This is truly the end of an era."

Christopher closed his eyes and racked his brains for an Iggy Pop song to fit the occasion. He believed that basically everything in life had a parallel in an Iggy Pop song, you just had to find it. He put his arm around Isolt and singing in her ear he led her inside the ship away from the egg of sorrowful night into the artificial, cruel light.

> I'm walking down the streets of chance,
> Where the chances are slim or none,
> And the intentions unjust.

Part Three

10

The English Boredom

CHRISTOPHER WAS unhappy at the prospect of a new city to conquer. He concentrated on Isolt's explanation of the underground system. As she talked, she saw names that conjured up images of the banality that she associated with this city: Ealing, Islington, Mile End, Swiss Cottage, Stockwell, Hampstead Heath. They took the yellow Circle line to the Embankment and shuffled down white-tiled corridors through grim-faced rush hour crowds, heavily burdened with Christopher's luggage. The brown Bakerloo line was less packed. Isolt stared past her reflection to the blackened brick tunnel walls. She listened to the robotic announcement at Waterloo: MIND THE GAP, it resounded soullessy, STAND CLEAR OF THE DOORS PLEASE. MIND THE GAP. They got out at Elephant and Castle, the end of the line. She had done this many times before.

Christopher was twisting and turning, avidly taking in his new environment.

"How come we're the only white people getting off here? What kind of place are you bringing me to? A fucking jungle?"

She looked at Christopher — a black raincoat down to his feet; black, baggy, ill-fitting trousers; wrecked running shoes; a navy sweater with wool balls hanging like dingle berries from the fabric; out of his filthy shirt-collar his yellow, dirt-ringed neck protruded, the skin texture between his collar bone and neck similar to a tiny loose triangle of testicle, as wrinkled and criss-crossed as elephant skin. His eyes were so deeply brown the dilated black pupil and the iris seemed one. His skin was yellow, his nose had blackheads and even the whites of his eyes looked red and grey. His mustache glistened with snot and sweat and his face was small, encircled as it was by his abundance of curly, jet-black hair — small and poverty-stricken, unenlightened and mean. Isolt surveyed this tiny Hispanic man from the North American Third World.

"The end of the line. Elephant and Castle. We're now at the mercy of the British. This is the empire that the sun never sets on. It never rises either. In fact you never see the sun here. This is an empire on its last legs; beware of that, it is as dangerous as a dying wasp at the end of summer. We are going to live with the poor, the immigrants, refugees, exiles. The Brits have a strong caste system here. They adhere rigidly to their own class and they despise outsiders. Xenophobia; anybody past the very white cliffs of Dover is a wog. We are no longer beggars, we are scavengers. You are a kind of dirty yellow and I'm just another poor Paddy and my color is green."

"All right, Paddy, I don't need a tour guide. I travel the world to get high." Christopher mounted the flight of steps, grunting. "Let's find these feeble friends of yours and abuse their hospitality."

But even Christopher recoiled on reaching the street. They could not take the bicycle on the bus so they walked about a mile and a half. He shook his head as they made their way past the huge grey tower blocks of council flats and grotty dwarfed pubs with names of royalty. There was a giant flyover on the Old Kent Road like a concrete bridge to relieve traffic. It sat in the middle of the road and stretched for maybe a quarter of a mile. It was ugly, intrusive and inhuman. Cars hating people. Sprayed in huge white letters on its grey side was the graffiti prayer, NO MORE FLYOVERS. They walked up Darwin Street and crossed over to East Street. He saw more monolithic blocks of apartments linked by cement walkways. They had names like Taplow, Little Wendover, Big Wendover, Ashendon. Ashendon was the first one he saw and so he thought of ash every time he looked at them. In the shadows of these monstrosities crouched older red-bricked post-World War II blocks of flats with wooden doors. Isolt assured him that he would grow used to it all.

"There's trash everywhere," he moaned. "The people look so sick and undernourished and downright nasty."

Isolt led him through a stinking cement entrance to a tower block.

ABANDON HOPE ALL YE WHO ENTER HERE was scrawled in white paint.

Christopher snorted: "A nation of comedians."

They stood waiting for the lift.

"This lift is known as the death ride. If you stand on the left it comes to a sudden stop. Everyone has to keep to the right and it rattles all the way." She smiled, enjoying his apprehension.

Jim Glass sat on a fold-up chair by the table with a cat on his knee. He was on the fifth floor of the Little Wendover tower block. The government built it in the sixties, those ugly sixties when they thought it would be a wonderful alternative to a sprawling mass of pokey little council houses for its ever-swelling population. They really might have believed there could be streets in the sky and communities would survive and thrive. Jim felt sorry for himself and his thousands of hapless neighbours living like rats in stacked-up cages. This particular flat was a squat. He had found it three years previously while staying in a Bed and Breakfast with his wife and their baby girl. His wife had made it into a home with stereo, rubber plants, bookshelves, sofa. There were two bedrooms; his little girl had a mattress on the floor and even a play-house with all her teddy bears in one room.

Their name had just come up for a council flat in the vicinity and though his wife was elated at the long-awaited security, he felt a little doomed. Absentmindedly he stroked Cloud, the gray and white tomcat. He felt like a cup of tea but was too lazy to make it himself. The kitchen was his wife's territory. He was not usually up before her but today they were expecting guests. A glimmer of a smile settled on his pale face. He liked Isolt and knew her well. He did not know Christopher. He had never seen Isolt with a man before.

Jim himself had grown up in a council house in Glasgow. He had three sisters, all doing well in their ascent into the lower middle-class. His mother was a stern and hard-working Catholic woman. His father, a Protestant, had long professed his hatred of Catholicism and his in-laws and remained at odds with his family because of it. Every week his mother would drag her little brood in their best Sunday suits to Mass and his father would curse them ferociously. Jim was the youngest and as far as he could recall his parents had slept in different rooms and never talked to each other. His father was increasingly alienated from the entire family and withdrew altogether from its activities. Jim could remember seeing the old bastard hunched over at the breakfast table, slurping his milky tea, or passing him on the stairs, a great blundering shadow. He had never in his whole life thought of anything to say to him.

Jim had begun drinking at the age of fourteen with his friends, and during his later school years drinking and reading books were all he did, much to his poor mother's chagrin. He played lead guitar in a local punk band but when they split, due to musical differences as he liked to say with a wry smile, he had never joined anything again.

On leaving school at the age of sixteen he did not actively seek employment but sat with a select group of unemployed local luminaries in the pubs as they spent their fortnightly dole checks obliterating mind and body with sloppy ales and biting whiskeys. The rest of the days were outstanding only in their titanic emptiness. Under the grey sky of a working-class Glasgow in an unyielding, cramped council house, lying hour after hour in his damp bed reading the classics of modern fiction, frightened at the lengths to which he had taken his own recalcitrance, subjected to his mother's scorn; his father was a bad dream, a belligerent ghost with feet in the fire and bigot eyes on the TV; his sisters dull, thrifty and bossy, leaving one after another for pastures not much less gray than his own. All his good friends were gone to London to look for work or were becoming junkies or growing stupid in the pubs week by week. He fled at the age of twenty-one to the continent.

In Paris he was content to be in exile. He was sensitive and dreamed of writing a great novel. A callow young man with no formal education and no funds beyond the first week, he fell among beggars. He was sickly and prone to bronchial trouble exacerbated by the many cigarettes he sucked to the bitter bone throughout his waking hours. He was a beggar now, determined to play the part, abandoning himself to all manner of fates. He relished the abuse and derision and stopped washing completely.

With a head full of lice and a soul full of venomous mirth, he impressed Isolt with his extensive reading and acerbic wit. She met him outside the Pompidou Centre when she was sixteen. She was just off the boat and had latched onto Irish Jim. Isolt secretly worshipped

Jim Glass, the Scotsman, for she fancied he was a poet as he read the same books as she and frequently scribbled in a notebook. Scottish Jim, unaware of his silent admirer, assumed she and Irish Jim were a couple. Isolt was glad of this confusion in retrospect as her infatuation dimmed and she found the courage to talk with him in a normal manner.

It was a habit of Jim's to save some money and take the train up to Brussels every few months. He would tear around the sparkling, clean capital of Belgium on a massive binge from pub to pub, searching for inspiration. On one of these occasions he tried to chat up a barmaid. To his surprise the barmaid not only responded favourably to his crude advances but returned to Paris with him that night.

She told him she was thirty-seven years old and was married to an Arab. She had two teenage boys. She said her husband beat her and was cruel but that he loved the boys. Her husband's family lived in the same house in Brussels and treated her like a slave. To them she was an empty vessel through which her sons had come. She began to drink heavily, soured by the thought of returning home. She was sick of it all and though she claimed she loved her sons she never mentioned them after the night they met in the bar.

Everybody in Paris was taken aback at Jim's cumbersome souvenir of Brussels. She was overweight, pasty-faced, old, and she wore thick-framed glasses. Her hair was mousy and hung shoulder-length with a severe fringe. She looked gloomy and mildly psychotic. Isolt had not met them then for she had only stayed four months in Paris before embarking on a journey that took her to Spain, Italy and onto the Middle East, where after much meandering she had settled in Israel. She heard later that everyone felt sorry for Jim, lumbered as he was with this hefty cargo. Jim, however, berated anyone who dared to suggest a severance of this unlikely relationship. Finally, he and Emma left for Rome.

They lived in a little two-person green tent pitched in a campsite in the city of Rome. They paid the rent erratically but the lady in charge took a liking to them and offered them a reduced rate if they would act as semi-caretakers of the site. Jim went on drunken benders, not returning for days on end. Emma wept in the cluttered tent, guzzling whiskey, lying on the blanket writhing in the oppressive heat, depressed and confused. One day Jim returned to find the manager shouting rudely in Italian and Emma lying in a wretched state, having not left the tent in days. The manager, a middle-aged Italian widow, and Jim dragged Emma out of the tent and locked her in the games room in the main complex. A doctor examined the filthy, distraught creature on the blistered ping-pong table among the Space Invader and pinball machines. When he announced that she was in about her fourth or fifth month of pregnancy, the widow gesticulated wildly and embraced the now subdued Emma. She led her off like a docile lamb to be bathed and groomed.

Jim was left in the shabby games room. It was the end of a beautiful August day; he stood swooning slightly in the wondrous effulgence of the evening. Inadvertently he began to sob and with his soft unworked hands, he spun the handles of an ancient table-top football machine. The ludicrous plastic dummy players cartwheeled through the blur of his watery eyes, spirals flying from side to side on the ball-less pitch, discs of meaninglessness thumping the air in perfect unison. He rocked the table back and forth, big tears plopping onto the shredded green baize.

He tidied their tent, cleaning out two giant black bags' worth of debris for her arrival back home.

Emma was a natural linguist. She could already speak Italian comfortably after six months and with her big belly on display she spun a whole plethora of stories around her dubious circumstances. She made good money begging and Jim never abandoned her for long periods of time again. Ignoring his reservations about her age and the possibilities of a miscarriage or a damaged fetus, she drank heavily and smoked like a chimney.

By December they were the only ones in the campsite. Coming home swaying and leaning against each other, Emma's coat stretched and buttoned crudely around her enormous belly, Jim frail, thin, full of drunken bravado, giggling shamefully, mocking the forlorn, green, little tent that stood alone and conspicuous in the empty field. The widow had given them the key and he cherished the absurdity of ceremoniously opening the giant, wrought-iron gates for himself and his pregnant mistress, locking them afterwards with the enormous key.

She gave birth, a pauper woman to a pauper girl, in the hospital in Rome while Jim was begging outside a cathedral on Christmas Day.

They took the child home that night and swaddling her in blankets placed her in a cardboard box among all the rubbish and mess in the tiny tent. Huddled under blankets they marvelled with flashlights at the tiny, snuffling animal they had created.

The two-person tent was now a home for three. Begging together as a family, Emma breast-feeding on the street, they touched the Italian soul for all it was worth. Unfortunately it was not worth enough for two drinking habits, food, baby equipment and rent. The hospital was persistent in pestering them for expenses incurred and the widow, frustrated and disgusted by this wayward family, felt they had squeezed all charity and good-will out of her. They had not paid rent in months and did not clean the toilets or cut the hedges as promised. She heard them return late every night, drunk as lords, clanging the huge gates and fumbling with the iron key in the lock. Once, she unzipped the tent and found the baby alone in her cardboard box, red faced, stinking and rashed from her unchanged nappy.

Emma, Jim and their unnamed, two-month-old bundle of joy were deported from Italy in March. Isolt met them in Paris and invited them to stay in her tiny room in the squat. She was with Becky at the time. They all lay in the same direction, cocooned in separate sleeping bags. The baby was put in an empty disposable-nappy box at their heads in case one of them crushed or smothered her in their stupors. The normally cranky Becky had taken it all in good spirit. She seemed delighted at the novelty of a baby in their midst and gave Emma advice on the rigors of child-rearing. The four had even gone out together to cafés with the baby in tow. This precarious harmony could only last so long in such conditions and one day Becky flung a used syringe into the nappy box, mistaking it for the rubbish bin. Emma flew into hysterics on discovering the bloodied needle next to her child's face and even the placid Isolt distrusted her friend's dubious excuse, never having known Becky to throw anything in the rubbish bin in her life.

They left for Glasgow as soon as they had begged enough money for the boat and bus. Emma paced the deck of the car ferry uncertainly. She took the ugly greed of the seagulls as a bad omen. Clutching her little girl tightly to her breast, she bit her lip, thinking of the trials looming at Dover. She had an overwhelming urge to throw her baby into the furling water so far below, and scurried inside for fear of succumbing to this murderous impulse.

As they sat on the night bus from London to Glasgow, Emma told Jim she would be embarrassed to arrive at his mother's house with a nameless child. Somewhere in the north of England they christened the child Justine.

Jim's mother was not impressed and relations deteriorated further when Jim was arrested for shoplifting that month. His father kept the TV turned up louder than necessary. Emma was shocked at his refusal even to look in the baby's direction.

They took off at midsummer to London, staying in B & B's and getting the dole. Jim married Emma in a registry office so he could claim for her and the baby as well. At last they found a squat and at first Emma cried seeing the state of it. She got to work, though, and made it a home. She cooked the meals and kept the place immaculate. Justine grew up speaking French in the heart of Elephant and Castle.

Isolt came from Amsterdam with Rory one spring after Becky died in Paris. She stayed in a squat in the area for a year, becoming a steadfast friend, before flitting off the next spring to Paris. Just a week ago, they had received a postcard heralding her imminent arrival. The postcard had a picture of the Saint-Michel fountain and Jim felt a pang of nostalgia for his old freedom and the charms of the nearby continent.

Emma had Justine in her arms and was distrustfully eyeing Christopher's tool-box and bicycle which now stood in her hallway. Since Isolt had seen her last she had changed dramatically. She had lost weight, her hair was dyed red and was down to her elbows. Instead of the thick glasses she had contact lenses. She stood a full head taller than Christopher and Isolt and a few inches taller than her husband.

"You look great," Isolt marvelled enviously.

Emma acknowledged the compliment with a dry smile.

"How long will you stay?"

"Not long, just till we find a place of our own — a week maybe."

"It could take longer than that."

"Hopefully not."

Jim was lurking in the background, slightly ashamed at his wife's lack of hospitality to an old friend, but he said not a word. They all sat down and Emma cradled the sleepy Justine resentfully.

"You've lost weight," Isolt said, trying to endear herself to this changed woman.

"I've stopped drinking."

"Really? That's great," Isolt nodded half-heartedly. "Do either of you know Christopher? He was in Paris for about six years. He wasn't really on the begging circuit but thereabouts."

Jim nodded, smiling softly. "Aye, sure I know, you were the wee American dealer. I heard a good deal about you."

Christopher sat on his best behaviour and rolled a joint.

"Can I smoke with the child here?" he inquired.

"Go ahead," Jim said. "I'll roll a cigarette if I may." He leaned over and snatched the tobacco packet.

"I don't smoke cigarettes any more, you know," Emma told Isolt.

Christopher rolled one joint for himself and one for the company as was his wont.

Emma relaxed after the joint and Christopher gave Justine a little teddy bear they had stolen in the boat gift shop.

"She has lots of teddies," Emma said, bringing Isolt into the adjoining room and showing her Justine's playhouse, which was indeed host to a multitude of stuffed bears of all shapes and sizes. Isolt was duly humbled at her own lack of originality.

"How will you subsist here?" Jim asked Christopher.

"Dealing is out for the moment as I've no capital."

"What do you think of the Elephant so far?"

Christopher smiled: "The Elephant. Is that the local lingo? Well it ain't Beverly Hills, that's for sure."

"Home sordid home!" Jim nodded, looking out of the window.

"I'm glad we've come in spring. Summer is right around the corner."

"Aye," Jim agreed, still a little stunned by Isolt's new boyfriend. He was a hard-core street man if ever Jim had seen one.

"What are the winters like here?" Christopher asked.

"Ach well, not too bad; cold, though, and long. It doesn't snow every year. I didn't even have a pair of gloves all last year," Jim said, still staring out of the window, and then added as a mournful after-thought, "But it would have been nice."

Isolt and Christopher sat on the couch. The family had gone off shopping at East Street market. Christopher looked about him.

"This sure is nice for a squat. Fucking lovely."

"In England squatting is different. Once you break into an empty place and change the lock it takes six months to evict you through the courts. You can have electricity and hot water quite easily. There is a squatting agency on the Old Kent Road run by a bunch of anarchists. They even have a newsletter they deliver squat to squat. SHIP it's called, or have they changed it to SNOW? Anyway we'll go there tomorrow. I know a few people around here, all of them squatters; they might hear of places through the grapevine. I have a feeling Emma is not too disposed to our arrival. She's lost weight, given up all vices and is now a good mother. She's not the same old Emma." Isolt sighed sadly.

"What's the cat's name?" Christopher said.

"Cloud. I hate that cat. He never leaves me alone."

Cloud eyed them disdainfully from an armchair. Christopher shook his head and folded his arms. "The things I could do to that cat."

Isolt knew Elephant and Castle. Christopher contented himself to look and learn. She called in on people, sharing her cigarettes and hash in exchange, she hoped, for information on abandoned squat-table flats. First call was 28a Innis House on East Street, her old squat where now an Irish girl and her boyfriend stayed in the one-room studio. The Irish girl made them tea while her unruly dog Glip flung himself with abandon at them and tried to hump Christopher's leg. Her boyfriend was a short, black man with bleached blond hair. He sold Christopher some codeine DF118 tablets and they were on their way. 33a Darwin Street was their next destination, where an English girl and an Argentinian biker girl lived and fought over the same man, Sea-mus the Irish Bastard. They swapped news and tried Innis House again, this time encountering a bumbling, blond, bearded, good-na-tured, stuttering South African refugee whose dark squat was crawl-ing with reptiles, including several snakes draped on the furniture or huddled in corners. He showed Christopher his light blue stateless person's passport and told him, "I was so a-a-angry with my p-parents for moving to South Africa. They said they felt limited in Scotland. I s-s-said s-s-so you came here to limit s-somebody else!" He laughed feverishly, driving his long fingernails through his blond hair.

They visited Niki the Greek with one arm who shared a squat with a broken, alcoholic, illiterate Irishman and a grey-haired, crusty old queer with watery eyes and shaky hands, who slept on a mattress in the kitchen. He told them to try Kinglake Street where Oliver's new room-mate was dealing now. They called it a day and returned without many prospects but bolstered by all the chatting, tea, hash and cigarettes they had consumed on their mammoth squat crawl.

Emma had made a vegetarian soup. Isolt had not expected to be fed but Jim insisted. She felt uncomfortable in the house, though Jim tried to assuage such doubts. Justine was a quiet, mannerly child who played alone in her room for considerable lengths of time. Emma would not allow a TV in the house as she believed it was detrimental to Justine's development. Jim had a considerable collection of African music which was constantly playing in the background.

Down in the pub that night Jim admitted to Isolt and Christopher that he was bored stiff and had not reckoned on stultifying domesticity so few years after escaping his own version of it in Glasgow. Christopher listened intently and shook his head, sipping his mineral water.

"Do you write any more, Jim? I never got to read any of your stuff," Isolt asked.

Jim's face was downcast. "Ach, no. Emma got me a typewriter a while back and I wrote out little sketches. I've almost given up on that idea, to tell the truth."

Cloud was as inhospitable as its mistress. It hissed in Christopher's face as he sprawled out on the couch that night. Christopher grabbed it by the scruff of its neck and threw it against the wall. The malevolent creature spent the night dive-bombing from the back of the couch onto Isolt's chest. Christopher eventually got up and slapped it hard, locking it in the bathroom. They heard it tear down the shelves and screech menacingly.

Isolt sat for two days in the social security office making a claim. On the second day she was next to a young man who could neither read nor write very ably. His T-shirt had SUBHUMAN emblazoned on it. Periodically he sucked deeply from a plastic bag of glue and exhaled ecstatically. Isolt was helping to fill in his form while she waited for her number to be called. She surveyed his body: a spiderweb tattoo on the side of his forehead with a spider hanging down to his chin; several women's names in ink tattoos, Millwall football team, KUNG-FOO, MOTHER, a syringe at the appropriate vein, FISO tattooed on his neck, LOVE and HAT across the knuckles of his hand.

"Isn't it supposed to be LOVE and HATE?" she asked curiously.

"Wot?"

"L-O-V-E on one set of knuckles and H-A-T-E on the other. You have LOVE and HAT."

"Oh yeah, that." He stared down at his grubby hand sheepishly. "I started on the wrong finger."

"No!" Isolt was staring at his hand.

"Yeah!" He laughed. "I was fucked out of me head on glue and I started doing it, right? So I did the H A and fucking T, right? and then I ran out of bleeding fingers."

"And who is FISO?" She pointed to his neck.

"Psycho!" he stated emphatically.

"F-I-S-O, fiso." She was bewildered.

"Nah." He grew impatient with her. "Psycho! It's a trick spelling, innit?"

Isolt went back to his form. "Date of birth?" she asked hopelessly.

On the third infuriating day of wrestling with a tight-fisted bureaucracy, she was promised a cheque for a single woman in a squat, no rent allowance. It was to be delivered to Wendover in two weeks. They refused her an emergency payment. Those days were over. England was not the happy-go-lucky welfare state it had been. As she was Irish they owed her one, and if it came in the form of free money she was grateful to accept any such reparation.

She called into 28a and talked to Oonagh, the Irish girl. The wretched mutt Glip had a cast on its back leg. Oonagh agreed to lend this stranger a tenner until her dole came through. Isolt thanked her.

"We've all been there," she shrugged.

Isolt bought potatoes, carrots, onions and tobacco at the market and headed back to Christopher.

"Have you been looking for a place?" she asked him.

"No, man. I'm too hungry to use up my energy. Did you get some money?"

"The government won't cough up for two weeks. I borrowed some from the girl in my old squat and this is the result." She handed him the groceries.

Christopher took them off to cook. Isolt noticed several Perrier bottles beside his bicycle.

"Where did you get the money for Perrier?"

"I borrowed twenty quid from Emma. They got their dole today. It's all spent now, sweet thing, so don't bug me."

"On fucking Perrier." Isolt saw that his pupils were dilated and his movements cushioned. "You're high as shit."

"I ran into that crazy black man, Sinbad — Sinbad Coin to be precise, that's a crazy name for a black man. His people are West Indian he says . . ."

"What the fuck are you talking about?"

"The black guy with the blond hair. I asked him if it was natural. He didn't like that too much. Ha! Ha! He was giving the dog a good kicking in the arse, as they say here."

"You bought more tablets?"

"Yeah, bitch, and some high class water to wash them down with. Quit crowding me when I'm cooking. I need to concentrate or I'll fuck up your dinner and then you'll be whining."

"Can I have some at least? Please."

He gave her four. "This'll get you off. Now go away."

"Be careful, Isolt," Jim advised. "I hope you know what you're doing."

"Christopher's cool. You should talk to him more, you would appreciate him. He's got some great stories about Detroit and the Army and Paris. When we were leaving Paris we passed this beggar by the steps of Saint-Lazare, a wretched man if I ever saw one, and Christopher was convinced he was Barabbas."

"Barabbas?" Jim looked incredulous.

"Who is Barabbas?" Emma asked.

"He's the murdering rapist the mob chose to free rather than Jesus," Jim explained.

"I want a green card. I can't think of any better plan than going to America. It's business," Isolt said.

"It looks like more than just that," Emma said.

"Who does he think I am?" Jim pondered. "Maybe Lazarus."

"And who is Lazarus?" Emma asked kneeling as she dressed the co-operative Justine in a pair of pajamas.

"When he was brought back from the dead he wept," Jim responded.

Emma glared at him and turned to Isolt.

"You know I don't like this shit-hole any more than Jim, but it is better than the streets. I won't have Justine grow up on the streets. I know you think I am boring but that's OK with me. Now I concentrate on her. Jim is not my dream man, my knight in shining armour, my Mr. Right. He will never work. He won't even lift his cup from the table and bring it to the kitchen. I do even that for him. It is lucky for a man of his means to have a servant, is it not? I do the laundry, the cooking, the cleaning, all, I do all. He barely looks at Justine, you'd think he was her brother not her father, he never talks to her or plays with her. He reads books all day and listens to his African music and once a week he brings her to the library. That's all. All his friends come here with their drugs and drink and they look on me as the proverbial nagging wife. I am just trying to do my best for this poor child who it is a miracle is alive after all I did and my age."

Justine, who had been standing half-naked with only her pajama-bottoms on, began to cry. Emma had inadvertently been squeezing her arm. Jim got up and in an unusual display of affection scooped her into his arms.

"Look what you've done now, Emma, for fuck's sake." He kissed her on the forehead: "There, there! Everything will be all right."

"Why don't I baby-sit and you two go out dancing?" Isolt offered. "Remember you said you wanted to dance, that you hadn't danced in years."

Emma shrugged. "London is not a dancing town."

Jim handed Justine back to her mother. "We'll find somewhere. Let's go out next week on dole day."

Emma led Justine to her bedroom. "You don't like to dance, you just want to get drunk and for me that's no fun any more."

Jim shrugged helplessly.

The next week they availed of her offer on condition that she did not let Christopher be alone with Justine. Emma was in her early forties now. She put on some make-up and washed her hair. She wore a white blouse, and a black mini-skirt and high heels. Jim shyly wore a clean navy shirt and black trousers. He was thirty years old. They left the apartment walking down the grim, endless corridor and trustingly descended in the filthy grating death-ride. They wandered rather sadly and self-consciously into the late spring evening in search of a place to dance. Jim had insisted that he would find such a place in the centre of London. A night with electric stars. He took Emma's hand tentatively and kissed it. A knight in tinsel armour.

Isolt was borrowing money in dribs and drabs from every acquaintance she had. The Argentinian biker girl furnished a tenner, her English room-mate a fiver, the South African, king of the reptiles, gave her three quid. She even rang up a cousin in the city and walked the five miles to his office to get a tenner, promising to ring home to Ireland and tell them she was all right — but she knew he would do this for her. They ate their usual diet of potatoes, vegetables and onions, all boiled in Emma's kitchen.

"Why aren't you getting thin on my diet?" Christopher mused. "Either there is something wrong with your metabolism or you're eating hamburgers on the sly. You still look awful. I'm glad you're growing your hair, with short hair you kind of look like a man."

Despite never exchanging a civil word, they were having sex every night on the couch, much to the consternation of Cloud.

Water dripped into a basin from a leak in the roof. It was a wet day and they were at SNOW, the squatting agency on the Old Kent Road. Christopher took all the leaflets and read them closely. There were huge maps of the local housing estates covering the walls, with red thumbtacks at strategic points marking possible empty council property. Isolt wrote down all the addresses on the margins of Christopher's newspaper. He was chatting with a middle-aged Russian with a woollen hat containing all his grey dreadlocks. Another anarchist holding the fort was familiar to Isolt. He was an old Scotsman called Billy and had once cornered her for a whole evening in his squat expounding on various subjects. She kept her back turned, eavesdropping a little as he ranted at length to two Italian junkies:

". . . the pigeon now is just a scavenger, a sky-rat if you will, all you foreigners like to stand at Trafalgar Square and be covered by the filthy diseased bastards. Have you taken a closer look at them by any chance? A very pariah among the feathered tribes is the pigeon . . ."

Taking Christopher by the arm, she led him outside. The sun was shining now and the ground was wet.

"See that laundrette? That's where we can buy smack. And see that building way up there beside the Gin Palace?" Christopher pointed. "The Russian bloke told me that the cops started watching the laundrette and were using that place as an observation post of sorts. A few hundred people were going into the laundrette every day and only a handful had washing. Using their remarkable powers of detection they put two and two together and tried to bust the whole operation but the observation point got fire-bombed."

"It's nice to see you so interested in local folklore, but we got shit to do," Isolt said.

"Let's check out all these addresses," he agreed promptly. "I want to find a home so I can occupy myself with bigger and better things. In fact that shall be my epitaph. When I die I want you to have that inscribed on my tombstone: ON TO BIGGER AND BETTER THINGS."

"Will I be around when you die?" Isolt asked.

"You might be the death of me. Now wait here a few minutes. How much money do we have?"

"No way, I've only a tenner. We have to eat."

"Always thinking of that big stomach of yours, aren't you? Have a little discipline. The full moon is approaching. I will be fasting, of course. You should join me. Besides, if you don't eat for a day or two and drink only water, you should feel the almighty buzz you get off the first joint after abstinence. Enough to send you to the moon, and I mean that literally."

"The only powder you'll get in the laundrette for a tenner is washing powder."

"The trouble with you, El Ribbo, is that you're so middle-class." He put out his hand. "Give it up!"

She relinquished the tenner. As he strode up the road and stood peering into the windows of the laundrette in his long black coat, he reminded her of an old, bent crow and she thought of him suddenly spreading his wings and taking off for the moon; sky-rat, a very pariah among the feathered tribes.

Emma had enough of Christopher constantly boiling potatoes in the kitchen and leaving a mess. They had grown lazy with their luggage and the living room was in a state of disarray. Their debt magnified and Emma began to question tobacco, Perrier and the *Daily Telegraph* as bare necessities.

One day Cloud was floating about the apartment hungrily when only Isolt and Christopher were there listening to some Dutch rock and roll guy called John Brood being blasted from the speakers. They munched on codeine tablets. The animal rubbed off her legs and meowed pitifully. Isolt went to the cupboard to find the poor cat some food, but when she got there the cupboard was bare. Isolt smiled to herself, stoned. And so the poor cat got none. Cloud stood rigidly in the doorway so Isolt, more persistent than her nursery rhyme predecessor, searched the fridge which was also bare. Finally, not liking the militant attitude of the cat, she opened the only food she could find, a can of peas. She poured the cold peas into the plastic cat dish.

"I'm going to my cousin to scab more money off him. It's a last resort. All reservoirs of generosity have run dry in Elephant and Castle and we haven't eaten anything but dry spuds in four days. I don't like to do this; my family don't hear from me in years and all the news they get is that I'm on the scrounge again with no fixed abode."

"Well, give them a ring and tell them you've hit some hard times. Play politics, girl, get some cash from them."

"Why don't you ring yours then if you're such a politician?"

"Quit bothering me. I don't know what's got into you these days. Have you just eaten chocolate? You get like that on chocolate, I notice. All birds do. I'll accompany you on your walk, will that cheer you up? I haven't been out of this slum since we arrived a month ago; this can't be all there is to London."

Isolt selected some clothes from her pile of rags and put them in a bundle. "I need a quick bath. I'm beginning to smell myself as I sit."

"Birds should wash. For a girl you sure are dirty, I must say. Men can go on long voyages without a sponge but birds pass their sell-by date fast. Men are built more efficiently. Birds should stay in the nest. They can't go a month without all kinds of discharge and all that good shit. Hey, bitch, what are you standing there for hanging on to every word? Go wash your funky ass. Frankly I want to be gone before our gracious hosts return and the vibes get ugly. I can't bear to watch you grovel to them either. This is a squat, damn it. All property is theft. How dare they think they have precedence over this place? But no, you're so fucking middle-class with your cousin in business or journalism or whatever the fool does, you ingratiate yourself to them and squirm when they hint at our departure. That doesn't ease matters; it only shows vulnerability. I don't give a fuck about them, the old dragon has that guy pussy-whipped to the max and their child is some kind of retard, it never reacts to anything. I don't have your convent manners, my dear, and I don't have any use for them in my life. I'm not running a popularity poll."

"You wouldn't want to," Isolt shouted as she sloshed about in her shallow bath.

When she came out, Christopher was reading his newspaper intently. She dropped the towel and put on her black leggings.

"Jesus, hurry up, I told you your body should never see the daylight." Christopher glanced over. "Damn, it's unbelievable that that's the body of a twenty-year-old. I hate to think what it'll be like at fifty."

Isolt pulled on her black T-shirt and then sniffed the air. "Jesus what's that smell?" She felt her chest. "Aggggh, yukkkk! Fucking hell!" She pulled it off and sniffed it. "The cat's pissed on my clothes." She ripped off her leggings.

Christopher was laughing. "Man, that cat watched you choose those clothes and leave them in a heap. I saw it come over with a mean look on its face and squat on the pile without even bothering to glance in my direction. That cat must hate being given some lousy cold peas for supper!"

Isolt chose another shirt and pair of leggings. She laced up her Doc Martens.

Christopher stood up. "I'll avenge you, sweet thing. Can't have the cat think he's boss here." He took the cowering animal by the scruff to the kitchen and shoved its face under the tap in the sink. The cat clawed and fought but Christopher squeezed its neck and held it steadily under the gushing water. Isolt intervened, trying to pull

Christopher away, and when that failed she turned off the tap. The cat panted and trembled on the floor. Christopher rinsed his scraped and bloody hands. He was exhilarated.

"Your friends may consider themselves CHRISTOPHERIZED."

Emma, Jim and Justine returned to find a black tide mark on the bath, their shampoo used up, clothes and newspapers scattered all over the living room, the stereo still on, their cat soaking wet under the bed and the peas they were going to eat for tea in the cat dish.

Oliver lived with a Rastafarian man called Caesar. He held court as the dealer while Caesar preferred to keep a low profile. The squat was in good condition, wallpapered and carpeted with a kitchen kept clean by Caesar who was fastidiously tidy. Oliver had a permanent leer. He finished every muddled pronouncement with the leer, as if it were an explanation in itself. He had a huge stomach, a red bulbous nose, a bald head with thin black hair hanging over big crooked ears, sunken slitty eyes, the diseased leer and ten fat warty fingers that rolled joint after joint in front of the TV.

"Who sent you?" he asked the first time at the door.

"Niki the Greek with one arm," Isolt said.

There were couches against each wall facing the TV. They sat on one and Oliver collapsed into another.

"You know, come to think of it," Isolt said, "I think I might have been here before a year or two ago. I came with Vinnie, the Irish dealer who lived in Innis House. I used to hang out with him a lot."

"Yeah, he was a good geezer all right," Oliver nodded. "But I think you must have been upstairs where Sam Steal the painter lives with Desperate Dave. I used to live up there with him but moved down here when this place was vacated. So you met Sam?"

"I must have. Only very briefly."

There was a knock on the door and Caesar got up and went into the hall. He returned trailed by a miserable-looking human being who reminded Isolt of Payman, enthralled by some ineffable anguish.

"This is Desperate Dave from upstairs," Oliver courteously introduced everyone. "This is . . ."

"Isolt and Christopher," Isolt said.

"Christopher is from America," Oliver said proudly.

Desperate Dave sat down. He wrung his hands.

"Sam's a lazy bastard, he won't go out and get any booze no more. Won't even walk down the bleeding steps and get some fags. Been lying in bed for a day now without budging. I'm fed up with him so I came down here."

Oliver said: "Oh yeah? Not like Sam Steal, he's always pacing and roaring and going into terrible conniptions up there. I've never seen him off the grog but mind you it's probably for the best, he hasn't had a dry spell for years."

A few days later they sat in the pub across the road. It was truly English in its peculiar dreariness and sense of strong inviolable working-class traditions. Oliver treated Christopher to a coke and Isolt to a warm pint of lager. Desperate Dave came in too and sat with them.

"Sam's a boring bastard. He hasn't even cashed his dole check, first time that's happened. He won't talk to me neither. I'm fed up with sitting up there drinking with him."

"Oh leave off it, will you?" Oliver said, getting irritated. "Forget about Sam a while. He's a fucking artist, mate. They're broody, you know what I mean? It's not easy to live with genius, Dave, you have to let him have his sulks and tantrums, all geniuses are like that." He nodded towards Christopher whom he always addressed over Isolt.

"I never met a genius," Christopher said, taking his straw out of his glass and wiping the rim with a napkin before he drank.

"Are you on the dry, mate?" Oliver asked him sympathetically.

"I haven't had a drink in six years or so. I wasn't an alcoholic but I prefer drugs," Christopher said softly. "Drinking makes people stupid."

"Sure it does, mate. Good for you." Oliver slurped his pint with ulcerous lips.

"I'll drink to that," Isolt said, and they all clinked glasses. "We should get our check in the afternoon post. It's about time."

"You don't seem American," Oliver said to Christopher.

Christopher laughed ironically. "No? Well, I'm not from New York or LA. I'm from Detroit. Motor City. You can't get more Detroit than me. Europeans have a kind of naive concept of what an American is."

"Yeah," Oliver agreed. "We think Yanks are dumb but I guess they can't be, seeing as they kick everybody's ass who gets in their way. I can respect that."

"Let's say we have a grudging admiration that thinly disguises a deep loathing." Isolt tried to rile Christopher.

"Listen to Paddy here. Don't let your old lady get away with that." Oliver winked at Christopher.

"The Irish," Christopher snorted. "The fucking super-race. How come so many of the super-race are over here then? London has the highest concentration of Paddies in the world. I know that for a fact."

Isolt shrugged. "The super-race has an unemployment problem at the moment."

"I'm not prejudiced or nothing," Oliver said, and ordered four more pints with all the indulgence of a grand old colonist. "Some of me best mates have been Micks and I loved each and every one of them, but in all fairness, the Irish aren't exactly famed for their intelligence neither, eh?"

Isolt took a deep breath: "The Irish are stupid, French are snobs, Caribbean people are lazy, Italians are slobs, Spanish are loud, Scandinavians are bland, Germans are violent, Swiss are elitist, Austrians are Germans in disguise, Greeks are greasy and the Turks are torturers, Belgian people are nondescript, Americans are phoney, Australians are vulgar, New Zealanders are envious, Nigerians smell, Canadians are just marginally better adjusted Americans, Japanese are ants, there are far too many Chinese, South Americans are thieves, Pakistanis are greedy, Indians are pagans, Arabs are molesters, Israelis are rude, Filipinos are born to be domestics, Welsh are losers, East Europeans are dowdy, Albanians are invisible, Sicilians are thugs, the Scots are as mean as the Jews, Iranians are fanatics, Koreans are the Irish of Asia, the Asians are all the same, the Irish are the blacks of Europe, Africans are savages. So where exactly does that leave the English?"

"Lords and masters!" Oliver said confidently. "You're the first normal Yank I've met. All the others lacked cop-on. That's what it is."

"How many have you met?" Christopher asked, perplexed.

"You're the first in the Elephant, that's for sure, you poor bastard."

"America is tough," Christopher said carefully. "Those TV programmes — deliberately misleading, over-sentimentalized because we are so hard-hearted. Remember this is the Devil's Workshop we are talking about, you'll see. Wait till you get there. It's the belly of the beast. Don't think you know anything about the US. It's bigger than you and more ruthless. It will hook you in and eat you alive and you will love it. You'll never want to come back. It's the dream-machine, baby."

"Then why are you in exile?" Oliver asked.

"I had enough. I was weary. But this young child here is just out of the cradle and wide-eyed, she's craving it all."

Desperate Dave, who had gone off to check up on Sam, came shuffling back as they were debating whether to buy another round.

"There's something the matter with Sam," Dave pleaded desperately.

Oliver pulled his huge body out of the chair and waddled off after him, puffing and panting up all the cement steps. Isolt and Christopher followed. Oliver went in alone and came out after a few minutes.

"Yeah, there's something the matter with Sam all right, you pillock," Oliver almost gloated. "He's dead."

Desperate Dave quivered weakly as Christopher held on to his arm to support him.

"Sam's brown bread, mate!" Oliver leered. "Brown bread!"

The huge body of the fifty-five-year-old Sam Steal the painter was carried down in a coffin and cremated somewhere in London by his estranged upper-class family. Desperate Dave never recovered from the discovery that he had been partying with a corpse for seven days. He could not stay there any longer and moved in with two Kurdish brothers down the street.

Isolt and Christopher had at last found a home. They moved in the day Sam Steal the painter was cremated, changing the locks and their dole address. Christopher stole two rolls of wallpaper from Emma and Jim's cupboard.

Sam Steal's possessions and clothes were still there. His unfinished picture was standing on an easel. His photographs were on the wall. They moved in among this past life and left it all intact out of laziness, superstition and mock deference. They felt more like curators of the Sam Steal museum than inhabitants of their own place. The mattress where he had died still bore a death indentation and a curious smell so they leaned it up against the wall. They found an old pool table which they covered with some spare carpet and used as a bed. The bath was full of painting materials and bricks. There were three bedrooms. The one with a hole in the roof they called the element room since they were on the top floor and the atmosphere therein was entirely indebted to the atmosphere thereout.

Isolt was out most days looking for work. Christopher spent the days rooting in the skips and bringing home modest treasures. He proved quite ingenious, putting a makeshift radio and tape player together so they could listen to the World Service and BBC Radio 4 all day and night. They put the fridge in the corner and cooked on a little one-ring camping gas container he had brought from Paris. He had stolen a saucepan from Emma and they ate off paper plates with their fingers and drank from paper cups.

Apart from the front door there was only one door left on its hinges. The boiler in the kitchen had blown up, the walls were blackened and every surface had a layer of grease. They put a curtain over the door and taped it to the frame and never entered the kitchen again. The rest of the walls were covered in ugly violent red and black murals by Sam the painter. Christopher was too short and inexperienced to put up the stolen wallpaper in whole strips so he cut it into large rectangles which he stuck on the wall.

Emma, Jim and little Justine called over after a month had calmed their nerves and soothed their tempers. Isolt was down at the job centre trying to set up an interview. Christopher crept into the hall and peered through the peep-hole.

"It's us," Emma shouted impatiently. "*C'est nous!*"

Christopher, remembering the stolen wallpaper and the saucepan, panicked and ran to the living room. He started tearing the rectangles off the wall in a frenzy. They heard him thrash about demonically like a bee in a biscuit tin and departed in bad sorts. Relations were effectively terminated between the two parties.

Isolt came home and Christopher was sitting by the easel with the unfinished last work.

"Look, I'm painting the street outside."

Isolt looked and saw a rust-coloured stripe drawn through Sam's otherwise chaotic abstract work.

"See, that's the buildings. There's no other color for the sky."

"What about windows?"

"I never thought of them."

He leapt up to attend to the pot of boiling potatoes on the gas ring.

The floor was covered in strips of white wallpaper, the walls now even uglier with bits of wallpaper dangling from the murals like half-picked scabs.

The block of flats was flanked by scaffolding. On those beautiful summer days, Isolt and Christopher would bring the armchair cushions out through the living room window and sit on the scaffolding smoking joints and listening to plays on Radio 4. Christopher told stories and surveyed his new dominions. Isolt, listless and self-enclosed, chain-smoking and consuming beer, barely listened. The curators of the Sam Steal Museum rested among the fragile, drunken ghosts of his life's last belongings, his presence washing over them like fermented, stale smells. He had failed and no one came to look and wonder. Guards of his legacy — a worthless little girl and a low-life Lucifer.

11

No More Flyovers

CRUCIFY HER with little birds' beaks. Little beaks through her hands, silencing their faint overlooked song, tiny wings spluttering in the drizzle-driven air. With an anchor weigh her down, she's bending back under low-lying skies, fighting with moves as lazy as honey these dark rivers inside.

This for the pock-marked branch of the family tree: the bride in her muddy dress writhing in the tangled ditch, the groom gone mad in the itchy little town which threw them up like early flowers, died before full bloom. The father taps his foot in the hall, a rattle in his chest, bloated into a terrified statue by the black swarms approaching from eastern hills.

They came at heavy dusk whirling towards sullen lights.

Crucify her with broken spines of old women. Earthquake sighs in windowless corridors of power, spaghetti junction graveyards cut out from stone, this world that once raised you has left you alone, cut off from the aching streets, whittled to the bone, lava trickling in veins, crusted at holes in her palms, she's going down further than where the dead lie, flip her over as she pushes past a house where night falls nightly, linger for a breath by your bride and groom. Stolen children, hands crossed in laps, screaming like birds.

Crucify her down by the seashore. The salt stings the wound, the yellow foam infects the sore. With an anchor weigh her down, she's bending back under drizzle-driven skies, struggling against these sorry rivers inside.

*

Isolt woke up and got dressed to go to her temporary clerical job. Christopher lay on the pool table observing her. It was a beautiful early August day. There had been a heat wave that year and they were enjoying a long, hot summer.

"It's a nice day to get married, you old hag," he grinned. Isolt smiled and gave him the money needed to tie this strange knot.

At work she and two other temps took an early lunch and rushed to the registry office on the Walworth Road. She was worried that Christopher would take the money and run off to France and so she was relieved to see his bicycle locked to the railings outside the building. He was eating peanuts out of a pharmaceutical bag and had created a puddle of shells on the floor around him. They were married without much ado. Christopher kept his fingers crossed throughout the vows.

Isolt walked back with her two co-workers and gave back the ring she had borrowed from one of the office girls. The boss had put flowers on her desk. She sat beside the fax machine in the afternoon and one of the girls cooed, "Oooh! It doesn't seem right; faxing on your wedding day."

Isolt laughed, embarrassed at all the attention.

She returned home that evening and waited for Christopher so that they might have a personal celebration, for she was under strict instructions not to utter a word to any of her friends. She had bought a ginger cake in the newsagents and she put two candles in it. Placing the flowers on the mantelpiece she sat on the armchair in the living room smoking. There was a one-eyed cat from next door that prowled on the scaffolding and she almost lured it inside for company. She read a library book on the Ancient Greeks and ate from the ample supply of fruit in the fridge. She nibbled away at the cake. Finally, she burst into tears and stomped out, slamming the door. She blubbered all the way across the sun-scorched green and over to Darwin Street. Sally, the English girl, and her Argentine friend were home bitching about Seamus the Irish Bastard. They took her in and she told them the whole story. Cecilia put on her thigh-high leather boots, packed on some orange foundation and painted her lips slut red. She pronounced all men scum and the three took the underground to Camden Town to frolic with the Tuesday night Hell's Angels till the wee hours.

Christopher was adamant in his refusal to return to his bride that night. He would help her get her visa and then send her packing, but he had no intention of consummating the marriage. There was something in that piece of paper and the sexual act that was irrevocable. The Romans got you in the end and the woman was yours till death do you part.

He was lonely and would have liked the company but he was high and moderately content. Wheeling his bicycle along the road he stopped to roll a joint in front of the flyover. All of a sudden he was struck by the tragedy of the graffiti: NO MORE FLYOVERS scrawled in seven-foot letters on its grey flank. The flyover was so piteously ugly and so obviously an obstruction in the community that he laughed out loud, incredulous. Here he was, a middle-aged man from Motor City, momentarily taken aback by the effect of cars on people.

Racing through the traffic as the lights came on he took off towards the heart of London. He pedalled over the great bridge on the Thames towards the Houses of Parliament and past Big Ben. He flew past New Scotland Yard and on and on down Victoria Street. Peacock — his claws clutching the rubber pedals, his marvellous wings guiding the non-polluting vehicle towards no particular destination, just the thrill of the lonely ride, his blue-feathered neck craning forward, his beady eyes streaming crocodile tears. There was no full moon, just a shining fingernail-clipping in the sky, but Christopher rode and did not have to fly tonight. He was a groom, finally legal on this his chosen continent after years of deportation fears. The cross would be easier to bear. "No more flyovers, motherfucker. I am thirty-four next week. My life as Christ is over. No more flyovers, the age of Christ is dead."

And so he rode his bicycle gleefully while Rome burned.

Isolt got a permanent job as a chambermaid in a block of luxury apartments run by Saudi Arabians near St James's Park. Christopher handed out flyers for a Romanian Fortune Teller at Piccadilly Circus but argued with the mean old gypsy and then retired. Most of the time he preferred to potter about the house waiting for Isolt to return. He formed a routine for everything and insisted that they adhere rigidly to it. His attitude to the vicissitudes of daily existence bordered on ritualistic. They did not have sex after the marriage;

whenever Isolt attempted to make a pass at him on the pool table he would scold her.

"Now, now, Isolt, don't get frisky."

On the Walworth Road there was a camping equipment shop where they went to replenish their gas can for cooking. One of the employees was a short red-headed girl who beamed radiantly at them in a most unnerving and singular fashion. She told them her name was Veronica and that she was engaged to an army man. She began clandestinely to give them discounts on their gas and Christopher was delighted, considering it a minor conquest of the natives.

Isolt struggled with giant hoovers, pushed trolleys of cleaning equipment through long, dark corridors, lugged black bags of rubbish down to the basement and hurled them like featherweight carcasses into the skip. She mopped the giant lobby, moved tables and chairs, made king-size beds, scrubbed sinks and bathtubs, lifted hair from the drains, scraped shit from the white enamel bowls, polished windows and bedside tables, picked clothes from the floor, swept crumbs off kitchen surfaces, scoured congealed food from oven tops, poured bleach into the fridge. She wore a cream overall coat and her army boots.

Often she would be trapped in the lift with some of the wives choking on perfume, dazzled by heavy gold jewelry, shiny silks, gaudy leather jackets and fur coats, sparkly red snake-skin stiletto shoes, glossy pink lipstick, orange foundation glaring off puffy cheeks, jowls jangling loosely, rose spangled blusher streaked over wide open pores, shimmer blues painted on their eyelids, parading in schools down the windowless gloom of the brown corridor like tropical fish, armed with bags of rice, always rice. It left a turgid sock smell lingering in the air.

Alas, Christopher did not fare so well in his quest for employment. He went to a few interviews but was basically unviable. He had no real appetite for menial tasks and he loathed authority; obeying orders degraded him and unfortunately the sinecureship he sought did not exist for his kind.

At night when she tried to snuggle up to him she met only with rebuke.

"I can't have sex, sweet thing, it detracts from my personality and besides I don't like to get my fingers dirty."

She sometimes cried beside him on the hard table and he ignored her. She had to get her visa and get out of this penurious existence before she lost strength and wilted without exploiting her youth. A young bride writhing in the tangled ditch.

One fine crisp autumn day, Isolt called in sick to work and walked naively into the labyrinth of United States Immigration and Naturalization Service. She took the number twelve bus from Oxford Street back to the Walworth Road clutching a handful of forms, ill-equipped to deal with such monolithic bureaucracy. And so she began to dance the dance of marriage certificates, birth certificates, bank statements, police reports from all countries of residence, translations of foreign documents, notaries public, chest X-rays, AIDS tests, medical certificates, photographs, passports, white blouses, tight skirts, high heels, taking a number, endless queues, raising her right hand, swearing without profanity, wads of cash handed over without so much as a squeak. Dancing bewilderedly through the maze, feeling tiny and belittled, unable to see a way out ever, not knowing how to go back. A tick kicking, pirouetting and leaping on an elephant's ass.

One day, after a particularly unsuccessful bout of wrestling with bureaucracy, she left the embassy glancing up warily at the menacing iron eagle perched on top of the fortress-like building, eyeing her like prey. When meandering hastily through the crowds at Marble Arch in her high heels she stumbled and fell, grazing her knees and ripping her tights.

Christopher looked startled when she entered the squat. He saw her bloody knee and jumped up in alarm.

"Are you all right? Have you been raped? My God . . ."

"Go get some smack. I passed all the junkies at the bottom of Kinglake but I didn't want to score in my state of mind. They're out for a feeding regular as clockwork, just like the fucking sea-lions in the zoo." She handed him forty quid and he went running off down the road without even stopping to put on his jacket.

She felt better an hour later and peeled off her tights, tearing them out of the congealed gash. Christopher boiled water and putting salt in it he cleaned her knee, dabbing it gently with cotton wool.

"I need a holiday, Chris," she moaned softly.

Christopher smiled and put a Motown tape in his makeshift recorder. "You make me feel like a natural woman," he crooned with the music and did a little stomping dance on the floor.

It was an unrelentingly grey morning and Christopher was stubbornly refusing to allow Isolt to carry any luggage on their week's holiday to Amsterdam.

"It's bad enough for my image that I'll be arriving in Goes with a bird in tow, but not with a bird with baggage. It fucks up my aura. I lose power. I've got an image I need to keep up. I'm sort of a mystery man, a voyager, a stranger in the night. A small-time user, two-time loser. Jumping Jack Flash. The Hoodoo Man. Jesus H. Christ to you, my girl. A woman makes me look kind of dumb. It weakens me. You're here on sufferance as my apprentice but no baggage. No way!"

Isolt stuffed her coat pockets with a handful of clean knickers, make-up, comb and toothbrush and toothpaste, passport and cash. Christopher caused further delay by insisting on rolling a joint before departure. They missed the bus at Victoria bus station and ran to the train station. Christopher almost boarded the wrong train and Isolt had to drag him off and load him onto the right one.

"I got to take a piss."

"The train is moving and there's no toilets, just hold it in."

Christopher pissed on the floor of the train and they moved to another booth.

"Jesus, it's like travelling with a five-year-old," she sighed.

He descended at a station halfway to the coast to look for a coffee machine and Isolt had to get off the train when she realised that he was not coming back. He finally arrived with two Danish pastries in plastic wrapping.

"Breakfast," he said enthusiastically.

"We've missed the fucking train."

"Let's go home and try tomorrow. All these happenings are bad omens."

"No. All these happenings are you screwing up. Jesus, I don't know how you ever made it out of Detroit."

"You can take the man out of the city but you can't take the city out of the man."

"Yeah, yeah. We're getting on the next train. No more shenanigans."

They arrived at Sheerness and leapt into a taxi, arriving in the port just in time to see the ship glide graciously out into the English Channel.

"Sheerness!" Isolt shook her head.

Sheerness was dormant out of season. The amusement parks stood frozen and forlorn. They bought two bottles of codeine cough medicine and downed the odious syrup by the stony seashore. The waves broke like gunshots on the pebbly beach. Isolt made sure to be at the car ferry entrance a good hour before the evening departure.

"Should be changed to Sheer Hell," Christopher quipped.

The boat was hours late and Isolt took the opportunity to wash her hair with soap in the women's toilets. Christopher observed the motley crowd that gathered for this, one of the less popular Channel crossings. There were two Dutch hitchhikers with giant rucksacks.

"Look at that. I think it's a disgrace for a girl to have her sleeping bag out in public view," he commented.

"It's not in view. It's rolled up and attached to her bag. What do you expect her to do for the journey? Ingest it?"

"Well, everyone knows that that's where she sleeps tonight, so to speak."

"So?"

"It's just a mite unseemly, that's all."

Isolt gave him a look of incredulity.

"I'm an old-fashioned anarchist," Christopher told her.

In the early Dutch morning light, Christopher knocked clamorously at his friend's door in Goes. These were the lads from the Versailles squat. Vagrant apostles from the good old days. He wished Isolt would hold her head up when she walked; she looked so hunched and battered, as if she'd seen the troubles of life but had garnered no wisdom. Birds should have easy lives, otherwise it showed up to their detriment in their posture and expression. These men had seen him with the slim, graceful, tall, skittish, temperamental thoroughbred, Marie-Claire. Maybe they would understand if he explained the marriage deal. His fingers had been crossed and his dick had never entered her odorous chasm since.

Within minutes of arrival Tony, shuffling and grey-faced in a tatty towelling dressing-gown, told them that he and the lads were all trying to get off heroin.

"We're just trying to get back on it," Christopher retorted.

Tony laughed ruefully. "I suppose I could postpone my cold turkey for a few days if you've got money."

They went next door to a middle-aged dealer from Guyana. Isolt got higher than she had been in her whole life. She thought she was going to pass out. The dealer tried to chat her up and she was paranoid that the lads had made a deal behind her back. She tried to go to the toilet to get her head together and splash some water on her face but he got up too and insisted on showing her about his apartment. Christopher and Tony were catching up on old times and paying no attention. He was showing her his giant Van Gogh Sunflower poster when she made a dash for the sink and puked onto his dishes.

"Do not worry, cutie . . . As I was saying, of course I do not want to deal heroin forever, it's not my style. But you see, back in my country my daughter she die and I do not have money to bury her, so my aunt she die too and we bury them in same place, same box, it is terrible you know. I have night dreams, my little daughter she is nine year old. She come to me and say Father, I have no room." He pounded his chest in anguish. "So I leave my country and come all the way here and I have to make the money. I can not live with my own self any more, I am a man in torture."

"How very sad," Isolt said brusquely and went back to the lads. He followed closely.

"Yes, so I come to the Netherlands with heroin to sell so I can dig up my baby girl and bury her in her own box."

"Jesus, I thought we'd never get out of there," Isolt said when they were back in Tony's apartment.

"Smack, crack and hash to kick-start the day," Tony smiled at her.

"Talk about breakfast in Babylon." She raised her eyebrows.

"And lunch in Sodom and dinner in Gomorrah," Christopher said gleefully.

*

After three days in Goes with Christopher's friends they hitched to Amsterdam and had dinner in the train station cafeteria. It was the only place Christopher ever ate when he was in Amsterdam. He could get a whole plate of potatoes and vegetables for a few guilders and he liked the large booths and anonymous surroundings. They went to a café afterwards and bought some hash. Isolt sipped a beer and Christopher a Perrier. They sat in silence side by side looking out of the window onto the dark narrow street.

Isolt had worked in Amsterdam for a few months after Becky's death in Paris. Three years ago she and Rory had worked at the train station luring backpackers to hostels and receiving commission per head. The pittance won at the end of each evening was hardly enough to buy tobacco. Certainly it did not compensate for endless hours waiting on the chilly platforms. She had earned a living in the same way in Jerusalem a few months before meeting Becky, though in a sunny bus station and not a wintry train station. It all amounted to the same thing in the end; waiting and hustling. That night she impressed Christopher by leading him to a run-down hostel behind the train station, straight through the bar without blinking an eye and up the threadbare stairs to dark rooms with several bunk beds crammed in whatever space there was. They chose a room with a few people asleep in the beds and they took a bunk bed by the door in case a quick escape was warranted. Christopher got into the same bed as Isolt. There was an old Spanish-looking man in the bunk beside them with huge bandages swaddling his feet. Christopher commented that he could be his father. He kept coughing harsh pneumonic coughs, rising up in agony every now and then to splurge phlegm into a plastic mug. Prostrate, he emitted a strange purring sound as his lungs rattled with a deathly wheeze.

Isolt rested her head on Christopher's chest and he put his arms around her. She felt at peace and full of love for him.

"You're a nice girl. I don't want to hurt you." He kissed her.

They consummated their marriage in a muffled embrace under the torn white sheet and thin brown blanket while the tourists snored and the old man rose and sank excreting bilious fluids, his oblivious eyes cast in their direction, blinded by the massive effort of his dying.

For the next few mornings the honeymooners rose and crept surreptitiously out of the hotel. Isolt would sit quietly in a French café on the Damrak. Christopher would go to the Zee Dijk bridge and score heroin, returning promptly to his young wife. They would empty half of the contents onto the glass-top table and snort them with haste, downing espresso and exiting into the foggy mornings to stroll about town.

They wandered for hours, their hunger killed by the opiates. Christopher put his arm around her and even stole a cheap camera from a chemist's shop to take her photograph. He would not let her take his picture.

"It might fall into the wrong hands," he said.

In the evenings they ate potatoes and vegetables in the train station and sat in a café listening to music, smoking joints and finishing off the heroin. On the last night they arrived at the hotel too late and the door of the bar was locked. They tried to sleep huddled in an alcove in the train station but the police threw them out. Gathering cardboard and newspapers they walked glumly through the red light district wondering where they might crash on this cold autumn night.

The whores sat in the windows like commodities. One fat girl in a leopard-skin leotard lay on a bed eating a banana and listening to a walkman. Shifty-looking people sidled up behind them whispering.

"Coke, smack, hashish, acid?"

"Jesus, do they have all that on them?" Isolt asked, baffled.

On the Zee Dijk bridge the police were hassling dealers. Two undercover cops with long hair and tatty sheepskin coats had one black guy against the wall and they took down his trousers — exposing his shriveled genitals to the night's snickering onlookers. Dealers took advantage of this opportunity to sell their wares and pickpockets lurked in the shadows. REAL FUCKY FUCKY one neon light flashed on and off and in the neighbouring establishment pictures of naked little boys enticed men to go behind a red curtain. An unshaven, middle-aged drunk came out of an alley holding a small girl, who looked about eleven years old, by her scrawny shoulders. She wore a green sequined tight dress and her chest was completely flat, her blond hair was dirty and tucked behind her ears, she had sores all around her mouth. She looked slyly at Christopher and the man said, "My daughter, eight years old, a virgin, ten guilders my friend, for you ten guilders." He perspired and squeezed her shoulders.

Christopher shook his head in disgust and handed him a note.

"Here, have the money. Put your daughter back to bed. She doesn't belong out here. She could get AIDS."

The man snatched the money greedily and disappeared in an instant. The neon flashed on and off all around, there were lewd whispers from doorways.

"Man! This is Babylon. This fucking city is all about canals, cobblestones, whores and boy-fucking," Christopher said.

Isolt was shaken by the lurid vision of the man and the girl. Christopher snorted in derision, "Save your sympathy. It's probably a scam. See those scabs by her mouth? Nobody wants to fuck that diseased little bitch. Why do you think he came up to me with you around? There are plenty of suckers out there who would give money just not to do it, I bet, and then feel noble all night."

"Just like you."

"No, sweet thing. I give money to all beggars and I have every respect for a scam like that. I don't mind paying but I don't fool myself neither."

"I got to piss," Isolt said.

They stopped by the Holiday Inn and saw that the receptionist had momentarily abandoned her or his post. They dashed down a corridor and Christopher eyed the toilets.

"These are big enough to sleep in."

That night they slept on their cardboard and newspapers, curled around the toilet bowl in a locked wheelchair cubicle. They left Amsterdam the next day, hitching to the Hook to get the car ferry.

When autumn ended and winter had begun, Isolt walked up the Old Kent Road after work filled with uneasiness. She always felt wary about the future when the seasons changed for the worse. The cold air scraped her cheeks with menacing asperity. The rubbish was wet on the streets and it piled up in the gutters, at the bus stops, and against the buildings in sodden heaps. All the shops had iron grills over their windows and suspicious Pakistanis behind the tills. Whey-faced toddlers, staring placidly out of the elasticized hoods of their quilted anoraks, were pushed in go-cars down the street by young mothers with pinched faces. A tiny Chinese woman stood on tip-toe behind the high counter of the take-away watching the big TV screen as the

Berlin wall fell down. Isolt turned the corner onto Kinglake Street where the junkies were lined up against the wall, docile and huddled under umbrellas. Only in England would junkies have umbrellas, she thought. Kinglake was grim and austere and the grey stretch of sky pressed heavily down on the red brick blocks of flats. Flats were burnt out and some had windows boarded with plywood. There was blue graffiti on one board reading: FIGHT WAR. A fat black boy stood over his huge Rottweiler as it squatted on the muddy, green patch in front. He glared at Isolt with unguarded hostility.

Her mind was fraught with memories of past winters. Hunched over metholated fires with Becky. Eating stones on a cold beach in France. Crouched behind dustbins with Freddie dead in the cottage. The big dog's sudden barking rocked the darkness plaintively. She had come so far for nothing. She was not in love. A siren pierced the side of the night and fear and horror poured from the open wound. Isolt climbed the concrete flights of steps and plunged her key into the wooden door.

The news was on and Christopher motioned her to be silent as she entered. She swept the papers onto the floor and collapsed into the armchair. He listened excitedly to the news that the Cold War was over. Isolt closed her eyes and rooted down the side of the chair for her novel.

"I can't believe it! And in my lifetime," Christopher exclaimed, walking over to get the saucepan.

Isolt shrugged; she couldn't care less. She never read newspapers.

"One war ends and another one begins. 'The beggars change places but the lash goes on.'"

The cyclops cat from next door came in through the stuck window and stretched out in front of the electric fire. Isolt dug her head into the book and tried to read but re-read a sentence ten times before conceding defeat. As a child she had never felt such despair. It was only when she discovered what it was that the world wanted from her as a woman that she began to hate herself and the world. She curled up on the chair and covered her face with her hands; she dozed off listening to Christopher rustling, clanking and flinging himself from room to room as he cooked the supper.

12

Magician and Tinker

THERE WILL HAVE BEEN life shot through by darkness. There will have been the end of pain through too much pain. She will be God down the Old Kent Road wincing at the creation of her own dilemma. They have one soul, communal and at times startling, held in place by the rough scaffolding of their poverty. They were treated like rats, fed like rats and like rats they were housed somewhere towards the end of time, a small place to be. When they treated each other like rats a newspaper article was written, a tribute to the world's attentiveness. They, undeserving heads bowed, forged a crooked dream in the fire and took it to the heart of London, on red buses that hurt their eyes. Racing towards the lamp-lit Thames, they plunged their stunted bodies in, slunk back home in defeat, back to the dens where they laughed, blinking and spluttering back into life.

And Lazarus clenched his face in panic, he has forgotten how to die. We will take him by the hand and remind him. Softly now, poor Lazarus, we are taking you home. Your broken bones collected and returned by ugly people at bus stops, like sick birds.

Who are they? The strange drug-induced demons, that seemed worn out and familiar. The monsters grew tired of their roar. Turn on the television to turn the world away. With one touch their monsters tumbled, fragile as dry sticks.

She heard noises and stole out into the hall. Gazing at the rectangular universe through her letterbox. The dark orange street. The dulled red-brick flats. The road eaten by road works. Two men fighting. She watched it in slow motion, then crawled back to the damp bed. Her neighbours were all gasping. But no fresh breeze blew down the Old Kent Road. Here they live in a tunnel, silhouetted by the light that seems to be shining behind them. Always behind them.

Groping the walls of this slippery tunnel, searching for doors. Gasping for breath in untidy ranks. Here the breezes are nuclear. Here there are no pretty English gardens. They are in exile in their wallpapered sitting rooms. Here they wake up with nuts and bolts in their mouths and a glass of hepatitis by the bed. Which one of them will be so brave — to fight the world with cardboard limbs?

The little girl was an old man. Standing in the launderette with her mother. Standing on chicken-bone legs. Staring at the machines with greasy eyes. Isolt thinks of faraway lands and grows cold at the sudden thought of his grubby, tobacco-yellow hands rolling her a cigarette, staring out of the window with searching eyes, infinitely doomed. She is deformed by her fascination of being alive here.

She was born beside the sea. And how she misses the sea. The vast oceans of solitude. The waves breaking like gunshots on the pebbly beach. The sea rolls in gutters and sinks in drains.

Who is she? Who can sit perched on a single thread, linked from tower block to tower block? Balancing with the empty grey sky. Magician and tinker. She does not believe in God but she believes in the loneliness and fear of dying that made God. Who is she to hate? Always at war. Who is she to boast of the awfulness?

She was awoken again by the cats. Their distorted wails punctured the night. She lit a cigarette and lay in the glistening darkness. Sadly Lazarus sulks at the other side of the room. Deep in thought. He has his suitcase packed. Waiting in a slow torment, unnerved by the cat's call.

One warm summer evening she wiped the hair from her eyes. She saw a young man looking old, standing shivering at the corner. Christopher waiting for the dealer, his body soaked in sweat and stale neglect. She decided to defect. North of the river her eyes strained to see the pretty things, but she was dedicated to the inverted beauty of the Old Kent Road . . .

> The mildewed sink,
> And the sleep in the eye of the sun in the morning
> The cracked plaster on the walls,

Sunrise on the Old Kent Road,
The naked bulb throwing shadows,
The battered faded walls catching them,
The bare trees interrupting the evening,
Weaving anguish into the sky,
The orange peels in the cereal bowl,
Ash in the egg shells,
Breakfast things uncleared,
An arrangement of wilted flowers in the window,
The well dressed girls in the Gin Palace,
Bored out of their tiny minds,
The black child with bare legs in winter,
The windswept rubbish parading down East Street,
After the market has been rained away,
The unhappy Pakistani sipping weak tea in the morning,
Her disappointed face looking back at her from the broken,
make-up stained mirror.

Does she belong to it? It is growing old. And she feels she is receding. She sleeps and dreams all the time. Returning and thinking. Was she happy in the womb? Because she did not know. And can you dream there? What can you dream of there? Because she did not know. The warped sound. The unnatural scream. Scouring the darkness, infecting her speech. The manky cats are singing her dreams.

Suddenly she is sick and cold. She begins to dream that she is walking down the graffitied underground passage to Elephant and Castle tube station. The Wicklow mountains loom. A wild, rocky valley, waterfalled and green, reaches out its huge craggy hand and snatches her back to Ireland, where for years she stands in a smoky dole queue realising the harness of hunger, the disturbing effect of a ruined city, Dublin, derelict, downtrodden. The sea sweeps her back, carries her away, away from the sea, to London, where it's only a river. It's only a river.

Here rarely a Mr. Right. Here often a Mr. Willdo. They laugh in bars with him. Have his children. Fight and die. But it's not too bad. They can disco dance in clubs with him, to disco dance music. A sailor would look out of place down the Old Kent Road. For where is there to go? And where the ship? They are no tender people. They would take the eyes and more, return to you the yellow sockets, licked clean of juice and pulp. Life is hard and the people are liquid. They are frozen in moulds; yet deep in the ice, hearts beat. If not tender then able. Able to laugh with Mr. Willdo. Able to hug their children, "There, there! Everything will be all right." Everything?

There are awful days without money. Without that no food or cigarettes. No bus fare to look for work. Days of sitting and going nowhere. Tired and weary, relieved when night comes and she can creep back to bed. What gets her through those days? When she can remember better? In crowded schools swearing to be brilliant. But never refugees, immigrants, exiles.

Though she had never laughed so much. Christopher and Isolt in the squat night after night. She had never laughed so much. Sweet Lazarus, you shall not die tonight. But suicide comes in short, sour snaps. So wrap yourself around that thought, console yourself.

They walked through concrete laneways looking over their shoulders. They bought a Chinese takeaway and sat on the crossway of tower blocks. Watching the London lit lights, an orange sky. Full moon on the Old Kent Road.

Putting the seashell to her ear, her eyes are open. No feeling now. It is too late and this must be home. So take off your old raincoat, put some pictures on the wall. Buy curtains on East Street and settle down. The shabby ranks of the defeated are all your friends, their poverty burning in a slow blaze. How nice to huddle around an electric fire and listen to the clicking of the glowing bars. And she is all over now, she is all gone away, she is nobody home. She is growing old. She looks at Christopher asleep beside her. She tries to lie down, she wants to run away, she feels she is falling, she watches and waits. All the stormy scenes when she could not even work up a mild breeze. Oh most useless God! There is no glory in pain and poverty. There is only pain and poverty.

13

A Cold Wind Blows

SHOPS WERE closed, cars were overturned and burning, gangs of young men went marauding down the Old Kent Road wielding clubs and other primitive weapons; natives trembled in their homes. Christopher and Isolt sat drinking tea around a table with Oonagh in 28a Innis House.

"They take their football seriously here," Christopher remarked casually.

"It's always like this when there's a big match. Millwall is the local team. It's tribal," Oonagh explained. "I feel especially vulnerable being on the ground floor. They could smash that big window and then where would I be? I certainly don't have the cash to fix it."

"The Brits have the worst reputation for it too," Isolt said, sipping her tea. "Especially on the continent. Years from now they'll be legendary figures just like the Vikings. A rabble of hooligans arriving by car ferries to rape, pillage and plunder."

"Stop!" Oonagh laughed. "Mustn't laugh. Glip! GLIP!" She grabbed the unfortunate mutt and tried to extract a shoe from his mouth. "GLIP!" She pounded her fist on his coarse, sandy head and then tried to pry its mouth open. Finally she waved a biscuit in front of him and he dropped the shoe and went to grab the biscuit, but Oonagh put it back on the table: "No Glip, not for you, you mangy cur."

"Why does your wretched mongrel always have a cast on its leg?" Christopher asked.

"He doesn't always have a cast on his leg." Oonagh sounded offended. "Since he broke his leg the first time it must be weakened. I get Sinbad to bring him for walks and it breaks when he jumps walls and stuff."

"Why does Sinbad have that name?" Christopher asked.

"'Cos he's a pillock!" Oonagh said matter-of-factly.

"Seems like all the blacks here have wild names," Christopher continued. "Sinbad, Caesar, Napoleon, Nelson."

"Why, what sort of names do they have in America?"

"Oh, I don't know." Christopher then lit up: "But I did go to school with some called Roosevelt, Lincoln and Washington."

"Read what you like into it," Oonagh said. "More tea?"

"Why does Sinbad have blond hair?" Christopher persisted in his aimless interrogation.

"Why do you think? Because he bleaches it, that's why."

"So he's not an albino. That puts that theory to rest," Christopher smiled. "Why on earth does he bleach it?"

"'Cos he's a pillock," she stated emphatically.

"If you took a photo of him the negative would at least be normal." Christopher slapped his thigh laughing. Oonagh threw her eyes up to heaven.

Isolt took showers alternately in Oonagh's and Sally and Cecilia's. Christopher did not avail of their hot water.

"I take a bath once a month whether I need it or not," he claimed. This was untrue.

On a few rare occasions Isolt witnessed him in the dark bathroom standing in front of the sink. He took off his shirt and pulled his trousers down to his ankles displaying his yellow frozen buttocks. He filled the sink with cold water and, dipping the soap in, lathered his body in a frenzy. Then, unplugging the sink, he splashed himself frantically with running water. He pulled up his trousers and, stumbling out of the unlit bathroom back into the living room, found his shirt and hunkered down in front of one of the electric fires, trembling violently, his teeth chattering.

Isolt watched him shiver and deigned to make a suggestion.

"You should boil a kettle of water if you want to strip wash."

Christopher growled, "Mind your own business, El Ribbo. I warn you only once."

"Or is it penance for all your sins?"

"You are my sin. My Mary Magdalene."

Isolt shook her head. "You can reserve that role for your anorexic Marie-Claire. I'm not looking for a saviour. I represent strictly pagan elements in this sordid little affair of ours."

At night he would climb on top of her and withdraw before he ejaculated. Kneeling on the pool table with his dick squeezed in his hand, he would moan, "Oh! Not again! Back to square one."

Isolt saw Jim Glass sitting in the library on the Old Kent Road. It was inevitable that they would encounter each other at some stage in the area and the library was an obvious place. She had seen him once in the market but he had been with Emma and Justine and she had been with Christopher and she had felt intimidated at the idea of a reconciliation in the midst of such a crowd.

His light brown hair was cut short as usual and he sat frail and hunched at a low table as he read. Justine was on her knees colouring a picture with crayons. Isolt hesitated and then sat down in an empty chair beside him.

"Hi, Justine. What are you drawing?"

Justine looked up and did not answer.

Jim closed his book and turned towards her.

> "Frisch weht der Wind
> Der Heimat zu.
> Mein irisch Kind,
> Wo weilest du?"

"Good to see you, Jim," she answered unsmilingly.

"Where is your Tristan then? Back at the squat?"

"Christopher is not my Tristan."

"I'm relieved to hear that. Though rumour has it you married him."

"I did."

"Why, Isolt? Why?"

"I want to go further and I needed a green card to explore a third continent."

"No," he said tenderly. "You are naturally brave. You wanted to walk into the forest where it was the thickest."

"And who are you to judge my actions?"

"I don't judge you. I merely feel obliged to point out your motives so that you may tread carefully. You are embroiled in some strange pageant. Don't deceive yourself as to your own role. Christopher has serious delusions. He is a dangerous man."

"He thinks he is Christ," Isolt said, smiling. "He says Christ forgot to tell the world about proper diet and he was sent to impart the information. He wanted me to be Mary Magdalene but I gave that sublime honour to the woman he really is in love with, an old girl-friend of his. He had his Barabbas who was to remain in Paris when he was compelled to flee from the Dutch avengers. He even has a Veronica who may be called to mop his face with a cloth on his path to Calvary but in the meantime provides us with discount gas. And you of course are Lazarus."

"Come back to tell you all, I shall tell you all," he said.

They were laughing and she almost kissed him.

"So how's Emma?" she asked abruptly.

"Awful, as a matter of fact. Something snapped, and I don't blame you for anything, but that whole sojourn of chaos triggered something; it was definitely a catalyst I'd say. Maybe that's why I think yon wee Christopher is a malevolent force."

"Why, what happened?" Isolt asked, shocked.

"She went off the rails when you left. I don't know why but she started drinking again. At first I welcomed it. I thought it was back to the good old days, though I seriously doubt we've ever had anything resembling good old days. Then she would cry all the time. Get drunk and cry. It's a mess. This poor mite here . . ." He gestured toward Justine. "I have to take care of her and I'm not up to it. I confess she goes unattended half the time. Sometimes Emma is passed out like a big old sow in bed and I am reading and listening to music when I realise the child hasn't eaten all day. I scrape money together, what little of it either of us hasn't drunk, and I bring her back a bag of chips."

"Jesus. What happened?"

"I don't know, I don't know."

"She must go to a doctor."

"Aye. But what can he do for drunks like us? I want to leave, Isolt, but I don't have the guts. That's the truth. Not because I'm noble and a family man but because all the world out there is empty."

Justine was staring vacantly into space. She was unkempt and pale.

"I look at the road, the great highway. I think of all the places it leads to, all the great cities, all the lush jungles, the mountains, and I am afraid all is dust, the trees are rotted, the mountains hollow. Poverty and obscurity reduces them all to clay."

"Write, Jim," Isolt implored. "Maybe that's what you have left."

"I'm no longer young." Jim shook his head. "Even your friend Becky was better off than I am. She left her family but I have no metal detector to root out my salvation from so much clay. There are no beginnings out there. I have lost."

"Becky died. You never struck me as a loser."

"I have been outwitted by circumstance." He got up and the ever-docile Justine put her crayons back into a tin and took his hand.

"Come around sometime, Isolt," he invited as he departed. "You'd be a ray of light in the gloom."

Isolt sat for a while upset by the encounter. Then she picked up Justine's drawing. Abstract scribbles of orange, yellow and red, as if she had looked into the face of the sun.

Isolt received her elusive green card before Christmas. She felt jubilant as she had finally succeeded in doing something complicated to ameliorate her situation. Now she had to save her money and go. Seamus the Irish Bastard had stayed with them for a week. Having a houseguest brought Isolt and Christopher close together, united as they were against a common enemy.

Seamus the Irish Bastard lingered on like a bad smell. Christopher and he argued and debated constantly over the most trifling inanities.

Christopher tried to help him find a squat but Seamus was lethargic and came home after his job as a security guard just to loll about on a chair and get stoned. Christopher sent him to SNOW, the squatting agency, and he came back triumphant.

"I found a place, man, it's fucking lovely too."

Christopher and Isolt were happy. Seamus threw a tiny burgundy leather jacket at Isolt.

"Here! I found it there. I thought it would fit you. Keep it, it's a present."

Isolt held it away from her with two fingers.

"It's for a kid," she said. "I don't want it."

"This place has furniture and all. It even has a washing machine."

"A washing machine?" Christopher was wide-eyed. "No shit!"

"Yeah, a fucking washing machine, man," he enthused, "and a TV and blankets and everything."

Isolt and Christopher looked at each other in disbelief.

"Seamus," Christopher grinned, "that sounds like somebody's house."

"Nah," Seamus protested. "There's no one there. I've watched it for a few nights. No lights on and nothing in the fridge."

"A FRIDGE?" exclaimed Isolt.

So Seamus went and changed the locks to his new abode and settled down for a good night's sleep. Two days later, however, he was rudely awoken by a mad woman.

"Who the fuck are you? Why are my locks changed? I had to climb in through the bloody window. I'm calling the police."

She was wielding a frying pan and brought it down on his back with a resounding whack. He slithered whimpering out of bed.

"Don't kill me. I thought it was a squat. I'll leave. I'll leave, let me go, you bitch."

"A squat! How dare you! I go on holidays to Benidorm for two lousy weeks and when I come back a bleeding Irishman is in my fucking bed."

Christopher and Isolt were perturbed to have him back in the fold and never let him forget the whole affair.

"Goldilocks the Irish squatter!" Christopher re-christened him.

Seamus ashed his cigarette on the floor, much to Christopher's chagrin.

"Well, I guess you know your house is a dump," he said sarcastically, "when your friends think nothing of ashing on the floor."

Seamus left after a month when he met a woman down in the pub and moved in with her and her three teenage children. Isolt and Christopher heaved a sigh of relief and got a Chinese takeaway in celebration of their regained privacy.

On Christmas Day Isolt left Christopher stewing in his own juices and made her way across the frozen landscape to Little Wendover. There were a few people, dressed awkwardly in cheap suits with gifts in gay wrapping paper, exiting the lift. It stopped on the second floor letting an old woman with a beard step in beside her.

"Happy Christmas," Isolt said.

The woman nodded and they stood to the right as the contraption rattled upwards.

Emma was sitting on the couch; she looked old and her face was puffy but she appeared sober. Jim poured Isolt a scotch and Isolt kissed Justine.

"Tiens! C'est quelque chose pour Noël."

She gave her a colouring book which Justine took readily.

"Et aussi . . ." Isolt gave her a bright red, tin fire engine. *"Pour ton anniversaire."*

Justine dropped the colouring book at once and snatched the fire engine in delight.

"Say thank you, Justine," Emma intoned from the couch.

Justine, who was wearing a dark blue dress for the festivities with a matching blue bow, ran and hid behind her father. They all laughed.

The doorbell rang and Charley, a Nigerian friend of Jim's, arrived. He brought a pudding and a plastic tea-set for Justine. Snow from Cameroon arrived with some more booze, African tapes for Jim, a hair slide for Emma and a goat-skin drum for the excited Justine. Emma had cooked soup and vegetarian meat loaf.

"So you're still a vegetarian," Charley said tactlessly as they all sat in the living room with their plates on their knees.

"Yes," Emma said. "Even though I'm this fat again and drink like a pig."

"A fish," Jim corrected her. She glared at him as he gulped down his soup with his eyes cast downwards.

"I'm sorry," Charlie said. "I didn't mean it like that."

"But you are right, Charlie," Emma acknowledged. "If it wasn't for this poor child I would kill myself today."

"She looks lovely." Isolt tried to liven things up. "I've never seen her so animated."

"Justine is a normal little girl," Emma glared. "She doesn't speak a lot I think because of the conflict of two languages. She understands French better and speaks words here and there but in time she will have both languages, which will be very useful when she is older."

They all nodded, eager to agree.

"Justine Glass," Snow said, patting the child on the head. "A beautiful name."

Isolt helped Emma put four candles in the cake in the kitchen.

"What about your other family?" Isolt asked. "Do you ever write to your boys?"

"It's better they think I'm dead," she snapped.

It was only when Justine was tucked into bed and her door closed that Emma took a drink. "I swore I wouldn't ruin her birthday," she explained to the embarrassment of the others as she swallowed a hefty scotch and poured another.

They drank and talked, then Snow sang a song from Cameroon, and Charley, not to be outdone, launched into a few melodies from his own native land. Isolt stood up and tried to recite a poem but Cloud kept screeching and interrupting. She got exasperated and looked to the others for help, but despite their admonishments, Cloud would start a rumpus as soon as Isolt opened her mouth. Emma sang some Flemish tunes very sweetly to calm everyone down. Jim, who was a good singer, gave a moving rendition of "I'll take you home again, Kathleen." He stood by the wall, his delicate lids closed over his blue eyes, his body eerily still and his whiskey motionless in his hand. His voice, stronger than his frail frame, swallowed up his whole presence.

> I'll take you home again Kathleen, across the ocean
> wild and wide.
> To where your heart has ever been since first you were
> my bonny bride.
> The roses all have left your cheek, I've watched them
> fade away and die,
> Your voice is sad when e'er you speak and tears bedim
> your loving eyes.
>
> And I will take you back Kathleen,
> to where your heart will feel no pain,
> And where the fields are fresh and green,
> I will take you to your home Kathleen.

When he finished singing, they sat moved in their drunken melancholy, these refugees, immigrants, exiles. Emma's eyes were moist but Snow himself, who had a wife and child back in Cameroon, wiped salty tears that streamed down his cheeks.

"Ah, Jim, you are a strange man," he said. "You make me cry."

"Our lives are hard in this foreign land. This is our Babylon," Charley agreed, finishing his drink.

Jim laughed. "Jesus, I didn't mean to depress yiz all."

He went into the kitchen and poured the brandy over the pudding and set it alight. Emma turned the lights off and he stood in the frame of the kitchen door, holding the burning pudding before him. The small blue flames licked the surface and they all looked at it, mesmerized for a while in the hushed atmosphere.

One cold January night, Christopher and Isolt were fast asleep curled up on the pool table that jutted out so unceremoniously into the hall. There was a loud banging on the door.

"Christopher! Christopher! Are you there?"

It was an unfamiliar British accent. Christopher motioned Isolt to stay quiet. He sat up as still and alert as a deer. There was some commotion outside. Then the glass in the toilet window was smashed. Christopher grabbed the knife he kept beside him and ran to the door, throwing it open. Three men raced down the steps. Christopher managed to grab one and stab him in the side. Isolt looked over the balcony and saw two men run away around the corner. One of them she recognized as Seamus the Irish Bastard. Christopher kicked the other guy down the stairs. He came pushing past Isolt and stared at his hands which held the bloody knife.

"What happened?" Isolt's legs began to shake.

"I stuck the fucker in the kidneys."

"I recognized Seamus the Irish Bastard. They were up to no good." She closed the door behind them.

"The stupid fucker is trying to break in and steal shit after all my hospitality." Christopher washed the knife. "They won't go to the cops but they might try to get me back. Damn! Is there no peace on earth?"

"He's so stupid. He knows we don't go away much and there's nothing to steal."

"Your countrymen are a treacherous lot. I wish I had my chair leg handy. That was in the other room. Fuck, I shouldn't have stabbed him. I was half asleep."

"At least the scaffolding is down," Isolt said. "Is that the same chair leg you had in Paris? How did it get here?"

Christopher snorted. "You took it, El Ribbo."

"What?"

"You took it. I put it in your bag when we left Paris. You carried it all the way."

"I had to carry all the heavy shit," Isolt grumbled.

"You are my beast of burden." Christopher turned on the light in the living room and began searching for his hash. "You are so simple-minded, El Ribbo. So fucking middle-class."

Jim Glass went running through the streets clutching his little daughter to his chest. He leapt up the concrete stairs two at a time, only managing to avert a bad fall by his outstretched hand. He hammered on the wooden door. Christopher opened it suspiciously.

"What do you want?" he asked, without stepping aside to let them in.

"I want to speak to Isolt. It's an emergency," Jim said breathlessly.

"An emergency?"

"I haven't time for your shit now," Jim snapped, shouting: " ISOLT, ISOLT."

Isolt was at the door in a flash, her mouth falling open when she saw his expression. He thrust the child into her arms.

"Take care of the wee one. I have to go. I'll explain later."

Isolt nodded, dumbfounded.

"Don't leave her alone with that bastard," Jim shouted as he ran down the stairs.

There had been a hurricane the day before. A terrible wind had seized the city, thirty-six people had been killed, trees had been uprooted and a red double-decker bus had been blown off a bridge and into the Thames. Justine had hidden in her little play-house with all her teddies and her parents had fought bitterly in the next room. Jim had threatened to leave and Emma had said that she would kill herself if he took that course. She had struck him with her fists and he had curled into a ball on the floor, shielding himself with his limbs. Emma had left in a drunken fury, running down the dark, emptied streets as the storm died. She was in a state of great agitation.

A man approached to calm her. Emma felt him closing in, she felt smothered by his concern, she turned and slapped him hard across the face. He tried to grab her hand but she started screaming.

"Leave me alone. Get your hands off me. *Laissez-moi tranquille!*"

He backed off, holding his hands in the air in a gesture of surrender. She walked and walked, tearing at her clothes and talking to herself.

The police picked her up by the banks of the Thames threatening to throw herself in. They took her to St. Thomas's Hospital where she was sedated and put under observation. She had no identification and at first refused to give her address. It wasn't until the next morning that Jim was alerted by the police and decided to spare little Justine the whole hospital drama.

He entered the huge hospital and walked through the crowded lobby looking for information. Emma was awake when he came into the ward. She lay in bed staring at the ceiling. At first she would not look at him and he did not know what to say. Then she turned her head away and looked at the wall.

"Sorry," she said very quietly.

Jim squeezed her hand.

"I feel so ashamed. When I awoke I wished to be lying under a guillotine and hoped my head would be chopped off."

Jim smiled but she was not looking at him.

"Don't leave us, Jim," she said meekly.

He was silent.

"If you have to go, take us with you," she pleaded.

Jim sat by her side as she slept, still lingering under the effects of the sedation. He noticed the roots of her hair were brown for two or three inches before the red dye. The words of the song kept coming back to him in a distorted and terrifying form.

> And what became of you, Kathleen?
> You moved as a winged demon through the cruel air.
> And I will not take you home once more,
> Your hair full of spiders,
> Your heart soaked in despair,
> Living over the hall of our warped tower block and far away,
> No happy ever after there.

Isolt brought Justine to work. She explained to her Saudi employers that there was a family crisis. The Arab men made a great fuss of the wee girl, giving her sweets and a lollipop. Justine sucked sullenly on the lollipop and held onto Isolt's hand with an unshakeable grip. She followed Isolt about all day. Isolt gave her a cloth and told her she could make herself useful, but the hapless creature just held the cloth and refused to let Isolt out of her sight for a minute. She and the other women took their break in an empty apartment. Justine fell asleep on a bed and they advised Isolt not to wake her but to finish the chores alone. Isolt was preparing to enter the lift when Justine came tearing down the corridor in fright. She hurled herself at Isolt and Isolt cradled her.

"Hush. I wasn't going anywhere. You can come with me."

Justine, cranky and sleepy, leant against the wall, staring at Isolt as she hoovered and made beds. She was a rather bland child, pasty-faced with shoulder-length mousy hair and pale green eyes.

Isolt had to carry the four-year-old all the way home on the tube and the bus and the length of Kinglake Sreet.

"She's a dead weight," Isolt groaned.

She put the sleeping child on the armchair and shook her arms, which had gone numb.

"So those Romans saddled you with their retard without so much as an explanation," Christopher commented. "What if we're stuck with her for life? How will we put the brat through college on your meagre wage?"

"I have to run out and get tampons. Watch her for me and don't molest her."

"She's not my type," Christopher smiled.

When Isolt left Justine woke up and looked about her, startled. Christopher nodded at her from behind his newspaper.

"*Isolt va revenir bientôt,*" he said gruffly.

The child sat and stared at him resentfully; she twirled her hair with one finger. Christopher raised his eyebrows and shook his head, emitting a low whistle.

"Oh, man!" he said as he resumed reading his paper.

Jim arrived that evening and told them what had happened. Christopher was tactful and courteous. He cooked potatoes and broccoli for them all and insisted Jim smoke a few joints.

"Look, I want to spend the night at the hospital," Jim said.

"But she's OK," Isolt said.

"I know. I just want to be there. I want to talk to her and stuff. It can't wait. Can you stay the night with Justine in Wendover? I'll give you the keys. Both of you can go there if you want. I'm sorry for being so rude earlier, Chris, I was just in a right state. There's cat food in the press too."

"Cloud," Christopher exclaimed, beaming. "Cloud."

"When will you be back?" Isolt asked. "I can't take her to work with me again."

"I'll be back tomorrow morning, maybe even late tonight. I really appreciate this."

Christopher and Isolt went with Jim to Wendover. He tucked Justine in and read her a story and then he left. Isolt fed Cloud who sat deadly still when she saw them enter Emma and Jim's bedroom.

Christopher lay in bed next to Isolt.

"So we're back in Bend-over are we?"

Isolt smiled and kissed him; he pretended to flinch and wipe the spot childishly.

"This is kind of cosy," he said. "Legally married and our kid next door, dreaming sweet dreams."

"Jesus, I wouldn't want to see Justine's dreams and that's for sure," Isolt said. She tossed and turned a bit. "I have terrible cramps."

"I can't have any sympathy for you, it's a woman's burden."

Isolt lay there feeling the iron claw drag at her womb; this time it felt like lead weights had been hung on all her thousand tender tendons, pulling and stretching her insides. She could bear it no longer. "I'm going to check if they've any painkillers in the bathroom."

She left the room and tiptoed across the living room, Cloud observing her from the same position as earlier. Isolt took four tablets and returned.

"The cat's maintaining some strange vigil outside."

"Do you think Jim is with Emma tonight?" Christopher asked suddenly.

"No," Isolt said. "He's gone out drinking, I suspect."

"That bastard. I don't know why you consort with such low life."

The next morning Isolt got up and there was a small animal turd right in front of their bedroom door. Cloud was nowhere to be seen.

*

There was a pleasant surprise awaiting her return from work the next week. Irish Jim sat in her armchair chatting to Christopher. He got up and they kissed twice Parisian style. He was looking healthy, his complexion had cleared up and his brown hair was quite long and tied in a ponytail. Gone were his denim jacket and heavy metal patches; in their place was a leather biker jacket with no markings. He had both ears pierced and had tiny black and white ying yang studs adorning them. He wore denim jeans and a dark green shirt. Isolt laughed.

"You look so different," she remarked.

"Cleaner, huh?" Jim laughed sheepishly.

"The Germans have smartened him up," Christopher told her.

"You've been in Hamburg all this time?" she asked, sitting down on a stool.

"*Ja!*" Jim said.

"*Ja.* I gather that is the extent of your German," Isolt said.

"You never give up, Isolt, do you?" Jim smiled at her.

"Nothing so sour as a sharp-tongued woman," Christopher said sternly.

"I'm in an alcoholic mood," Isolt said. "Let's go get drunk."

"I thought you were saving, young girl?" Christopher frowned.

"I've money," Jim said hurriedly. "Christopher has been telling me about the local lovelies. I'd like to meet some."

"I see," said Isolt. "Well, I'm sure I can round some up for you, though it's early."

"We'll have a head start," Jim said.

They were quite drunk by six o'clock and Christopher was sober but sucking on a codeine bottle and so content in his own private euphoria. They ate in a pizza place on the Walworth Road and Jim kept urging Isolt to ring some of her female friends.

"I'm not your pimp," she snapped and he blushed and shut up.

"I have tidings of joy, by the way," he said, pulling a triangular wedge from the pizza and drowning it in salt, pepper and cheese. "Remember Dutch Mark?"

"Yes." Christopher was alert. "I had some altercations with him concerning certain illegal substances."

"I know," Jim said.

"How did you know?" Christopher asked sharply.

"The grapevine," Jim said nonchalantly.

"Go on. What's the fucker up to now?"

"He was opening some restaurant in Amsterdam and he finally raised the cash. A month before it was opened he decided to go off on a last fling and went to Kenya. He was drunk in a car with two Germans and they drove off the road into a ravine and were all killed. One of the Germans was driving."

"That's karma for you," Christopher nodded with satisfaction. "He tried to forcefully extract funds from penniless beggars and got Freddie murdered."

"Well," Jim said, "he got his come-uppance to be sure."

"He tried to hoodoo the Hoodoo Man," Christopher said.

"And you can't do that." Jim winked at Isolt.

"I could go back to Paris," Christopher said. "No need to remain here. Eh, El Ribbo?"

"I'm going to the States," she told him. "You can do what you like."

Christopher bristled: "Behave yourself, young lady."

Jim looked from one to the other and smirked.

"Where's your wee dog?" Christopher asked.

Jim flinched. "Dead."

"That's a shame. I'm sorry," Christopher said.

"How did she die?" Isolt asked.

"I walked to the shops and I had her on a lead. As soon as I came out of the shops the hurricane had hit the street. It was like walking into a wall of wind. Sheba sort of blew away, I held as tightly as I could to the lead but I was dragged too. It was like flying a fucking kite, I swear. I tripped and let go the lead. She flew against a wall with such force. I can't believe it . . ." He couldn't go on. Isolt and Christopher could not contain their laughter.

"Oh, I'm sorry, Jim," Isolt laughed. "But it's just so ridiculous."

Jim stared at them: "Thanks for the sympathy. You've obviously never been close to a dog."

"It's not that," Isolt protested, "it's just the story itself." She laughed again.

"I had to shoot a dog once in Detroit. I know how it is," Christopher said. "Any news from Paris?"

"Yeah! Melonie goes back and forth quite a bit," Jim said, pulling himself together. "She's become quite a dealer."

"A bird dealing," Christopher snorted in disgust. "Especially Melanoma herself. What a thought. Dealing is strictly a man's territory."

"Rory has buggered off to Spain with some chick. Larry's still hanging out, Black Jack's still giving everyone a pain in the ass, Fred's gone back to Scunthorpe and Cloggie's gone back to Holland. The usual stuff."

Christopher went home afterwards and Isolt took Jim to Oonagh and Sinbad.

Oonagh opened the door. "We're fighting. Come back later."

They rang Cecilia at her boyfriend's place.

"I'd love to," she said, whispering. "I'll make an excuse and escape. He's in a foul mood."

They took a bus to the centre of London and waited for her in a pub around Covent Garden.

"I hate London," Jim said. "The pub atmosphere is dismal. All the pubs look the same on the inside. It's good to get out of Hamburg though. That hurricane was a disaster. People were killed. It was like a bomb hit the place. Those winds scared me. Everywhere I went reminded me of Sheba. I still find dog hairs on me. That dog was like my girlfriend."

"The hurricane hit here first, it was a mess, Emma went crazy for its duration. It's good to see you Jim, it really is. I can say that now I'm drunk. The last time I saw you was when we stole Kim's money and you left on the train for Hamburg. Talk about depressing."

"Yeah? Did you miss me?" He grinned.

"Not half as much as Kim," she said.

Cecilia arrived wearing a fake fur tigerskin coat and a large pair of black sunglasses. She sat down glancing about nervously. Her lipstick extended beyond the outline of her lips. She had a cigarette in her hand.

"God, we had the most awful row. He tried to drown me in the sink. Yesterday he stuck a cigarette out on my tit."

Jim looked her up and down lasciviously; she noticed this and sucked in her stomach and stuck out her chest. Isolt glowered jealously.

They spilled unceremoniously onto the street at closing time and sent Cecilia off.

Isolt and Jim took a taxi to Sally's house on Darwin Street.

"Can we stay the night?" Isolt asked her.

"My God. Everybody's at it, even you," Sally said.

They lay on Sally's fold-out bed in the living room, kissing, for a long time.

"You don't have to do it if you don't want to," he said.

"I'm just scared."

"He won't find out," Jim said. "Come with me to Hamburg. Pretend you're going to America."

Isolt lay naked looking at the flat ceiling above.

Irish Jim stayed with Emma and Jim Glass. He didn't have the stomach to stay with Christopher and Isolt because of his hatred for the former and his now undisguised love for the latter. Isolt went to him after work every day and they had sex each time. Emma and Jim encouraged the adulterous exploits of their old friend and always found a pretext to make themselves scarce at some time in the evening.

Jim told her he had been in love with her since he had met her in Paris, when she was sixteen years old, just like the song, sweet sixteen. But he thought she was into Jim Glass and then she had left for Israel. He told her the time on the beach in the south had been something he had longed for, but he had been too injured to do much and could have killed himself when she had gone back to Paris the next day. He had sulked and grieved until Rory made him go back to Paris to get her but then when he arrived he found her living with Christopher, of all people. He couldn't believe it, they were such an ill-matched couple. He had to get away and forget her, so he arrived in Hamburg determined once and for all to rid himself of her image. He could not. He saved all his money, bought new clothes, washed his hair and took the boat to London to find her and try and wrench her away from his arch-rival. This was the happiest time of his life. Isolt crawled all over him, she stuck her tongue into his mouth, she sat on top of him and engulfed him, her hair stuck to her forehead with sweat. He wanted her to come live with him in Germany. He had a part-time job as janitor in a school and she could learn German. They could share a place with Jim Glass, Emma and Justine. She would be safe with friends and Christopher would never find out. He would protect her. He sucked her nipples, they rolled over. Isolt laughed, she did not feel ugly, he loved her, he lusted after her body, he thought she was amazing. She pulled him closer, his long hair fell on her face. They came.

Isolt took a bath with him every day and he carefully washed her body of all juices. She did not hold her stomach in, he loved her big, ripe belly and fat thighs, he stroked her and licked her. He had a spotty back and a scar across his face, neither was perfect. It was a new feeling to have someone single her out and love her; she could hardly believe it had happened.

They made plans for Hamburg and she told him she would follow in two weeks. She had to give notice at work and that way Christopher's suspicions would not be aroused. Jim had a friend in the U.S. and he would get him to send a few postcards to Christopher from there. He wanted her to come at the end of the week with all of them. He thought it was a mistake to procrastinate. How could he bear a two-week separation after waiting so long? He kissed her forehead when she was dressed, he held her jacket for her as she put it on. They hugged, she buried her head in his chest — if she left suddenly Christopher would go crazy.

Jim walked her to the corner of the off-license every day. He watched as she went up each flight of stairs, he hated to see her go in the door of the squat into enemy hands. He wanted to run up and rescue her. He wanted to be with her every minute. Soon everything would be all right.

Emma was in better spirits and seeing a doctor regularly. She dyed her hair and was on the wagon once more. They had decided to forego the offer of the upcoming council flat and return with Irish Jim to Hamburg. Emma was reluctant and frightened but determined to keep her family together at all costs. Snow had gone to Africa to get his wife and child in Cameroon and they would pass the squat on to him.

"You know, with the wall down and everything, Germany is the place to be," Jim Glass enthused. "I've heard all these stories of how the East Germans left their kids and their homes to scramble to the west. Greed abounds but perhaps we can take advantage of it. If all those houses are abandoned then there must be plenty of places to squat."

"And I suppose we just move into their place and bring up their children?" Emma said sceptically. "They all run to the west and we run to the east. We defect."

"The world order is shifting. England is not the place to be," he responded.

Two days before they left Isolt sat on the couch watching them organise it all. Snow was standing awkwardly in the living room. His young wife stood out of the way in the kitchen. She paced up and down, sliding her feet along the floor without lifting them, holding their baby which was only a few months old.

"We're going to leave it all to you, Snow," Jim said affably. "All I'm taking is a few clothes and my tapes. You can keep my books and sell them if you want."

Emma nodded. "We can sell you the stereo and the fridge which are the only things of value. You can keep the cooker, it was here when we arrived anyway. The beds are just mattresses we found on a skip and Justine is allowed to take only one teddy. She'll have to make that choice, God knows how. Your son can have the play-house and the rest of her toys."

"Thank you, thank you." Snow's eyes were moist.

"Isolt, you can have Cloud, I know how fond you are of the animal."

"That's all right, I'd hate to uproot the creature, it would be too traumatic."

"The stereo and fridge we can give you for one hundred pounds. It's a good machine and the speakers are brand new."

Snow said, "Please, no. I have not the money after my trip. I know you need it so much. Please sell them outside. You have been so good." Snow was at a loss for words.

Jim Glass wanted to hug Snow but he was not a physically affectionate man and just clumsily patted him on the back.

"You know," Isolt said, "you are going to try Eastern Europe. That is considered the Second World. Africa is in trouble now. It is the Third World of the Third World. All the wars are bringing famine, no end in sight. And there shall be wars all over the Second World that the First World will try to contain, and wars all over the Third World that the First World will ignore. The fates of the Second and the Third Worlds are in the hands of the First World and the First World is terrified that immigrants will spill starving into their territory and reduce their share of the wealth.

"Meanwhile the population of the earth is sky-rocketing and they say all the wars in the next century will be resource wars. Populations are restless and shifting, changing colour. You move from the First World to the Second World and Snow moves from the Third World to the First World and shortly I will move to the richest country of the First World which uses up the majority of the whole world's resources. I'm sure that we'll all remain poor, and there is only one world."

"Thank you, Isolt," Snow said. "You really make me feel better."

The two Jims decided to sell the stuff on the fringes of the market and they carried the fridge out with the help of Snow. His wife, who hadn't a word of English, began to shout at them in her own language. Snow tried to calm her and she retreated and stood very stiffly and obviously frightened. She was very deeply black, her hair was cut close to her head. She was only sixteen years old and had never been outside her small town. Snow had taken her to the vast metropolis of London where the trees grew out of cement, where they would have to live in poverty at least until he completed his medical studies. Grey was the colour she saw and felt everywhere, cold grey, like the ashes of a long-dead fire had been smeared all over the barren, built-up landscape.

Isolt carried two speakers and Emma the stereo. They left Justine in the flat with Snow's wife. When they returned after two hours in the market, bubbling with the success of their wheeling and dealings, they found Justine and Snow's wife and child fast asleep on the mountain of teddies in the little play-house.

Isolt went to Victoria bus station to see them off. She held onto Irish Jim tightly and he kept kissing her. Emma and Jim Glass each carried large suitcases and backpacks. Justine had her chosen teddy, which Isolt noticed was not the one she had given her, but she had the red fire engine Jim Glass had diplomatically told her she could take. The child was as placid and restrained as usual; she trotted along trying to keep up and never whined once.

They embraced as the luggage was put in the side of the bus.

"It will be a long journey. Bus, ferry, bus again," Isolt said.

Emma nodded. "Thank God Justine is an angel. You must join us soon, Isolt, and leave that dreadful man behind you for good. Thank you for everything, you have been a good friend."

They hugged and kissed.

"Good-bye, Justine, *au revoir.*" Isolt kissed her and the child returned her kiss with damp lips on the cheek. She held the teddy up and Isolt kissed that too and then the fire engine. Justine then held up her plastic drink container but here Isolt drew the line.

"No, Justine, not that. Now *sois sage* for your mother and *bonne chance.* Maybe you will speak German too, huh?"

Jim Glass came forward and they embraced with emotion.

"I love you, Jim. You are a great man."

"Come to Hamburg soon."

"I will if you promise to write some stories."

"I can't promise that, Isolt. Poor Isolt, you have too much faith in me. Every time I attempt something it only fills me with deep shame. It takes a certain kind of courage as well, you know. Courage to be exposed as a fraud if it all falls through. I had aspirations but there is no longer any inspiration or ideas. Why? I don't know. Maybe I'm just out of practice; more likely I was never in."

"Don't worry, Isolt," Emma said, "I wouldn't allow him to pawn his typewriter. I have packed it and it is so heavy he will have to write something just out of sheer guilt that I am carrying it all this way."

Irish Jim kissed her on the lips. She hugged him with desperation.

"Take care, Isolt. You must write and tell me exactly when you are coming. Have you got the address?"

"It's in my address book."

"Don't lose it."

"I won't."

"I know you, you're always losing things."

"I'm a loser."

"Don't tell Christopher anything, just leave. Tell him you're going to America and you'll be back. Be careful."

"Yes. Don't jeopardize yourself," Jim Glass added.

"I love you," Jim said, kissing her again.

"It's been a month of hurricanes." Isolt nodded. "I hate goodbyes. Get on the bus before I cry."

"No need to cry," Irish Jim said. "Sure won't we be seeing you very soon?"

"Two weeks. I guarantee."

"It will be the longest two weeks of my life."

"You two are disgusting," Jim Glass laughed.

She watched them board and find their seats. Emma and Justine sat together, Jim and Jim behind them. Isolt couldn't bear it anymore. She waved quickly to this fragile family and her lover and they all waved back; then she left the bus station in anguish.

She was hidden amidst the crowds on the street as she saw their bus pass by. She stood rooted to the spot as it cleared the lights and disappeared, heading for the highway. The great highway that runs from east to west, west to east. *Frisch weht der Wind.* A cold wind blows. A month of hurricanes and highways, a whole lifetime of them. How could something so simple have got in such a turmoil? They were all only animals searching for food, but she had perhaps expected more, and now, delayed by her meandering journeys, she had reached the food only to find it stale.

14

Jerusalem Lit

THE DAY stitched him up in silence. That week the one-eyed cat from next door had fallen out of their bedroom window while trying to catch pigeons. It plunged five floors to its doom. Christopher heard a squealing noise, climbed off the pool table and pushed through the clutter to the window. The cat was writhing and gasping below. He ran out of the squat and down the brick stairs and around the back of the building. Its back seemed to be broken and its four legs were splayed. There was nothing he could do to assuage the inexorable pain; the one eye was rolling in the socket in ugly delirium. He had softened since his time in Europe and was reluctant to kill the agonized creature. He looked about for help but the street was empty. Christopher lifted his foot up in the air and stamped down hard on the animal's back. He heard the sickening snap of cat bone and took his foot off. The thing was still alive. It trembled and emitted faint squashed eerie squawks like a heavily breathing bird. Christopher's forehead creased into a dark frown and he crushed the skull with his heel. He wiped his shoe on the grass and went back upstairs.

Isolt came home that evening and told him that she had bought a ticket to Hamburg and would fly from there to New York. He watched her pack and he couldn't utter a single word. The cat had got his tongue. The day had dried his tears, denying him that relief.

He played his Iggy Pop tapes for solace and insight.

"You can't go."

"What?"

"You brought me to this stinking land and you have a responsibility. You can't just leave me all alone."

"Since when did you care about me? I've got a ticket. I'm leaving tomorrow."

"I love you, Isolt."

She looked at him. He was extremely agitated. His eyes were wide and grasping for reason, his lips quivered and his hands were clasped together, crooked finger entwined in crooked finger, almost in prayer. She walked over to him and at once he leapt from the chair and flung his arms around her.

"I'll miss you, Christopher."

"You must come back. Promise, promise."

"I promise."

"I love you."

That night they had sex on the pool table and Christopher came inside her.

"What did you do that for?" Isolt asked angrily.

"It's high time I grew up. Maybe we're ready for a family."

"Jesus, you've gone mad." She slithered out from under him.

"You're no spring chicken, El Ribbo. I reckon you should be about ready to have babies in the next forty-eight months, fifty at the latest. Anything later than that will be at your peril."

Isolt struggled to the toilet and came back.

"I'd like a photo of you to keep," he said.

"You have a couple from Amsterdam."

"No, I want naked ones. I'm your husband after all, and wouldn't you prefer me to jerk off to you than some other bitch?"

Isolt climbed back onto the table.

"Frankly, no."

"Just let me take one."

"No way."

"I wouldn't let them fall into the wrong hands."

"No, no, no, no, no."

Isolt got up. Christopher was in the living room. The electric fires were all lit.

"I've made some tea. Sit down."

He fussed around her. The room was tidier than usual. It was her last day and so she approached everything gingerly.

"I'll write every week and I promise I'll come back."

Christopher cleared his throat. "That won't be necessary. I've come to a decision."

"What kind of decision?" Isolt drank her tea.

"If I let you go you won't return. I know the nature of women. Also you could get fucked by someone else and you are by law my property. I couldn't live with it if you got jumped by another bastard."

"I'll give you my word I won't fuck anyone," Isolt said warily.

"No, Isolt. You won't have the option to betray me." He held her new leather backpack up in the air.

"Give that to me." Isolt stood up.

"I have your ticket, passport, US immigration documents, address book and money."

Isolt was frightened.

"Christopher, I . . ."

"Enough!" he shouted. "I don't want to hear your lies and false promises. I have a legal right to you. You are my wife. You are not going anywhere."

"Please, I . . . the bus goes in two hours. I'm all packed. Come with me if you like. I'll buy you a ticket too."

He seemed to consider this, then shook his head.

"Maybe. But right now I'm confused. I have to think. Settle down, El Ribbo. You're not going anywhere. Shit, I shouldn't call you El Ribbo, things are going to change around here. You're my wife. That puts you above other women. I apologise for all the disrespect I've shown you. I will change, you'll see, Isolt. You'll be proud of me and if ever you're down I'll keep you laughing. I'll tell you jokes. I know I haven't been such a good lover. I just kind of use you to jerk off but I won't be selfish. I'll even muff dive, I'll suck your pussy, huh? Would you like that?"

"You can't hold me against my will."

"Yes, I can. You are my wife."

"So you keep telling me, but that was a marriage for green cards. You kept boasting how you'd kept your fingers crossed."

"Yes, but we consummated it. That's what counts." He laughed. "The Romans have got us in the end, eh?"

Isolt was flabbergasted. They sat in the living room all day. She watched the alarm clock and saw the hands rest on the exact minute that the bus left for Hamburg.

"What if I just get up and leave?"

"I'll kill you," Christopher said, showing her his knife.

Isolt put her head in her hands and tried to think.

Christopher wore her backpack even to the toilet. When he left to go get water across the road he locked the door so that she couldn't open it from the inside without a key. She considered screaming for help out of the window but she couldn't go anywhere without her money and documents. A man fixed his car on the street below and some dogs ran about on the patch of muddy green. Christopher returned and came in, bustling about.

"Get away from the window."

"Why? Afraid I'll get shot?"

"Ha! Ha! Very funny," he said. "Listen, I've been thinking. You must have been polluted by all that junk food you eat. I think I have to clear out your system. It's a full moon tomorrow night. We will both fast for forty-eight hours starting from now. Then you will adhere more rigidly to my diet than you have been. It will enable you to see things clearly. You gobble up too much bread. I believe wheat is a depressant."

"I'm not depressed, Christopher. I'm being held hostage. How long can this go on for?"

"As long as it takes for me to be satisfied that you won't stray from the path of righteousness."

They smoked a joint and Isolt wanted another one immediately so he rolled a few more. They drank water. In the evening he laid down the sleeping bag in the dining room. Isolt watched him with dread.

"I'm not sleeping with you tonight. I can't."

"OK, OK. But you have to lie with me, here and not on the pool table."

"Why?"

"The floor is more solid."

"Please, Christopher, let me go," she pleaded.

"You're my wife. The only possible way I could let you go is if you told me you had fucked someone since our marriage. Then I'd have no interest in you."

Isolt thought about it.

They lay in the darkness on the hard floor under a blanket. One electric fire glowed orange near their feet; they listened to the clicking of the glowing bars.

"Christopher — I have been with someone."

There was silence.

Christopher sat up and asked when.

"Two weeks ago."

He lay very still and then said, "You actually fucked."

"Yes."

"Did you get a nut?"

"Yes."

"You never did with me."

"No."

"Did he go down on you?"

"Yes."

"I bet you liked that. You always wanted that."

Isolt was silent.

"How many times?"

"I don't know."

"You don't know? What the fuck does that mean?"

"I can't count. A lot."

More silence. Silence stacked upon silence, grim silence, wizened silence, you could hear a cat drop.

"I mustn't love you as much as I thought," Christopher said, "'cos I'm not strangling you at this very minute."

He wasn't strangling her, he was crying. Isolt felt sorry for him.

"I did love you, Christopher, for ages, but I didn't think you loved me. That marriage is just a piece of paper. I don't set store by those things. I'm not a Roman, we live outside the law, we weren't lovers, we just had a strange companionship. Let's . . ."

He crawled on top of her. With one hand on her chin pushing her head back, his eyes full of hate, he grabbed her breasts roughly, tearing away her clothes. She tried to push him off but he was very strong.

"Open your legs," he shouted, prying them apart.

He grabbed the knife and held it in one hand and forced his way into her. She felt a ripping pain and tried to focus on the blade gleaming in the orange glow of the fake fire. She sank in an underwater horror, submerged in stagnant, thick fluid, choking in the slime. He climbed up and knelt on her shoulders. She writhed and pleaded but he came all over her cheek and it ran and caked into her ear and her hair. He would not let her move to wash but held her in an iron grip, hissing and raging threats into her ear. If I get through this alive, she thought, I will be strong. She lived, forcing her way through the barrier of every second, and tried not to go mad; but parts broke down. Sometimes she sank back into the stagnant slime and clinging, ooze-drooling seaweed dragged across her exposed neck, she felt herself tilting upside down in the mire. I am dying by drowning, she thought.

The screeching, manic, hard-rock Iggy was played without respite. The next day they didn't eat. They drank water and smoked hash. He forbade her to smoke tobacco on its own. He took his clothes off and paced the room naked, brandishing the chair leg.

"I have nothing to lose by killing you. I have nothing. Domestic murders don't count for much. I can handle prison. I'm disciplined. I'd get respect inside for killing you. Now you have to stick by me, I made you a woman, I'm going to kill you. There's no such thing as rape in marriage. Having one wife is kind of obscene. A man should be allowed a few wives. You alone are like having a Porsche. Somebody's scratched my Porsche. I won't rest till he is six foot under. I'm thinking though, I'll have to kill you too. I should have three wives, Candy Brown, Marie-Claire and you. Candy 'cos she could score anywhere day or night; Marie-Claire 'cos she was a good thief and a classy bird, and you, you? Shit, I don't know, 'cos you work like an ant, Ha! Ha! Oh, and your jokes, you had some good jokes. Tell me you forgive me for what I did last night. You must forgive me, I feel bad. It was undignified. I'll try to restrain myself. I can't guarantee you anything, though. It is my right as your husband, but maybe out of respect for you I'll deny myself my rights."

That night she covered her face with her hands as he crawled on top of her.

"Don't cry. Don't cry," he implored.

He came inside her.

The third day they were still together in the same room. It was the night of the full moon. Neither had eaten yet. Isolt was beginning to starve. Christopher closed his eyes — a peacock looked back at him behind his lids, so close, he felt there were two eyeballs under each lid. He had an erection.

Isolt gazed at him in shock. He had hit her on the head earlier with the chair leg. She was sore and her face was throbbing, between her legs there was more stinging and pain, she could not sit up straight. His white cheeks puffed out and his joints bloated. He opened his swollen purple lips, all his teeth had fallen out. A fat blue tongue vibrated in his ulcerated mouth.

Bzzzz! He was buzzing.

A mad wasp at summer's end. Hepatitis yellow and chimney black, wavering in an unsteady flight pattern. Programmed to die, a doomed wasp, lethal as the evenings get shorter and darkness approaches from all edges.

Bzzzz! It was a hideous sound and cracks were appearing in his face. His eyes swirled in the sockets of his skull and settled on her, his penis vibrated, he trembled and stamped his spindly black legs on the ground. A mad wasp at summer's end, needing to sting before he was wiped out.

Christopher rose out of the chair, naked. His eyes were closed. He ejaculated without touching himself, his arms cruciform, outstretched, in flight. The sperm sprayed onto the floor in a long spurt.

He looked at her and his expression was sad and a little ashamed.

"Oh, Isolt. When we are friends again I will tell you my greatest secret. I will share my raptures with you."

She lay prostrate on the floor and rolled onto her stomach.

"Christ, I could have sworn you were a fucking wasp."

Her stomach rumbled.

"Tell me. Tell me who he was. Tell me and I'll feed you."

He tapped her shoulder with the chair leg.

"At work, someone at work."

"An Arab?"

"Yes, yes, he was staying there for a month, he's back in Oman."

"What was his name?"

"Ali."

"I'm going to kill you."

"Food, Christopher, give me something to eat."

"Not yet."

Isolt groaned. This was the fourth day. Christopher ate fruit and crackers from the fridge but would not share. He began to board up the toilet in case somebody got in through the window.

"That bloke I stabbed may be back."

All of Isolt's friends had said their goodbyes and thought she was in Hamburg. Jim and the others would be expecting her. No one knew she was here.

For the moment Christopher was singing:

> They call me Mr. Dynamite
> I blow things up in black and white,
> An end to your charade
> The button I have made
> Must be pushed.

The hash had run out and Christopher left the squat with her backpack, leaving Isolt locked inside. When he returned he told her to tidy herself up.

"We're going downstairs to Oliver. This is a test, Isolt. I want you to behave yourself because if you don't I won't be responsible for the consequences, you dig? You are not to ask for anything to eat. If you try to run I will catch up with you and kill you. I don't think that I have quite decided on what terms you may stay alive, that is if you are to live. Have some smack before we go, it will soothe your nerves, put you at ease. I'm sorry I'm digging in to all your funds. What's mine is yours and what's yours is mine."

On the way down the stairs he put his arm around her neck and held her close to him.

"You're suffocating me," she complained.

"Sorry." He was self-conscious.

Oliver opened the door and let them in. They sat on the couch and

Oliver weighed a chunk of hash on a small tin scales. The TV was on and Isolt felt weak and tired. Caesar looked at them both and shook his head.

"What's up with you two, man?"

Christopher laughed. "Nothing, we've just been taking it easy and hibernating awhile."

"We heard some strange noises and a lot of thumping," Oliver leered. "Boy, you two sure go at it."

"Well," Christopher smiled, "you could say the nature of our relationship is under discussion."

"Want some tea?" Caesar asked.

"Do you have any Coke?" Isolt asked suddenly.

Christopher nudged her with his elbow.

"Actually, I do." Caesar nodded. "Believe it or not."

He brought her back a can of Coke. She began to drink it, savouring the sugar.

"I've a joke for you, Caesar," Christopher shouted to Caesar in the kitchen.

"Do I want to hear it?" Caesar shouted back.

"Go on then," Oliver said.

"Why do black people smell?" Christopher shouted.

Isolt threw her eyes up to heaven. Caesar didn't respond.

"Go on." Oliver's eyes gleamed.

"So that blind people can hate them too," Christopher stated with a note of triumph.

Oliver yelped and slapped his thigh. Caesar came back with three cups of tea and put them down on the table.

"I've heard it before," he said.

Isolt went to the toilet.

"She looks sick," Caesar said.

"What's been going on in that love nest of yours?" Oliver leered.

Christopher shrugged and sipped his tea. "You know how women are, time of the month and all that good shit. Thanks for the tea, Caesar."

"Yeah, cheers mate," Oliver said.

"You're welcome," Caesar rolled a joint with his long, deft rubbery fingers.

Isolt was puking in the toilet. She hadn't eaten in days so it was just the Coke that spewed easily from her mouth; it was so fresh that there were still bubbles in it.

Oliver was leering at her when she came back.

"Hey, Isolt, tell me this . . ."

"What?" She sat down exhausted.

"If little girls are made of sugar and spice and all things nice, then why do they stink of fish?"

Isolt stared blankly at him as the three men's laughter swelled in the smoky air around her.

The moon was a lunatic's lopsided smile. Christopher was nailing a blanket over the window. He sang as he worked:

> There is no reason for the sky,
> When I'm on fire from your lies,
> So if I win this fight
> They'll call me Mr. Dynamite.

Isolt told him stories to keep him distracted.

"When I was a child I was all right. I was happy when I was three feet tall. I used to think about the world and I thought it started from the road outside my house on the housing estate. That road I thought never ended because it linked to the main road, which led to the sea, and the sea bore the cars and people to the new road on the other coast and on and on. The road outside my house led to every other road in the world, even though we lived on an island. It led eventually to the great highway that lay outside your house. The highway that haunts you every waking hour. Roads were like water; all linked from muddy lanes to spaghetti junctions, just as every little stream leads to the ocean."

"Yes, yes, I know about the highways, the cathedrals of America," Christopher said. "But enough of all that. Your childhood stories bore me."

"I know everything about your life. Your mother's death, your grandmother, your drug dealing, your army service, Puerto Rico, Europe, Marie-Claire — I know it all. Night after night you repeated those stories till they almost felt like my own, but you don't even know if my parents are alive or dead or how many brothers and sisters I have."

"I know enough to see there is not much to know, El Ribbo. Nothing you say would be a secret to me."

"You were born with a caul, you'll never drown at sea but careful crossing all the roads of the world, you might be run over by a car."

"You know, all the lads around here just think you're some kind of rich kid. When I told them you were going to the States they assume that daddy pays for it all."

"They know I work."

"I know, yeah. I know you're not like that at all, I kind of feel bad when Oliver makes a discourteous comment. He's down on the Irish, you know. He never says anything when you are there but when I'm down there getting stoned during the day he makes comments all the time."

"I don't expect that much from these people."

"I know, I know, of course. I guess it's the books and the way you speak that makes them think you've got a daddy who you can run back to and who gives you the readies."

"God forbid a woman survives on her own," Isolt said.

"Well, a bird shouldn't really. When we have children, if any are daughters I will have to deal with them very differently than from what you've been dealt with, that's for sure. If they come home with make-up I'll scrape it off their faces with a wire brush."

"You're absolutely right," Isolt said. "Look what happened to me."

He got up and shouted, "You betrayed me. You put out for a man you did not belong to. You gave him what was mine. I feel violated, the penalty is death."

Then he sank back into the chair. "Oh, Isolt! Tell me some stories, keep me laughing, it's your only hope, I can't control myself."

Isolt saw he was holding the sides of the chair and was embroiled in some dark struggle. Evil could be a bedmate with pathos; evil could also be shrivelled. As she attempted to shake it off, a hatred which she could not match crept behind his eyes, and he flung himself slurpingly onto her neck, suckling into her skin, burrowing deep inside her to devour her guts, raping her insides.

"I have the smell of death on me. The smell of death since birth."

There is a death beat running through. Hide.

"Isolt, you really should stay with me. You never were pretty and soon you'll lose your youth. I can see lines under your eyes and around your mouth and coming down from the side of your nose. The hard life is beginning to show all over you. Jesus, look at all those lines, probably the smoking you do, it creases you up. By the age of twenty-five you're going to be ragged. My days of lust are over. I'm prepared to be a family man. You are unattractive, poor, female and unskilled, there is not much future for you out there, but with me you will always have support, a helping hand so to speak.

"There are so many weirdos out there willing to take advantage of you. Look at Seamus the Irish Bastard, we feed him, give him shelter and he tries to break in and steal from us. Think of all the times you go and whore yourself for some man and get it thrown back in your face, I know that hurts, sweet thing.

"By rights you should be a virgin for me; most men in the world have that honour but the West has lost its way. You are a sinner but I will take you as you are if I am sure you can be repentant. Already I see improvement, no I really do, tomorrow I shall feed you some fruit. I will be able to make you as slim as you always wanted, as every bird wants, take some of that chubbiness out of your person. I know that's what every bird dreams of. Nothing more ungainly than a sharp-tongued, ugly woman, is there? Trust me."

"You've been watching too many cartoons," Isolt said.

He allowed her to eat an orange and a pear that evening. He cooked up some spuds for himself, which she eyed hungrily. He had no cutlery and he ate out of the saucepan with his hands. She remembered times when she tore a piece of styrofoam off a fig carton and used it as a rude spoon. God hurl you to oblivion with no cutlery, she thought. What she used to admire as a rejection of materialism she now interpreted as a savage rejection of joy. He created a self-enforced prison surrounded by ugliness, thriving on friendlessness. Night after night full of rage and jealousy he drove his soul to extinction.

Isolt watched him as if for the first time and could not fathom how she had ever got involved. The good old days in Paris when he slithered about the city with his little tartan shopping cart, containing an ounce of this and an ounce of that, cleaning his teeth with mango stones and making her laugh. In a continual stupor, stealing and begging, no whining, threatening or squealing. Now there was just brute force, threats and rapes in the dead of night.

She hated him and hoped he would kill himself. She had been blind in her dealings with him and now it was too late. Catastrophe comes like lightless ships in the dead of night, sailors with their tongues cut out, eyes red from rage and frustration.

He felt hatred burn like lava, spasms of bewilderment interspersed with flashbacks into the horror of his life, the sleazy violence of his past and the ugliness of his present surroundings. The curator of the Sam Steal museum eats with no utensils, has no hot water, his wife has betrayed him.

He took her to Leicester Square on a red bus. She made no attempt at escaping. They went to a film of his choosing and Isolt kept her eyes closed through most of it, both to spite him and because she was drained and unable to respond to the barrage of guns, car chases and violent sex that the U.S. offered the world on its chipped cultural plate. He led her by the arm through the crowds and she walked as if in a trance. Sitting in a hamburger restaurant where he had ordered them both dry salads, she snapped out of her lethargy. He drank a big chocolate milkshake, he spilt his water over the table and tucked his napkin into his collar.

"I thought you didn't touch animal products," she said in disgust.

He reached his hand over to hers. "Don't hate me, Isolt. I'm doing all this because I love you."

She thought to herself that he was just a filthy junkie with his trousers hanging halfway down his arse. His breath smelled of garlic and he had bad body odour. She pitied him intensely, averting her head from the spectacle of his poverty.

For the next three days they did not leave the squat. She only knew that three days had passed by the tiny triangle of light where the nailed-up blanket did not cover the broken window. Grey was the day and grey three times, black came twice as night. She lay on the floor by the fridge in the filth. Christopher paced and screamed, cried and raped, held a knife to her, laughed loudly, threw a hammer at her. She was a witch, a whore, a bitch. He was going to kill her.

On what she believed to be her eighth day of incarceration, she watched him sit on the chair beside the grey triangle. He was naked. He was humming and sobbing at the same time and his dick was hard. After that she lost her fear. When the grey turned to black and he tried to fuck her again she was not afraid of the knife, the hammer or his fists. She took him by the ears as they lay side by side and slammed his head off the ground. She squashed her face against his. "If you touch me again, I'll kill you."

Later he said, "I can't believe you spoke to me that way. You're usually so passive. I've never seen you really energized about anything. I made a woman out of you. Remember Marie-Claire when she kicked the door so hard? We were cowering inside? She wouldn't have done that, only for me. I made her strong and now you. I want my women able to stand up for themselves."

Isolt sat up and had a cigarette. She flicked the ash towards the ashtray but it missed and landed soft as soot on the floor. Christopher grew enraged.

"You always flick the ash without paying attention. It's a filthy habit and I won't stand for it," he fumed. "You have no respect for the ash."

The next morning he got up and announced that he had decided not to kill her.

Christopher put the chair leg away.

"I have no further need for my magic wand."

"Can I go now?" Isolt asked.

"We must draw up a contract," Christopher said as he rooted in the debris for a pen and paper.

"I have such mixed emotions. Have you now realized the enormity of your actions? You said you were in love with me in Amsterdam and certainly I was with you, so this can no longer be considered a paper marriage, or let's say *mariage blanc* as this plot was hatched in France. Were you just taking the piss out of me? Because two months later you committed adultery.

"Unless you can put me away for more than ten years then police action is absurd, young one. Are you going to get the pigs to protect you? But none the less if you agree to co-operate, Isolt, let me make this perfectly clear, I'll never premeditatedly physically or mentally harm you again. But it's up to you to stop taking the piss! OK?

"And just for the record I've felt a couple of boxes, apart from yours, in the past thirty months, kissed a girl or two and tried to entice two or three females up to the squat to fuck, to no avail however. But now I have my monk's hat on. I must be cruel to be kind so that you won't do this to another man. Consider the next six months a lesson in dues. I did not send you to work every day to fuck me around, young lady. My peace of mind and your tranquillity depends on our friendship which I ask you to work on. Don't try to run away, I know the ins and outs of finding the whereabouts of people.

"You are my wife and I'm sure the authorities will understand when I say to you that you will fear if you talk to the Arab once fucking more. You only think fear, I know that, only think. This is a very polite gentleman's warning. If I suss you and him are communicating then I'll put my battle fatigues on. I have absolute proof that the only danger me and my friends feel is if someone fucks with them. This is war, Isolt, war."

"What are you talking about? You're making no sense," Isolt said.

Christopher sat on the chair and took out a piece of paper with something scrawled on it in tiny letters.

"This is one of the poems I wrote this week. Remember when Freddie died I sketched? Well this trauma has caused me to write, but first I will explain a few things. I'm going to keep you here for six months to sort things out and to prepare myself for oncoming solitude, to ease my way into it. I've always had company in the last few years and it will be strange to have nobody. We won't have sex. You can come and go as you please. I will even allow you to take a break for a week, only if you return to Ireland and remain under your father's supervision. We'll work it out later.

"We still need each other for papers, there is no reason to think that we aren't in the same boat. All I'm asking is to have a little bit of faith in me and I'll show us the way out of this. And if you don't like the direction that I'm proceeding in then you may sleep elsewhere. I'm not as accomplished a poet as perhaps you are used to reading, so have pity . . ."

He cleared his throat and began to read loudly:

BACK AT SQUARE ONE
All right, the door is firmly shut, and that's done,
We had our fling and that was fun,
Is it wrong of me to ask you back to square one?
For lack of a better term, you'll probably forget me as I will you,
And it just may be before the month of June.
So before we're both put back on the shelf,
Can I not ask a compromise of yourself,
And that is to give my plan a wee chance,
And never will it be said we departed in black circumstance.
Because I'm now set on being just good friends,
I won't ever pour my heart out like that again,
And needless to say, and only if I may,
There's no place for that in square one.

He blushed and would not look at Isolt. He started rummaging around in the bag and extracted another paper.

"I'm embarrassed thinking that I'm bothering you unnecessarily, and of course now that I've my senses back I'm feeling very, very ashamed of myself and my conduct. I don't know how to put it in words or if I've even ever had this feeling before but it's awful. So if you can ever find it in your heart to forgive me, I'll do all I can to bring it out. That's all I want from this relationship and I'll take my leave. It's true, I'll simply bow out and fade away. No more trouble from me.

If your attitude and words are to be believed,
You are quite serious about wanting to leave.
The story goes, Adam's wife was fashioned from a rib,
Thus, spontaneously giving birth to woman's lib.
I've not yet mentioned her name
For fear of appropriating the blame
Or so the story would have us believe
It's her, and her alone that ends up a sleaze
The moral of this story escapes me, and indeed,
That bastard Adam should've stuck up for his wife Eve.

"Poems can be read between the lines, Isolt. If you think that these aren't pitiful and corny then comment on them."

"They're quite clever," Isolt said.

He lit up. "Yeah?"

"What made you change your tune?" she asked.

"If you were a human being of world calibre then I reckon I would batter you to death, but you are still an innocent kid out of her house for sixty months. Fucking an Arab behind my back. Yes, behind my back, you told me after the fact.

"If I never ask you for anything else in my life, I ask that you listen to my confession carefully. Why the change of heart? It's because this affair was getting too intense and out of hand with all the pain and hurt, crying, feeling bad, jealousy and coercion. I was frightened that I would kill you. Anyway my change of heart happened last night. I could finally hear the tone of your voice and broke — a turning point, El Ribbo, first time I cried for you instead of me.

"This was a sad chapter in my life. About our break: it's one hundred percent and I'll abide by it. We'll have to trust each other to protect each other's interest, but in your case you'll have to stay healthy.

"You are not obliged to sleep in the same space as I. When you leave in six months if you would like to divulge a phone number it would be appreciated, but don't feel obliged. Half my savings and house is yours as you wish. Things will be different, I swear to almighty God.

"I was dead wrong. I'm making amends and swear that I'll never hurt you again."

Isolt remained silent and fished in her head for an adequate response.

"I appreciate that." She trod carefully. "So what kind of contract do you want to draw up?"

"I'm going to work on it today," Christopher said. "Eat some fruit and roll a joint, relax, you're out of the danger zone."

"What do you mean by me having to stay healthy?"

"Ah yes," Christopher said. "This is important. I probably have AIDS. All my needle-swapping you know. You must have it too. I want you to have the HIV test."

"All right," Isolt said, and then added, "That's a horrible thought."

"I don't see how I could have avoided the disease really. Occupational hazard so to speak, but you should've known better than to sleep with a junkie without a condom."

Isolt lit up a joint and sucked deeply.

1. Isolt shall remain under either her father's or husband's supervision for the next six months.
2. Only Ireland is neutral territory and shall be the only place for a holiday. A week is the only amount of time acceptable for vacation.
3. Isolt will not work but will remain in her husband's care for the stated six months.
4. Isolt will undergo HIV testing.
5. Isolt will give all information on adulterer to her husband and will hinder no part of the hunting down and killing process.
6. All of Isolt's papers and documents will be monitored and in possession of her husband.
7. Isolt shall undergo pregnancy test and if positive will remain in number 29 for the duration of the pregnancy. If she insists on a parting of the ways after that, custody will go to the husband.
8. Isolt can come and go as she pleases but will spend every night under her husband's roof.
9. Christopher will treat Isolt with respect and dignity and she will not be obliged to provide her husband with his marital rights. Christopher will only comply with her sexual needs if she begs him to.
10. Isolt will not utter a word of the past happenings or of this contract to a soul on pain of death.

"For your perusal," Christopher said, handing it to her.

Isolt read it and nodded. "Fair enough."

They both signed it.

"Let's go out and celebrate," she suggested.

Christopher sighed. "No. Tonight we shall stay in."

"Well, I do feel like taking a wee holiday since I was psyched for the U.S. for so long. Ireland will be weird. I'll get culture shock after being away for five years. My family will freak out. My brothers."

"Sure, sweet thing," Christopher said. "I'll buy you an airline ticket. You won't even have to take the boat. That'll impress them, eh? Bring them gifts too."

Isolt stood up and went to sit on the armchair. It was the first time he had let her get up off the floor without his permission.

"Let's get some smack," she said. "If I'm going to be here for another six months I might as well do something with my time."

Christopher escorted her to the airport. They sat on the tube, he reading his newspaper and she looking out the window through her reflection to the black tunnel walls. Just like the good old days. They got off at the airport and checked in, weighing her luggage. She had a return flight to Dublin for a week and had stolen books for her family.

"Let's go and get a coffee," Christopher said.

She ordered a beer and rolled herself a cigarette.

"Damn." Christopher clenched his fists. "All those days when you were late home from work and said you had been hanging out with Irish Jim at Wendover. I should have known. You know I kind of smelt something but I thought it was just cleaning up after all those whoremongering Arabs. I put it out of my mind, I would have never guessed. How could you do it with those beasts? You fucking slut."

"I'm sorry," Isolt said.

"Sorry! Sorry! Jesus, you cunt. You don't even know how I'll make you repent."

Isolt glanced at the clock. "I want to buy some booze for my parents in Duty Free. I should head."

"OK," he said quietly.

They walked to the departure gate.

"What's in the bag?" he said.

"Books."

"I thought you packed them in your main bag."

"These are to read on the plane."

"They have newspapers on the plane and magazines and shit."

"I don't read newspapers and magazines and shit."

"What books are they? Let me have a look."

"You never cared what books I was reading before."

He laughed. "You really are a reader, aren't you? Ha! Ha! That's something else, El Ribbo, sorry I shouldn't call you that, I've never seen anything like it, you even carry a few for an hour flight. Fiction I bet."

"Fiction, and poetry for the intervals."

He laughed. "I thought as much."

"Books aren't good for an ignorant girl."

"Did I say that? Yes, I did. Well you should have listened to my gospel more closely, El Ribbo, you wouldn't be in this trouble."

They reached the entrance to the gates.

"Give me your address book," Christopher demanded suddenly.

"Why?"

"I need to check it for clues to his identity."

"I'll give it to you when I come back."

"No." His face was contorted with rage and he squeezed her arm. "If you don't show cooperation in every respect, you are coming home right now, young lady. I warn you. I'm not afraid of making a scene. And I will win."

Isolt reddened as she rooted in her bag. She gave him her address book and he pocketed it.

"You won't need it in Ireland. Right. I'll meet your plane on the way back. Don't pull any stunts, you hear? No matter where you go or for how long, I will find you. I will hunt you down and even if it is years from now, one day you will open your door and shit bricks 'cos you will know I'm there to kill you."

"Are we going to part on that note?" Isolt asked.

"No. No. Forgive me." Christopher was sweating. "I'm a wounded man. This week I'll fast and meditate and will be ready to be a good husband on your return. I love you. Tell me you love me."

"I love you," Isolt answered.

"Ah, I know that is hollow." He had tears in his eyes.

He kissed her on the lips. They had never kissed on the lips before. Isolt had always taken it to mean that he didn't love her. Now he kissed her and she hated him.

She walked through the gate without looking back. Christopher stood biting his knuckles and waving to her unseeing back.

She sat in various parts of the departure area for three hours reading a book. Her legs were shaking. She had watched Christopher stash her documents under the strip of carpet on the pool table when he believed she was asleep. That morning she had smuggled them into her bag when he was in the toilet. She was terrified he would check for them before they left but she had been lucky for once. She kissed the brown envelope with her US immigration forms.

She exited the airport warily, terrified of bumping into him at every turn.

There was a tiny monkey on her back. It kicked her neck and tweaked her hair. She pursed her lips and took out the tiny piece of folded up paper with the heroin Christopher had given her for the trip. The train carriage was practically empty and she snorted it surreptitiously. What if I have a habit? she thought in panic. It was the least of her problems.

Isolt re-entered London with a heroin habit and very little money in her pocket. There were parts of London she could no longer go to, a lover in Hamburg who expected her two weeks ago, a mad husband who would hunt her down and slaughter her, no job, no one who knew she was in the country, no addresses or phone numbers and all her luggage was now in Dublin.

So many times she had stood on the threshold of returning. Each time sensing the uselessness of this desire. She is an animal looking for food. Always leaving everything behind. The sullen future like a dull hole is her burden. The shadows are numerous and impenetrable, yet skies above are always blue, mocking her dreams of cold, steel rain. Once, when she was quite young, she had slept on the floor of her parents' room in a hotel, when the car broke down. Darling little lamb, and now she is punctured like an old man.

Through the scrubbed hills of the desert, she had left the city of thieves for the city of stone, looking for food. She had worked outside the city walls in the bus station, and how it hurt to see them all returning and embracing. She sold her welcome to open her eyes. Now her lids are cremated. She shall never rest again. How could she go home?

She had cleaned the stone steps of the house, left the bins out, made breakfast, but she could not eat. The last night she stood and saw the furious clouds roar past the three tower blocks. Huge clouds moving behind the stone blocks. Orange clouds, Jerusalem lit.

It had been winter by the time she got to Greece. Desolate. Empty beaches, few boats, stormy seas. Men had followed her with greedy eyes. They asked her home. She, bent, angry, bored, afraid. *How can you take me home? I left many years ago. My brothers are grown. If one sat here now I would not know him. Maybe you are my brother. You have searched long. Have you really come to take me home? Take a train, take a boat, take a plane, cradle me from oceans and mountain wind, protect me from those who take me to their houses. My brother, how old you are now. Take me home. For I do not think I can go alone.*

Where is the direction of the female mind? Hers is imploding all the time, pointlessly. There is room for tragedy in this world, she has caught glimpses of it. She is glad at the greatness of some minds. She has no right to tragedy. She is not a lion. A darling little lamb to be slaughtered, asleep on your floor. She is not the eldest nor the youngest, but she is asleep on your floor. Who are you and who is she? Before you have to die remember to tell her where it all belonged, and where you were all coming from? Fifteen years old, in a hotel, asleep on your floor.

Things have not been all right. She has been dazed. She watched in disbelief her life unfolding. The realisation that something is moving her apart from herself. Something is tearing her away from herself.

She loved you. She loved you more than the world you gave her to.

Take this bread and eat it. May the Lord have mercy on us all. This valley of tears no bigger than her clenched fist. The banished children of Eve are sending no more postcards home. Fruit of thy womb could not find root in these caves, so barren the soil we never expected to tread, so dulled the vision when the snakes had fled.

She left her guardian angel in the sink, when she took it off to wash the blood from her hands at the train station in Nice. Pray for us now and pray for us always. Keep secret the hour of our death. And turn out the lights in our souls the moment we leave the world lest others are stillborn in terror of our ghostly thoughts. May the Lord have mercy on us all. Take this wine and drink it. Forgive us, for we know not what we are doing and we know not where to go.

God is an animal that died alone in desert sand storms or under cold banks of snow, or in the green fields while the rain fell down, a long, long time ago. You can not wake the good God up. We have all been born with homeless souls.

15

The Long, Wet Shadow that Lay Between All Land

THE STEAM rose thickly from the scalding bathwater. Cecilia opened a bottle of gin and handed it to Isolt, who took a hefty swig and stared dubiously into the steam. She was fully clothed but her feet were bare. Her toe had barely touched the surface when she withdrew it, grimacing.

"Ouch." She drank some more.

Cecilia grabbed the bottle and gulped heartily before handing it back.

Isolt stood at the top of the stairs in her cousin's North London flat.

"Jump!" Cecilia urged.

Isolt groped for the gin and drank some more.

"Do you want me to push you?" Cecilia asked, a little too eagerly.

"No," Isolt cried. "Don't you dare. Don't come near me."

She removed herself from the precipice and went into the bedroom, lying flat out on the bed.

"When Seamus the Irish Bastard got me pregnant I drank gin and he kicked me in the stomach and threw me down the stairs."

"Did it work?" Isolt asked, half afraid.

"No."

"No." She sighed with relief. "At least I don't have to feel guilty for not hurling myself down those wooden stairs."

"You'll have to go to the clinic. It's all free."

"Oh God. I'll be mortified, what will I say? They'll think I'm so stupid. Maybe I should try the stairs."

"Pregnancy is not the end of the world."

"It is for whatever's growing inside me."

"I've had three. The first was the hardest but after it was all over I was so relieved and I came home feeling happy. I had done something positive. I went out to the Angels Club and did heroin all night. I couldn't tell them what happened, murder and all that. They'd kill me for doing heroin too. They hate that. You know I told them what happened with you and Christopher, but they agree with him, you were his wife, you fucked around. Legally he can do what he wants. I'm sorry you can't stay with me but Thump said he wasn't running a shelter for battered women."

"I'm all right here," Isolt said. "My cousin's cool."

"Thump rang me at my father's this morning and told me I'd really cheapened myself last night."

"Why? What were you doing? They're Hell's Angels for God sake. You're meant to be cheap."

"He sees me sitting on an old drum outside the club wavering from side to side and says, 'Cecilia, just look at you, you are a victim, a victim.'"

Isolt laughed.

"Do you know, Isolt," Cecilia suddenly sat up on the bed, "you look much better these days. You've lost a ton of weight. It suits you."

"I ate nothing but oranges for two weeks," Isolt protested.

"God, do you know I'm almost jealous."

"Of course — kidnapping — not the desirable way to diet but certainly the most effective."

"I know . . . still . . ." She hesitated. "Your skin is pale, not so ruddy, and you look less dumpy."

"Dumpy?" Isolt asked. "As in Humpty Dumpty?"

"I didn't mean to offend you," Cecilia said. "It was a compliment."

"Well, if I eat only oranges and crawl around on the floor I will remain pale and thin. No way, Cecilia. I've got to eat, build up strength for the revolution."

Cecilia drained the last of the alcohol. "We've finished the gin."

"Go get another bottle. The water's cooled down now, I want a bath."

Isolt shuffled into the room naked under a blue paper gown, the ground cold as a frozen tongue under her plastic, blue feet. She hooked her feet into the stirrups with her legs wide open. She felt achingly exposed and vulnerable as the nurse and doctor walked about the room without glancing in her direction. All the pressure to keep that part hidden and now it was open and no one looked. She started crying; the grief was for herself. The anaesthetist looked in surprise and he nodded to the nurse who came and held her hand. The anaesthetist would not hold her hand but the nurse would. It compounded her sorrow.

She awoke stricken with violent cramps and was allowed to lie a few minutes extra in bed. The nurse helped her down and she hobbled off to a cubicle where her clothes were crumpled in a bundle in a wire basket.

Christopher's child had lived as he often wished he himself had lived. It had been born all at once in death. The only fright, the instruments of termination. The first pain had been the end of all pain. Barely formed, a living tissue of cells, it had been pulled into the world dead. The whole universe with its limited capacity for mercy neither welcomed nor mourned this truncated existence. It was a mother's gesture of mercy to herself. A gift solemnly offered to an esurient future hungry for sacrifice.

Cecilia walked by her side, impossibly high stilettos cracking on the pavement, eleven inches taller than her companion and wearing a black cat suit and a fake fur tigerskin coat. Men admired from all angles and Isolt was amused.

"I can hardly imagine what it would be like not to be invisible. Men actually turn to look at you."

"It's better to be looked over than overlooked," she answered promptly.

At the pawnshop Cecilia pushed some of her mother's jewellery into the hatch and the man behind the glass took it off to be evaluated.

"My mother left me this in her will," Cecilia explained. "This is about the last of it."

"I lost my mother's ring," Isolt said.

Isolt looked up at her towering friend. Her make-up was caked too thickly, dark sunglasses shielded her eyes, her face was contorted from the smoke, but she kept the cigarette hanging from the side of her mouth as she drummed her chipped scarlet nails off the counter. The ash fell into the hatch but she appeared not to notice. When the man returned they agreed to the price and as she flashed him a perfunctory smile there was red lipstick smeared on her teeth.

Her cousin's house was situated beside a small patch of woods. Isolt was once again homeless, deposited on someone else's sofa with all her earthly possessions in a little mound piled up on top of her new rucksack; still circling tethered to her stump of poverty, lethargy and doubt.

Isolt fantasized that Christopher died. She imagined herself, the young widow on the car ferry, terribly alone, with the little pot of ashes on her knee, cringing silently in the drone of the ship's engines.

She would magnanimously, and also to satisfy her curiosity, contact his old girl friend Marie-Claire. They would bond instantly and take the RER to Versailles, for this is where he was happy for the only time in his life. It would be spring and the cherry blossoms would bloom rapturously. They would find the three-storey house where the old squat once was. In a stranger's garden Humpty Dumpty and the anorexic scattering the grey weightless remains of the Hoodoo Man, sadly hoodooed.

In a dream she is handed an innocuous basket. She takes it with her into her house in Dublin. There is a giant toad inside. It begins hopping maniacally about the kitchen, bounding off the sink, the ceiling, the shelves, breaking all the dishes, bruising itself and becoming bloody. It hops two metres up to the light fixture and there is a splintering of glass and then darkness. Isolt crouches with her hands over her head, terrified at this grotesque, huge creature slapping and panting and dismembering itself as it bounces off every surface in the black pitch of the room. Christopher raged through her unconscious

cutting down trees, burning everything around him, until the landscape was bare and smoking and she was exposed.

Her heart stopped as the tube train cranked into the grotty Elephant
and Castle station. She stood by the doors watching the smattering of
passengers disembark and move towards the exits; she walked briskly
looking behind her every few steps; alone in the lift she took a deep
breath as the doors opened, thinking momentarily that he would be
standing there. He was not. She plunged into the harried dusk of
the intersection and scurried towards the underground passageway.
Changing her mind, she trotted to the bus stop, believing it a safer
option. She mounted the bus and deliberated on the most concealed
seat. Choosing the upstairs, she peered out into the dying light, con-
tinually expecting to see him race for the bus. He did not.

As she ran through the gasping light of evening, she anticipated a
hand on her shoulder every step. She knocked on 28a Innis House
and saw Oonagh's shadow fill the hallway behind the frosted glass.

"My God. The dead arose . . ." Oonagh said.

"And appeared only to a selected few." Isolt immediately stepped
into the hallway.

"Come in, why don't you?" Oonagh said sceptically. "I never
thought I'd see you again. You shouldn't be down here at all. Do you
want a nice cup of tea?"

They walked into the big one-roomed squat and Isolt looked
around nervously.

"I know this sounds dramatic but can I close the curtains?"

"If you want," Oonagh said, disappearing into the kitchen.

"Where's Glip?" Isolt asked, pulling the curtains over the big window, glancing warily at the suddenly dark street outside.

"I'll tell you later. First you tell me what the fuck is going on
between you and Christopher. I'm kind of insulted you didn't call
around sooner. There have been speculations as to your whereabouts.
You told me Hamburg but Christopher said you disappeared to
Ireland and never came back."

Isolt took her tea and sat on the couch. Oonagh sat on a chair and
began rolling a joint while smoking a cigarette.

"I tried to go to Hamburg to the Glass family, you know the
Scottish bloke with the Belgian wife and kid. They were staying with

this other guy Jim, an Irish guy, the one you met that Sunday we all went drinking in Camden. I had a ticket and everything, then Christopher took a notion that we were to play happy families and wouldn't let me go. He held me hostage for two weeks and then freed me on condition I return to my family in Ireland, namely my father, stay a week and come back to him. He escorted me to the airport but I didn't get on the plane. I've been staying with a relative in North London since. I've been saving money doing this scam with Cecilia and am trying to decide where to go now."

"Jesus, woman. Did he beat you? Did you get raped?"

"I don't know. I suppose you could say so."

"At least you're alive. You don't know how lucky you are. Women are murdered like that all the time."

"The lesson of the blind midget."

"What's that?"

"Don't feel self-satisfied by comparing yourself to the most dismal bastard."

"Well, listen here, Christopher kept calling over to me, almost every day. I didn't know what was going on but he kept insisting you were in Ireland and when you came back you'd apply for a council flat and have kids and live happily every after."

"My flesh crawls."

Oonagh laughed loudly. "I kept saying: 'Are you sure? Are you sure? Did Isolt tell you this?'"

"What did he say when the week was up? Did he come round again?"

"Yeah, he was angry, he said he was preparing a letter to you and one to your father to tell him all about it."

"Oh God."

"He said once your father realised you were married he'll insist on you returning."

"So," Isolt said, "at least he thinks I'm in Ireland. Maybe I'm going to have to speak to my family after all. I'm sure my cousin has told them already, though he doesn't know about Christopher, not the details anyway."

"Well, you should. What if he turns up in Ireland? He said he would go over and get you if you weren't back in a month."

Isolt put her head in her hands and groaned.

"Why don't you keep in contact with your family anyway? Did you run away?"

"Initially kind of. I was sixteen. I came over in the summer to improve my French and told them I had a baby-sitting job lined up. I just fell into the whole lifestyle, you know. Time went on and I couldn't bear to ring and talk to them. I was afraid they would somehow make me come home. I just left it for years and then it got harder and harder and I never did write or phone them. I didn't know what to say."

"That's so selfish." Oonagh shook her head disapprovingly. "They must be out of their minds. I bet they think of you every minute of the day."

"Well, I have four brothers who are much younger than me and two older sisters. That should keep them occupied."

"Still," Oonagh said.

"OK, OK. Now I'm going to pay for it, aren't I? I have to ring and announce, 'Hi Mammy and Daddy, it's me, the prodigal, the third born, third female in a row, the short fat one who disappeared all those summers ago. Well, I'm just giving you a buzz to warn you of the impending arrival of my psychopathic husband who might just kill you all in your sleep and to forward all the hate mail I receive from him to my cousin's address.'"

Oonagh was laughing and Isolt ruefully began laughing too.

"That guy Jim came around too last week."

Isolt sat bolt upright: "What?"

"Are you all right? Here, have a puff of this." She handed Isolt the joint. "He called in, I think it was Tuesday, looking for you."

"How did he behave? What did you tell him?"

"I don't know, he's kind of quiet. He didn't stay long, just for a cup of tea. I had nothing to tell him, he said he'd been around to Christopher looking for you but Christopher refused to give him your Irish address. I said that you had originally been off to Hamburg but I didn't know anything else. He said he came to check if you were all right. We both decided there was something fishy going on, he couldn't believe you'd gone to Ireland, then he wondered if Christopher had murdered you. I had to laugh. He said he was going back to the squat to investigate, then he left."

Isolt sat dumbfounded: "Poor Jim."

"Yeah, that was decent of him to come all the way to London from Germany to check up on you. He must be in love, eh?"

Isolt closed her eyes in silence and then asked: "Where's Glip?"

"Glip? Oh yeah, well, I have news as well. I threw that waster Sinbad out. He was just using me. I sussed what he was onto. I heard from all these acquaintances that he moves about London scrounging off different people until he burns the area out then he moves on and eventually when all is forgotten, he arrives back in an area and people greet him like an old friend. He's got it down to an art. The bastard, if I had a gun I'd shoot him on sight. I need to get out of this place, it's doing bad things to my personality. I'm letting my friend Frances have the place. She just finished Art College in Dublin and is coming over here to work. I'd offer it to you but it wouldn't be wise."

"Where are you off to then, home?"

"After you?" Oonagh laughed. "No, I can't go home. Ireland's OK for Christmas but there's no jobs there. Everyone I know over there is unemployed. I'd love to but there's no point. I have to work, I couldn't stand just being on the dole in that weather. Most of my friends have emigrated anyway."

"Where, then?"

"India!" she said proudly. "I'm off to India next week. Look, I had to get injections." She rolled her sleeve up. "I'm terrified of going on my own but I have to get out of here and far away."

"God, you're so lucky."

"Come with me."

"No, I'm off to America before he cops on and reports me to immigration. I've always wanted to go to America."

"Yeah. I was over there for a year but I got deported."

"How?"

"I was working in Boston and I came back for Christmas to see my mother because my sister had just emigrated to Australia and she was going to be on her own. On the way back I flew to London to avoid customs in Shannon; I was staying with Sally and Cecilia in Darwin Street. I tried to re-enter and they stopped me at Newark. God, it was fucking awful, they interrogated me and shouted at me and escorted me in handcuffs to the plane. I felt like a common criminal. When I sat down the bloke beside me was staring. I burst out crying and told him I'd just been deported. He was an Arab, I forget where from, a businessman, he bought me drinks all the way back and tried to console me. He even gave me his card if I needed anything. One time I actually went to tea at his family's house. His wife and kids were so nice. Ha! Ha! Life's so fucking strange, the things we do, the places we end up. I'd left all my belongings in Boston. All my clothes and my leather jacket, lost forever. When Sally came home from work she said, 'I thought you were going to America?' I told her I'd been."

Isolt laughed. "And Glip?"

"Glip." Oonagh took a deep breath. "I couldn't find anyone to take her. She had such a bad reputation. Poor thing, she was just stir-crazy, I reckon. I had to keep her in the hallway all day when I was at work, otherwise she'd tear the place up. I was too lazy to walk her. It's not good for a dog, cooped up like that. In the end I brought her to the vet and had her put down. It was for the best."

"Thus endeth Glip."

"Thus endeth Glip," agreed Oonagh.

"I bought a book on India. It's too boring though. Maybe it will all make sense when I get there. They worship elephants. Can you credit that? Elephants with six arms. Crazy people."

"I don't know. We worship a torture instrument. Wherever we were, in every room, over my parents' bed, around our necks, a tortured man, dying in agony and it was our fault. I'd have preferred a six-armed elephant any day."

Oonagh convinced Isolt to go to the pub with her. Fortified by the joint and hankering for a drink, she agreed. From a corner on East Street, Isolt could see the Sam Steal museum in the distance. A light was on.

"If he only knew how close I was," she shuddered.

"You'll go back," Oonagh said. "You won't be able to resist it. It was the most intense thing that ever happened to you and it's hard to go back to normal functioning without the drama and adrenaline."

"I hope you're wrong. Though I kind of know what you mean. Christopher was always cruel to me but I was fascinated by him, and all the mind games and point scoring can become addictive. It's horrible but it's exciting or different anyway; after a while you use it to define what you are."

In the pub Oonagh said: "Maybe you're the type of woman who's attracted to it."

"No, that's bullshit. There's just a lot of men out there who abuse women. My friend Becky I told you about, she was running from her husband who beat her; Melonie, the fat girl, she had to leave the country because this guy was going to rape her; Cecilia gets abused regularly. It happens all the time, it makes me wonder about men, what are we to them?"

"When he raped you did you fight?"

Isolt sighed. "No. I was too scared."

"I can't imagine that. I would fight and kick for all I'm worth. I'd rather be killed."

"I fantasize about killing him all the time. You know I feel I should buy a gun and if any man ever tries it again I'll just shoot him in the head. Because he would be the man I was frightened of all my life."

Oonagh nodded. "For me it was my father."

Isolt was shocked. "Jesus, and did you fight?"

Oonagh shook her head. "I was too young."

"I hate Christopher. I hope he dies screaming."

"I go home to see my father every Christmas, I buy him socks and after-shave. My three sisters too. I've never told anyone that before. I'm drunk. Don't tell a soul, please."

"I won't, and you don't tell anyone about me."

"What now?"

"We'll survive and endure," Isolt said.

"No. I meant I've finished my drink! It's your round, and get me peanuts too. Dry roasted."

Isolt embraced Oonagh at the bus stop after closing time. Oonagh gave her an address of a friend in New York where she could stay the first week.

"Good luck. You've got my parents' address in Ireland. I'll ring them and tell them to forward all mail. Give it to Jim if he comes back or write to me if you ever hear word of him again."

Oonagh nodded. "Good luck. Here's a 53 bus now."

"Have a good time in India. You're a brave woman."

"Aren't we all?" Oonagh said as Isolt stepped up to buy a ticket.

Isolt sat on the top deck as the bus passed the giant flyover and left the Old Kent Road. She almost felt a nostalgia for the area but she was drunk.

*

Daylight stamped the night out. With new faith she rose and went into the street, smiling at the sun shining on the red brick buildings, thinking perhaps she should be out early every morning, it could feel so good. She took the tube to Heathrow airport and flicked through the book her cousin had given her to a particular passage he had marked. She smiled; it was *Ship of Fools*.

> We travel around through every land
> We seek through every port and every town
> We travel around with great harm
> And cannot reach
> The shore where we should land
> Our journeying is without end
> For no one knows where we should land
> And has not one peaceful day, one peaceful night
> To wisdom none of us pay heed.

Becky's ship had sunk, Freddie's ship had sunk, even Sam Steal's ship had struck the rocks and gone down; Payman had had to walk the plank, his presence no longer tolerable on his own mutinous ship. Christopher's battleship was searching to destroy and she still was on her raft, drifting. She closed the book in anticipation of her stop.

The plane was overbooked so she accepted an evening flight in exchange for monetary remuneration, glad of the extra cash. She read her book and strolled aimlessly about the terminal.

Isolt entered the stomach of the airplane. She felt apprehensive about immigration at the other end of her journey. She had carried all her documents in her hand-luggage, even the giant chest X-ray she had miraculously smuggled past Christopher. "Christopher." The very name dropped into her pool of consciousness with a sickening splash. He was a malevolent spectre that hovered over her; she could see sunlight in the distance but the chill of his shadow moved as she moved, pushing the benign light away.

When the film ended she rose with the rest of the rabble to queue for the toilet, bladders synchronized perfectly — after take-off, after the meal, after the film, before the landing. The line was long and as she waited beside the safety door she cupped her hands around her eyes, as blinkers against the plane's illumination.

Pressing her face to the glass, she peered outside, searching the black beyond the iron wing for shapes in the darkness. It was almost by chance that she cast her eyes down towards the earth and saw no solid thing but witnessed the dark Atlantic. The rapture of the depthless powers roaring below her, impervious to any fate, murdering century after century without comprehension. The long, wet shadow that lay between all land. Day and night and ceaseless seasons fell unremarked on its surface. The silent creatures under water passed life-cycles in the gloom with no need for philosophical quests nor capacity to break one another's hearts. Countless skeletons from ragged coffin-ships lay on the tenebrous pitch of dank sea bed, coldly eroded in the unearthly chill. They were her ancestors, severed branches of the tree, forgotten, mute, faded out of the pattern before the end. The rain kissed the window, it stuck its tongue through the thick glass and licked her with spirit.

Part Four

....

16

Darkness Approaches

CHRISTOPHER WAS crouched in his squat like a clenched fist. The smoked-out city changed texture and wrapped around his face like a damp rag. The bastard TV had finally gone dead after months of threatening. This was more awful than he had imagined; he had lost patience and was now hysterical.

The TV had been given to him at summer's height by an Italian junkie girl. He had carried the bulky antique two miles, sweating in the muggy heat. He had lugged it up the six flights of brick pigeon-shitted, syringe-strewn steps of his block. In the beginning the picture was green and jerky. He sat in front of it with the chair leg in his hand. The picture would narrow to a tiny box, darkness approaching from all sides. If he didn't bring down the stick on top of the TV with a resounding thud, the screen would go blank. It could take hours of dedicated nurturing to bring a picture back after that. The door could not be answered and he relieved himself into empty Perrier bottles that were strewn across the floor. If he watched for too long, sparks flew out of the back. The radio/tape player had similar modes of behavior. No one else could operate or utilise any of this machinery; few could even recognise it.

He sat among his creations feeling like a crazed inventor. He attended to them in their terminal sicknesses. He mourned with fury when they gave out the last sputters of an over-lived life, their swan songs often explosions that put the fear of God in him.

The TV had a warped screen. When characters stood in the middle of the screen their faces were stretched and distorted. He often let out shrieks of laughter at the particularly grotesque ones, especially the women, their deformities unbeknownst to them as they rattled off all their inane TV talk while their foreheads ricocheted off the horizon.

Towards the end the picture had become so unclear it was hard to tell a close-up from a crowd scene. Images were distorted, green and fuzzy, with darkness approaching from all sides. He sat in front of it and just listened to the voices, with the chair leg on his lap to fend off oblivion. Now there was not even a whimper, the poor creature was finally dead. He kept it in the room anyway because it gave badly-needed shape to the setting. An ancient tribal image, the armchair in front of the TV. Otherwise the room was just debris and a fridge in the corner. He could find no comfort in that.

Now there was silence. A smooth smothering silence that crept into the cracks and pores of everything. He fidgeted with the wires on the radio but a panic was building up in him. He felt a sick rat crawling up the wall of his stomach and falling, crawling up and falling over and over again, worms in his skull sliding over each other, multiplying by the minute. He had to get out of the squat now. He stumbled to the door of the living-room and undid all the bolts through watering eyes. He crashed through the debris of the hall but he had boarded up the toilet a week ago. He vomited in the hall before he could make his escape.

Even still he felt nauseated. He couldn't find the key he needed to open the front door. The other two rooms were full of junk. One had a hole in the roof. The element room. It snowed and rained in there. The sun made it stink. The master bedroom, where he and his wife had slept, now had pigeons nestling in the crates and under the tables. He could not bear to sleep there ever again.

The thought of Isolt quenched his desire to leave. Life was un-imaginable without her. In the living room he leaned out of the window. It was getting cold. The moon had a piece missing. It looked as if it had been wedged into a crack in the sky, yellow and moth-eaten, a shabby moon squeezed into the night. The pigeons were fighting again in the master bedroom. He felt like going in with the chair leg and smashing them all to pieces. Without the TV all he could think of was Isolt.

The floor and surfaces were strewn with pages of letters to her. Most were never sent. When he was in a stupor he put random pages in envelopes and posted them off to her parents' house. Where was Isolt? Nobody would tell. Their mutual acquaintances had conspired against him. Everyone had abandoned him. No post came since she left and only troublemakers called at the door. Troublemakers with their troubled lives, they always wanted something from him. He never wanted to give but at times craved even their company. These were troubled times. After all these years nobody was left but his monkey. No sound but the cars and trucks that rode the great highway in his skull. He had to contend with the solitude, now that all the apostles were enthralled by their own lives in faraway cities around the globe. Their number never reached twelve and they never followed nor listened very long, they were unacquainted with each other and did not think of the role they had been bequeathed.

He had had an ear infection for months now; he tore distractedly at the scabs, wincing with the pain of it. This was all her fault. The broken TV, the festering ear, the vomit in the hallway, the chipped moon. The bitch had torn down the ramparts and let the enemy flood his castle. The penalty was death.

There were eviction orders served to him every couple of weeks. They said they evict on Tuesdays. Every Tuesday he sat crouched on the chair waiting for the bailiffs. He would take a small bag and sleep in the streets if he had to. At five to midnight he would say to himself, "I guess not this week."

There was nowhere to go. All cities were shut down. He had lost his footing. The only luck was bad luck. When he had been truly down and out in Paris something had always come up; once a man dropped two hundred francs from his wallet on the Metro and nobody had observed this but Christopher. The gods had given friendly signs and he had people to talk to. Now for months nothing but misery and destitution and hunger. Freddie the Giant had cried for him when he had told him his life story, a grown man had cried for him, a good man. His lips were eaten by rats. The silence here was awful and his ear was bleeding. Infected pus was draining from his ear and tomorrow was Tuesday. Could he survive a winter on the streets? Where had his wife gone?

The night beat on. He trudged up and down the room, pieces of debris cracking beneath his feet. He hated this place. Even when she went away for a little time, it had been awful to be alone here. Maybe he should have told her that. He pictured her coming, knocking at the door, crawling on her hands and knees begging him to have her back. There should have been something, otherwise invisible, that would surface when he fell this low, to give him hope when all hope was gone. He thought hard but could only see her face and dream of smashing it beyond recognition.

The place was haunted and cursed. The floor beneath him was damp and rotting. He wondered if they could salvage this place when they threw him out. It had not been cleaned in years. They had never entered the kitchen after sealing it up the first day. He still did all the cooking on his camping stove on top of the fridge in the living room. Veronica the devoted camping-gas girl no longer gave him discounts, even when he begged and showed her all his change; she seemed frightened of him now. The ugly, violent red and thick black-lined murals of Sam Steal were still on the wall, a manifestation of his ghost; he could swear the lines moved and changed position. Why couldn't they leave him alone in this place he hated? The floors were so rotten he would one day fall through and land on the lap of Oliver downstairs.

Oliver grew fatter and uglier every time he saw him. Christopher could always hear the muffled sounds of his TV on all day. All the people in this area were casualties, stumbling around, shell-shocked from some part of their lives. This was a sorry place to end up. Christopher was as lonely and despised as the rest of them. Isolt had made her escape without him. He reeled in abandonment.

Christopher had taken all the photos he had of her and cut out the face. He had sent them to her parents' house with obscenities scrawled on the back: "I kill you die whore," "Death to cunt," "You are a dead hag," "I will be the way you die count on it." And he would, he would be the way that she would die, it would be his consolation prize. He kept one unflattering photo that Isolt had hated. It made her look fat and her face blotchy. He kept this to remind him that he had not lost a lot. You ugly cow, he said to it every time he saw it, you ugly cow, I'm going to make you regret you were ever born.

This was the room where he had kept her locked up when he wouldn't let her eat. She smoked joint after joint and pleaded with him and sobbed. He cried too and sat shriveled and naked with the chair leg in his hand and an erection. "Look what you've done to me," he implored, begging her to understand. "Look, I've tears running down my face and a raging hard-on. How can a man cry with an erection? Look what you've done, Isolt, you're killing me." Couldn't she see her childish cruelty had huge consequences? She had looked at the erection and at the chair leg with pure hatred for him. She had not looked at his tears.

He slammed her head with the chair leg when she tried to stand up. "Keep on the floor, get up when you are repentant." She scrambled off whimpering in the debris. A truly pathetic sight. He slammed her again to fend off oblivion. Darkness was closing in from all sides. When they first met she had said: "Don't worry about me. I'm the most easy-going person you've ever met." It had made him believe that a life together could have somehow been possible. She never whinged or whined and seemed happy getting stoned amongst the debris with the whole place rotting underneath them. Happy as a pig in shit. Pig Isolt. They were the perfect couple, how could she leave him?

She had promised to return. He had a copy of the contract, signed. He had been astounded by her wickedness and treachery. "Next time," he wrote to her parents' house, "you will get more than the chair leg Sweet Thing" and in the same breath he enticed her to return. He began to get a hideous, dark, choking feeling when he realised she wasn't coming back. He plotted suicide for days but abandoned the notion for revenge. He would not die till he had been avenged. Christopher, the great explorer and entrepreneur, whacked down in full flight by a wee simple-minded girl. He had friends in high places. You can't hoodoo the Hoodoo Man.

He rocked back and forth. In a demon's voice he began to sing favourite melodies:

> There's nothing in my dreams but some ugly memories,
> Kiss me like the ocean breeze.

The night tore on in fever and outrage. There would be many nights like this, wallowing in the silence left over by the dead TV. Fingerprints in blood from an infected ear would stain and streak the walls as he hurtled himself from room to room grasping for balance. Eventually he would even take on the pigeons in a bloody, messy battle. Holocausts would reign in this tiny place, apocalypse after apocalypse. Everything now in the debris, vomit, shit, dead birds, bottles full of piss, ash, apple cores, dismantled machinery, death threats to his wife, eviction orders, codeine cough medicine bottles, newspapers, syringes, crumpled-up tinfoil, scraps of clothes.

And in moments of rare lucidity, Christopher could look with forlorn detachment, devoid of self-pity, only bewildered by the length and depth of his sorrowful existence, at the festering heaps of debris. Remnants of the empire.

17

The Great Highway

IT WAS September and Isolt chose to leave New York on the fourth anniversary of Becky's death. She packed her bag and performed a customary search of her tiny room in the apartment she shared with a few other people. She found some condoms under the bed which she pocketed and a tiny bag of cocaine with just enough for one last snort. She emptied it onto a book and took out a dollar from her pocket, already rolled from last night's revelries; she snorted the powder and went into the hallway. The apartment had an old comfortable feel, as if all the ghosts were lounging about well-fed and content to observe passively rather than disturb. Isolt turned on the TV — she had got used to having one after so many years without. All the monumental news events of the past six years she had only heard about through word of mouth. Her consciousness was different; she was not party to her peers' communal visual memory. Flicking across the channels she finally switched it off. She walked through Alphabet City; for the New World, it certainly looked very old and used.

She was communicating with her family once more and had promised to visit at Christmas. In return they had forwarded Christopher's letters, mostly crude death threats. There was not an hour that passed when she did not think of him and nightmares plagued her when she drifted off in the darkness, his wings shadowing her. She felt revulsion but no pity. He would be all right, he would get along, he was Jumping Jack Flash and he was Jesus Christ. She did not doubt his tenacity and instinctive ability to survive and thrive through all his deranged misery; he would wheel and deal his way into some wretched niche eventually.

Her real sadness was for Irish Jim. She knew of no way to locate him. She returned often to the memory of his departure, a face waving from behind the glass. And she would always wonder what happened to them all, the Glass family and Irish Jim, her friends. She would not see or hear of them again. They were all tinkers with no fixed abode. The connections were severed; this was another continent and she could not search for them from here. She had lost them as the bus turned the corner, moving into the unknown and staying there forever. Think of the sound "tink," shallow and brief.

At Astor Place she took a subway uptown and walked to St. Patrick's Cathedral. Standing inside with her rucksack on her back she contemplated the Pieta, grieving mother holding dead son, bereft in a mother-hating, son-killing world. The divine mercy was conditional. The God had slaughtered the Son, thirsty for life's blood, and pierced the mother's heart with all the swords of sorrow he could muster. Christ running from his abusive father, absent most of his and Mary's life, Adam giving birth to Eve, the tree of life bearing poisonous fruit.

A priest droned on, standing at his exalted altar, fenced off from the congregation, working himself up to perform the putative cannibalistic gesture of devouring his own God. The people in the cathedral knelt in submission. Tourists wandered the side-aisles peering curiously at the proceedings, laden with shopping bags, bewildered sheep destroying the world. The homeless dozed in the pews at the back. Drone, devour, kneel, submit, shop, destroy, doze. Outside the planet was being wasted and mothers who should have been its natural protectors were crippled with mourning for their sons' misdeeds, for all the corpses sprawled out on their knees.

All is lost for them but Isolt has her own knowledge, she has found the accumulated truth in all those books she reads. She is Humpty, round and fat and small like an egg, with her house on her back like a snail. A snail-egg, she has left the womb, cut the cord, leaving a trail of silver slime as she sludges on across the damaged planet, her mind saved by the knowledge of the catastrophe, the who and what and why of armEGGeddon.

The poor people shuffled from icon to icon in the hushed awe of the cathedral, captives in Babylon, a strange land. Periodically songs break through, riding on air-currents across the river, telling secrets. It does not have to be this way, the poor do not always have to be with us, the son does not have to be slain, it was not your existence that drove the nails through. It was the vicious intent of the father. It's only a river; it's only a river.

Isolt stands confronting the statue, an egg awaiting release through rage. A daughter on the outside, cavorting in the margins of civilization. A female fooling around on the outskirts of time, an eager exile fondling the sphere of loneliness, watching closely but not waiting any more. Her raft has no anchor, she can sustain no stowaways. Her eyes are still absorbing and observing, and she would not exchange them for all the security and spurious strength in the world. She is hard-boiled in the scalding waters of knowledge, a Humpty who will not sit on the wall but who will roll, strong as a small steel ball, sustained by fragments of memories, her past always ongoing somewhere in her giant oval head. The wombs of all her ancestors are cushions for her when she needs a rest from fighting the world with cardboard limbs. She nestles against their pink slobberiness, the older ones dry and tough as leather, she nibbles at them, teases them, playfully juggles them, roots around inside of them, garners solace from their squeaky, rubbery company, and when she is dead she will join them in her daughters' heads.

Isolt walked through the sleazy, edgy streets to the Port Authority bus terminal. She bought a ticket to New Orleans and stood waiting, lighting a cigarette with the matches from the restaurant where she had worked. The people on the bus were mainly African-American, but there were four beefy white soldiers with shaved heads jostling each other and talking loudly; one winked at her as she struggled down the aisle. There were many lone mothers travelling with small children who were already cranky and whining. The driver was a lanky African-American with a shiny jacket and dark plastic sunglasses. Isolt found a seat by the window and a large woman with a plastic shower cap on her head sat beside her.

The bus left New York and headed south. She gazed keenly out of the window and held her book on her knee. The woman beside her had a metal detector stowed under the seat. Isolt grew dizzy at the implications — Becky winking at her across worldly dimensions.

When the woman waddled to the toilet she ducked her head under the seat to inspect the miracle. It was a carpet sweeper.

I should have lit a candle for you in the cathedral, she thought, to light your darkness wherever you are, in gratitude for the warning you gave me; you could have warmed your dead hands over the puny flame, where you are must be cold and still. I will always remember, you live in my past — in a cold still place in my head you survive as long as I'm alive. And she saw Becky stare back from the void, her face drained and yellow, her eyes angry as she stretches her bony fingers to snuff out the unwelcome flame. She shuns the light and cares not that the planet will not be saved, for who can ever prove organic life has priority over ash? It makes no difference to the universe, but we are egoists, instinctual beasts, pigs trundling forward to feed on the swill of life.

The hours passed as the continent unraveled outside the window. It was dark and the driver kept his sunglasses on. Isolt could see only her own reflection in the window until the lights were turned off and people tried to sleep in the cramped seats. A baby cried. Strangers sleeping by strangers, they hurtled through the wide open American night.

Isolt was awake, her head turned towards the window; her slumbering neighbor encroached on her space and she was somewhat squashed against the wall. The woman's plastic, crinkly head fell on her shoulder and remained there. Isolt did not dare to move, but cherished the unwitting devotion. Jerusalem, Tel Aviv, Athens, Paris, Nice, London, Amsterdam, New York — she had approached all cities with Dublin as her foundation and now New Orleans as destination. She could recall them all. The streets worn thin by feet and wheels. The feet worn thin by streets and streets. And Isolt knows.

She could reduce the streets, fitting the tower blocks into her pocket, and shops are but dust that float in rays of light.

In the smoldering night unawares, a small steel ball is let loose in her head, rolling and falling from one spot to the next. Days when it cruises without hitting anything, days when she cannot sleep for the noise it is making and the labyrinth it found when she was three feet tall; oh, she was tough and funny. Unspectacular nights when it lodges and never moves, nights that jolt it free to journey on, clanking down, and down, through an infinity of memories.

No kind of love can save her now. But she can follow the steel ball. Until she is an old lady, until she can no longer stand it, until she can no longer stand the cold, when she cannot stand up without falling down, until she will be wrapped in ambulance blankets and carried across the concrete flyover, onto the teeming highway, trailing the traffic and the evening coming down, the lights tentatively turned on, the roaring cars and heaving trucks, all those lives on the move, all those lives wearing the street down.

And Isolt knows that loneliness is the great highway that runs from east to west, full of wonder and banality, alive even in the dead of night, carrying all the tiny brokenhearted children from home to broken home.